Simon Williams

The Spiral Heart

BOOK IV OF THE AONA SERIES

The Aona Series by Simon Williams

Oblivion's Forge
Secret Roads
The Endless Shore
The Spiral Heart

Foreword

I'll save the extended acknowledgements for the final book in the series, but in the meantime I'll simply dedicate this to the readers who've discovered and enjoyed the Aona books. When you spend so much time in the inner world, it's a joy to find that your work is appreciated in the outer one.

APHENHAST

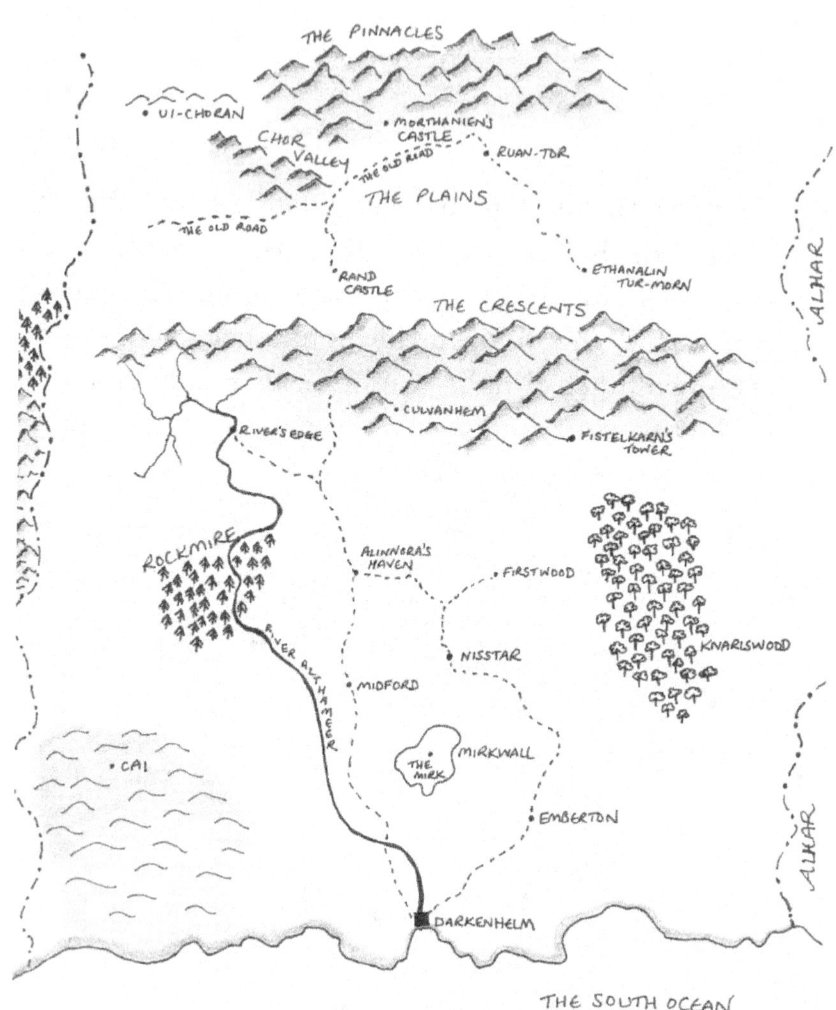

THE PINNACLES
UI-CHORAN
CHOR VALLEY
MORTHANIEN'S CASTLE
RUAN-TOR
THE OLD ROAD
THE PLAINS
THE OLD ROAD
RAND CASTLE
ETHANALIN TUR-MORN
JALHAR
THE CRESCENTS
CULVANHEM
FISTELKARN'S TOWER
RIVER'S EDGE
ROCKMIRE
ALINNORA'S HAVEN
FIRSTWOOD
KNARLSWODD
RIVER ALTHAMEER
NISSTAR
MIDFORD
THE MIRK
MIRKWALL
CAI
EMBERTON
JALHAR
DARKENHELM
THE SOUTH OCEAN

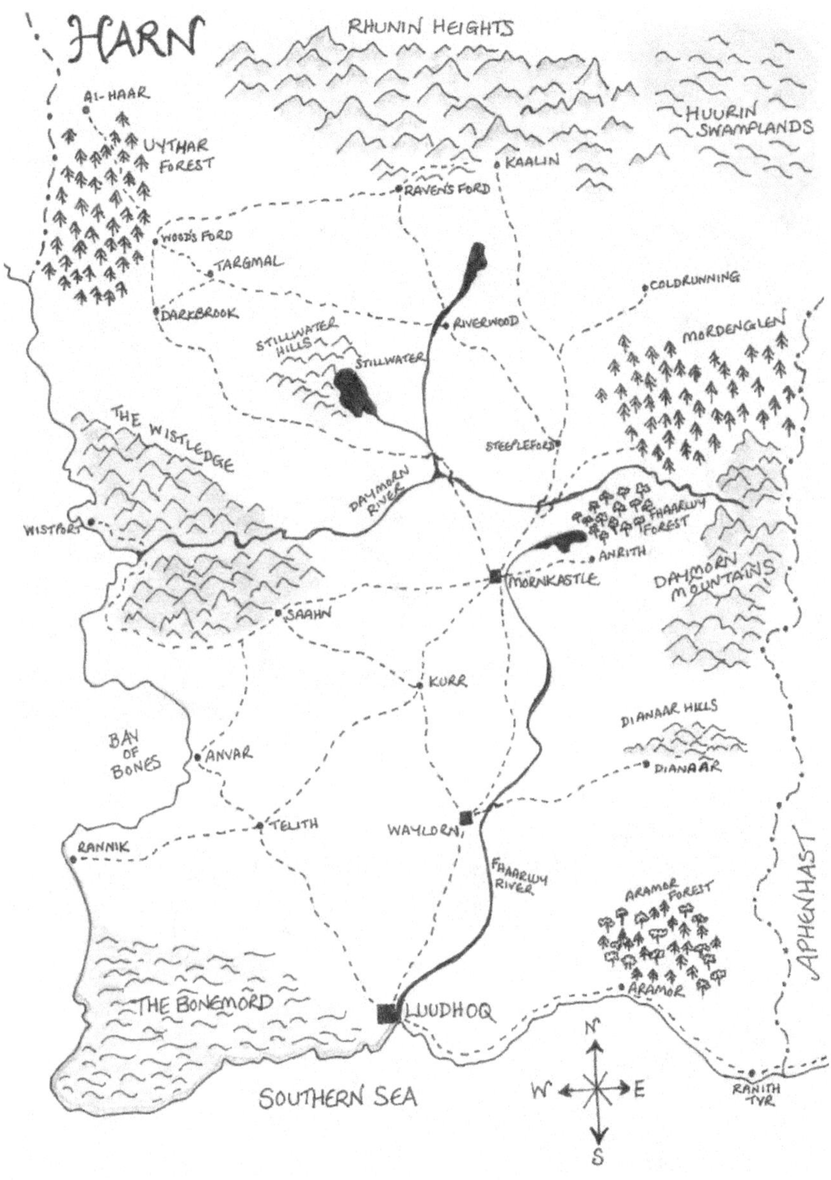

HARN
RHUNIN HEIGHTS
HUURIN SWAMPLANDS
AI-HAAR
UYTHAR FOREST
KAALIN
RAVEN'S FORD
WOOD'S FORD
TARGMAL
COLDRUNNING
DARKBROOK
RIVERWOOD
MORDENGLEN
STILLWATER HILLS
STILLWATER
THE WISTLEDGE
STEEPLEFORD
DAYMORN RIVER
FHAARLUY FOREST
WISTPORT
ANRITH
DAHMORN MOUNTAINS
MORNKASTLE
SAAHN
KURR
DIANAAR HILLS
BAY OF BONES
ANVAR
DIANAAR
WAYLORN
RANNIK
TELITH
FHAARLUY RIVER
ARAMOR FOREST
APHENHAST
THE BONEMORD
LUUDHOQ
ARAMOR
N
W E
S
SOUTHERN SEA
RANITH TYR

I – A Violent Path

I

Rocan found a new companion as he roamed the dismal corridors of Mirkwall awaiting the arrival of the starspawn. It took the form of an almost human woman, naked and covered in thick, coarse hair. At first he merely endured her curious attentions, but soon enough he found himself enjoying the company, albeit on a listless and distracted level.

For a day she followed him from a distance, drawing slowly closer like an animal whose need for food slowly causes the ebbing away of its natural fear, until eventually she dared to touch his arm. Rocan considered cutting her to pieces for this bold transgression, but in truth her temerity impressed him. He held the night-black blade of his sword to her neck, which she lifted and bared eagerly as if having her throat slashed by this weapon would be the greatest of honours.

"What do you want with me?" he demanded, but she did not reply. Perhaps, like some others of the *kin*, she had lost the ability to speak. Whatever the reason for her silence, she nevertheless made her intention clear: she went down on all fours and presented her rear, where her hair had become foul with a sickly wetness.

"Follow me," Rocan said, his desire quickening as he smelt her dense, meaty odour.

He led her to the set of rooms he had claimed as his own quarters, and then he unleashed the savagery that had burned in his heart ever since he had first touched the sword and learned its recent heritage. He discovered that the creature had vocal chords after all, and she used them to scream and bellow, pain and lust and agony and ecstasy tumbling over one another in a continuous, chaotic melee.

Finally, as his body spat its seed into the unknown darkness of her womb, he screamed out Suli's name over and over. The rage overcame him to such a degree that the beast-woman hurriedly detached herself and crawled away to the nearest corner, leaking blood and semen and casting fearful glances in his direction as she whispered wordless subservience.

He left her crouching in the shadows, and then he wandered through Mirkwall, roaming the high, windswept levels as well as the lowest reaches where damp seeped throughout the foundations. Many times he found his hand upon the hilt of the sword. He gripped it so tightly that he thought his knuckles might burst through the tight, cold skin that held them. *My gift from Ilumor,* he reminded himself. *It seems only fitting that I use this gift to kill him. Something has infected his nature. He masquerades as* kin *but he has become something else. Whatever the infestation is I must put an end to it, or at least make it leap from his body and show its true form.*

He imagined Ilumor's body falling limply to the flagstones like a fleshy sack as the hidden enemy revealed itself. He imagined himself cutting it to fragments, darkness slicing through the substance of which it was made.

I will be Lord of Mirkwall, he told himself. *Lord of the Mists. Banisher of the Destroying Light.*

He smiled to himself as he rounded a corner to find himself back at the walkway on the edge of the battlements, and then the smile hardened as he saw Ilumor walking in his direction, his cloak wrapped about him.

"Rocan," Ilumor murmured as he stopped a few yards away. Drizzle fell incessantly and a thin stream of rainfall leaked from the gutter above them on the parapet. "The waiting is worse than the battle, is it not?"

"Always." Rocan's hand hovered near the hilt of the sword. *How quickly can I cut him?* Rocan wondered. *How can I make him bleed his secrets onto the stone?*

He could not remember what happened next. It felt as if that moment, during which he drew the sword and lunged at Ilumor, erased itself from his mind. Perhaps the sword itself made the choice to attack. Whatever the truth, in the blink of an eye he had gone from standing on the battlements to fighting the master of Mirkwall.

Ilumor howled in pain as the blade cut through his side. Rocan stepped warily back as Ilumor pressed his free hand against the gaping wound to try and stem the flow of blood. This was not blood the like of which Rocan had seen before. It shone with an otherworldly brightness in the afternoon gloom, and as rivulets of that fluid inevitably found their way between Ilumor's shaking fingers, they ran not only down as expected but also sideways and even upwards.

Rocan took another step back, even as his instinct screamed at him to finish Ilumor off. *Whatever strangeness floods his veins, it can't harm you. You are* kin! *You survived the great battle in the north against the starspawn. All that stands before you here is an imposter, a creature masquerading as* kin, *a false follower. Cut him to pieces.*

But he stood transfixed as Ilumor's wound glowed crimson and then slowly faded. Even for *kin* his healing was rapid. His eyes, as bright and bloody as that brief opening in his flesh, surmised Rocan. A terrifying light shone behind them, and Rocan wondered what might have happened had he cut through Ilumor's skull. Would he have perished then, or might he somehow have survived that also, the illumination healing his brain and fusing together the jagged pieces of bone that housed it?

"In another time I could have tolerated your treachery," Ilumor told him. To Rocan's ears it sounded as if Ilumor had two voices, one low and sibilant and the other high and clear. "We're all creatures of opportunity. But to attempt murder as starspawn assault our fortress? Who do you truly serve, Rocan?"

"I serve our masters the Earth Lords, as you well know." Rocan's skin crawled with heat even as his teeth chattered. He took an unsteady step backwards and almost slipped on the wet flagstones. "Who do *you* serve?"

Ilumor said nothing. He came charging at Rocan, who found himself unable to lift the black sword in time. With the force of that sudden assault, both men struggled on the balcony's edge for a short while. Then Rocan slipped again and lost his balance. That misfortune was itself enough for Ilumor to push him over the edge.

Rocan fell through the mists in silence, to the marsh far below. Ilumor leaned over the edge, watching as he flailed and thrashed desperately for a moment before sinking.

II

The waters had barely settled over Arrko's son when the sound of a single, low blast of a longhorn cut through the damp air. Ilumor felt a chill of excitement as he hastened towards the northern end of the castle which he knew the *marandaal* would be approaching. The starspawn had awoken something in him that he did not find entirely unwelcome- a sense of fear, of possible mortality.

When he reached the battlements he found numerous kin gathered. Some even awaited their enemy at the foot of the great wall, having made their way down to the edge of the surrounding marshland in eagerness to clash with them. Ilumor was likewise eager, but his intelligence lent him a dread that, judging by the shrieking and baying of the multitudes far below, the lower *kin* could not even imagine.

Most of the higher *kin* gathered on the ramparts of the fortress, some on the same level as him and some clustered together on others. The air crackled and hummed with a vast energy that set his teeth on edge. Above and

10

before him the ever-present swirling Mirkfog had taken on a yellowish hue, and although it remained as damp as ever it felt sharp and almost noxious, as if the very act of breathing this dense and sorcerous air might blister his insides.

Then, no more than several hundred paces away from the castle walls, six concentrations of light emerged slowly from out of the mist. A deafening roar rose up amongst the entire gathering of *kin,* a cacophony that defied description and almost obliterated Ilumor's thoughts. He could not have shouted orders amidst the din, but he had no need to. Every creature gathered here knew on some level what was required of it, regardless of its intelligence and no matter its heritage- human, *luyan, crommar,* bestial, sorcerous or unknown.

Nearer still the *marandaal* came, and the marshland all around became bathed in their otherworldly illumination.

They walked into a seething mass of creatures seeping with the Old Powers, and Ilumor saw a chaos of light and shadow unleashed in an instant. Keening shrieks of rage hung in the dank air. He directed his own river of power towards the *marandaal.* It leapt and poured from him, unstoppable in the face of the Great Enemy, until finally, with the battle not yet won he collapsed to the wet stone, a turmoil inside him that he knew came from the alien light that wrestled with the Old Powers through every vein in his body.

III

Ilumor woke in his quarters to the sound of someone or something whispering to him. At first he couldn't properly identify the maker of those sounds, but then it stepped from out of the deeper gloom, a *kin*-creature that might once have been a human child but which had far too many limbs- some more well-formed than others- and a small second head that protruded as a growth from the larger one, sharing the same scaly, thick-veined neck.

I am dying, it whispered, lidless eyes wide as it regarded him.

Ilumor sat up slowly, resting his arms on the damp mattress. Ignoring the mysterious creature that stood nearby, he closed his eyes and allowed his *kin*-sense free rein to roam the great castle.

He quickly discovered that Mirkwall was a lonelier place than before. Here and there he saw, heard and smelled small groups of *kin,* many of them wounded. But where previously many hundreds had occupied even the furthest-flung corners of the fortress, now perhaps several dozen still lingered. There might have been more survivors at first, but those too badly wounded to heal themselves or be of further use would have been consumed. He found one pale, hulking creature whose bloated stomach held the half-digested pieces of two smaller kin.

Of the *marandaal,* he saw no sign. Only the countless bodies and body parts festooning the silent corridors and battlements remained as evidence that the starspawn had come to Mirkwall and attempted to destroy all within it.

I led the defence of our home, he thought. *Despite Arrko's mad son and his plans for me. But I fell before the victory was complete.*

He opened his eyes suddenly. Where was Rocan? Had he perished, drowned in the marshes? Or had he survived? *I saw him drown,* Ilumor recalled. *But then I too seem to remember drowning in the marsh, for a little while.*

The *kin* creature whispered to him again. But the words it now uttered convinced Ilumor that only a crude vessel stood by his bedside, doing the bidding of some far higher entity.

You are no longer needed here. The words drifted over to him, a whisper in both ears and inside his head. *The battle is done with.*

Ilumor did not know who or what spoke to him, but at first he assumed that with the starspawn driven back, his lords had a new task for him and a new place to which he must go. He sat up, attentive. "My lords, ask and I shall gather the survivors, and..."

Impossibly strong, one of the *kin*-child's more muscular arms whipped forth, and a hand like cold iron seized his windpipe. The grey-lipped mouth opened a crack, and through that narrow aperture Ilumor caught a glimpse of a savage white light, a terrifying brilliance that he knew from his tormented dreams and which, inexplicably, knew him inside and out, through all the untold centuries he had lived.

"They no longer hear you." The voice was clear now, as bright and as powerful as the force that writhed and roiled within its hapless container. "You cannot call to them. I have made it so."

The hand released him, and he fell back on the bed, unable to speak.

"There is a weakening, Ilumor. When order is allowed to unravel, when the heart itself can change, the great darkness will arrive sooner. It will achieve permanence. I have already chosen you to walk the outer path on my behalf, yet events move ever further beyond control. You must walk the innermost path also."

Ilumor tried to understand. "Do you..." He coughed and swallowed painfully. "Do you mean places other than this? The secret places known only to the guardians of Aona? The Endless Shore? The Silver Road?"

"The Green Road."

Ilumor felt a chill scythe its way through him. He had heard plenty about the Green Road, though not for over three hundred years. It was thought that this mythical place was reached by several of the First themselves, unknown to the *choragh*. In time, of course, they too learned about it, but according to most of the tales he had heard they had never been able to reach it. This was around the time of the Fading, when the First and their immediate descendants became the dominant force in the north of Harn, despite having to flee the south as the Seven and their minions the High Watchers arrived. The *choragh* became weaker and retreated to more distant places, away from the Younger Races.

"I have never walked the Green Road," he managed to say. "I have heard of men and women who could. But no one has reached that place for many centuries. I would not know how. It's as far beyond my reach as the stars themselves."

"One other has walked the Road already. She is in great danger."

"Are you not all-powerful? Can you not protect her?" Ilumor feared a painful reprisal as soon as those words swiftly left his lips, and it was not long in coming. This time the hand seized his head, and he screamed in agony. It felt as if his brain was being scorched black. When finally the creature released him, he convulsed for a long while on the bed, mouth opening and closing as his entire body seized up with waves of pain.

In time, the ordeal subsided. His assailant loomed closer. "You were mine once, Ilumor, before you became theirs," it said quietly. "Of course, you remember nothing of that Age."

He tried to speak, but all he could taste was hot blood at the back of his throat.

"I could boil you alive in your fluids," it continued. Light flared up within the creature, momentarily displaying a crude patchwork of veins. "But you have work to do. You will be led towards the path you need to take. You will find the child and you will protect her at any and all costs."

Ilumor said nothing. For a moment he thought of calling to his masters, using every last ounce of energy he had. Perhaps they would heed his call and something would happen in response, something to deny this entity. But the idea died as swiftly as it had been born as he recalled the words his tormentor had spoken. *They no longer hear you.*

I will wait until it leaves, he tried to tell himself. *It lies, in order to bend me to its will. Regardless, I can't walk the Green Road. Even my Lords can't reach that place.*

The creature turned and left him without another word. Ilumor lay for a while and willed his heart to be calm. Cold and rational thinking lay beyond his reach; black emotions surged through his mind, and above them all a simmering rage at his endless slavery. For centuries he had accepted the yoke of the Earth Lords and had appreciated the rewards of his servitude. But *this*- an unrewarded subservience to an unknown entity that sought not only to control him but to torture his body and his very being for the slightest transgression- this was an agonising misery the like of which he could never have imagined, and from which he could envisage no escape.

The hand of the choragh *never struck me in anger unless clearly justified,* he thought when finally he was able to think at all. There had been times, long ago, when he had enjoyed the rewards his powers had provided for too long a time and at the expense of the greater, far more important matters- using those powers for the advancement of the causes favoured by his Lords. When that happened he had been set back upon the right path. But they had never needlessly tortured him.

He went outside, where the rain had turned to snow which spiralled silently through the mists. The Mirkfog looked thicker than ever, above and below. Ilumor breathed in the still, harsh air and closed his eyes, attempting silently to reach out beyond Mirkwall, through air and over land and water, seeking his masters. But all he could feel, all he could see in his mind's eye was the mist and the snow.

They no longer hear you.

Ilumor did not understand how that could be. Somehow he had been tainted by the alien presence. It shone through his dreams; it had poured into his veins, turning him into something that was somehow both greater than and less than the *kin*. It claimed to be the voice of Aona herself. But if that was so, then why would it cut him off from his masters, who themselves were the guardians of Aona, and had been for thousands upon thousands of years?

He walked back inside and headed along one of the longer routes back to his quarters. *I must find a way to speak to my Lords,* he decided, *or find a way for them to discover what has happened here.*

Sometime later, Ilumor found himself standing at the top of a deep stairwell. An icy draught issued from out of the dark, disturbing thick white cobwebs that festooned the walls. *I don't recall seeing this before,* he mused, and immediately the idea occurred to him that this might be a subtle ploy to lure him away from the Mirkwall he knew, to a place where the light that tormented him ruled unquestionably. *Whereas here,* he reminded himself, *the* kin *still wander and the power of the Earth Lords holds sway- in Mirkwall if not inside me.*

One of the kin *must go to our Lords and explain what happened,* he thought suddenly. *If I cannot, then it must fall to one of them must carry out the task. The strongest and most quick-witted of the survivors.*

He turned abruptly and walked the long cold distance to the eastern wing of the great fortress where groups of *kin* huddled, licking their wounds and awaiting a sign from the *choragh* or Ilumor. He found one such group, a motley assortment of creatures that turned as one as he walked into their chamber through an archway. Even the lupine beast that was busy ransacking the opened body of a fallen comrade looked expectantly at him, a long piece of intestine held like a plaything in its mouth.

"If *any* of you receive a sign from our Lords, seek me out immediately," he said, as he surveyed each one of them in turn, wondering which of them might be least ill-suited to convey his message to the *choragh*.

Those who could, meanwhile, nodded their acceptance at his instruction. Ilumor heard one of them, a female covered mostly in thick, matted hair, also growl a word. He listened attentively as she repeated it, and thought it sounded very much like *Rocan*. Ilumor's gaze wandered down to her bloated belly, and he smiled as he sensed the coiled sliver of life nestled within. "Now there's a swift pregnancy," he noted. "Your progeny will be fatherless. Rocan went mad and threw himself down into the Mirk." *More or less,* he mentally added.

The beast appeared to understand, for she uttered a low howl as if lamenting the demise of Arrko's son. Ilumor had to agree that his death had been a waste in some ways. But perhaps the night-bladed sword had maddened him. The object might well have worked its insidious effect upon many of its wielders down the centuries- he had even learned the fate of some of them.

Ilumor turned to another of the *kin,* a wiry, muscular man dressed in rags who squatted down on the floor, passing a dagger from one long-nailed hand to the other and back again. "You," Ilumor said, making his decision there and then as he sensed the sharpness of the *kin*-man's intelligence. "I have a task for you."

"Name it and it shall be done." The *kin*-man bowed his head.

"Leave Mirkwall. Head north-and-west, avoiding any starspawn that may linger. Find the largest group of *kin* that you can, and in so doing you should find a way to convey a message to our Lords. The message is this; something has happened in Mirkwall that requires their intervention."

Ilumor paused. "No. Something has happened to *me* that requires their intervention. Something is wrong. One of them must come to Mirkwall." Ilumor gestured to the archway. "Go now. Do not return until the message has been passed."

Ilumor could not find his way back to his quarters.

Realising quickly that the unnamed parasite had woven some spell about him, he worked his way from the inside out, or attempted to. Yet when he turned what should have been a final corner, beyond which a doorway would lead him out into the mist, he instead found a black stone wall, cracked and dusty with age no matter how recently it might have been spirited into place.

It occurred to him suddenly that perhaps he ought to have commanded the *kin*-man to lead him out of Mirkwall. The request would have seemed odd, but it would not have been questioned. Only the *choragh* questioned higher *kin*. It would at least have allowed him to put distance between himself and this twisted version of the fortress which only he had the misfortune of enduring.

I'll go to them now, he decided, and he retraced his steps as best he could.

But time slipped by alarmingly. When he finally reached the chamber where the group of *kin* had been resting, he found only Rocan's lover and an infant, dark with clumps of hair and caked blood, sucking or perhaps even chewing at its mother's heavy breast. Mother and child looked up at him at the same time, and Ilumor saw fear and hatred wide and clear in their eyes. The *kin*-woman snarled at him and her offspring took up the act, displaying a set of sharp, glistening teeth as a trickle of milk and blood streaked languidly down its chin.

He turned and once again attempted to navigate his way to his quarters. When he could not, he instead made his way down towards the main exit doors from the castle, but they no longer stood where they ought. In their place a stone stairwell he had never seen before invited him down into unknown depths.

"I would not walk your Road even if I were able," he called out. "I am a lord amongst the *kin*, and favoured by the Guardians of Aona themselves."

"You are lord of nothing," a voice spoke up behind him. Ilumor jumped and turned to see the *kin*-man he had sent to convey his message to the *choragh*. He had, apparently, been prevented from leaving and- judging by the lurid gleam in the man's eyes- subverted in much the same way as the mutated child.

"You continue to fight against me," it accused him.

"For as long as I draw breath." But fear took flight in his heart when it asked, "How much pain do you think you can bear? You *are* mine, but for as long as you think you are not, you will be punished. You will beg to die, but I cannot let you until your work is done."

"I belong to the true guardians..." he began, but his words became a scream as immense pain built in his groin and he fell forwards. He could feel himself being crushed. His vision became infested with a deep red smear as wave after wave of agony crashed through him. For a moment he passed out, and when he came to he was he kneeling before the *kin*-man's compromised body.

Ilumor spat blood upon the cold stone. It gleamed fiercely in the failing light, hot and bright. "What... have you done to me?" he croaked.

"I have remade you," it said softly. An unseen hand caressed his cheek and Ilumor flinched from the touch. "By destroying me?" Still he could not keep the fury from his voice, but in the aftermath of those words he feared whatever torture it might choose for him next. He could feel blood and even flesh sliding down his legs, the torn and mangled remains of his genitalia.

"I have not made an end of you. That time will come, but for now you have a journey to make." So saying, it pointed to the stairwell.

Ilumor got to his feet and began making his way down the staircase with painful slowness. When he happened to look up, he saw that the light had gone from its container. The *kin*-man stood staring into an indeterminate distance, dull-witted and slack-jawed.

Ilumor walked on and down until his legs almost gave way. He rested with his face pressed against the cold, damp stone each time they threatened to buckle and send him tumbling down into the dark, wishing that he could melt into its mass and be crushed, and never have to walk another step. More than once he contemplated allowing himself to fall to wherever the bottom of the spiral lay, but he knew that the road ahead had become inevitable. Even if his bones were broken and his innards smashed to pulp he would be forced to stand and walk, little more than a *diafagh* as step by awkward step he staggered on, wracked with endless pain.

The steps ended eventually. A passage led away, and this gradually widened until he emerged into what looked like a cobbled yard behind a tall building. One lamp lit the alley that connected the yard with a street. Night had fallen.

No, Ilumor thought suddenly as he looked into the sky. *This is not night as I know it.*

No stars dotted the cloudless sky, nor could he see either of the moons. A faint green glow with no apparent direction or source suffused everything here- not only the featureless sky but also the silent buildings and, he felt certain, this entire nameless city.

I am here, he thought in wonderment, and stood contemplating that fact for what could have been an age. The world around him gave no sign of changing as time went on, leading Ilumor to believe that in this place, like the Silver

Road and the Endless Shore, time held its breath, or was entirely absent.

IV

Ilumor soon learned that the city was devoid of any sort of life that he might comprehend. It had no citizens, no overlords. Law and reason had no presence here, no reason to exist. And yet as he walked the dimly-lit and oppressively silent streets, he saw entities that bore vague resemblance to creatures, moving swiftly from place to place as if carrying out unknown errands. All of these mysteries kept their distance. He saw shadows deepen until they became gaping holes from which he hastened away. Sudden light flared up for brief moments, pouring from the windows of buildings or from cracks in the ground. He shied away in fear, recognising its nature- for it was the same unspeakable illumination that had become a part of him, casting itself upon the darkest recesses of his body and mind.

Eventually even the silence was broken, and he heard a rhythm that might have been thunder or the crushing fall of a thousand great boulders. It shook the ground. It forced open great chasms in buildings and the ground on which he walked. Somehow it sounded portentous. The noise became chaotic, urgent, and the rhythm broke into random thumps and vast groans that emanated from out of the fissures torn along the streets and the dim sky above at the same time. Ilumor had a sudden urge to run, to leave behind the awful sights and sounds of this place, but he knew that fleeing was not possible. In all likelihood the city perimeter would widen at the same rate that he tried to rush towards it.

Instead he stopped walking. His heart still thumped audibly, and Ilumor imagined that with every beat the light hidden behind the surfaces of this world pulsed to the same fearful rhythm.

21

A sound like the snapping of rotting wood or bones came from behind him. He could not bring himself to turn and look directly behind, but when he glanced to his left he saw a great shadow move slowly over the ground.

Move!

He obeyed the inner voice without a moment's hesitation, and strode across the ground towards a vast bridge. Two thousand hands or more below, a winding river glittered faintly, marking out the division between two jagged cliffs. Spurs of glassy rock and petrified trees jutted out from either side of this deep valley. From some of these he saw figures hanging, and despite the gloom his *kin*-eyes picked out the dismal state of these entities in all too perfect detail. One had great feathered wings that bent backwards, pulled so fiercely to either side that they half-revealed the flesh of the torso. Another had thin branches of stone, or glass, or wood, wrapped around and threaded through its body, which hung like an ancient, withered offering over the river far below.

They were not alive, nor had they ever been. He felt certain of that. Yet he also knew that they represented something about Aona herself, or the creatures that occupied the waking world. Beings that were spat out into the daylight and wandered through their lifetimes to finally become consumed by earth or fire, nothing more than tiny parts of an eternal cycle that had no known purpose.

His gaze was drawn to a path that led off the bridge and down the side of the valley. "No," he whispered as he felt himself being compelled to walk along it. "No!"

The route down to the river was perilous. In places barely wide enough for him to step along it, the path changed direction, turned sharply around and even ascended on occasion. Every time he stopped to rest he could feel intense heat or cold radiating from the rock face. He wanted nothing more than to lean against it to rest, but dreaded that he would either burst into flames or become stuck to the rock and freeze solid.

"I hate you," he whispered at one point, and immediately felt a stab of fear as he wondered what violent response his tired rage would elicit. But nothing happened. He remained standing on the path, trying not to touch the rock face looming to his right or look down into the chasm where the still-distant river waited.

When finally he reached the valley floor he sank down by the water's edge, listening to the flow of the water. For a moment he thought he could see stars- familiar stars by which one might navigate- somewhere within the water. But a moment later the river caught only the faint green hue of the sky from far above.

Finally he struggled to his feet and began walking alongside the river. *I must be headed in the right direction,* he reasoned, *or else I would be forced to reconsider, or beaten by some invisible force.*

The sides of the river valley grew closer together and became smoother. Up ahead Ilumor saw vast columns of black stone on one side. When he drew closer and peered up he saw that they looked like statues. *But who could possibly have carved them?* he wondered. *Is everything here created by Aona herself, or are other forces at work?*

He stopped to gaze up at them a while longer, drawn to their sombre, forbidding faces. For a time he remained transfixed, and wondered what the architect of these great monstrosities looked like. He could not have said how long he stood with his head uplifted to the dim heavens, but a sense of utter wonder came to him. If the Green Road was truly Aona's inner heart, how and why did this environment appear as it did? Had it always been thus, or had it evolved over time, and if so then from what? Did Aona herself control all that appeared and happened here, or was much of it random?

Ilumor had been *kin* for a very long time- even he could not have said how long exactly- and he had certain knowledge of how worlds came into being, cooled and condensed and eventually, if very particular conditions were met, harboured the first signs of life. But Aona was far beyond such understanding, and perhaps also beyond the understanding of his former masters the *choragh.* This world did not obey universal laws that were observed throughout the Existence. It- or *she,* he told himself- was not simply a world that harboured life, but life herself.

And yet she is responsible for the light that ruined and enslaved me and tortured me almost to the point where I thought my mind might snap, he recalled. *And so she is a hateful mistress, generous only with her punishments.*

He stopped that train of thought suddenly, again fearful of instant and savage retribution. Yet none came. *It will come when I no longer expect it,* he decided as finally he looked away from the immense structures bordering the valley and began to walk again.

After a time the valley widened and the great slopes on either side fell away, so that after a while Ilumor found himself walking over open land. He stopped several times, so exhausted that he thought he might be unable to continue of his own accord and would need to be forced along this preordained path instead. Yet somehow he stood up and walked on each time, his legs shaking with the effort.

Suddenly he felt the faint caress of a cool breeze, and he stopped to look around and then up into the sky.

Stars, he thought, staring at the forest of pinprick points. He almost smiled with relief, but a shard of bright pain began to build inside his head. It disappeared only when he began heading west across the open grassland, shivering in the wintry breeze.

II – Light Without Shadow

I

Caul looked up apprehensively as the weaponsmaster Lerim walked over. Even here in the soft physicality of the Silver Road, Lerim's steps were sure and far from soundless. The silvery light that suffused this realm bathed him on all sides, lacking direction. Caul could not get used to the effect. It bore a slight resemblance to the illumination yielded by Ildar on an especially bright night, except that here in this twilit netherworld Ildar never appeared, nor did the red moon Archaon, nor even the familiar stars of the sky under which they had all been born. Nothing that they could name occupied the sky. This was an inner world, where the pinpoint lights of the great Void remained forever absent- a faint shadow of Aona which made for a sterile place where day and night and perhaps time itself meant nothing.

Lerim stooped near, a grim expression upon his hard, lined face. "Even here," he said quietly, "I feel the movements of the Old Dark. I don't need your talents to sense them. They are out there, some drifting without purpose- but the more predatory amongst them watch us. Once or twice I've seen them for a moment. Sometimes, Caul, I even sense their hunger. Are they drawing nearer?"

Caul nodded. "I don't doubt it." Not only had he felt the transient malevolence of *kin* and other servants of the *choragh* moving in and out of the Silver Road, he had caught glimpses of some of them in considerable detail even from what appeared to be a great distance, out in the great plains beyond the woods. Of course, distance did not mean quite the same thing here; its measurement was ambivalent at best, so he could not tell how near they might be nor how easy they might be to wound or kill. Many of these physical manifestations vanished soon after they appeared, and he had wondered if some of them might even be echoes of whatever journeys such creatures happened to be undertaking in the Aona of true colour and substance.

But as Lerim had pointed out, these echoes affected them all. The Silver Road was far from safe. It crawled with many kinds of evil.

"We had no choice but to open the pathway," Caul reminded the overlord. "They came from all sides like a swarming pestilence in the dawn. You saw for yourself that their host ran many rows thick. Close on two thousand swarmed the barricades with higher *kin* amongst them, driving them further in their bloodlust."

"I saw them well enough. But sometimes I think we should have stood our ground and taken down as many as we could," Lerim said bitterly.

"I doubt your wife and children would agree," Caul interrupted him, "now would they? We cannot wilfully hasten our own ruin. We're sent back into the earth when the earth is good and ready."

Lerim scowled. "Never mind your philosophies. How long until the others of your circle are strong enough to lead the return?"

Caul shook his head. "There'll be no going back to Cai, Lerim. The *kin* will have made it their own, subverted the very material of the place. If we return..."

"*When* we return."

"...it will be to some other place. Perhaps the Wistledge."

"We're not on good terms with the westfolk, Caul. You know that."

"Are we on better terms with the *kin*?"

Lerim fell to brooding silence. "Inform me when the circle is strong enough," he said eventually.

Caul watched him leave, grateful that he didn't have to suffer the man any further for the time being. Lerim had always carried a restless and bristling anger, and the forced flight of the *du-luyan* from Cai had worsened his nature. He saw it as some sort of affront to his honour. Caul did not like weaponsmasters in general, and certainly he had never supported their ascent to high office amongst the *du-luyan* people. Once, perhaps, their profession had been a noble and principled one- certainly enough of *du-luyan* history indicated that much- but those he had known personally were nothing more than glorified assassins and murderers. Most of them made a living from the sale of their skills to humans, *luyan* or whoever else wanted to get rid of someone who had slighted them. Misguidedly they believed that their bloody deeds spread respect for their race; Caul saw only the spread of fear.

He's like his little brother Iyoth, Caul thought. *But at least those of us who love peace are well rid of Iyoth. He never did return to Cai, and if he returned now...*

Caul smiled and shook his head, imagining Iyoth and Lerim together battling the *kin,* hacking in hopeless rage at dead-eyed *diafagh,* their blades whirling uselessly through the air, all their potent skills of no regard whatsoever to the Old Dark.

His thoughts turned inevitably to the fate of their people. The circle of six warlocks of which he was a part had expended vast energy in opening a way through to the Silver Road, allowing an escape route for the *du-luyan* of Cai. Of the six, two had died shortly afterwards. The four who remained would have to somehow open a way back into the world they knew and Caul doubted that they had the strength between them, especially if they tried to reach the Wistledge- a far less familiar place than Cai.

Caul feared that it might not even be possible to control the path of their return, when eventually they did make the attempt. *We could find ourselves anywhere if we struggle to maintain the connection,* he thought. *One of the cities ruined by the* marandaal, *perhaps- or even somewhere out in the vastness of the ocean.*

But we can't stay here. This place will madden us in days. Not that we can even measure days in this place.

He wondered suddenly why the *kin* had come to Cai in such great numbers. If something about the place was important to them then Caul certainly was not aware of it, and he knew his history and lore as well as anyone.

That would be to find out if and when they returned to the world they knew.

Caul went to find the others in his circle to seek their opinion. A dark thought occurred to him as he walked the dark narrow paths between clearings of the silent forest. *I condemn Lerim for thinking we should have stayed in Cai to be honourably slaughtered, and yet a part of me hopes that we perish in attempting to return, rather than remain in limbo in a shadow world washed free of colour and natural life.*

He found Merithen first. She sat on a boulder on a rise that overlooked open scrubland. "I see them everywhere," she said without preamble as he came to stand nearby. "A few are nothing more than passing shadows-some construct or other of this place. But others are linked somehow with the *kin*. They observe us."

"And yet they keep their distance," Caul observed.

"For now, although I fear their reticence will be short-lived. More will find their way here, and numbers will fuel their courage." Merithen glanced at him, looking troubled. "Our combined presence serves only to tear at the fabric of the Silver Road, Caul. I have been here once before, and this place has changed."

"In what way?"

"It's weaker, more tenuous somehow. Less predictable. Did you know that a sinkhole opened up in a clearing not far from here? It swallowed an entire family."

Caul shuddered, yet pointed out, "Are such things so unusual, even here?"

Merithen looked away. "They were, once. But this sudden cavity- as far as we know, it had no measurable depth. Those who tumbled into that abyss are likely falling even now, and forever more."

He tried not to think about that. "Then we need to leave before we're ready. Even if some of us are killed by the act of opening the pathway."

"I don't think we will ever be ready. Where would such a pathway lead?"

"The Wistledge, perhaps. If a bargain can be struck, it may be that we'll be allowed to remain there awhile. The war will come of course, but at least we'll be there to fight it."

"We may not be strong enough to open the gateway, let alone maintain position on the other side, or its shape and form. It would be liking grappling with both ends of a snake at the same time."

"Yes. I'd thought about that. But we have to try, Merithen. The Road will destroy us otherwise. This is no place for the living. Not even the *kin*."

She nodded and got up. "Let's find Arian and Rend, and hear what they have to say."

"It must be done," Caul said quietly as he followed her.

They found the other two surviving members of their circle sitting together, studying a map which they had laid flat with the aid of two stones. Arian and Rend glanced up at their approach, and Arian, the youngest of their number, pointed across the clearing to a tree whose branches, unlike those of its neighbours, rose upwards into the monotonous sky as if each limb sought desperately to avoid proximity to the ground. *The swallowing earth,* Caul thought, *and the chasms with neither light nor end. This place is madness.*

"Something bleeds from its bark," Arian told them. "It isn't sap, nor is it anything we've seen before. One of the children called it *Aona's tears*. That may be an unwitting truth for all we know."

Caul imagined the world caught up in a frenzy of wild, fearful grief and lashing out at itself, slowly eating away the very heart that sustained it.

"The rules that have kept this place together wear thin," Rend added. Caul thought he had aged a couple of decades during their time here. "It's time for us to open a pathway and leave."

Caul looked at Merithen, who stared thoughtfully down at the ground for a moment. "We may all perish, if we leave so soon. How do we know we can hold the pathway open until everyone is safe?"

"We can't," Rend said simply. "But we have no choice. Will you wait until the ground on which we sit disappears, or the sky itself lowers and thickens to suffocate and crush us against the earth?"

Merithen nodded slowly. "Then let's do what we need to do."

Soon all those who had survived the escape from Cai gathered just beyond the woodland, close to the open ground where they had arrived. "We will attempt to direct our pathway towards the Wistledge in Harn," Caul spoke up. His voice sounded oddly flat and still, as if he spoke in a closed room rather than a great open space. "We will ask for shelter from our cousins there."

A murmur of unease rose up immediately. The two communities were separated not only by distance but by an enmity that had seethed for decades. Originally a disagreement between two ruling families, it had been allowed to continue and worsen like a festering wound for many years. Time and distance had not tempered it.

Yet not one of them argued against the decision. They could see for themselves that the time had come to flee the Silver Road. No matter the unease and mistrust between the two *du-luyan* communities, the Wistledge was the only place where they might find some measure of safety. Certainly they couldn't live near to human or *luyan* settlements.

Caul, Merithen, Rend and Arian linked hands and stood facing one another. Each of them could see the Powers stirring in the eyes of his or her companions. *May we all live another day under skies we understand,* Caul thought, willing himself to be as calm as possible.

As the roaring darkness of the Powers surged through their blood, a shimmering commenced in the open land before them. Caul did not need to open his tight-shut eyes to see it. He could tell by the murmurs of those all around them.

As had been agreed beforehand, the four of them concentrated on the same focal points within the Wistledge, places that they could visualise. They had all been there at least once, as part of the various diplomatic missions that had been attempted over the years. Caul pictured in his mind the sharp contours of Highpeak, the greatest mountain in the Wistledge range, and the Daymorn River as it cut through the deep valleys, heading towards the west coast of Harn.

When finally they stepped away from one another, he could barely stand. An archway of diffuse, wavering light stood before them, its height and width changing slightly from moment to moment.

Lerim was the first of them to step through, and down the pathway beyond the light- a pathway that, if fortune favoured them, would lead to the Wistledge. *His fear of this place pushes him onwards,* Caul thought with faint contempt.

As on their journey to the Silver Road, the four of them who were strong in the Old Powers waited, keeping the gateway as stable as possible as everyone else filed through. Many of their people were obviously frightened, and the younger children had to be calmed, yet everyone did their best not to let that fear consume them. Finally, as the last of their people made their way through the shimmering archway they stepped after them.

The pathway glowed almost as if light emanated from the ground itself. All around them the Silver Road grew somehow fainter, yet at the same time darker than ever, as if they had only just avoided a great black wave washing over the fragmenting landscape. Caul fancied that he heard faint cries of anguish in the distance up ahead, but he forced his thoughts away from those sounds. The distance itself could be mere paces away or half a world- measurements twisted themselves in knots in this place, and they more than likely became even less predictable as the Silver Road's state grew more calamitous.

When finally they stepped off the pathway at its end, a more familiar night scene awaited them. Ildar's light bathed the open grassland and the steep, jagged mountains that rose in the west. *The Wistledge,* Caul thought, his relief almost overwhelming.

As he looked around, however, a chill went through him. Not everyone had emerged from the pathway. Perhaps a quarter of their number were missing, and cries of distress grew as the people of Cai realised this.

"We're not alone," Arian said quietly at his side, and gestured to the rocky outcrop less than a hundred paces to the west.

As if in response to her words, at least two hundred figures rose from behind the rocks, their dark leather armour gleaming in Ildar's light. Caul heard the sounds of their own people drawing longknives and scimitars all around. *This will be a bloodbath,* he thought frantically, and immediately shouted, "Don't attack! Lay down your weapons! This is *their* territory, not ours."

Most of them acquiesced, as *du-luyan* folk of the Wistledge approached, many of them armed with loaded shortbows. At the head of these people walked a tall, narrow-faced man with thinning hair. He regarded them balefully. Caul's heart sank in the face of this quiet resentment. *We had no choice,* he told himself.

"A blatant shattering of the fragile peace between us," the man spoke up eventually. "Will one of you step forward to explain this? Where does your leader conceal himself?"

Lerim stepped quickly forward. Perhaps the insinuation that he hid amongst his people goaded him into the act. "I am Lerim, weaponsmaster and head of the Kamoalan family," he said. "I lead these people. The Old Dark came in vast numbers to Cai. We had no choice but to leave."

When the other man stared at him, Lerim quickly added, "Better that we live to fight the minions of the *choragh* another time. We remained awhile in the Silver Road to recover, but..." He glanced at Caul and the others of his circle. "It is breaking apart. The world itself is starting to collapse."

The Wistledge man smiled at that. "What would you expect? The starspawn have reached Aona. It is up to us to defend her against them, for the sake of all things."

Caul watched as the bowmen moved around. Something about the look in their eyes unnerved him. He glanced back at their leader. *He is* kin, Caul thought suddenly. *How could I have not known? Some sort of cloaking is in place, but the mask is not secure. And there are others too- scattered amongst these people.*

Only Arian stood near enough for him to whisper to. "I think they mean to kill us all," he murmured. She merely nodded, tight-lipped- then whispered back, "*Kin.*"

Despite his exhaustion, Caul felt the Powers begin to stir within him, a deep, ancient fury directed at all those who would turn the world dark. Arian glanced across at him, and he could see the same in her eyes.

Then a hail of arrows flew through the night.

II

In the eruption of chaos that followed, time almost stood still. Caul felt helpless, watching the scene as if he was nothing more than a spectator.

Somehow none of the arrows found him, but it was only when he saw the oncoming *kin-* they were no longer *duluyan,* he told himself- rushing at them in a mass of whirling blades that he shook himself free of his torpor. He stumbled backwards as the Old Powers streamed from him, almost beyond control. Several foes fell to the ground nearby. One of them shook wildly, a black liquid streaming from between his chattering teeth as he tried to withstand the invisible onslaught. Another, a female with a shaven head, almost reached him but fell back screaming, choking and clawing at her throat until it split and burst open.

Caul was vaguely aware of Arian cutting down their enemies nearby. She was a far superior fighter to him, and she danced amongst their foes, wounding and darting away too quickly for them to reach her. *She must be shielding herself somehow,* Caul thought as he caught his breath. When he looked around in each direction he saw that some of their people had already fled. Others fought, but their foes numbered far too many and he suspected that others waited somewhere, ready to pour forth should they be needed.

But if there are then they won't be needed, he thought, staring in dismay at the bodies of his people who had already fallen. *We need to flee as well.*

"Arian!" he shouted, as he used what strength he had left to hold back the tide of *kin.* She came to his side and seemed to understand what he wanted to tell her.

Something loomed nearby. Caul turned sideways to see a lumbering creature bearing down upon him- a *duluyan* man but taller and wider than he ought to be. Twisted musculature bulged from his naked torso and veins pulsed madly in his arms as he reached towards Caul. He would have been too late to withstand the attack but for the arrow that suddenly appeared embedded through the man's eye and deep into his brain. As he fell to the ground, uttering a roar of agony, Caul turned and paused only to make sure Arian was at his side. Neither Merithen nor Rend could be seen. *Perhaps they've already fled,* he thought, as he and Arian turned and ran.

As they disappeared into the night, a dismal realisation tormented him. *Now we're reduced to nothing. In the Silver Road we were at least survivors. We had one another. Now most of us lie dead and the remainder are scattered, fleeing through the dark.*

We'll be hunted. The kin *will track us through the woods and over open land, across water, even over land that we burn and leave behind us as ashes. They'll track our fear, and they'll find us. And this is my doing.*

They ran on into the night, and the sounds of rabid butchery faded behind them.

III – The Fortress of Miracles

I

Anlerran stirred suddenly. How long had she been standing here?

The great hall lay empty and her audience, to whom she had pleaded so desperately, had departed without the slightest response to her words. Might her arrival here have caused a rift amongst the *illeagh*? She feared that it had.

"Is anyone still there?" She spoke softly, nervously listening to the harsh echo her voice made. No reply came.

Anlerran didn't know what else to do. She turned and made her way down a dark stone tunnel that led away beyond one of the archways. From time to time she felt faint, so she stopped for a moment each time and reached out to support herself against the cold wall of the passageway.

She walked for a long time, taking one turning after another at random, heading along lonely passageways, up and down dusty staircases and occasionally into rooms whose walls gaped emptily at her. She listened intently but heard only the sounds that she herself made. She looked for footsteps in the dust but found none except her own.

Eventually Anlerran reached the top of a flight of stairs and found a half-open door that led into a furnished bedchamber. She wandered slowly in, noting the lit lantern, prepared bed and a view through the window on the far side of the room of a grim mountain scene that stretched away into the dusk. After a moment, remembering her state of nakedness she took one of the rough, thick blankets from the bed and draped it around herself. The woollen fabric made her skin itch but the warmth was a relief.

Anlerran could not be sure how long she remained standing there, looking through the window and allowing

36

thoughts to come and go, but eventually she turned, certain that she was no longer alone.

Someone stood in the doorway.

As soon as she set eyes upon the figure standing on the threshold she knew instinctively who it was. She watched, wide-eyed and tremulous as he walked slowly over to her. He was handsome in an otherworldly way; his eyes changed colour from a peaceful lilac to dark brown as they gazed upon her, so dark that they looked almost black before they changed to pale lilac again. His skin, almost translucent like a *luyan* man, appeared delicate but also marble-like, as if he had somehow been chiselled from the stone of the *illeagh* fortress. Brown hair reached down in waves as far as his shoulders, yet even that was not entirely one colour- Anlerran caught a glimpse of many others as he moved.

"Anlerran." He whispered the word as if he scarcely believed that she stood before him. "Do you know who I am? Ah. You do. I can see as much."

"You're... you're my..." Anlerran shook her head, feeling faint.

She jumped, startled as he clasped her hand for a moment. "My name is Elluron. And yes, I am your father." His expression grew sad as he let her hand go. "I abandoned you. But you already know that, I'm sure."

"You left me in good hands." Her voice shook.

"I watched you from the shadows in the Great Hall," he said. "I listened to your impassioned words. I wanted to reach out to support you then, but that would have done no good. My opinion counts for little here, so it would not have helped. But in any case, I found myself entranced by the words you spoke."

Anlerran suddenly realised what that meant. "I was naked!" She could think of nothing else to say, but felt embarrassment bloom in her cheeks.

Perhaps also embarrassed in his own way, Elluron hastily wandered over to the window and looked out. "Many of the *illeagh* have given careful consideration to your words. It may be that some of them even choose to rise against the *marandaal* and the *choragh*."

Anlerran's heart thumped wildly. Could that be true? Had she truly been able to convince some of them? She could hardly dare to believe it. "We have no hope without them," she said. "I'm certain of that."

"As am I." He sat down on a chair by the window. "I hid myself from the world for a long time, Anlerran- and yet I know more of it than you may suppose. More recently, I've travelled and learned. I've seen the chaos spreading in the east. A united Harn must face it, but for Harn to be united your companions will need to take Luudhoq, and bring the Seven and their Watchers to their knees- because the Seven will *never* ally with you."

He smiled grimly. "I'm sure your Watcher companions already know that they will need to return to that citadel. You can only unite Harn by ridding it of the warring factions. *Your* people. A single cause; one land, one people." He stared meaningfully at her. "Give them something to hate more than one another. Then and only then may you turn your attention east, where the *marandaal* spread from the void."

Anlerran could not help but stare at him, transfixed. "I can't believe I'm talking with you," she whispered finally. "I can't even believe that you're standing here."

"I came not to lecture you on the obvious but to beg your forgiveness, Anlerran."

She blinked. "My forgiveness?"

"As I said, I abandoned you. I don't deserve to be forgiven for that, but I'll ask regardless."

"I hadn't even thought about forgiveness," Anlerran said, and shrugged, feeling oddly embarrassed. "I only heard a little of the story from Ruhal. But I would like to know why you gave me over to Joran and Emelle to bring up."

"We felt that it was the safest option for you. Your mother and I were being hunted by *choragh-kin* as we passed through the lower Rhunin. Too many of them, and the *illeagh* would not come to our aid. We knew that whatever happened to us, you had to survive. I am half-*illeagh,* and your mother was a descendant of the First. Your path, if you grew to adulthood, was always destined to be remarkable."

They talked for a time. The sky grew dark outside and the wind sighed around the fortress, lashing dry, powdery snow against the window. Anlerran learned that her father had spent his years here alone for the most part except when the *illeagh* chose to study him. He talked about his travels through Alhar and Aphenhast and other places that Anlerran had never heard of. "The world is mostly empty," he observed, "but I found evidence that it was not always thus. There are vast empty lands where ruins still half-stand, a rich history being slowly buried and forgotten."

Anlerran also discovered that mother had gone her own way, heading into the far north-west beyond Ai-Haar, and had not been seen since. Elluron would speak only little of her, and would not explain her decision. Anlerran saw that the memory pained him and resisted the temptation to ask further questions about her.

She talked about her life in Mordenglen with the man and woman who had brought her up as a child of their own, and with difficulty related to him their eventual fate. Not wishing to dwell on that day, she also relived some chosen memories of happy occasions- one of the various gifting-days through the year, or another event that held a special place in her heart. Her father listened attentively and in quiet sadness for the duration.

Observing her distress, her father lowered his eyes when she stopped. "Your guardians stood in harm's way that you might survive. May the Powers grant you justice for their deaths, Anlerran."

"May they grant me revenge," she replied quietly, and he said nothing to that.

"Where are my companions?" she asked him suddenly. "Are they being treated well?"

"Of course. I will take you to them. I'm sure you will have your clothing returned as well."

A thought occurred to Anlerran. "Will you come with us, when we leave this place?"

"I cannot remain here and watch you leave," he said, "now that I've met you." An intense look suddenly flared in his eyes. "I fear not knowing what might happen to you. Remaining here and not going with you, now we've met again…" He shook his head, closing his eyes for a moment. "I could not bear it a second time, nor could I forgive myself. So, if you… if *Ruhal* allows it…"

"I'm sure that he wouldn't refuse something I desire so much," Anlerran replied with a tentative smile.

Elluron took her firstly to the chamber that had been set aside for her use. Anlerran's cleaned clothes had been left neatly piled on a chair. He left her to dress in privacy, and once she was ready he took her to another area of the vast fortress.

The two of them stood at the top of a flight of stone steps that spiralled up through an immensely tall tower fashioned of black stone riddled with washes of grey and white. Anlerran had scarcely had time to notice its cold beauty. The last fifty feet or so of the ascent had been bitterly cold; no glass covered the gaps in the walls, and a howling gale swept through. The view outside, bathed in Ildar's light, was both breath-taking and dizzying. Anlerran gazed in silent awe at the mountains above and below, and at cruel-looking sculptures of ice worked into shape by the unrelenting wind. Everywhere she looked, unusual constructs of stone and ice stood.

"I have looked out at scenes like this for many years now," Elluron said, which did not explain why he had brought her up here. Then he turned to her. "I enjoy the solitude. I'm neither one creature nor the other, Anlerran—truly a half-and-half, a mongrel. The *illeagh* do not know what to do with me, I suspect. I have no place amongst others, only a place such as this that I myself choose."

"Then neither do I," she said, shivering.

"But you do, Anlerran. You've lived with humankind for all the years you can remember. I've travelled amongst them occasionally, but you were *raised* as one."

"Does that, then, make me more human?" Anlerran did not see how it could.

"Perhaps it does, at least in terms of how others see you." He gave the harsh mountain landscape a final look and they made their way slowly downstairs. "Do I seem odd to you? I suppose I must."

"No more than I imagined," Anlerran said. "Less so, I think. I had many pictures of you in my mind. You seem more... human than I expected."

"I am told often by the *illeagh* that I think like one also," her father remarked. "The observation is not intended as a compliment."

As they reached the base of the staircase a sudden question occurred to Anlerran. "Which of them was human? My grandmother or grandfather?" she asked him.

"Your grandmother," he said as they headed on along another passageway. "I will tell you all about her another day. About him, I can tell you nothing."

"And your childhood?"

Elluron glanced only briefly at her. A look that might have been one of fear flickered in his eyes. "Truthfully, I don't recall any sort of childhood anymore. Those memories have faded."

Staring at his back as they walked, Anlerran wondered how many incredible tales he had to tell about the places he had been and all the things he must have witnessed. *I've so many things to ask him,* she thought, *and I don't know what to ask first.*

They arrived in a hall where fires had been lit in great hearths set into each wall, and chairs and a table arranged near to one of them. Anlerran's companions waited there, some sitting and others standing. Ruhal paced restlessly back and forth.

"Anlerran!" he exclaimed as they walked in, and before she even had time to react he strode over to engulf her in a hug that threatened to crush her ribs. As she breathlessly disentangled herself Anlerran glanced quickly at her father, on whose lips she saw a ghost of a smile.

Anlerran sat in one of the empty chairs, and after being prompted by Ruhal she began to describe what had happened to her since their separation. She told them about the speech she had made to the *illeagh.*

As she finished her story Anlerran realised a stark truth. From here, whether or not the *illeagh* aided them, she and her companions would head back into Harn and continue regardless, because nothing remained in their lives except their quest to raise a united Harn against all that would destroy it. They had no allies as yet and a multitude of enemies, but if they gave in they would be destroyed.

Anlerran blinked back tears that welled suddenly, and looked away as despair threatened to overwhelm her.

Water had been provided in another of the halls nearby. Observing the companions' wariness of this offering, Elluron insisted that it was safe to drink. "The *illeagh* would not think of poisoning any creature- why stoop to such a low pursuit? Should they wish to, they could crush the life from you in an instant rather than leave you to linger in suffering. To kill elaborately is not their way, I can assure you."

"The *illeagh* do not eat," Elluron told them when Jahar asked if food might be provided. "At least, not in any way you could understand. So you'll find no food here unless you care to forage or hunt. I suspect there's nothing for leagues around here that you would care to eat or could even stomach. The water is snow-melt, and as you may have noticed a healing ingredient has been added."

"What is it?" Lura asked, setting her flagon aside although she had already drunk a large amount of the water.

Elluron shrugged. "I honestly do not know. But it will help heal and strengthen you."

Later, Elluron showed them to the chambers nearby that had been set aside for their use, and then left them.

Ruhal lingered for a moment and glanced at her as she was about to enter her room. Anlerran stopped and looked back at him. *He wants me,* she thought, and for one mad moment she considered inviting him in. Perhaps he saw the almost fearful indecision in her eyes. "Sleep well," he said finally.

"I'll try," Anlerran murmured, and made her way into her bedchamber, uttering a sigh as she closed the door behind her. *What am I doing, thinking such things?* she asked herself. *I can barely look at him. I can't be sure what he'll see in my eyes.*

She soon fell asleep despite the unyielding mattress, and the multitude of thoughts rushing through her head concerning the *illeagh,* her father and the things he had said- and the dark muddled knot that was all she could see when she tried to contemplate the future.

Anlerran's eyes suddenly flickered open and she sat up, looking around the room. Nothing had changed, but on a sudden impulse she felt a need to get up and see for herself. The lantern had burned down almost completely and thick, dark shadows danced languidly on the walls. Anlerran reached the far wall and touched her palm against its cold surface, unable to stop staring at it.

And the world melted away.

The vision into which she sank swallowed her whole, and she succumbed to it as if her body had been pulled through a sudden softness in the ramparts of the *illeagh* stronghold. Her terror quickly faded as the scene of internal workings, the sound of a monstrous thumping heart, and the feel of its steady, ancient pulse- *powering the entire castle, she thought for a moment*- gave way to something altogether more mundane.

She stood in the middle of a vast field, in the pouring rain. Before her, a great castle rose into the sodden sky, dark grey against a lighter grey. People came and went through a multitude of tall, ornate gates.

They seemed to be celebrating something.

She turned around in confusion and wiped wet hair out of her eyes. Chain armour weighed her down. Chain armour? she thought, confused. Why am I wearing chain armour? Where am I?

A more terrible question followed: who am I?

She could see other figures nearby. Many had been wounded, some grievously. A few sat and wept, head in hands. Her gaze was drawn to a du-luyan *woman, tall and fierce, and a human soldier who stood with her, head bowed in exhaustion.*

Someone loomed nearby. A man- a lean luyan *warrior. "Jula," he said softly. "Do your wounds still pain you? You need to rest."*

Jula blinked and shook her head. What had just happened? Some kind of lingering spell? Not choragh *work, to be sure, but perhaps from one other of the Blood?*

It will take a while to trust, she thought tiredly, and we still spy upon one another as the trust slowly builds. I must go to speak with Lurin and offer the hand of friendship- or at least, a lasting pact, now that the enemy has been chased back into the desolate places of the world.

"Harrik," she said to her companion as they made their way slowly towards the nearest castle gate, "I think some spell ails me. As if…" She stopped. "Someone is watching through my eyes! One of the Blood? Or something else?"

Harrik turned her gently to face him. His eyes looked deep into her own.

Suddenly they narrowed in shock, and he uttered a single, unknowable word…

Something flung Anlerran backwards across the room. She hit her head against the floor. For a moment, raging pain assailed her. Colours and lights swam at the periphery of her vision as she curled up on the cold stonework, gasping and shaking. She understood nothing of what had happened, yet its enormity chilled her even as she lay crying on the stone tiles and her consciousness faded in and out.

Yet when she came to a little later, she lay on the mattress again with nothing but the strangely distant memory of a dream remaining in her head.

II

Anlerran woke into the morning with a pounding headache, which thankfully eased as she dressed and then left her chamber to look for her companions. She found those who had already woken up waiting in the nearby hall. Looking around, she saw that Culos was nowhere to be seen. *I failed to notice his absence yesterday,* she thought, feeling a little ashamed. *We would have perished without his help. We certainly would never have reached the* illeagh *fortress. I should see if I can find him. But this place is so large, I doubt that I can. I might just become lost. In any case, maybe his journey is over with. If that's so, what will happen to him? Will I see him again?*

She wandered for a while, and to her relief she eventually she found Culos in an open area high up in the *illeagh* fortress, where a wide balcony jutted out over a precipice that yawned far below, ringed by icy spurs and spiked, rocky structures that loomed from out of the surrounding mountainsides. The collision of harsh white and deepest black made Anlerran giddy as she stared out at the unforgiving mountain slopes falling away to the sunless valleys far below.

Culos stood on the edge of the balcony, calmly looking out into the distance as if the vast drop to the landscape below meant nothing to him. Grey clouds scudded through the sky; a bitterly cold breeze tugged at Anlerran's clothing and at the dog's fur, yet unlike Anlerran he appeared to be oblivious to the cold.

Finally he turned and wandered over to Anlerran, who knelt and hugged her companion. "I was hoping I would find you," she whispered. Culos licked her ear and whined softly.

Finally she turned and left, heading back through the silent passageways. Culos padded along at her side, moving in near-silence through the shadows.

As the companions gathered in the hall later, Elluron walked in from one of the archways, bearing what looked like a thin, cylindrical piece of grey-coloured metal. As he showed it to them, Anlerran saw that one half was smooth and reflective in appearance, and the other half had tiny grooves cut into its dull surface.

"Early this morning, I was commanded to meet with those of the *illeagh* who have agreed to rise against the *marandaal*," Elluron told them without any preamble. "They gave me this."

"What does it do?" Kelandra asked even as some of the others immediately looked to each other, shocked that a decision could have been reached so swiftly.

"It calls them, if broken in half," he said simply. "It can be used once only. Thereafter it falls to dust, its power used up entirely. If we use it, then they come to us." He gave a wry smile. "We should take great care as to when we make use of this device."

Ruhal frowned. "What then, if we *do* use it? What happens when the fight is done? And is it their intention to fight against the *marandaal* in some other way as well, regardless of whether or not we call them?"

"I asked similar questions," Elluron said, "but received no answers. They give only the information they wish to give. That is their way and it won't change."

"How many of them have chosen to assist us?" Ildoron asked.

"I can't say exactly. They believe perhaps a third of their number."

"How *many* is that?" Ildoron persisted, a little more sharply.

Elluron stared at him with a thin smile. "Watcher, truthfully I don't know how many of the *illeagh* exist. The fortress stretches far underground, and into the great mountain to the north. It is larger than its dimensions, you might say. I am not one of them; I do not know the great majority of their secrets and wonders. To the *illeagh* I am a visiting curiosity, an anomaly."

"How can it be *larger* than its dimensions?" Lura asked.

"Aona made it so," Elluron said simply. "How is anything that seems impossible, still true? On rare occasions Aona herself intervenes in the natural order of things. That is why I stand before you here and now; I am the product of such an intervention- a creature that should not be. And Aona intervened a second time." He gestured to his daughter.

"I will keep it safe." Elluron put the metal cylinder into an inside pocket of his cloak. "They have asked that we leave tomorrow morning."

"How do we know that their help will be enough to make a difference?" Lura asked.

He smiled at that. "We don't. We can only hope. And their assistance does not come without a price, even for the *illeagh*. They are not immortal in the sense that you may understand. The world can change them, can even take from them. Then elder races are a part of Aona. Even the *choragh*."

The world can take from them. Anlerran shuddered at that notion without knowing precisely what it meant, and later that day she found herself thinking of the dream- the *vision-* from the previous evening. It had not faded as she expected. If anything it felt sharper now than it had then.

She sought Jahar's company and quietly told the warlock as much as she could about what had happened. He listened in grim silence until she finished.

"Far worse could have happened." Jahar scowled. Lowering his voice, he continued, "Perhaps, in such places as this, time is *thinner,* for want of a better word. It sounds like a vision dream of sorts, but somehow you reached back into the past... into the time when the First had overcome the *choragh,* overthrown their ancient masters." Watching as she gaped at him, he guessed her question and added, "I know because those are ancient names, well-known to those few who have studied the history of that Age. Distant folk from a distant time. But that must never happen again. *Ever.* To reach back and touch what once was is to put in danger all we know."

"I didn't want it to happen," Anlerran reminded him. "It was beyond my control. How can I prevent it happening again? I have to sleep!"

A sudden thought occurred to her, though she dared not mention it to Jahar. *Yes, perhaps such a link to the forgotten Age could cause terrible damage. But could it not also be of good use? Knowing what we do now, could we not use that knowledge to forestall the terrible events that have taken place over the last few millennia?*

Then a darker thought occurred to her. *Are such events destined to happen, preordained by powers higher than us? If such happenings are somehow thwarted, do they happen at a later time regardless? Is touching the past like stealing from a higher power, inviting terrible retribution?*

"Never," Jahar said, staring at her as if those very thoughts were written plainly upon her forehead. "Do you understand?"

"I understand, Jahar." Anlerran looked away, unsettled by his look. *What can I do,* she asked herself, *except remain awake?*

"Jula was of the First," Jahar told her. "A woman who had gained the ability to wield the same natural forces that the *choragh* and *illeagh* alone had controlled. This would have been well over a thousand years ago."

Anlerran shivered, trying to comprehend that yawning gulf of time and all the untold generations that linked her with Jula. *What if I had lost myself in the distant past?* she wondered. *What if I had remained there, a lost and silent presence behind Jula's eyes, eventually fading?*

Somehow she managed to push that thought aside. *If something like that happens again, I must find a way to wake. But how will I do that?*

"What can I do?" she asked.

He would not meet her eyes, and Anlerran thought he looked as afraid as she felt. "I don't think there is anything you can do," he said finally. "Except hope."

But he was not done with her yet. "We walk a constant precipice- all of us. We must never lose sight of *why* we are together, *why* we fight this fight, though we are now condemned exiles, wanted by all the corrupted powers that have divided Harn since the end of the Age of Blood."

Anlerran nodded, moved by the vehemence in his words. "I still burn with the desire for vengeance," she murmured. "That's why *I* intend to..."

Jahar interrupted her. "Vengeance. Justice. Sometimes we each have to work out the difference for ourselves. If we succumb to the baser emotions, we become no better than our enemies."

Baser emotions? What does he know of what I feel?! But with an effort Anlerran held her tongue. She recalled how he and the others had been imprisoned by Inerdyr's lackeys, held in the stone tower to go mad with pain and thirst and slowly rot away, forgotten by the world. Would they resist the bright, hard temptation of retribution, if ever the great warlock knelt at their mercy? *I wouldn't,* she thought. *I would gladly watch his head leap from his shoulders, even if I didn't swing the axe myself. And I'll wager Jahar would as well, no matter what he says.*

III

When Anlerran returned to her chamber to sleep later that day, she found Ruhal waiting outside the door. Something about his manner quickened her pulse, and for one mad moment she thought about turning and swiftly walking away. *But I'd end up running,* she thought. *I'd look like a frightened, lost girl. I won't show such a meek face to him, but neither will I flee.*

"I wanted to talk with you," he said bluntly by way of greeting.

"Talk with me?" Anlerran looked into his eyes and then swiftly away. *I may not know the world's ways, or those of men,* she thought, *but by all the Powers I know what he wants, and it has little to do with talk. What I don't know is whether he intends to take it regardless of whatever I say.*

She made her way into her chamber and half-turned as he followed her in and shut the door behind them. "I have to know," he said hoarsely. "I have to know if you want me."

The afternoon light had grown dim. Anlerran warmed her hands by the lantern at her bedside, watching with alarm how they shook.

"I... I've never..." She swallowed and turned round, wiping away prickles of sweat from her palms. *I'll wager he knows that much already,* she thought suddenly. "I don't know," she blurted out, and then put her hand to her mouth, horrified at the way her voice had sounded.

Ruhal blinked in confusion. Perhaps that was the last thing he had expected her to say. Anlerran would realise later that this was the moment when she decided that she wanted him to stay with her. Something about this great hulk of a man, caught between raw lust and a strange awkwardness, drew her to him.

"Yes," she said in a quiet voice.

Anlerran said nothing more. She feared that if she did it would sound like nonsense. She began to remove her clothing, her eyes fixed upon him the whole while as he did the same, without looking away for an instant. Anlerran stared back into his eyes, transfixed by the sheer hunger in his expression. When she lowered her gaze, her pulse quickened even further. She could feel the heat of embarrassment in her cheeks.

They lay upon the bed. Ruhal reached to one side and pulled the covering blanket away entirely, throwing it across the room where it lay until the next morning. "My only love," he whispered as he loomed above her.

Anlerran opened her legs, almost jumping out of her skin when she felt him between them. Her eyes met his. As he pushed himself inside her, pain flared up and was gone a moment later. She wrapped her arms about him as he thrust slowly, listening to his almost desperate breaths until finally he gasped and rolled to one side, covered in a sheen of sweat.

They lay in silence close together. Despite the comfort and warmth, the strange glow she felt, Anlerran could not help thoughts of the coming day creeping back into her mind. *Here we are, hiding in our burrow until the morning comes and brings with it a reminder of the darkness we must fight against.*

As she drifted off into slumber, Anlerran murmured to him, "Your only love?"

"Yes," he whispered back. "Above or below the earth, forever."

Even as she pondered those strange, fierce words, sleep reached up and pulled her away.

IV - Desperate Steps

I

Ileana gasped and grimaced as she washed with the cold water from the pump. When she turned around, shivering, and padded across the floor to the bed she saw Jak sitting up and staring in horror at the patch of blood on the sheet. "Did I hurt you?" he blurted out.

No more than usual, she felt like saying, but stopped herself. Making him feel hurt and guilty would do neither of them any good. "It's moon-blood, Jak," she said with as much patience as she could muster. "It happens every Ildarian month from the time a girl becomes a woman." She stared at him and shook her head in disbelief. "Did your father never teach you about that sort of thing?"

"No. He never really talked about women. Not like that anyway." Jak looked down and Ileana saw a look almost akin to disgust on his face. "Powers, Ileana, I've got your blood all over..."

"Go and wash yourself if you find it that terrible!" she almost shouted, and sat on the side of the bed, turned away from him as she began to get dressed. *If he tries to make up by grabbing my breasts like the last time he made me angry, I'll hit him,* she fumed.

But he didn't. He lay down and when she looked around he appeared to be slumbering. *Either that or he's sulking,* she thought.

She relented soon enough. It wasn't Jak's fault that he hadn't been taught certain things. It wasn't even his fault that he said and did the wrong things at the wrong times. Ileana reckoned all boys and men were clumsy like that. "I'm sorry," she said quietly after a moment, but then she heard him snoring faintly.

Ileana could not even contemplate going back to sleep. She had far too much to think about.

She still entertained fanciful thoughts of escape, although her careful explorations of the castle had yielded nothing that offered even a glimmer of hope. *If I stay here then everything will be lost,* she told herself every morning, and she told herself that same thing now. She couldn't say how that would happen, but she felt certain of it. To worsen matters further her initial feelings of unease about Inerdyr and those close to him had only grown stronger as the days went by.

She had met Ayvin, the grey and grim commander of Inerdyr's militia, and it hadn't taken her long to figure him out. He was a careful, calculating man, cold and with no heart to speak of. He would not stoop to help another person no matter what dire situation they might be in, unless the act offered him some sort of advantage. He was a man of reason and ambition and nothing else. Ileana wondered how such an empty creature derived any enjoyment from life.

And then there was Jaana.

Ileana had sensed Jaana's proximity even before she arrived at the castle, and the prickle of unease that she felt at first had grown into a ball of fear that she carried around inside her all the time. Jaana was a descendant of the First, a manipulator of the Old Powers, but Ileana sensed a simmering darkness to the woman, a hatred that festered and grew slowly but surely.

Maybe terrible things have happened to her, Ileana had reasoned at first. *People are shaped by the things that happen to them. She hates the world and its people because of some injustice.*

But she then reminded herself that she too had suffered in her past, and *she* wasn't full of hate like Jaana. *Maybe I've dealt with things better than she did,* Ileana considered, *but it's strange how I could have done that. I'm much younger than she is. I don't know what happened to her, but was it really so much worse than the things that have happened to me?*

As for Inerdyr, Ileana avoided him as often as she could. Thankfully he seldom sought her out- instead he sent Jaana to talk with her- but she occasionally saw him, and if he happened to glance at her, more often than not an odd half-smile could be seen on his lips, as if he was amused by something or perhaps looking forward to some imagined day when Jaana finally succeeded in befriending her. She also saw him talking to himself more than a few times, and even running his hands along the masonry of the buildings and nodding to himself as if in appreciation of the craftsmanship. Ileana could not bear to be in the man's vicinity even for a moment, not only because he frightened her but because of the vile stench that accompanied him- sometimes blood, sometimes excrement, sometimes even the pungent odour of rotting meat. Ileana could only imagine why he would smell like that, and tried her best not to think about it.

Meanwhile, Jaana's clumsy attempts to win her over were easy enough to resist. The woman would comment time and again how the two of them were really the same and that Ileana needed to be trained to develop her powers properly under Inerdyr's guidance. Ileana couldn't imagine anything worse than being trapped in a chamber with Jaana and Inerdyr, and she had found excuses to decline the offer each time it was presented. *I feel too tired to focus,* she had said one time. *I think whatever powers I had are getting weaker* had been her reason on another occasion. Those excuses had sounded lamentably awful even to her own ears, and Jaana became visibly angry and frustrated each time, hearing the lies for what they were. But apparently Inerdyr had still not commanded that she be forcibly brought to him.

Still, I think that time will come soon, Ileana thought as she finished dressing and wandered over to her bedchamber window which overlooked one of the inner courtyards.

Her thoughts wandered back to her dream from last night. Vivid and frightening at times, it had also exhilarated her beyond measure.

She hurtled through a forest in almost absolute darkness, until eventually the trees thinned out altogether and she had found herself at the top of a vast hill. The rise sloped down towards a distant city she didn't recognise. The sky looked strange, although she couldn't say how. Neither of the moons had risen, nor could she see any stars in the sky, although there were no clouds either. The light was good enough to see by, although it was impossible to say where that light came from.

I could run forever, she remembered thinking as she stood at the top of the hill. I could keep running, faster and faster if I needed to, and never get tired.

At the back of her mind a nagging suspicion remained that this was not a place of dreams but something else.

She saw faint lights appear and then vanish in different places around the silent city. Ileana knew when she looked at them that these were not the lights of civilisation; they had never known human hands. Some of them burned brightly, others gave out only a faint glow. She saw a few of these curious illuminations move from place to place as if borne by unseen entities around the shadowed streets of the distant metropolis.

Ileana felt a sudden, powerful urge to discover that place, to walk the streets and be bathed in the strange luminescence, and so she had started running down the hill. The further she ran, the faster she moved, until the ground became a blur under her feet. Her steps became vast leaps, impossible to control. It was as if the city pulled her in more and more powerfully as she drew nearer to it. At the same time, the ground underfoot changed, becoming more like a flowing river of green-hued water. When she looked down, she could see not only into its depths but beyond them, into a spacious realm far beneath where distant points and clusters of light gleamed. The strange thought occurred to her that she was looking down into a patchwork map of the entire Existence- all the stars and strange worlds that hung in the cold darkness. Finally, as she reached the bottom of the hill and sped towards the city walls, she looked up and saw a great iron gate, rusted and topped with vast spikes, opening as if to invite her into the silent interior of the metropolis. And in the shadows of the nearest street, something moved from out of the stone itself...

"What are you looking at?"

Ileana almost jumped out of her skin, and rounded on Jak. "Gods, Jak! Don't *do* that!"

"Do what?" he asked, perplexed.

"Sneak up on me." Ileana took a deep breath to try and calm herself.

"I didn't," he asserted. "I already asked you the same thing twice, but you weren't listening."

"Well I didn't hear you." Ileana shivered. The images of her dream faded to the back of her mind as she watched heavily-armed guardsmen patrolling the courtyard far below. *If ever I find a way of escaping, it won't be that way,* she reminded herself. *So unless I learn to fly, or I find a secret tunnel leading out of the castle...*

She almost laughed out loud at that. *A secret tunnel? Inerdyr isn't stupid no matter what else he might be. I doubt there are tunnels, secret or otherwise, leading out of here.*

A fragment of her dream drifted back- an image of the darkly mysterious world through which she had run, and the seemingly endless depths and dimensions of that place. For a moment she felt certain that something desperately important lay buried in the dream, something intangible that she could sense just as a whisper or a fleeting glimpse. But that instant came and went.

They stood and watched a little longer as Ayvin and Jaana came into view, riding slowly through the courtyard towards the outer gateway with a small retinue of militiamen in tow. Ayvin, dressed in a light blue cloak over his leather armour, sat upright and rode easily. In contrast, Jaana slouched a little as if reluctant to be part of their venture, and Ileana could tell even from her distant window that the woman rode uneasily- badly, even. *Maybe she'll fall and break her neck with any luck,* Ileana thought, but a moment later she felt ashamed at herself for wanting for such a thing to happen to anyone, even Jaana.

"They're going out to the villages again to recruit more folk for the war," Jak noted.

"They needn't bother," Ileana said. "What use are people armed with sticks and knives going to be against the *marandaal?*" When Jak glanced quizzically at her, she continued, "Do you remember what I told you about Ethanalin Tur-morn just before the Gate opened? All the mad people and the chaos? And then, when it did open..." She shook her head. "I didn't look, but I could feel what was happening. Hundreds died there and then, maybe thousands. The whole *town,* Jak. Forcing ordinary people to be part of some army to defend Harn... it's just pointless bloodshed, nothing more."

"Inerdyr will want you to be a part of that war," Jak said quietly. "And you're anything but ordinary."

"I won't have anything to do with his plans." Ileana turned to him, a sudden certainty in her heart, though she had no idea where it could have come from. "We *will* escape, Jak. You and I, and Amethyst and Vornen. The four of us will get out of here. We *will.*"

He didn't believe her, of course. She could see it in his eyes, a flat disbelief- but worse than that, sympathy.

II

Ileana had guessed Jaana's mood correctly. Travelling around the villages of the district with Ayvin was the last thing she wanted to do, but Inerdyr had insisted that she accompany him and his men. "You can sense others who are strong in the Powers," he had reminded her, "so you will go with them, and if you *do* find any, bring them back."

"Perhaps then we won't need Ileana," Jaana had suggested. She didn't really believe that- the girl almost seeped with the Powers- and Inerdyr had disagreed in any case. "She is essential regardless of your findings. Continue your attempts to befriend her, or at least break her down. Sooner or later she must realise that she has nowhere to go, and that her destiny is tied with yours- and that of every other Descendant we find. All you're dealing with is the stubbornness of youth. She'll grow tired of her little rebellion in time."

I think we should be harder on her than that, Jaana had wanted to suggest, surprised and a little irritated at Inerdyr's patience where the girl was concerned.

Morning wore towards noon and a pale sun cut through high ice clouds, offering no warmth. Jaana stared at the track ahead of them and found herself reminded of her previous existence as a nomadic healer wandering from settlement to settlement. Sometimes she had been able to help but more often than not she had left the village under a cloud, having failed in what she had considered her duty.

And then, when people had inexplicably begun falling into fevers or madness...

Then I knew that whatever I did would never be enough, she thought. *Better to be a warrior, and use what powers I can as a hammer against those that would destroy us. Not that I ever thought of myself as a warrior back then. I was weak and spineless.*

Jaana found her thoughts disturbed. She could feel Ayvin's cold stare upon her without needing to turn her head halfway to look. "Does something bother you?" she asked eventually.

"Bother me?" He laughed at that, an empty sound. "No. Although some time ago I had considered bedding you, if you must know..."

"How nice of you to tell me," Jaana said icily.

"Oh, just a moment of madness. Your company has taught me something in that regard."

"Has it? How so?"

"I think you prefer women. Especially that pretty *luyan* girl with whom you spend so much time."

Jaana couldn't help but give him a sharp look then. Finally she shrugged, turning her attention back to the way ahead. "If you must know, I prefer my own company above that of most others. But in any case it isn't a matter of *preference*. It isn't a choice."

Ayvin frowned. "I don't see anyone forcing you."

Jaana shook her head. "I may as well try to explain the Powers themselves to you, Ayvin. And since when has that stopped men like you forcing themselves upon women regardless?"

"Oh, I would rather it be a pleasurable experience. Besides, I expect you're as sour between the legs as you are sour of expression. I would advise you to put on a more conciliatory manner as we go amongst the villages. And remember, be aware. The moment you even *think* someone may be a wielder of the Old Powers, you tell me."

Jaana sighed. "I'm aware of what must be done."

She thought again about the task that lay ahead. *We could raise an army of a hundred thousand,* she thought, *but the end result would be the same. A man or a woman with a sword or a bow is of little use in the war to come. Those weapons cannot harm the* marandaal. *Only the Old Powers can touch them. Only the Old Powers can send them hurtling back into the void.*

"There must be dozens, perhaps hundreds of Descendants of the First in Harn alone," she spoke up after a while. "A small army that would be far more potent than this far greater one we hope to eventually muster."

"Inerdyr has commanded that all those who can wield a knife and throw a punch be enlisted eventually." Ayvin shrugged as if he didn't see the reasoning behind the order. *In that at least, we're agreed,* Jaana thought.

"There is at least one more Descendant we're aware of," Ayvin continued after a while. "She travels with the band of outlaws and Watchers in the far north. Inerdyr has sent men to kill them and apprehend her."

And who will be first amongst us, if several others are found? Jaana wondered. *Inerdyr has all but promised me that role, but what if others find favour with him? What if one of them is stronger, more worthy?*

By the fading light of the afternoon they arrived in Farrow Field, a village that nestled in the grasslands next to a small, winding river. Most of the hundred or so houses were huts of packed earth. The few stone dwellings that Jaana could see were set aside from the others. She wondered if these were the homes of the elders or senior families, as was often the case in mid-Hastian communities through which she had travelled. *Whatever hierarchy they observe here,* she thought, *I recognise the stench of the place. Gods, it's like being back in Aphenhast.*

The dozen or so people who were out and about stopped their tasks and put down anything they were carrying, waiting as the riders came nearer and Ayvin finally called a stop. Judging by their wary expressions they knew who these newcomers were or they at least recognised the banner carried by one Ayvin's men. Nevertheless, Ayvin decided he had to inform them. "I am Ayvin, commander of

Lord Inerdyr's forces. You may already know of the grave threat facing Harn from the east."

Grubby children squatted half-clothed in the mud and stared wide-eyed at the horsemen. A few of the villagers exchanged quick glances. But the silence wore on, and no one spoke.

"We are recruiting for Lord Inerdyr," Ayvin continued finally, a note of frustration in his voice. "Warden Jerrim is responsible for this area. Who knows of his whereabouts?"

"Lord Warden's headed over to West Stonewood a league that way," a pregnant woman standing by the entrance to one of the houses ventured. She pointed to the west. "There's been a disturbance. Folk going mad." She touched the bulge of her stomach as if to ward such madness away from her unborn child. Jaana found herself idly wondering if the insanity that afflicted lightdreamers- if that was what lay behind this disturbance- could pass from mother to child somehow. Might it even be possible for unborn children to know of the *marandaal* and be afflicted by them on some level, even as they lay in the womb?

Her gaze took in those who had gathered nearby, and then other people further away. She looked at each of the small dwellings. This village was larger than some, yet small enough for her to know that no one here could wield even a tiny fragment of the Old Powers. She would have been able to tell by now.

As if he had sensed what she was doing, Ayvin glanced across at her. Jaana shook her head curtly.

"West Stonewood, then." Ayvin did not seem displeased. "At least there's an inn worthy of the name there," he added as they rode through and out of the village.

Dusk had fallen by the time they reached West Stonewood, a larger village with stone buildings including an inn, stable and smithy. Ordinarily it might have been a more civilised place, but as they stopped and dismounted near the stable and Ayvin called out impatiently for the stable hand to attend, Jaana saw three people standing in the middle of the street, watching them. Cast half in the fading light day and half in the soft glow of the nearest torch, they appeared eerie and unmoving, as if they were statues wrought from an unknown material.

No, she realised after a moment, feeling a chill within her. *They're not looking at us.* Their heads happened to be turned in the direction of the newcomers, but they were not looking at them or indeed anything else.

They see only their dreams, Jaana thought as a cart rumbled along the road and the driver shouted a curse at the obstacles in his path, cracking his whip across the face of one of them. A dark gash opened up across the man's face but he didn't even flinch. Lines of blood streaked down his pallid cheek.

One of them, a woman a little older than Jaana, suddenly shrieked, "They will *burn* the darkness from you!"

Ayvin, who had been talking with the stable hand, did not even turn to look as he calmly asked the stable boy, "Why are they not locked up?"

"Not sure what crime we might charge them with, m'Lord," the lad mumbled, wide-eyed and watchful as the woman turned one way and then another as if to search for an absent companion, scratching so hard at her scalp that Jaana wondered if the skin might come away. "Some headed north, decided to form their own little gathering. No one knows why. Warden and his men have gone after them."

"Not sure what crime you might charge them with?" Ayvin echoed. "Have you any imagination at all? Lock them away. Put them to the sword." He shrugged. "It's in your interest to be dictated by common sense rather than pity. They cannot be cured." He glanced at Jaana. "Inerdyr told me that you once tried to heal lightdreamers, but you could not."

"I could not," Jaana agreed flatly. Then, without thinking she added, "Their minds are no longer their own. They cannot be mended."

"There we have it then." Ayvin turned to one of his men, a hard-faced, shaven-headed young man called Cal. "They disturb the peace with their madness. Put an end to them. Do it quickly. Make it a mercy."

Cal neither questioned his commander nor even hesitated. Jaana had not expected him to. Perhaps he had been impatiently waiting for this moment. He sauntered over to the three, and his sword cut bloody arcs through the gathering night, slicing through the woman first. Jaana watched, fascinated that the three lightdreamers had not even been aware of the approaching danger. Even when the woman had her coarse shouts cut short her companions continued to stare blankly and looked around as if they saw something quite different to the middle of a village street.

Then they were down in the cold dirt.

A mercy, Jaana thought, echoing Ayvin's words. *They were vessels of those who seek to destroy all Aona. A mercy to cut them loose from the light, so that they may eventually pass back into the earth.*

Cal walked back and carefully wiped the blade of his sword clean with a cloth before discarding the rag. "Their blood carries a poison," he explained to the others. Then he looked at Jaana. "Isn't that so, witch?"

"It's likely," she said, not knowing if it was or not. She gave the bodies in the road one more glance and then looked away. *A mercy*, she told herself again.

"Reckon the Warden needs to explain why they're left wandering the streets and worrying folk," Cal added, addressing Ayvin.

"He will be made to when he returns," Ayvin said, and strode impatiently into the alehouse.

Jaana had a room to her own that night, which was exactly as she wanted it. She endured jeers and japes from Ayvin's men- though not from the man himself, who did nothing more than smile thinly and give her a coldly disinterested stare- as she left their company and headed upstairs to sleep. "Maybe we should find a whore for her!" one of them laughed.

Maybe you should, Jaana silently retorted as she opened the door to her bedchamber. *A whore would be a far less tiresome companion than any of you.*

As she drifted to sleep, it occurred to her that she had made the right choice not to ask Lyya to accompany them. Lyya would have attracted a worrying amount of attention from Ayvin's lecherous thugs- not that Jaana worried about her not being able to take care of herself- but she would also surely have objected to the killing of the lightdreamers. *I didn't like it especially,* Jaana thought, *but we live in a time when ill deeds must be done for the greater good. Perhaps an infection does indeed run through their blood, as Cal suggested- not that he would know. At the very least, the Lightdreamers spread worry and panic amongst those who have not been afflicted, and fear is a disease in itself.*

She remembered visiting the sanatorium building in the Hastian city of Nisstar with Fistelkarn, Tyrameer and Ludas. It seemed an eternity had passed since that day. *The authorities kept the lightdreamers locked up and offered them no treatment,* she reminded herself. *They should at least have slain those who had no hope of recovery and no hope of a life without remaining trapped in some hellish dream.*

Only a short while passed before another group of lightdreamers arrived in the area. Jaana listened to the sounds of their shrieking and shouting for a long while, hoping that the noise might die down. It did not; although they wandered up and down the street their babble and chatter continued unabated, and Jaana felt the cold anger inside her harden further. Why had the Warden and his peacekeepers not apprehended these mad folk? She was surprised that Ayvin or one of his men had not already risen from his bed and marched out to put them to the sword. Had they all corked their ears? She suspected not. In all likelihood they had stumbled into their bedchambers blind drunk and were sleeping too heavily to be disturbed even by the ramblings of afflicted.

Wearily Jaana sat up, listening to one man's braying laugh and a woman shouting out something that sounded a little like an old Hastian prayer. "They will cleanse everything!" she proclaimed after her recital.

Why should Ayvin's men sleep soundly while I have to bear this insanity? Jaana thought, slipping out of bed and putting her shirt and trousers on. She took her knife from its belt pouch and stared at the blade.

The lightdreamers are cursed, she reminded herself. *Whatever they may say or do, they endure lives of confusion and misery.*

Mercy.

She got up and wandered over to the window, drawing back one of the curtains a little way. The laughing man stood with his arms upraised to the night sky as if to coax his supposed benefactors from their unknown location in the heavens. He was naked from the waist down, and one of his legs looked so painfully thin that it was difficult to see how he could even walk. The woman had quietened but continued to look all around, over and over, as if she hoped for some unfortunate passer-by to preach to. A little boy stood nearby, silent and head bowed so his face could not be seen. Jaana wondered if he too was afflicted or if his crazed parents had hauled him along on their night-time misadventure.

They are not sane. They recognise nothing of their lives that were.

They are no longer people.

Jaana clutched the handle of her knife harder than ever, until the blade shook in the dim light. *It would be a kindness to silence their cries,* she reasoned. *Certainly Inerdyr would agree with me. I would not be condemned or punished for releasing them.*

But she turned and went back to sit on the edge of her bed, moving the knife from one restless hand to the other. She itched to use the weapon, yet she knew that she would be likely to lose any struggle if they suddenly fought back. Finally, enraged at her weakness and indecision, Jaana flung the knife across the room where it embedded itself in a half-broken chest of drawers.

She undressed and threw her clothes to the floor, and then lay down again. After a while the lightdreamers moved on, but even after their noise had faded Jaana imagined herself striding outside to deliver peace to those creatures. *I'd slit their throats,* she thought. *I'd slit them ear to ear and watch their blood gush forth as if they were pigs at a slaughterhouse. Or I'd drive the knife straight through their eyes...*

She slept, and similarly grotesque images later became part of her dream.

Jaana woke suddenly and sat up, her breaths fast and laboured. The horrors of her dream swiftly faded, but her eyes were drawn to a faint presence across the room by the window. As she stared at it, the apparition gained a little in form so that it looked almost human-shaped. Early morning sunlight filtered through the curtains and where it touched this ghostly form, faint tendrils of smoke or mist drifted upwards as if the oncoming day threatened to burn away its existence.

Jaana.

The solitary word echoed in her head, desperately sad and reproachful. Jaana knew the voice intimately. She had known it for as long as she could remember anything at all. Grief that she had hoped to keep buried for the rest of her days welled up suddenly, and even though she knew that she saw and heard only what her tired mind created in its confusion, a part of her still believed that this vision was real.

"Mother..." She could barely even whisper the word.

What have you become, Jaana? The faint words conveyed a sense of fathomless sadness.

"What... what do you mean? I..."

But as she got up and began to walk towards the window, all traces of what she had seen vanished, and Jaana was left standing and staring at dust in the air.

IV

Ileana gazed up at the ceiling of her bedchamber. Unable to sleep, still she could not stop her vivid dream from the previous evening from seeping through her thoughts. Her mind recreated each moment over and over to the point where she ran, seemingly unable to stop, towards the dark gated city.

It's as if I haven't finished, and I have to relive the dream until I do, she told herself. *The dream is a puzzle and I have to work it out somehow.*

But she couldn't even begin to work it out. The hours wore on, and eventually, despite her restless thoughts, Ileana drifted off to sleep.

She woke standing by the window, her hands clutching the ledge and her heart pounding as if it had grown to three times its size. The window was open, although she felt certain that she had closed it before she and Jak went to bed. Maybe Jak had opened it. But why hadn't he awakened her, if she had been standing here dreaming as the chilly night air swept in?

"Jak," she murmured, turning slowly round. "Why didn't you..."

But Jak wasn't in bed. The bed looked as if it had been made by the chambermaid and then left. It didn't look slept in. She couldn't see Jak's clothes anywhere on the floor as she wandered slowly over.

The idea that he might have got up, got dressed and left to wander around the fortress was madness enough- they both knew that exploring the place was a bad idea and doing so at night bordered on suicidal. But the idea that he had not only tidied the bed but also left her standing by the window without so much as a word...

No, Ileana decided. *Something else has happened. Either some sorcery has spirited him to some other place, or...*

...or I'm the one who is somewhere else.

She turned fearfully to the window and stared out into the night, across the courtyard and towards the gates. She could see no guards on duty. Perturbed, she allowed her gaze to head upwards into the sky where she could see nothing but a uniform darkness.

Ileana tried to swallow down the terror that threatened to overwhelm her. What was this place?

She looked down at herself. She was barefoot and wearing one of the nightdresses that Inerdyr's servants had provided on their arrival, but none of her other clothes could be seen anywhere.

A faint breeze rustled the curtains. Ileana thought it felt unseasonably warm. *I must be still dreaming,* she decided. *This isn't even winter.*

She had no idea how long she spent just standing by the window. A number of times she looked outside and then turned to look around the room, as if by observing one scene she might somehow cause the other to change and become familiar.

Almost without thinking, Ileana began to walk slowly over to the door. To her bemusement, when she turned the handle the door opened outwards instead of inwards. She peered out into the corridor outside. The room where Amethyst and Vornen slept was on the same side as hers. She padded down the corridor as far as their door and knocked softly on it; then, when no response came she knocked again a little harder. "Amethyst," she called out, although she didn't dare call too loudly and the strange sound her voice made caused her to shudder. The deep, utter silence that quickly swallowed it up was unnerving.

Ileana could hear nothing from within their room, even when she cupped her ear against the door and listened intently. She couldn't hear the steady, faint rhythm of breathing that would be expected if they were fast asleep.

They're not in there, she told herself, feeling a pit open in her stomach. *Jak, Amethyst and Vornen, probably Lyya, Fauli and Jaana as well... they're probably not anywhere in this place. There's just me.*

I must still be dreaming, she asserted once again. *All I need to do is wake up.*

But everything around her felt too real, too *solid. Wake up!* Ileana urged herself sharply, but she couldn't. She took a step back from the door and looked up towards the end of the corridor where the lamplight faded. She thought for a moment that despite the utter silence someone or something whispered faint words, repeated over and over and in a language she couldn't understand. She was briefly reminded of her time with Amethyst and Vornen in the vast underground caverns beneath the Crescent Mountains in Aphenhast, when she had heard the strange language used by some of the lower *kin*. Sometimes it had sounded as if their words came from out of her own head.

This was different though. She felt oddly certain that whatever these whispers sounded like, they were not made by any sort of living creature- and the insanity of that idea did not make her any less certain of the fact.

Suddenly more afraid than ever, Ileana turned and made her way quickly down the stairs at the near end of the passageway. Her bare feet slapped loudly on the marble steps as she descended. She hurried on from the base of the stairs, along a number of passageways and through half a dozen or more silent halls before abruptly she came to a large room that she could not remember having seen before. Its ornamentation looked quite unlike that of any other room in the fortress, so much so that it appeared to be part of another building entirely.

You have to stop these mad thoughts, she told herself, staring around at the overly ornate furnishings coated with bright, delicate gold leaf that stood in every part of the great hall. On the far wall a vast mirror of polished glass hung, and Ileana slowly approached it, marvelling at the detail afforded to the reflection of everything in the room. *It looks more real than the hall I'm standing in,* she thought, and the idea made her uneasy. *How can that be? How can a reflection be more real than whatever it's reflecting?*

Yet she walked a little nearer, staring at herself.

And then her reflection *smiled* at her.

Ileana shrieked, and tried to turn and flee, but her feet felt as if they had become part of the floor. She swayed and almost fell, yet some invisible force held her up.

Ileana's mouth felt dry; she could only stare in terror as the apparition drew nearer to place its hand against some invisible barrier. *The glass,* Ileana thought. *But if it can break the glass, or force its way through...*

It could not. It drew back, and a flurry of wildly different expressions suddenly crossed its face- *her* face.

Malevolence, rage, cunning- sorrow, fear, desperation- Ileana could barely look at the surge of uncontrolled emotions that distorted the features of her reflection, even as her own remained still in shock.

It's not me, she told herself over and over. But then she thought, *It's what I could be, if I was trapped here. And maybe I'm the only living being in this hell, so perhaps that's why the only being I've seen is myself.*

Ileana found herself free at last. She turned and ran back to the archway through which she had entered the hall, but it no longer looked the same. The few torches that remained lit sputtered and flickered, casting mad shadows across the walls. Portraits leered accusingly at her as she staggered along. She searched on either side for doorways, but they no longer existed.

Wake up! she screamed to herself, but she could not.

Then she fell through a part of the wall against which she hammered her fists. It ripped before her onslaught as if it was nothing more than thin, dry fabric. She fell forward, and tumbled down a short flight of steps.

When Ileana picked herself up, her eyes were drawn to a passageway further along from where she stood. A row of windows on one side allowed pallid greenish light to seep through, and when she reached one of them and stared through the small square aperture, she saw open land stretching away on all sides. Great mountains, thick forests and sprawling cities, vast lakes and wide rivers that wound through the landscape- all of this she saw in minute detail, as if the very act of gazing upon each facet of this tapestry focussed her eyes and allowed her to draw closer even though she remained behind the stone wall of the tunnel.

I'm not in Aona at all, she thought, unable to believe what her eyes showed her. And yet at the same time she felt sure that she *was*.

It's a hidden place, a voice from within her whispered. *A world within the world. Something to do with the Old Powers. Maybe only those who are strong enough can reach this place. But what purpose does it have?*

Then a far more troubling question came to her. *How do I find my way back? I'm not dreaming. I can't just wake up and be back in the world I know. If I could I would have already woken up by now.*

Panic rushed through her, and Ileana threw hesitation to the wind. She ran headlong down the corridor, and it stretched out before her, seemingly endless. Thoughts rushed through her head, of Amethyst and Vornen, and Jak.

Jak, she thought miserably, imagining him waking up with the bed cold beside him, perhaps thinking at first that she might have gone for a morning walk. *I have to get back to him!*

"No!" she screamed out loud, and as she did, Ileana saw a faint gleam of light on the other side of the passageway, where a wide crack ran up part of the wall. The light transfixed her. She felt immediately certain that whatever lay behind this part of the wall was a different place entirely. *I recognise the light!* she thought. *It's the familiar light of the world I know.* Those words sounded like the panicked ramblings of a lunatic, but Ileana believed them. She began hitting and kicking at the wall, repeating those words again in her mind.

Pieces came free from the wall, and she attacked it with even more force, bruising and cutting her knuckles. Eventually she had made a hole big enough to force her way through. She had no idea what lay beyond, only that it provided an escape from this place.

She struggled through, and fell into the light.

Ileana sat up suddenly, gasping as desperately as if she had been forced underwater. She knelt by the window of her bedchamber. Immediately she looked around and took a deep, tremulous breath of relief as she saw Jak's familiar form. He was lying on his side, partly covered in bedsheets, still asleep and snoring faintly.

Gods, I found my way back, she thought. *I found my way back!*

She got up and walked unsteadily over to the bed to lie down. Jak muttered something in his sleep and smiled faintly when she curled up against him and kissed him tenderly on the cheek. *You don't know how close we were to losing each other,* Ileana thought, stroking his hair before she lay down on her back and waited for her body to calm itself.

The memory of everything she had seen and experienced in that other place remained in her mind in exact and vivid detail. That fact alone convinced her that it couldn't possibly have been a dream. After a while, too restless to sleep, she sat up on her elbows and looked around the room, looking for tell-tale signs of cracks where a hole in the wall might have appeared and then sealed itself. She found none, but Ileana knew that whatever sorcery had carried her to that other world and back here again was so powerful that it could do whatever it did and disappear, leaving no visible trace.

Before long other, dangerous thoughts crept into her mind.

What if I could reach that place again somehow?

What if I could travel through that place and come out again somewhere totally different?

She knew that she was simply being young and foolish and that even contemplating the idea was ridiculous. She had only found her way back here before through sheer luck, and that other place was full of nightmares. What if she became trapped there?

But the possibility of escape had ensnared her imagination. It would not let go, and Ileana wandered slowly over to the window to stare out beyond the castle perimeter as far as the eye could see, to the distant places where free people lived their lives.

V

After returning to the castle that evening Jaana found Lyya sitting and reading in a chair near the hearth in one of the smaller halls. Flames leapt and fresh pine logs crackled and split in the heat. Another chair had been positioned nearby and Jaana wondered for a moment if Lyya had placed it there in the hope that Jaana would find her and sit with her upon her return, or if someone else was to take that place.

Lyya heard her approach and looked up. She closed the book and put it to one side. "Did you find what you were looking for?"

"You mean descendants of the First?" Jaana shook her head and wearily seated herself. "All we found were filthy peasants and lunatics. Still, I expect Inerdyr will send us out again in a different direction tomorrow. And then again each day until we find folk who are worthy of the journey and the effort."

"Filthy peasants and lunatics," Lyya said flatly. "I remember a time not so long ago when you had kinder words for those less fortunate."

"Kind words never healed anyone."

Lyya smiled at that. "I believe they can, Jaana. Among my people, healers have shown that there are times when simple kindnesses *can* help those who..."

Jaana sighed so loudly that Lyya didn't finish. "Please spare me your *luyan* philosophies, Lyya. We are recruiting for war." She paused and thought for a moment. *I should not be harsh with her*, she thought. *In fact, even if she objects to our journeys to the villages and our treatment of the lightdreamers, still I would rather have her with me than be alone. Perhaps I can even show her the necessity of what we*

75

do. But she'll have to keep her temper under control at all costs.

"I'm sure Inerdyr would allow you to come with me next time," she spoke up. "Being left to wait here can't be enjoyable for you, and I would welcome the company. I would welcome *your* company."

"I should like that," Lyya admitted. "But I fear you won't listen to what I have to tell you. Certainly you won't like it."

"I'll listen to you," Jaana countered, "and we're allowed to disagree on things now and again. Why don't you tell me now, and then you won't have to again later. We can argue if need be. I would rather we do it now than when we're away in some dirty guest-house where we can't even bathe."

Lyya looked troubled. "I'm worried about you."

"*Worried* about me?" Jaana laughed and shook her head. "I'm favoured by the lord of this castle, Lyya. He knows what I am, he recognises what it is I must do- what we must all do, one way or another. Even Ayvin and his curs dare not touch me. You have no need to be concerned. If anything it's that insolent little bitch Ileana who should be worried."

"You misunderstand me. I'm worried about what you're doing to yourself. You're walking into an abyss, Jaana. A great chasm from which eventually you'll find no way out."

Jaana felt a prickle of unease. She could think of nothing to say, but for a moment the memory of waking up earlier in the guest-house bedroom in West Stonewood came rushing back. The faint ghostly form, a figment of her imagination that might have looked like her mother, just for a moment in the sunlight.

I miss her, she realised. *I will always miss her. It's no wonder that I'm prone to imagine that I see her from time to time.*

Lyya got up and walked over to kneel before her, then reached forward to clasp her hand. "Jaana, I love you. But I fear for you. Can you not see what is happening?"

"I..." Jaana blinked, struggling for words. "If you're really that afraid, then come with me when we next head out to the villages. Watch over me if that allays your fears."

"I will," Lyya said softly. "I have no choice. But I don't think it'll be enough."

Under a cold sky the following morning Lyya rode alongside Jaana and behind Ayvin. She kept her eyes steadfastly on the land ahead, gritting her teeth every time she heard one of the men utter a coarse comment about either herself or Jaana, or worse, both of them in the same sentence. She gave no outward response to their jibes, but could not help but imagine turning and riding up to each of them in turn, slashing their necks with her longknife. *Men like that don't deserve to live,* she thought hotly. *No luyan man would ever utter such hateful words or threats. No, if a man of my people detested someone so much, then the target of their ire would be dead in a moment. We don't waste time with idle words, and neither would I in dealing with these fools.*

But there were too many of them. Given the opportunity provided by any transgression they would kill her slowly in front of Jaana. Lyya tried to banish the image of herself being held down on the ground and raped and beaten again and again with Jaana forced to watch. *Be calm,* she instructed herself. *For your own sake and Jaana's, be calm. Outwardly at least. Remember why you're here.*

Ayvin took no part in his soldiers' japes, but neither did he do anything to curb the activity. He had said no more than a few curt words for the entire ride so far, and Jaana had been just as withdrawn, so Lyya was surprised when Jaana suddenly spoke up as they drew near to the village of North Vale. "If we find anyone with a talent for the Powers, then don't speak against whatever we need to do." She gave her a sidelong glance. "I know you, Lyya."

"As you wish," Lyya said unhappily.

North Vale sat between two low grassy hills, and nestled next to a lake on one side. To Lyya it appeared squat and ugly with its hard stone and straw buildings that humans were so fond of creating. She hated even stepping inside such places, but supposed that she would have to at some point. Her sense of smell was as potent as that of any other *luyan* and she quickly caught a multitude of odours on the breeze- rotting vegetables, horse dung, a barn of silage, a flyblown carcass somewhere in one of the fenced off fields behind the settlement. As they stopped and dismounted, the stench of human excrement wafted across from several of the nearby houses and she almost gagged.

"Where is the elder of this place?" Ayvin called out. Moments passed and finally a man with a leathery complexion slowly walked out of one of the huts, leaning on a stick. "That would be myself, m'lord," he said guardedly as he drew near.

"Gather together everyone who lives here. I don't wish to stay longer than I have to." When the old man gaped at him, Ayvin continued quietly, "There cannot be more than two hundred people in this place. Is it so difficult? Gather them all. Bring them here. That is an order."

The folk of North Vale gradually learned of the command and made their way towards the waiting soldiers. Their reluctance was total. Lyya saw wariness and suspicion in the eyes of those who gathered nearby. Fearful parents drew their children close. Their offspring stared wide-eyed at the armed men in their midst, more fascinated than afraid.

"Everyone is here," the elder said quietly once the crowd had grown half a dozen rows thick. "What do you want with us, m'lord? If someone is accused of a crime, it's reported to the Warden or one of his men..."

"Be quiet." Ayvin turned to Jaana. "Look at them all. If there are any here with even the slightest talent, point them out."

"I already know," Jaana said. "There is one- and only one. Him." She pointed directly at a boy of perhaps twelve or thirteen summers standing by his parents. Lyya saw the look of shock in the boy's eyes. "What does she mean?!" he blurted out, and turned to his father. "I've done nothing wrong! Tell them, father! I've done nothing wrong!"

"Explain yourselves," his father spoke up roughly. He was a heavy-set man obviously used to hard labour and lifting. Lyya saw his fingers stray to the handle of the long axe held in his belt. "My son speaks the truth. He's done nothing to warrant your displeasure, Lord Ayvin."

"Oh. You know my name."

"Most folk in the middle lands know your name, and that of your liege lord." He stopped suddenly, perhaps aware that insolence would do neither him nor his offspring any favours. "I am only saying that he's committed no crime, m'lord."

"I didn't say he'd committed a crime." Ayvin turned quickly to Jaana. "You're certain?"

"I'm certain. He's strong," Jaana confirmed, and a whisper commenced amongst everyone who had gathered. Lyya's sharp hearing caught the word *witch* at least three times.

"Good. Then our journey to this cesspit was not in vain." Ayvin turned back to the boy's father. "Your boy has a talent in the Old Powers."

The effect of those words was instantaneous. Folk standing nearby shrank away from the family as if they bore the rotting plague or tonguedrop. A murmur of shock ran through all those gathered. "Take them all away!" a woman screamed from near the back of the crowd, and Ayvin smiled at that. "We *will* take the boy," he said.

"You will not," his father replied immediately. "Begging your pardon, m'lord, but..."

"Wait. You tell me what I can and cannot do and then presume to beg my pardon?" Ayvin shook his head. "You're as stupid as you look, clearly. " He turned to two of his men. "Bring the boy."

As the men strode forward, the boy's father stepped in front of his son and hefted the axe in one smooth motion. *Oh no,* Lyya thought, her heart sinking. Her mouth felt dry as she watched the men draw nearer. Swiftly she turned to Jaana, who glanced back at her, sighed and spoke up suddenly. "Ayvin, tell your men to stand back. Let me speak with the boy's father."

"What will you do, witch?" the villager retorted. "Wrap a spell about me so I freely give away my only son? I'll never do that."

As Ayvin commanded his men to step back, Jaana drew a little nearer. "There's a war coming," she said quietly. "A war against the starspawn. The rumours from Aphenhast are true. All those with strength in the Old Powers are to be brought together, trained and raised as weapons in the fight to preserve the world itself. Do you understand?"

He simply stared at her, but Lyya allowed herself a quiet sigh of relief as he returned the axe to his belt.

"*I* am like your son," Jaana continued. "I have strength in the Old Powers. Do you think we mean to harm him? Hardly! He will be of the utmost importance in our fight. He will be trained and eventually become a master of his abilities. He will be far safer at Inerdyr's castle than here, certainly." Her gaze took in the suspicious stares of North Vale's people. "The air is heavy with ignorance and superstition. He has no place here now, and without being schooled in restraining and focussing his abilities..." She shrugged. "It would be dangerous for him. He would more than likely burn himself out, or accidentally destroy something or someone, assuming that one of these gaping fools doesn't kill your son first."

As the father and mother looked helplessly at each other, Jaana turned her attention to the boy. "What's your name?"

"I... I... my name..."

"His name is Parril," the boy's mother spoke up, her voice quavering.

"A good name. An ancient name." Jaana nodded. "We will send word to you when you may visit your son. In the meantime, he'll be well looked after and will want for nothing."

"You give your word?"

"I give you my word as a Descendant of the First," Jaana said, inclining her head slightly. The words caused another murmur of consternation amongst the villagers, but Lyya, far less impressed at the title, thought she had heard a slightly mocking tone to Jaana's words.

Parril was allowed a tearful farewell, and then they turned and left. As they did so, Lyya glanced back and saw the boy's parents standing together in the muddy track, already alone. Not a single one of their neighbours consoled them. The crowd had disappeared far more quickly than it had congregated.

They'll be driven out, she thought as she turned away and rode on. *If I know human nature- and I know it as well as any* luyan *woman can- the others will consider them outsiders now, diseased even- harbourers of a dangerous warlock. No matter that their son has been taken from them.*

They rode for what remained of the day, stopping only for lunch. Dusk had fallen by the time they arrived back at the castle, tired and saddle-sore. Ayvin accompanied two of his men and a subdued Parril to Inerdyr's chambers. "No need for you to attend," he told Jaana. "Were I you, I'd get some sleep. We'll be out again tomorrow. South-east, I'd say. Inerdyr will want more than just the one."

"You did well today," Jaana told Lyya as they sat in Jaana's room a little later.

Lyya blinked. "I only accompanied you, nothing else."

"And that was all I asked for. It made a difference to me." Jaana glanced across at her. "And you did well because you ignored Ayvin's idiot thugs, or at least you didn't respond to them."

"I wanted to," Lyya said grimly. "Believe me, I wanted to. But that would have ended badly for us both."

Jaana nodded. "Let's not think about that." She paused and then added abruptly, "Are you still worried about me?"

"I don't think you are being true to yourself. You were a healer, and that was your calling in life. Now you see yourself as a warrior."

"I've embraced the powers that were always a part of me," Jaana replied, scowling at her. "What else was I to do? *They* represent my calling in life. They are a part of my deepest nature, more than struggling as a simple healer ever could have been. Half the people I sought to cure died anyway, Lyya. What little reputation I had was undeserved. But now I can make a difference in the war to come. Would you have done any less, in my position? I think not."

Lyya saw the dark look in Jaana's eyes and said nothing more on the matter.

As she lay down a little later Lyya found herself thinking of the boy they had captured. Presumably he would be trained by Inerdyr, or perhaps by Jaana. She tried to banish from her mind that look of terror in his eyes when Jaana had identified him as strong in the Powers, but couldn't. *What will Inerdyr do with him?* she wondered. *He has been patient with Ileana, even though she refuses to so much as talk about the Old Powers. She feigns tiredness or inability. Will he be as patient with the boy? What will he do to him, to awaken his talents?*

She imagined that Parril must have spent much of his short life forever looking over his shoulder, always wary and fearful that someone might have worked out that he was different to everyone else, no matter how careful he might have been. And now his worst nightmare had been realised.

Jaana is becoming hard like a stone, Lyya thought, but at least today she showed there is still a tender soul inside her. "You did well also," she pointed out. "You prevented bloodshed. Ayvin's men would have cut down Parril's father without a second thought."

"I did that for you, Lyya. I would never have heard the end of it if I hadn't at least tried to intervene."

"Well anyway, your words convinced them. I hardly think the boy would be easier to train if he had seen castle men butcher his family."

"True enough. Regardless, what's done is done for right or wrong, and we have another Descendant. At least, I'm fairly certain that he is. He's strong enough, that's for certain."

They said nothing for a long while. Lyya lapsed into thought, and when she looked across again, Jaana had fallen asleep.

She stayed awake for a while, feeling suddenly alone in the silence. *You're drifting from me,* she thought, looking at the sleeping woman. *If we lived in a different time we could enjoy a peaceful life together. Instead Aona stands on the brink of destruction, and your Powers rise to defend it.*

To defend the world, and take you away from me forever.

V - Transformations

I

Twelve riders drew to a halt in Kaalin's central square. Some of them slumped visibly in their saddles, wearied by the long morning's ride. The steaming breath of horses and men rose into the chilly air as they listened to the absolute silence.

"Do you hear it?" Hanric said presently as he surveyed the utter abandonment. Thin-lipped and with short-cropped grey hair, Inerdyr's henchman made a picture of chilling hostility as he took in the scene of wooden huts huddled together that made up this sorry excuse for a settlement.

"I hear nothing, m'lord," one of his men ventured cautiously.

"Precisely. You hear nothing." Hanric's hands tightened on the reins of his horse until his knuckles became almost as white as the snow. The rage was upon him again- the *dark ocean* he called it, for it often felt as if he was drowning in that fury, dragged further and deeper down into a bestial state that reduced him to something that was both a lesser and a greater man. *It has been too long,* he silently remarked. On the same night that Inerdyr had sent him on this mission, he had taken a young man from one of the villages near Mornkastle, violated and beaten him until even his own mother would not have recognised him, and left him naked and shivering- and probably bleeding inside as much as outside- in a field to freeze to death. That had satisfied his lust and his rage for a short while, but it would always return.

Hanric wished that Inerdyr had allowed him time with Sarros in the dungeons before his departure, but he had not. Instead some time with Sarros would be his reward for bringing back the heads of Ruhal and his followers.

Except the Descendant, he reminded himself. *I've no use for the bitch, although the men might- but Inerdyr wanted her brought to him unmolested. I suppose there's sense in that.*

The Warden of Steepleford had told them that Ruhal's group had headed north, directly towards this Powers-forsaken outpost town, but Hanric did not need to search the entire place to know that they had long gone.

Nevertheless they began a cursory examination of the nearer communal buildings, looking for clues as to which direction the mercenaries had taken. In the darkness of the stables they found the frozen, butchered bodies of horses. Hanric took a close look at each corpse, breathing in the now-faint iron odour of flesh. The insides of the creatures had been largely ransacked, their genitals mutilated and their eyes put out. He squatted in the hay, frowning as he tried to work out what had happened here. One of Ruhal's companions was a sorcerer of some repute- had he slain the creatures in order to evoke some spell or other? Or was this something even more mysterious- the work of the Watchers from the Black Citadel perhaps? Inerdyr knew something of the Watchers' powers and would have been able to work out the intent behind this butchery. But of course, Inerdyr was not here.

One of his men-at-arms, a swarthy fellow called Tomas, commented from behind him, "Strange that they would slay their own horses, m'lord. Unless the settlers did the deed."

"And why would they do that?" Hanric demanded without bothering to turn around. "In fact, who said these were the mercenaries' horses?"

"Why would *anyone* butcher horses if not for meat?" Tomas replied. "Clearly this was not done for food. Great evil passed through here if you ask me."

"Agreed." Hanric stood up and strode out into the open air. "Why are there no people here? Have Ruhal and his followers spirited them away somehow? Did they kill them all- and these horses- and then bury them somewhere? The snow's less than a hand thick, not enough to hide bodies. The ground's too thick to bury them. There's no pyre nearby."

"Reckon he's simply made them all his new foot soldiers and carried on to the next village," Tomas said.

Hanric thought about that. It made little sense that the traitors would have fled as far north as this to begin with- if they travelled any further north they would be in the Rhunin proper and no one could survive long in the mountains during the winter. They could have reached half a dozen other settlements further south and west in the time it would have taken them to reach this place. And yet the few sightings reported back to him spoke consistently of their heading directly here.

They searched the meeting hall next, and there in the frozen gloom they found the bodies of many townsfolk. "It would seem they encountered some resistance," Hanric mused as he walked amongst the frosted corpses, turning a number of them over with the toe of his boot before bending down to peer more closely as one of his men held a lantern near. "They gave no quarter, as you can see. Men, women, children- families died together in this place."

"Brave of them," Tomas commented, "to stand against the Warden of Mordenglen and his followers, *and* Watchers of the Black Citadel."

"Brave and foolish. They are not warriors. These folk are made for tilling the land in the warmer months and hunting game, nothing more than that." Hanric stopped and prodded the body of a little boy whose hand still clutched a dagger. The child's mouth remained stretched wide open as if he had died screaming. "Look here, all of you. This child tried desperately to defend himself against them- but what chance would he have had against Ruhal's mercenaries, let alone Watchers?"

Hanric stepped back and watched as his men stared at the body. He could almost feel the hardening of their anger against the traitors, not that it needed stirring up much more.

He studied each face he found amongst the cadavers in the hope that one might turn out to be Ruhal or one of his followers- human or Watcher, it didn't matter, unless it turned out to be the Descendant of course. But he remained disappointed.

Noon had not yet arrived, so the day still held sufficient light for them to make good headway south-west. Hanric named this as their chosen direction. "We'll reach Raven's Ford by nightfall if we make haste," he said, "and two days after, we should arrive at Riverstone. It's up to us to tell as many folk as we can what happened here. Ruhal Dalmorn and his followers will butcher anyone they see standing in the way of their rebellion, anyone who dares to stand against their madness. We'll recruit in Raven's Ford if there's any folk worth having."

Many of his men nodded soberly. They wore dark expressions. Hanric kept hidden his contempt for their feelings. The slayings had clearly upset them, particularly the less experienced fighters who had seen few scenes like this.

Some of the men Inerdyr had assigned to this mission were nothing more than castle guardsmen, good for little more than opening gates and leading processions. Hanric had thought about questioning the sense of sending such men on this mission but had decided against it. He had witnessed Inerdyr's wisdom being questioned before, and it had never ended well for those few brave enough to do the questioning.

II

They pushed the horses as hard as they were able for the rest of the day, and true to Hanric's word they arrived in Raven's Ford with the light still full.

Hanric's iron gaze took in all those who gathered after his men arrived in the village. He waited for the crowd to grow a little larger, and then spoke up. "Some of you may have heard of Ruhal Dalmorn, the Warden of Mordenglen. He is now known to be a traitor to the Free Territories, a usurper who seeks to bring chaos and ruin to you all. Clearly he and his followers have not yet come here- I see men of fighting age amongst you, for a start- but I assure you that they *will* arrive. Now hear this: there are *Watchers* amongst his number. Servants of the Seven, from the distant Black Citadel."

A murmur of confusion and fear rose up. Hanric allowed it to seethe and pass back and forth for a moment and then added, "Yes. They are real." He amplified the statement with a grim nod. "A great evil walks through the Free Territories. Ruhal is intent on sowing seeds of discord amongst the people of each and every settlement. They will come here, and..."

"Why?" one old man asked. Leaning on a sturdy wooden staff he peered up at Hanric, shielding his eyes against the low late sunlight. "It would make no sense to do such a thing. Wardens are protectors of their territories, sworn to uphold order and justice, and keep the peace throughout the Free Territories. A Warden can only raise an army with the agreement of the full Council."

Hanric frowned. "I am not here to reason or debate the state of the man's mind. Ruhal is a renegade Warden, and I hear he's to be stripped of his title. I am here to simply give you the facts and warn you. Already they have slain many people up in Kaalin. Ask any one of my men here, they'll tell you the same story."

"M'lord speaks the truth," Tomas spoke up unbidden. "Women and children cut down without mercy. No other band of travellers was headed that way. Only them. Whatever you may think of this Warden, he and his companions are enemies of the Free Territories."

"What protection can you offer us?" the old man demanded. "Will you be sending men to defend Raven's Ford? Or will you stay here yourselves to apprehend these rebels?"

Hanric stared at him. "It is up to every man and woman in every settlement to rise up against those who would commit treachery against the Free Territories. Have lookouts posted. If you see them coming, send a messenger on horseback towards Riverstone, for that's where we're headed. If we are gone from there, then they should head on towards Northmarch, but be sure to tell the people of Riverstone first. Is that clear enough?"

Idiots, Hanric thought contemptuously as some of them stared mutely back at him, while others whispered or even argued amongst themselves. A few hastened away, perhaps to warn other villagers who had elected not to attend. *What use will these folk be against Ruhal's mercenaries and Watchers? They'll flee or beg for their lives, or sit in the dirt and soil themselves.*

Then again a few of them could be useful, he reasoned. *Those who can fight alongside my men.*

"Anyone who can wield a sword or bow and wishes to join us will be handsomely rewarded," he spoke up. "Step forward if you're man enough. There'll be thirty silver stars for each man who joins us, to be paid when we cleave the heads from these outlaws. And plenty of food and drink." *These folk look hungry,* he considered, *and the harvests have been poor everywhere this year.* "The same if any of you honest folk who remain here kill one of them," he added. "All I need are the heads."

After a moment, three men stepped forward, then another two. Hanric disregarded all but two of the five. One was a slim, dark-haired man of perhaps thirty summers, with a longknife in his belt, who looked useful. The other was a nervous-looking lad of perhaps fifteen or sixteen with straw-blond hair, and handsome. Hanric looked him up and down, and felt a familiar stirring in his groin. *He'll do,* he thought. *I can't imagine he's much of a fighter, but it's not battle I have in mind for him.*

"You- and you," Hanric said, pointing to each of them in turn. "Come forward." He dismissed the others with an irritated wave of the hand.

A woman pushed her way frantically through to the front of the crowd, her skirts trailing through the mud. "Please, m'lord, my son Leon, he doesn't know what he's doing..."

The boy turned to her with a scowl of embarrassment, and Hanric said, "Seems to me he knows well enough what he's doing. He's a lad you can be proud of, woman. He wants to help us bring the traitors to justice. Isn't that right, Leon?"

Leon bobbed his head eagerly and threw a dark look at his mother. Hanric noticed with amusement her obvious distress. *I may or may not return him to you in one piece when all this is done,* he thought. *But is that not the likeliest fate of heroes?*

They left the village a short while later. Hanric demanded that two horses be taken from the village stable- two of only three- for their new recruits, but as it happened one of the horses belonged to the older recruit in any case.

Much remained to think about. Offering silver or gold for the heads of the traitors was one thing, but how likely were the people of Raven's Ford to even attempt an attack when Ruhal's outlaws rode into their village? *No,* he thought. *They'll be cut down. Perhaps some of the men will be taken prisoner, or agree to swear fealty to Ruhal.*

But whatever happens, the story of any further misdeed will spread swiftly if someone manages to escape.
And someone usually does.

III

As they rode that afternoon Hanric learned more about Ferrin, the elder of their two new followers. Ferrin revealed himself to be a man of some intelligence. He was polite but not fawning, and he held at least a few opinions that Hanric found himself agreeing with.

"There are some people who are, in truth, nothing but a burden upon others," Ferrin remarked. "What is best for the Free Territories? That those who deserve life are better able to live their lives. Those who cannot or will not contribute to the greater good- their lives should be forfeit."

"There are too many such people," Hanric observed. "Weak fools, snivelling and whining and expecting without giving. Put them to the sword I say."

"One only has to look at the way animals behave," Ferrin added.

"Animals?" Hanric threw him a blank look.

"The weaklings of any litter die," Ferrin explained, "because that's the natural way of things. But societies of humans and *luyan* and *crommari* and others have developed ideologies whereby the weaklings are senselessly protected. Energy and resources are often directed towards those who are least likely to become useful to the society at large."

Hanric grunted and shook his head.

That evening, after they had set up the camp Hanric commanded both Ferrin and Leon to show their prowess with the sword by sparring with Tomas, who was considered the best swordsman amongst the men. As Hanric had suspected, Leon was a poor fighter, and fell twice simply from poor balance. Ferrin, however, was a master with the blade, perhaps the best Hanric had ever seen. In each of the

91

three rounds he took part in, he had Tomas down and yielding with the tip of the sword pressed against his neck. *He's quick,* Hanric noted each time. *That's the most dangerous thing about him. He's just a little bit quicker than anyone expects. Where did he learn such skills? Not Raven's Ford and that's for certain.*

"Come with me, Leon," he said afterwards, as the men were preparing the campfires and setting up the tents. "I'll show you a few things about swordsmanship to help you improve."

The two of them walked around the bend in the valley through which they had been travelling, until after several hundred paces the camp was out of sight. Hanric's men were well-versed in his desires and would already know the reason for his departure with Leon. Luckily for them, they were also sensible enough to pretend they knew nothing of the matter.

"Unbuckle your sword and place it on the ground," he said. When Leon had done so, Hanric continued, "I think you have potential, Leon."

"You do?" The boy brightened.

"Indeed I do. And provided that you do as you're told, I can make sure that you rise to the highest rank amongst the men I command. But you *do* need to remain obedient. I'll not ask much of you."

"I'll do anything," Leon said eagerly, and Hanric smiled. "Good. Take down your trousers and smallclothes- and you might want to remove your boots beforehand- and go down on all fours, facing away from me."

Leon stared numbly at him. "I... I don't know..."

"It's very simple, Leon." Hanric took a deep breath. "Do as you're told, and you'll be well rewarded. If you continue to feign stupidity or disobey a direct instruction, it *will* end very badly for you. I would like to return you to your mother one day, Leon. You'd like to go back to her when all this is done, wouldn't you?"

"I think I'd like to go back now," Leon said in a small voice.

"It's a little late for that, I'm afraid, as you've willingly given yourself to my command. Now, I heard you say a moment ago that you would do *anything*. So are you going to do as you're told?"

He waited impatiently as Leon removed his clothing as directed and knelt down, shivering. Hanric spat on his engorged phallus. *"Don't scream,"* he murmured as he pressed himself against Leon. "That would make me *very* angry."

Leon mumbled something incoherent. *He's crying,* Hanric realised. *Well, I'll allow him that as long as he's quiet about it.*

Suddenly he felt the hairs on the back of his neck stand up. In a moment he became absolutely certain that someone lurked nearby watching. Coldly angry at the dwindling of his manhood, he tugged his smallclothes and trousers up, tying his trousers before turning round.

Ferrin sat cross-legged on a boulder, grinning widely. Hanric thought furiously for a moment that he ought to widen that grin even more and carve the man's face to shreds. But even in the madness of that moment he knew that Ferrin was a likelier winner of any such duel. He had seen him fight, had observed with hot jealousy the liquid grace of the man. *I thought I was a useful fighter with any weapon,* he thought, *but he would be a step ahead of me no matter what blade I chose.*

"Please, don't stop on my account," Ferrin said mildly, even as Leon tearfully pulled up his trousers with shaking hands. "I was going to talk to you about something, but it can wait. We each have our urges after all."

Hanric turned to Leon. "Go sit with the men, and keep your mouth shut." As Leon made his way back to the camp, still crying, Hanric turned his attention to Ferrin. "Well?"

Ferrin steepled his hands and pursed his lips thoughtfully. "If you will accept them, I would like to call some friends of mine to our cause. I promise you, they would be eager to help us find and kill these outlaws. They've never had a chance to slay Watchers before. They would be *most* interested..."

"It's not such an easy matter," Hanric cut across him roughly. "If you knew anything about such creatures then you wouldn't speak so lightly of the task. Why do you think we're recruiting anyone who's of any use?"

"Do I speak lightly? Please, forgive me." Ferrin inclined his head briefly. "However, I can assure you that if this were a routine mission I wouldn't have joined you. I would not have been interested, and neither would my friends."

Hanric stared thoughtfully at him. "You're not from Raven's Ford, are you? Where are you from? And how did you become such a proficient swordsman? Who did you train under?"

Ferrin blinked as if taken aback. "So many questions! No, I'm not from Raven's Ford. I happened to be passing by. I'll answer your other questions another time if I may. Now- will you allow me to call my friends to your cause? You need only say the word."

Hanric thought about the offer. The young man's insolence angered him, but he *was* a fine bladesman and no doubt possessed other useful talents besides. He wondered if Ferrin might even have some minor talent in the Old Powers. Perhaps *that* was how he was so swift in combat, dancing around his foes as if to mock them.

"Anyone you bring to this task will take their orders from me," he began, but Ferrin shook his head sadly. "No, no. They won't. I am responsible for them- their leader, if you will. They answer to me. That's the way it must be. But we *will* follow you, and we *will* help you do what we need to do. We're also *very* self-sufficient and we won't beg for any of your men's supplies. Most importantly, we won't run." He gestured towards the distant encampment. "*They* might. They're simple men, far from home. But we know the lie of this land intimately. Say the word and I will bring them with the dawn."

"Wait." Hanric scowled, considering. "I have two conditions. A Descendant of the First travels with those we seek. She is not to be harmed in any way, but returned to Inerdyr."

Ferrin nodded. "I'm aware of her. I give you my word, neither I nor those who follow me will harm her in any way. Nor will we harm the *other* Descendant. Well, in truth there are three if you include her father, although he has no notable powers of which we're aware..."

"What? Another..."

Ferrin smiled as Hanric stared at the ground, contemplating the swelling of his prize. "What brought them together?" Hanric said finally, bewildered.

"I have no idea. Maybe nothing more than simple chance." Ferrin gestured for him to continue. "Fate is a most curious companion. But please, go on. You had a second condition."

"I..." For a moment Hanric could not remember. When he did, he felt the heat of humiliation flushing his face again, and his expression grew dark as he replied. "If I wish to have my way with the boy, *stay away* from me. You *and* your friends, if they arrive. No watching, no interference. A man deserves his privacy to do what he must."

"I agree, and apologise." Ferrin nodded. "I give you my word, Hanric. We will leave you to satisfy yourself in peace, as is every man's right. And so I ask you again- may I call to my companions and bring them under our banner?"

"You may." Hanric strode back towards the encampment without a further word. Ferrin watched him leave, and laughed silently to himself.

As daylight grew from the east, nightmares arrived in the shapes of Ferrin's followers.

The two men on watch shouted their warnings and drew steel, bringing everyone else swiftly awake. Hanric had his sword in hand even before he was fully alert, but as he lurched unsteadily to his feet and peered through the cold gloom at the figures approaching the edge of the camp, Ferrin stood up and raised his hands to calm everyone.

"All of you, put your swords away," he said quietly. As the men stood and looked indecisively at one another, Ferrin's companions moved a little closer and Hanric saw them in better detail.

"Powers," he whispered faintly.

There were three of them, and each one could only be described as an abomination.

One had two mouths, both of them wide open and baring an array of needle teeth. Another appeared more lupine than human, its face covered in hair. The creature's bright, feral yellow eyes stared around at the men as if it hungered for their flesh. The third was a woman who appeared to have no skin whatsoever and was entirely naked. Her flesh gleamed faintly in the gathering light.

"Ferrin," Hanric managed to say eventually. "What are these creatures? Send them away or I'll command my men to slay them."

Ferrin turned slowly to face him. "Do you not recall our agreement, Hanric? These are the friends of whom I spoke. They mean no harm to your men. They are here to help us. Is your memory so short?"

"These are beings fashioned by some kind of sorcery," Tomas spoke up shakily. "They are unnatural."

"They are touched by the Old Powers," Ferrin admitted, "and you *will* require their help if you are to overcome the likes of Watchers and Descendants. Will you shun them simply because they look unlike you?" He turned to Hanric again. "We'll have the heads of the traitors, and the two Descendants tamed and shackled. Don't lose sight of your goal, Hanric."

Hanric remained silent for a while, considering. *A sack of heads,* he found himself thinking, *and not only one but two Descendants. Inerdyr will reward me well.*

"Keep them away from us," he said finally, unable to stop staring at the silent monstrosities.

"Of course. You may not care to know their names, but I'll give them regardless." Ferrin gestured to the man with the double mouth first. "Vylan," he said. Then he turned to the wolf-like creature. "Klaan." Finally he pointed to the skinless woman. "Ithia."

As if he had simply commented on the weather, Ferrin then sat and bid his followers to do likewise. Not one of them said anything.

Later that morning, Hanric and Tomas planned the day's ride using the maps they had brought while the other men began saddling up. Ferrin sauntered over to give some advice about the lay of the land ahead. Leon watched the activity, and saw that all of Hanric's men still nervously avoided Ferrin's followers. *Monsters from the old tales,* he thought, but a part of him didn't truly believe it. He recalled Ferrin's question to Hanric's men. *Will you shun them simply because they look unlike you?*

They're no worse than Hanric, he thought, throwing a hateful stare in the commander's direction before looking quickly away lest he be found out and punished. *Hanric will probably try the same thing tonight,* he reminded himself, and took a deep breath in an attempt to stop himself from panicking.

Leon suddenly found Ferrin standing by his side, and jumped, startled. He had thought he was still with Hanric and Tomas. "Put this in your pocket," Ferrin said quietly, and Leon looked down to see in his hand a small, black-bladed knife with a bone handle. He flushed with embarrassment and looked away. "I can look after myself," he said quietly.

"Remain a fool and your life will be a short one," Ferrin said. Something in his voice made Leon look back at him. Before he knew what he was doing he had the knife his hand. "Put it away," Ferrin murmured. "You'll know when to use it."

As Ferrin wandered away, Leon thought for a moment he could feel the knife become hot, but before he could pull it from his pocket the sensation had passed.

"How will your three keep up with us?" he heard Hanric call across to Ferrin as they were about to ride. "You needn't think they're sharing the saddle with any of my men."

I know the answer, Leon thought. *They'll run alongside, and keep up easily.*

"They can run all day if they have to," Ferrin told him, "and they'll still be ready to fight whatever needs to be fought come the day's end. Ever faithful and never tiring. Can you ask for more?"

During the morning, Leon glanced to his right to find Ithia running alongside. *The horses don't fear them,* he thought, as his mount cantered on ahead without turning her head. *Why would that be?*

"You must be Leon," Ithia said, without sounding the slightest bit out of breath. Leon was startled. For some reason he hadn't expected her to have the power of speech. He nodded guardedly, clutching the reins a little more tightly.

"Do you find me repulsive, Leon? Only you stare ahead as if this endless snowy moorland is of special interest."

He swallowed and forced himself to look at her. For a moment he thought it odd that Ithia's eyes should be so beautiful when the rest of her was a horror. "I've never seen anyone like you before," he ventured at last. "Or anyone like Klaan and Vylan. Are they... I mean, are they..."

"Human?" Ithia laughed. "Yes and no, Leon. We are all *kin,* but not all entirely of human origin. Klaan is the product of a liaison between a human woman and a greatwolf. The Old Powers ran strongly through her, and fashioned a miracle of sorts- their lustful copulation made an infant."

"If that's true, then he's an abomination," Leon said. He felt sick inside.

Ithia grinned. "We're all greater or lesser abominations, Leon- yourself included."

"I don't understand."

"Not yet. But you will."

"What about Vylan and yourself?" Leon asked, uneasy at her words and the vague threat they might hold.

"We were both human. Well, we still are in a sense. We breathe, eat and drink, shit, all that you might expect. But we've become more. We've been made again."

Leon could think of nothing to say. Perhaps bored with him, Ithia increased her pace and ran ahead, her fleshy form stark against the snow.

That evening, after camp had been set up and fires were burning, Hanric walked over to where Leon was sitting and crouched down. "Time for your training," he said. "Come on."

Hanric did not even bother to insist that Leon bring his sword with him. Leon got to his feet, his pulse already quickening. He glanced across at Ferrin, who gave an almost imperceptible nod.

There was still enough light in the sky to walk by without the need for a lantern or torch. Hanric led Leon to an area of ground behind a small copse of trees, where they would be unseen by anyone back in the camp. Leon began unbuckling his belt, fumbling as his hands shook. But Hanric spoke up: "Not this time. I want to see what you're like with your mouth. Kneel down in front of me."

Leon did as bidden, watching as Hanric untied his trousers and pulled down his smallclothes. At the same time the bone-handled knife grew hot in Leon's pocket. *Use it now,* a voice told him. *Use it now before it burns through your pocket and into your flesh!*

Leon had never used a weapon in anger. He had no idea what he was doing. He pulled the knife from his pocket, and in a sudden, spasmodic movement he put every ounce of his energy into a slashing cut aimed at Hanric's stomach.

That the blade held a taint of some sorcery now was beyond doubt. It tore through Hanric's leather jerkin as if it gave all the protection of paper, and deep into the flesh of his stomach.

Hanric stood in open-mouthed astonishment for a moment as Leon stumbled backwards and scrambled away a short distance, both elated and terrified by what he had done, fearful that he had failed to wound his tormentor sufficiently.

Hanric took a couple of steps forward, rage in his eyes as he pressed his hand against his stomach and blood ran swiftly between his fingers. Leon somehow managed to stand up but his legs almost gave way immediately. Wildly he thought, *Now he's going to rape me and then he'll slit my throat and leave me to the carrion. But I'll be at peace. I'll be at peace. Let it end!*

Leon's legs continued to hold him more or less upright, but Hanric's did not and he fell to one side, shuddering. His leather fell apart as if all the stitching had vanished, and then his innards began to slip from his body. *Offal,* Leon found himself thinking as he watched them glisten in the failing light, rolling slowly out to nestle next to his swiftly shrinking phallus.

Hanric attempted to grin up at him through the haze of agony. "My... men," he whispered. "They'll kill you..."

Leon darted nearer and sliced the knife through Hanric's insides, dizzied and sick as he saw again how easily the blade cut through flesh. *It's as if it falls apart at the touch. The meat of this monster is soft. Who would have thought killing could be so easy?*

Even through his intense nausea, bright and gleeful thoughts came to him. *I'm a man now, Lord Hanric. I've disembowelled you. I'll leave you awhile to linger on. I heard that this sort of death is especially painful.*

Hanric uttered a faint choking sound, as snow started to spiral down.

As he stared at the gory results of Hanric's mutilation, certain that he would violently throw up his meagre luncheon, Leon heard a voice speak up behind him.

"There's a good riddance," Ferrin said.

Leon whirled round to face him, dropping the knife in his panic. "Please," he begged. "Please don't tell anyone!"

Ferrin smiled and shook his head. "Boy, why do you think I gave you that blade? It was for you to exact vengeance, and that's what you've done. I would have killed him at some point if you hadn't made such... interesting work of the task yourself." Ferrin pointed at Hanric. "Stare into his eyes, Leon. Quick now, while he still lives. You want to see his pain and rage before he passes away, don't you? You want to see the impotent fury in his eyes?"

Leon took a deep breath and looked towards Hanric. Their eyes met for a moment, and Leon saw such utter, unbridled hate that he almost gave out a panic-stricken scream. But instead a rage rose within him, and he walked until he was next to him and then thrust his thumbs into Hanric's cold blue eyes, pressing them down and into his skull. He didn't stop until Hanric was still and lifeless under his shaking hands.

Leon jumped when he felt Ferrin's hand on his shoulder. He had completely forgotten that anyone other than Hanric and himself existed. "And so it ends," Ferrin remarked. "He'll harm no one else now."

"He said his men would kill me," Leon said. He couldn't stop staring at Hanric's bloodied eye sockets. For a moment he even felt as if Hanric was *still* staring at him, mad though the idea was.

"They'll do no such thing. They are my men now- as are you, if you wish. What do you say? The mission remains the same- to hunt and kill the traitors. The method may differ from what Hanric had planned. And there'll be danger involved, no doubt of that. But at least you'll have nothing to fear from those on your own side."

Leon knelt to wipe his shaking, gore-stained hands in the snow. "What about Hanric? Shouldn't we bury him?"

Ferrin shook his head. "A different fate awaits Lord Hanric of Mornkastle. Go back to the camp. I'll deal with the corpse."

Leon walked unsteadily away. He dared to look back only once, and when he did he saw Ferrin crouched over the body as if he might be breathing in the salty, iron odour of gore. Something about the scene unsettled him, and he turned away to quicken his steps towards the campfires.

Ferrin returned a little later, and observed Hanric's men in silence for a while before he said mildly, "I still see fear in your eyes, although my companions have done nothing to deserve it. You fear only because you don't yet understand. I, on the other hand, understand *many* things- and consequently I fear less."

Tomas met his eyes with a visible effort. "We live ordered lives in the middle lands. Sorcery is a tool seldom seen and strictly controlled."

"Is it?" Ferrin laughed as he settled himself on a boulder near the fire. "The Old Powers are a great river that flows where it will. We live in a time when they gather strength and reach out into the world, touching the people of Aona in new ways. The river cannot be turned. It will simply find a way past any petty resistance."

Leon watched as Tomas stole a glance at Ferrin's three followers. *He's frightened,* Leon realised. *He's a grown man, a hardened warrior, and he must have seen all sorts of terrible things. Yet he's frightened by something that he can't explain.*

But so am I. I was scared of Hanric. Now I've killed him and I'm scared of myself. I killed him and I enjoyed it. I enjoyed watching him die. I even enjoyed putting my thumbs through his eyes, even though I felt sickened by it.

Even after I killed Hanric I was still frightened of him. He was the sort of man who would do anything to anyone, and I feared he still might come after me even after it was impossible. That makes him a worse monster than these kin, *surely. Ithia, Vylan and Klaan don't terrify me.*

As if he was somehow able to read Leon's thoughts, Ferrin added suddenly, "In case you were wondering, Hanric will not be returning. Leon has slain him."

A stunned silence fell across the camp. Leon was sitting cross-legged on the ground, but he still felt his legs turn to mud. If he had been standing when Ferrin spoke, he would have collapsed. Instinctively he opened his mouth to defend himself- though he had no idea what he might say- but he had no need. "Leon is a loyal servant," Ferrin continued. "Hanric was a bad master. Does any man here mourn him?"

The silence persisted. Hanric's men looked at one another; not one of them looked able to decide what they should do. Ferrin's followers sat watchfully. They betrayed no sign of aggression but Leon had only to glance at them to know they were ready to fight if they had need to.

"I had to," Leon heard himself say eventually. He cringed as everyone turned to look at him. "I had to," he repeated, and then he looked down at the ground with the heat of shame rising in his cheeks.

"We all do what we have to," Ithia stated.

Leon fell asleep later, but woke suddenly after a short while. For a moment he thought that flames surrounded him, but then he realised they were only the flames of the nearest campfire, several paces away. Three of the men sat around it on one side, and on the other Ferrin sat cross-legged with his head bowed, apparently deep in thought.

As he began to drift back to sleep again a little later Leon listened to the men talking about Mornkastle- a place they visited often and which they evidently missed. Leon found the very idea of Mornkastle fascinating- a city through which the Unbuilt Wall ran, a place governed in part by the forces of the South and in part by the people of the Free Territories.

"How do such great enemies work together?" Leon mused, half-asleep.

"Work together? It's more of an uneasy truce, lad," he heard Tomas say. "Powers only know how it hasn't erupted into war. It almost has, on occasion. There's a story from well over a thousand years ago of two great armies approaching each other from the north and south. They reached each other at Mornkastle, which was a smaller place then. Hundreds of thousands might have died had war broken out, but instead a truce was devised. Even the Seven hadn't the stomach for a long fight against the Old Powers. So lives were spared, and lines drawn."

As Leon drowsily lay back, still vaguely listening to the quiet conversation, he fancied that he also heard a low, steady rhythm like a vast drum being pounded some distance away. If the men could hear it, then they gave no indication of having done so.

Leon listened to that strange sound as sleep enveloped him. His last thought as he drifted away was that although the rhythm emanated from some distant, ill-defined place, it followed and measured the beat of his own heart, as if the sound was somehow his own no matter how disembodied.

He woke again sometime in the middle of the night. Hearing a faint sound somewhere behind him, he turned his head to one side and almost cried out when he saw Ithia's face fill his vision. He felt the sour heat of her breath. She blinked slowly, her eyelids making an odd, sticky sound.

"Can you not sleep?" he whispered once his pulse had slowed.

"I can sleep well enough," Ithia said, "but I don't need to. Do you fear the future, Leon?"

"Do I..." He stared at her in confusion. "I don't know." Something about her bright, steady gaze unsettled him and so he turned away, wishing the conversation done with- only for Ithia's hand to touch his shoulder. A moment later he felt her entire body pressed up against his. The woman's unnatural warmth spread quickly through the two blankets he had wrapped around himself. "May I warm you?" she murmured.

"You already are," he pointed out, but she pulled the blankets from underneath him and moved herself under their cover before placing them over them both. "There," she said, and curled herself against him, breasts pressed against his back and one leg draped over his. "You can stop shivering now," Ithia added, but he already had. Despite his unease, the heat lulled Leon to sleep in moments.

The night had moved on and Archaon's reddish face fell swiftly in the west when Ferrin wandered over to squat down next to them. "He's mine," Ithia murmured, half in jest, and she extended an arm further around Leon's to caress his chest. The boy had cast aside their blankets in his sleep, no longer needing their protection from the cold. To Ferrin the pair of them looked like meat and alabaster.

"Will he become one of us?" Ferrin mused. "Or must we send him away to fight Ruhal's followers elsewhere, likely to be slaughtered?"

"That would be a waste," Ithia chided. "I see something special in him. I think you do also. Is he not one of the reasons why you were in Raven's Ford? Let him take the ceremony when the time is right." She pressed even more tightly against Leon, who sighed in his slumber. "I could be cradling a bundle of miracles, Ferrin. Let's hasten the day of their awakening."

Ferrin considered for a moment. "Let him take the ceremony tomorrow, if we're permitted," he said finally. "I will consult with our Lords if I'm able."

"So soon?"

"We have no time to *wait* for him or anyone else to consider their options. Sooner or later he takes the ceremony, or a far bloodier road instead. Those are his options, Ithia. They were ours once, lest you forget."

Ferrin left her then, and went over to sit by one of the dwindling fires. As he meditated cross-legged before the embers, his awareness of nearby places and events poured in and out of his mind, a flow of information, some of it useful and some of it nothing more than banal. The contingent of men and women from Frostgate and the *luyan* settlement of Hainur continued to grow in numbers, their intent to eventually move towards Ruhal and his followers when they were located. This had been Inerdyr's second plan in case Hanric met his demise, and Ferrin had visited Hainur himself recently to stir feelings up a little further. To the east, Raven's Ford had become a bitterly divided place, with some of its people still determined to oppose the rebels but others inclined even to follow them, or at least decline to take up arms in anger. Ferrin smiled as he considered Raven's Ford. If the Warden of Mordenglen and his people arrived there- and he had a feeling that they would- then the *kin* he had ordered to remain hidden among the settlers would strike against them when the time was right.

A while later, Ferrin stirred from his inner quietness and saw that Tomas was now on watch. "Did you like Hanric?" Ferrin inquired.

Tomas shook his head. "No one liked him. He met an end that many of us would have wished upon him- to be slain by Leon. Brave, that boy. Perhaps too brave."

"How so?"

"Why do you think we all put up with Hanric for so long? Because he was a loyal lieutenant and friend to Lord Inerdyr himself. If he knew the things that that man had done in his name... but he'd never believe it even if someone dared to tell him."

Oh, I think he might, Ferrin thought, *but whoever told him would likely still lose their head. From what I've heard, Inerdyr and Hanric were dissimilar only in the amount of power they each held.*

"If Inerdyr hears of what happened, Leon's life will be forfeit. Powers, *all* our lives will be," Tomas warned.

"He will learn soon enough," Ferrin told him, "but I wouldn't fear the wrath of one sorcerer, were I you. There are powers higher than his. Stay with me and my people, Tomas- and be a part of that which *we* are a part of. Then you need never toil under Inerdyr's yoke again."

But Tomas' fear spoke more convincingly to him than Ferrin could. He took one glance at the *kin* and went to sit further away.

Ferrin remained awake throughout the night. In the coldest hour there came a flapping of wings and a black shape descended from the southern sky. He turned and regarded the crow in silence as it stalked over to him, cocking its head to one side as if to ask where the correct recipient of its message was.

"I rule here now," Ferrin said softly, ignoring the uneasy looks from the three men who remained on watch. He extended a hand towards the bird and it hopped nearer and allowed him to untie the rolled-up message attached to its leg. Ferrin carefully opened it and read.

You have two tennights to bring back the heads of the traitors and bring me the Descendant. If you already have them, tell me. If you do not, then be aware that little time remains. Dissent must be destroyed.

The message was not signed, but Ferrin knew perfectly well that Inerdyr had written it. *You'll have your reply tomorrow,* he thought. *Other matters must be attended to first.*

V

Ithia came to sit next to Leon the following morning as they breakfasted. Even after days of her company he could not help but stare at her, revolted and curious in equal measure. That she required no clothing whatsoever in this harsh season was incredible enough, but her lack of skin he could scarcely believe. "It holds us together," he murmured as his gaze traversed the tight and intricate musculature of her face and neck, the soft fleshiness of her breasts and stomach.

"It doesn't hold me together." Leon visibly recoiled when Ithia flashed a grin at him, teeth white as snow against the angry crimson of her body.

"She's a marvel to behold, is she not?" Ferrin remarked without turning round, as he sorted through supplies that he'd found in Hanric's pack. "Ithia is quite aware of the cold, but it doesn't affect her. You'll see many a miracle in the tennights and months to come, Leon. The great magics of Aona herself create such gifts as these. Some folk have far better eyesight than they would naturally, enabling them to view objects or creatures in great detail from a distance. Others can run especially quickly or for a day and night without tiring. There are those who can move so quickly that you might only catch the slightest glimpse of them. Some can see the smallest amount of heat and movement in the darkest of nights, or... well, you imagine a useful power and it's likely that somewhere, someone will have the gift of it."

"What about you? What powers do *you* have?"

"Knowledge," Ferrin said simply. "Knowledge, and the ability to bring such folk together, to lead them and provide them with purpose."

Leon nodded. Knowledge and leadership didn't sound to him like exceptional powers, but he suspected that Ferrin had recourse to many others that he chose not to share or reveal. *I reckon even if I stabbed him through the heart it would keep on beating as strongly as ever,* Leon thought, *and the wound would close up in moments.*

"Ferrin sings the song of our Lords, the song of the world, and we listen," Ithia spoke up quietly.

"Well, he's a better leader than Hanric for certain," Leon declared.

"In his defence, Hanric has done more good in the days since his death than I suspect he ever did during his life," Ferrin said mildly. "But we'll talk no more of the past. Such wonders as I mentioned are seen more than ever now because Aona needs them. The world bestows great powers upon the chosen, so they may defend her against all her enemies. The starspawn, for one. For another, the mercenaries whom we hunt and their comrades from the Black Citadel, all of them steeped in evil sorcery. You've heard the stories of the Black Citadel, Leon?"

"I've heard many. Are they all true?"

"All those that matter, yes. The Seven who rule that place are surely the greatest stain upon the face of Aona."

"The greatest, and yet the least known," Ithia added. "By most accounts they came from another world, or from the void between the stars."

"And in that they share something with the starspawn," Ferrin added. He prodded at the fire with a stick of birch, and sparks rose and winked out in the chilly air. "A few little-known stories claim that the Seven *made* the starspawn, and then there are others that say the reverse is true. There's also the legend of a single world, a place from which the disease spread."

"Disease?" Leon frowned.

"The disease of the starspawn," Ferrin said. Leon nodded, not understanding the explanation.

Ferrin got to his feet, suddenly restless. Leon saw that Archaon had just dipped below the western horizon. "Meditate on that," Ferrin told him, "and you will begin to understand that although you may see monsters when you look upon some of us, in truth we are all healers."

VI

Ferrin left the camp a short while later and made his way up a hillside where gaunt trees bent miserably and the grass grew long. The stars winked out one by one as he continued his ascent to the summit where remains of an ancient fortress from the First Age stood. The wind sighed amongst the stones as he stopped and drew a deep breath.

The *choragh* had left signs that he was to come to this place, and Ferrin never missed such signs. They had a task for him. Perhaps it would mean a change to his overall plan.

A shadow moved amongst the stones. Sensing and recognising its true nature, Ferrin immediately sank to his knees and leaned forward until his forehead almost touched the ground. For a while he heard nothing but the rustling of the grass. The Powers writhed in his body like a thousand snakes, his proximity to one of the *choragh* agitating them to a level he seldom experienced. He could only imagine the forces that he might be able to seize and shape in this moment- but to give in to such temptation in the presence of one of the Earth Lords would mean instant death, or quite possibly a worse punishment. Ferrin recalled stories of several foolish, wayward *kin* who had done this in the past. The greater part of the Powers had been ripped from them slowly and agonisingly along with almost their entire personality. They had been left to wander the land as little more than *diafagh,* low and rotting beasts that nevertheless retained enough memory of their former selves to haunt them until their eventual demise.

Finally a whisper came across the morning air. *Look to me,* the Earth Lord commanded him.

Ferrin looked up, swallowing down his fear as he saw a cavernous gloom before him, an area where the gathering light of morning was entirely absent.

You are to go to the place known as Woods Ford. There you will summon the lower kin and make the necessary sacrifices. Preserve only those through which wild Powers run. All others, destroy.

He bowed low again and remained kneeling, looking down at the ground. "As you command, Lord."

We find your faith in the boy of interest, the voice whispered.

Ferrin almost panicked. *They already know,* he thought. *But then, why would they not?* Finally he managed to speak. "He can be of great use, Lord. Though he does not yet fully realise it, the Powers run strongly in him."

Then you will raise him as kin today, so he may prove his worth. Send him on his way into the woods to the east. Do not go with him.

"I shall, Lord." Ferrin felt a twinge of disappointment. He had witnessed a dozen transformations and each one had been uniquely spectacular.

You and he have conspired to slay Inerdyr's man. Therefore you will send back a message to Inerdyr. You will describe what has happened.

Ferrin felt a prickle of unease for a moment, but he retained his outer composure. "It will be as you command, Lord."

The *choragh* melted away into the dawn without him knowing. He only dared raise his head when the raging chaos of his blood lessened to a murmur, a sure sign that the Earth Lord had indeed departed.

When he returned to the camp, Ferrin took a scrap of paper from Hanric's supplies and wrote his message to Inerdyr using the small amount of mites' blood he had left. Writing it in Hanric's blood would have amused him, but of course that was no longer possible. He introduced himself, explained that Hanric had been killed- he did not say by whom- and stated that he had been instructed to take command of Hanric's men. Finally he informed Inerdyr that he had been given a task that would take them away from Ruhal Dalmorn and his mercenaries, and therefore he would regrettably be unable to continue the mission that Hanric had been given.

The crow still waited nearby, shuffling in circles and pecking agitatedly at the ground. Ferrin rolled and tied the message to one of the bird's legs. It needed no further instruction, and took flight as soon as Ferrin lifted it up. He watched it fly south until even his Powers-sharpened eyes lost sight of it.

He felt Ithia's approach- her radiant heat and the scent of her flesh- long before she reached him, but waited until she stood just behind him before he turned round.

"Is Leon to be raised?" she asked.

Ferrin regarded her for a moment. "He is." When Ithia smiled as if some victory had been won he continued, "Leon is not meant for you, Ithia, any more than he was meant for Hanric. We all fight for a higher cause. Put your desires before that cause and it will end badly for you. We have work to do in the name of our Lords."

"I understand that," she said sullenly.

"Then show that you understand. If Leon is destined to do great things, then step back in their name."

"As you say." Ithia turned quickly and walked away.

Leon looked up to see Ferrin staring intently at him. He sat up, pulling the wolfskin cloak he had been given about himself. Ferrin suddenly spoke up. "Are you ready to be made again, Leon?"

He felt a prickle of fear at the idea. "I don't know what that means," he admitted. "I'd rather go home to Raven's Ford. I'm no warrior." He stole a glance at the *kinman*. "I'm grateful for you helping me with Hanric..."

"We will all go home when our work is done," Ferrin interrupted patiently, "whether that home is the one we know in this life, or Aona herself."

"I don't think I understand."

"But you will." Ferrin clapped him on the shoulder. "It's time, Leon. So let's be about it, shall we?"

Full of trepidation, Leon followed Ferrin away from the encampment to the edge of a nearby woodland where the pines grew thick and close, powdered with the day's first snow. "It saddens me to say that I won't bear witness to the fulfilment of your transformation," Ferrin said as they drew to a halt. "All that remains for me to do is utter the word that sets you on your way. I'll be waiting back at the camp."

He studied Leon's look of boyish confusion. *Whatever innocence he has left will soon be gone,* he thought. *Iron from the flame, a fortress from crude stone.*

"I don't know what to do," Leon whispered.

"You won't need to. All you have to do is walk into the middle of the woods." He gestured to the line of silent trees. "Something will await you there. I have no idea what form it will take. Not all things are mine to know."

Ferrin cupped his hand to the boy's ear and whispered a word that Leon could not understand but to which he had an immediate reaction. Immediately Leon gasped and stumbled sideways. His ear felt as if something thick and slow-moving had been poured into it. A moment later, terror almost overwhelmed him, for that same entity had begun to move into him- yet when he grabbed his ear and pressed his finger into it he could feel nothing.

"What did you do?" he croaked, turning to face Ferrin, but the *kin*-man had already started to walk back towards the camp and gave no hint of having heard him.

Leon felt an invisible force turn his head to face the path that led into the woodland, and he began walking helplessly along it. Soon he was deep within the pines and heading deeper yet, towards whatever lay in the heart of the woods.

The silence remained almost absolute as Leon pressed on along the winding trail. The close canopy beneath which he trudged allowed no room for snow to fall through. He could barely see the way before him, but compelled as he was he had no need to. Whatever sorcery Ferrin had set in motion propelled him unerringly along and would likely have righted him had he stumbled and fallen.

Sometime later he arrived in a clearing where the grass grew long. A withered tree stood stark and bent at its centre. It looked as if lightning had struck it and scorched all the life away.

Leon felt something surge within him as he approached the tree. Then the first sound he had heard since entering the woods cut through the wintry air- a snapping and splintering of wood. The tree bent forwards and then back in a vicious movement. Then the main trunk split suddenly to reveal its blackened interior. Great slivers of darkness reached out swiftly to pull Leon even nearer. They dug into him, became a part of him. Leon screamed, his face turned upwards to the sky, as the Old Powers that had always been a part of him wrestled with those that now swam through his veins. His arms stretched out to either side. Had Ferrin dared disobey the *choragh* to witness the scene, he would have beheld for an instant a human boy standing and shaking, limbs twisted and bent, his appearance not unlike that of the supposedly dead tree before which he stood. The tree itself took on an almost human appearance, the branches now swollen with sudden life, their architecture more like that of heavily-muscled arms that writhed in rhythm with every involuntary shake of Leon's body.

Leon dared not fight against his transformation, fearful that if he did then the Powers would not remake him; they would burn him from the inside out and he would remain standing here as a smoking ruin until his body finally fell apart.

On a deeper level he knew these forces innately. From a very young age he had known he was different, that he could sense certain things that others could not. But he could never have imagined the sheer overpowering ferocity of the powers that now consumed him.

The black river carved its way through his being, as alien as it was familiar, unstoppable. When it reached his brain, Leon saw the sky turn dark for a moment and he beheld every star of the observable heavens. He sensed the individual rustling of every single blade of grass in the clearing, and knew how many there were. He could see and feel each of the seasons at the same time. Countless other revelations bombarded his mind, until finally his vision crumbled away and he fell to the ground, knowing nothing where a moment ago he had known almost everything.

VII

Ithia sat up suddenly, her *kin*-senses flooded with a myriad different sensations and emotions. "He's here," she whispered to herself, although the others heard her and Ferrin put down the wooden shape he had been carving for almost the entire morning. *Good,* he thought, sensing the truth in Ithia's words. *Only one day and he returns.*

A short while later Leon walked out of the moonless night and sat by the fire, a few paces away from everyone else. Ithia prepared to get up and go over to him but a single look from Ferrin made a quick death of her plan.

Leon did not say anything that evening, nor did he lie down to sleep later. *He may speak in time,* Ferrin told himself when he took the last watch before dawn's light and saw the boy gazing intently at the campfire embers as if he might divine something from their glow. *Or it could be that he will never speak again. Some of the strongest* kin *have been those who lose the power of the spoken word and gain other powers.*

Leon remained an enigma the following morning, but Tomas and the rest of Hanric's men had words to say. As the camp was being cleared Tomas said to Ferrin, "We will be heading south. Responsibility for the men lies with me, and if we're no longer putting down a rebellion then there's nothing here for us. We'll be going back."

"Riding to your deaths," Ferrin said casually, "to report a failed mission. I pity you."

Tomas stared meaningfully at him. "I have to give details to Lord Inerdyr of everything that's happened."

Ferrin shrugged. "Report whatever you wish. I suspect he'll be rather tired of reports from the north by the day you return. Of course, one can only imagine the punishment that your *Lord* Inerdyr will choose to inflict on you. The mad sorcerer, they call him in these parts. Amongst many other things."

Tomas stiffened, his hand moving to rest near his sword hilt. *Don't be a fool,* Ferrin silently implored him, mouthing a silent word with his hand covering his lips. A second word and Tomas' hand would remain forever melded to the weapon. "Perhaps you are allied with the mercenaries that we hunt."

Ferrin could not help but laugh. "No. Although there are in fact some similarities between us. None that you could understand however." Abruptly all trace of his good humour vanished. "Take your men and leave. Hurry south. If we see you again, we'll kill you all."

Tomas' eyes widened at that, but he said nothing. He and his men were soon packed and saddled up, and left before noon. Ferrin watched them depart, and for a moment he considered sending some of the lower *kin* or even *diafagh* after them, assuming there were any nearby to be summoned. Eventually he decided against what would amount to a waste of time and effort. It hardly mattered to him if Tomas reached Inerdyr's distant fortress.

After all, Ferrin reasoned, if his Lords had been angered by his role in Hanric's slaying then he certainly would have known by now.

VI – The Strange Weight of Innocence

I

I've been in worse cells than this, Nia thought as she sat on the wooden box and stared around the walls of her sparse but spacious prison. *Far worse.*

The journey to Darkbrook had taken almost two tennights, perhaps a little more. Nia had stopped counting the days long before they finally arrived in the town. Her journey had been uncomfortable at best, and when it ended and she was taken to the Lord Warden's fortress to await her trial, she found herself as relieved as she was tired.

Even now, with her trial imminent Nia felt a sense of relief as she waited, immersed in almost absolute silence. She held no illusions about being found innocent- she had only to look at the expressions of the people the Warden's men marched her past in the street, when those men took the trouble to explain who she was and the crime for which she awaited trial. The relief she felt simply because her time of reckoning neared, and instead of fearing the outcome she held out her arms to it. She would have pulled it closer yet, had she been able.

I hope they execute me simply and without fuss, Nia mused. Somehow she felt that they would. Darkbrook was a harsh, unsympathetic place- although much of that had to do with the climate and terrain- and its people surely felt only hostility towards a southern wretch brought here to face the justice of the Free Territories. But they did not seem like the types to torture her at length, no matter what she had done. For that much, she felt thankful. She no longer feared death- if anything she felt impatient for it- but she sought to avoid pain as much as any sensible person.

Her treatment at the hands of Ghoreth's men had been fair. The Warden himself had visited her twice. He

118

hadn't said a great deal, and on both occasions he spent most of the time frowning at her as if trying to figure something out. *I wish you luck working me out if that's what you're trying to do,* Nia had thought. *It's a trick I never managed. And neither of us have much time now.*

Her cell had no window, but she knew that the weather had taken a turn for the worse over the last day or so. The prison was located in a separate building to the rest of the Warden's fortress, and the jailers who called in on her occasionally had to walk across the courtyard. Short though the journey was, more often than not they arrived wearing a thick coating of snow over their cloaks and hair. *Winter is truly savage in these parts,* Nia reminded herself. *Here I am, in all likelihood condemned to die after my trial, and yet I'm sure dozens or more innocents in this town will die of nothing more than a lack of warmth over the dark months, and never see the spring.*

She felt suddenly sad that she too would not see the spring when it came. *I never cared to enjoy the changing the seasons when I had the chance,* she thought, *and now all of a sudden I'm starting to miss the things I never even thought about, much less appreciated. Flowers, the salt breeze coming in off the southern sea, that first warm day of the year...*

Nia sighed and shook her head. *Am I becoming a simpleton in my final days? Flowers, of all things!*

A little later the bolts on her prison door screeched as they were drawn back, and two men stepped in- the Warden and one of his soldiers. Nia read the look on Ghoreth's face and immediately felt cold inside. *This is it,* she realised, and suddenly it felt as if her trial- the beginning of her end- hastened her demise more quickly than even she wanted.

"Are you ready, Nia?" the Warden asked.

"I've been ready for days," she rejoined.

They walked with her out of the fortress grounds and up the wide town road towards a large, round single-storey building that made a faint but large shape somewhere up ahead. The blizzard was so severe that Nia could barely see more than several paces in front of her. The snow squeaked and crunched under their boots as they laboured along the street and then through a gateway into the grounds of the building. *The courthouse,* Nia thought.

Inside, the building was made mostly of dark hardwood, plain and unassuming in style. To Nia, who had occasionally seen the grandeur of Luudhoq's courthouses- made so apparently at the insistence of the Seven- it was little more than a large round barn with seats and tables. *Do they really deal in justice here?* she wondered as she looked around at the forty or so people who had gathered and stood around near the wall. *Or is this a charade that they intend to put themselves through as the appetiser before my hanging?*

Perhaps I should ask to be found guilty, she thought madly. *Might that hurry the process along? Surely then they would have no need to prove my guilt, if I've already admitted it? Is that how it works? No one has told me.* She glanced at the grey-robed man who sat at a high desk in front of her. *He must be the Overseer of the court- or whatever they call it here.*

The Warden, dressed in his cloak and wide-brimmed hat- *a little like a Watcher,* Nia thought briefly and not without a shiver- motioned for her to stand before the man, who viewed her with sad-looking, rheumy eyes. "Nia of Luudhoq..." He frowned, as if at some perceived irregularity of which he had only now been made aware. "Do you not have a second name? A family name?"

"If I do, I'm not aware of it," Nia replied.

"*My Lord Questioner,*" Ghoreth hissed, fixing her with a glare. Nia repeated his words, offering the Questioner a half-heartedly apologetic smile.

"Nia of Luudhoq, you stand before us accused of the murder of Xu'naal, sister of Warden Ghoreth, and formerly of the district of Darkbrook. Do you claim to be guilty or innocent of this crime?"

"Guilty," Nia said immediately, whereupon a murmur rose amongst those who had gathered around the fringes of the court. "Quiet!" the Questioner called, before turning to speak quietly with two men and three women seated nearby.

As Nia sat, straining to make out some of the words that were being spoken in the crowd- even now she held a morbid curiosity in her heart regarding others' opinions of her- Ghoreth turned to her and said quietly, "You are aware that the penalty for the crime of murder is death. There can be no other penalty. Do I explain this clearly enough?"

"You explain it with perfect clarity, my lord Warden," Nia said without a trace of irony. Then she added, "I want only for this to be done with. I'm tired- more tired than could ever imagine. I'll sleep at last, and you can do as you will with my body. I'm afraid there isn't much meat on my bones, so I doubt I'll be especially tasty..."

A hint of an amused smile briefly creased Ghoreth's lips. "We don't eat human flesh in Darkbrook, Nia. I'm afraid that's another of your Luudhoqian scare-tales."

"Throw me to the dogs then," Nia retorted. "I'm sure they'll be less fussy." She turned back to face the Questioner, whose discussions with his advisors had come to an end. "Rise, Nia of Luudhoq," he said, and when she did so he looked her up and down implacably and said to her, "In your own words, explain how you killed Xu'naal."

Nia's mouth fell open. She had not expected to have to offer any sort of explanation. "Is it not enough that I've admitted my guilt?" she asked weakly.

"No, it is not. Therefore, we will hear your story."

"I... used sorcery of my own against her," Nia said after a moment, and at the same time she wondered if they might believe those words if she happened to *shift* while standing before the court, watched by so many suspicious, predatory eyes. *Ah, but then they might keep me alive,* she quickly considered. *Barely alive perhaps, and that would be the worst fate of all. They'd do whatever they could to try and discover the secret to the* shifting.

Torture without end.

"You should be aware that attempting to deceive or speak anything but the truth in a courthouse of Darkbrook and its outlying territories is also a crime," the Questioner remarked. "I will however let the matter pass once only, given your obvious unfamiliarity with our law. I would suggest that you explain to the courthouse in as much detail as possible everything that happened from when Xu'naal had the misfortune to meet you, up to the point of her death. Be truthful, and leave no detail unmentioned."

Nia gazed helplessly around the courthouse. The people who had gathered to witness her trial stared back at her- some openly hostile, others simply curious, as if they were not so much angered by Xu'naal's demise as desperate to hear how the witch had met her end.

Very well, Nia thought. *If I must, then so be it.*

And so she told her story, sparing no detail. As Nia spoke her hesitancy disappeared and she almost forgot where she was. The terrifying scene of Xu'naal being destroyed by Yui's distant yet fearsome powers came back as vividly as if the scene replayed itself directly in front of her. She could even smell the mustiness of the cellar and the tang of murky preserving fluids in which body parts floated. The light around her seemed to dim a little as if to match the harsh and shadowy illumination of the witch's mutilation chamber.

She went on to describe how she fled Xu'naal's grim dwelling, and finished her recollection with a mention of how she had woken up the next morning without Yui's dim malevolence lodged in her head. When finally she could say no more Nia sighed and almost collapsed, leaning her forearms against the wooden stand.

The shocked silence in the wake of her story's retelling lasted for only a moment. Then the courthouse erupted into chaos. A few strident voices screamed that she was a liar and a murderer and should be put to death, whilst others appeared to be far more concerned that a sorceress of such power could be destroyed- and worse than that, destroyed from afar by a child in the distant Black Citadel.

Amidst the roar of conflicting voices the Questioner remained silent. His advisors talked into one another's ears- they had to because of the noise of everyone shouting their opinions to everyone else. Guardsmen stood warily between Nia and the crowd, hands gripping the pommels of their swords. Nia looked helplessly across at Ghoreth, but the Warden said nothing at all. She could not read his expression.

One of the advisors spoke briefly with the Questioner, and eventually the mayhem began to subside as it became apparent that Nia's judgement was about to be delivered.

"Nia of Luudhoq," the Questioner spoke up. "The courthouse of Darkbrook has found you innocent of the murder of Xu'naal. You are free to leave."

As the courthouse inevitably erupted for a second time, Nia stood and stared back at the Questioner and then looked to the Warden as if he might be able to explain the judgement. He raised an eyebrow at her look of stupefaction. "Oh," he said, leaning forward so she could hear. "You seem taken aback, Nia. Are you not, then, innocent?"

"I'm innocent of her murder, and I think you know it," Nia said. "But what use are innocence and freedom to me here? Death would have been easier."

"I don't doubt that. Death *is* easier than life. Would you prefer to return to Luudhoq? No, I expect not, given the potent enemy you seem to have made. Who is she in truth- some creature fashioned by the Seven?"

"She's just a human girl," Nia said. "Or she was. I don't know what she is now."

Nia was escorted by the Warden and his guardsmen out of the courthouse and back to the grounds of his residence. Nia felt a little safer once they had passed through the gates and a high wall and numerous guards separated them from the baying hordes that could still be heard across in the courthouse. Several angry and vociferous people followed them as far as the fortress gates to scream obscenities at her, until the guards sent them away.

"One thing you failed to explain," Ghoreth remarked. "How did you make such a potent enemy?"

"I tricked her into coming to Luudhoq," Nia said quietly, "and then I turned her over to the Seven. Or rather I turned her over to my employer, who then completed the task."

"Ah." He stared at her. "That explains why she wants to destroy you. And when she was thwarted, in her rage she killed my sister."

"I didn't know anything like that was going to happen," Nia said.

"No. But misfortune follows you like a lost dog." Ghoreth shook his head. "What's done is done. We need to decide what happens to you now. One might say you are a free woman, but matters are not that simple."

"They never are." Nia smirked unhappily.

"There are some people in Darkbrook who would beat you to a pulp on sight, regardless of the Questioner's verdict. Unless a decree is submitted stating that anyone so doing is himself or herself considered an enemy of the territory."

As Nia blinked in bemusement, the Warden continued, "I'm keen to know your story, Nia, and why you would hand over a young child to the Seven- and why you sought to flee your own lands, if it was not because of her."

Nia glanced towards the gates through which they had just walked, and Ghoreth laughed. "You'd rather take your chances with the townsfolk than tell your story? Without the formal protection of a decree, you'll be bludgeoned to death in moments. That may well suit you; it does not suit me."

Nia laughed. "This is your justice?"

"No. This is reality. You're an insolent southern woman who some people might feel has *escaped* justice."

"If I tell you, will you then let me go? The probability of a quick death outweighs my fear of a painful one."

"Perhaps. Or, I may offer you a choice."

"I'm not good with choices," Nia said. "Maybe you should make it for me."

"As you wish. But let's go inside awhile, and I'll hear how you came to be this sorry fugitive."

II

Nia was deeply reluctant to retell the events that had preceded and led up to her escape from Luudhoq, but Ghoreth clearly had no intention of letting her leave until his curiosity had been satisfied. When she did tell him her story, she left out how she escaped her prison cell, her discovery of the truth about the Watchers and the hidden race of folk within the Bonemord. She had resolved not to tell anyone about those things- and who would believe her anyway? She thought wryly to herself afterwards that omitting those parts had made her story sound far more credible.

"And so your mistress became a traitor to the powers of the Black Citadel," Ghoreth mused. "Did she see herself as part of a vanguard against the evil that runs through the veins of Luudhoq, I wonder?"

"I couldn't say." Nia had never for one moment imagined that Kelandra would make any decision based on a moral choice, until she had found for herself that the Watchers were not the creatures that everyone in the world bar the Seven had always thought. Might some faint shred of

125

humanity remain lodged somewhere within her? Something that Kelandra herself was not directly aware of but which had persuaded her into her course of action? The Watcher and her co-conspirators had chosen a path that cold logic would surely spurn as dangerous lunacy.

She served Harn above the Seven, Nia mused, *as did those who went with her. At least, that's what she believes. If they and those they sought to ally with all die, then that serves nothing and no one. But it's not my concern now.*

"Curious. I always understood the loyalty of Watchers to their sorcerer-lords to be total." Ghoreth's interest in the matter showed little sign of abating.

"As did I," Nia admitted, "although then again, I was only her servant." Not keen to discuss the matter further, she peered through the low window to her left. It overlooked one of the smaller courtyards and part of Darkbrook. The snow had turned to sleet, which had been falling without pause for the entire afternoon. The smaller earthy roads had already turned to muddy slush. Only two of Darkbrook's streets had any stone paving.

"You suggested I make a choice on your behalf," Ghoreth remarked, observing her watchful stare. "Have you changed your mind during the afternoon?"

Nia shrugged wearily. "I'm tired of decisions. I can never return to the city that I almost called home. Send me away if you will, or keep me here."

"I can offer you a wage and an apprenticeship as a scribe and informer."

"A scribe *and* informer?" Nia smiled at that.

"You seem well suited to a number of disciplines, Nia of Luudhoq. From what you've told me, you can read and write more than competently. How many people here do you think can do that? You also have a penchant for discovering secrets and unearthing information. Doubtless I'll unearth a little more about *you* in time."

"I don't doubt it," Nia said. *You'll never guess the things I haven't told you and you never will,* she mentally added.

"If you choose not to decide your own fate, then I'll take that decision out of your hands," Ghoreth continued, "You will stay here as a servant and employee of this house."

"As you wish." Nia paused, then added uncomfortably, "My words are not worth anything, but I'm sorry about what happened to Xu'naal."

"She was a cruel woman," Ghoreth reflected. "But then again, she was my sister."

Do you grieve for her? Nia wondered, but she didn't dare stir matters up further, and in any case Ghoreth had nothing more to say on the matter.

Over the next four days, she was given tasks to do. These were straightforward and mundane, but to Nia their humdrum nature felt almost a joy. For a while, immersed in duties such as looking up obscure laws in ancient books or counting stocks of one supply or another- counting and calculating was apparently another skill in short supply here- she even found herself distracted by this strange new life to the point of briefly putting aside much of what had gone before. When one afternoon she sat and rested on the stone steps leading down to one of the vast store rooms in the Warden's fortress, she contemplated the matter and realised that her new situation, and perhaps also her great distance from Luudhoq and all it held, had made her start to forget who and what she was. *Maybe I can become someone else,* she mused as she gazed up at a window through which bright sunlight poured. *Maybe in time I'll entirely forget who and what I was. That would be no bad thing. Perhaps I should have given myself a different name when I was first arrested by Ghoreth.*

Nia scowled suddenly. Thinking about a different name had made her think about her time in Arin's mansion, and she had resolved to try and forget that time altogether. *I wish I'd stayed,* she thought moodily, but then she answered herself back. *Don't be an idiot! The Seven's spies would have found you in no time, and your fate would have been far worse. As would Arin's.*

Stop thinking about him! she told herself, clenching her fists angrily.

Later, when she had finished her chores for the day and rested in her quarters, Nia lay down and willed herself to *shift*. But for some reason she couldn't. Strangely she felt no desperate compulsion to either. *Is it fading?* she wondered, and drifted off to sleep asking herself how she felt about possibly losing her miraculous talent. *I don't need it,* she reasoned. *It would bring nothing but trouble. Best that it fades, if that's what's happening.*

But her relief masked a strange sadness at the possibility.

Whenever Nia had to leave the fortress on an errand, Ghoreth commanded two of his swordsmen to accompany her. She had no idea if he had chosen these two specifically, but they were courteous, polite and distant, and the townsfolk kept a respectful distance from the three of them whenever they saw them. On one occasion Nia heard a mutter of *murderer* as she passed by a group of women gathered at a street corner, more than likely to gossip and complain about their lives. "Why, yes," she said, turning around to face them. "I've murdered many in my time, for nothing more than gold. Sometimes only silver."

She tipped an imaginary hat to them, enjoying their collective expression of wide-eyed outrage, even as one of Ghoreth's swordsmen glared at her and the other shook his head in disgust. But neither of them struck her. Nia suspected that the Warden had paid them an additional wage for the onerous duty of chaperoning the evil southern woman around their town.

"Turn the other cheek and say nothing to those who mark you as a murderer," Ghoreth said that evening. He had invited her to dine with him in his austere but warm eating hall, perhaps hoping to take the opportunity to forage around her past life a little more.

Ah, so my guards told him then, Nia thought. "But I *am* a murderer," she pointed out with a shrug. "I didn't kill your sister but I've dispatched others. This venison is the best I've ever tasted by the way..."

"Thank you." Ghoreth half-smiled and added, "I doubt many people could intersperse talk of murder and of food as glibly or easily as you, Nia."

"Perhaps not. Although food *is* a kind of murder, more often than not."

"Tomorrow, you need to go on a journey," he said, changing the subject abruptly.

"A journey? Will I be coming back?" She laughed uncertainly.

"Like it or not, yes. I'll be sending half a dozen of my guardsmen with you. I need you to head out east. Perhaps even as far as the Stillwater."

"The Stillwater?" Nia frowned. "I only know the name."

"A great lake that lies between the hills to the east, about thirty leagues from here. It's a place that most folk choose to avoid. Sometimes those few who do venture close to it speak of strange happenings that cannot be adequately explained, except as sorcery."

"Sorcery appears to be an explanation for everything in these parts," Nia said, and then looked uneasily at him. "I apologise, Ghoreth. I'm too free with my words. I should consider them more carefully."

"You should," he agreed, "because decree or no decree, someone may lose patience with you sooner or later. I would prefer that that didn't happen." He put down his knife and fork and sat back. "Regardless of local superstition, some stories about the Stillwater are unavoidable facts. The place has had an evil reputation for centuries."

"How so?"

"Three hundred years ago a town stood along its southern shore. For a while it thrived. But then, without any known reason, infants were no longer born alive. Every child that was conceived, was stillborn."

Nia nodded. *Hence the name,* she thought, but said nothing.

"Many were ill-formed or half-formed, as if some evil had found its way into their mothers' bellies," Ghoreth continued after a moment. "As you can imagine, the town was thought cursed. Perhaps it was something to do with the lake, or the nearby hills, or some terrible force under the ground. Nobody could say. Soon afterwards the town was abandoned. Only a few ruins remain there now. The stones lie overgrown. The name of the town is spoken by no one. There are things in this world that cannot be explained."

Indeed there are, Nia silently echoed.

"Anyway, there are new reports of... the Old Dark. There are also rumours of activities by forces loyal to Inerdyr of Mornkastle. Neither of those bode well. We need information. If trouble approaches, I need to know its nature."

"I'm not sure I know much about the Old Dark, beyond the superstitions of Luudhoqian people," Nia said carefully, "but I have heard much about Inerdyr."

"One thing is for certain," the Warden remarked. "He will have sent out militias to hunt down and kill your rebel Watchers and those who have common cause with them- especially Ruhal of Mordenglen."

"That would be a battle worth watching," Nia mused. "From a distance, of course."

"Inerdyr is not well thought of here in the north-west," Ghoreth told her, "although Watchers are even less well regarded- by those who think of them at all. As for

Ruhal and his followers..." He paused, lapsing into thought for a moment, and Nia waited for him to continue, mildly interested in what he might have to say about Kelandra's companions.

"Mercenaries," he said flatly after a while. "Heroes to some, villains to others. There are conflicting stories about Ruhal and those who have marched under his banner over the years. He is loved and loathed in equal measure. It's as if every man and woman in the Free Territories has an opinion about the Warden of Mordenglen, mainly because he has seldom behaved like a Warden."

"Kelandra seemed to know something about him that incited her to go against all that she believed in." Nia smiled, and then quickly looked away as he stared appraisingly at her. "The actions of a few often teach many," Ghoreth said finally. "Wouldn't you say?"

"I wouldn't presume what to say."

"I think perhaps these Watchers are more complex than we may have believed," the Warden ventured.

Oh, I'd say they definitely are, Nia silently replied, *but probably not in any way you can imagine.*

She ate the rest of her dinner in silence, and tried not to think about the prisoner in the Sanctum as roast meat yielded under her knife.

III

The following morning Nia was sent out with six of Ghoreth's horsemen to look for signs of raiders who had attacked farmsteads and smallholdings out towards the east. As she waited for her horse to be saddled up, it occurred to her that these enemies could be of any sort- renegades perhaps loyal to Inerdyr but with a freedom to carry out whatever atrocities they wished, or perhaps the Old Dark to which Ghoreth had referred. Nia wondered what Kelandra would have made of it all. To the dismissively pragmatic

Watcher almost everyone and everything north of the Never-Built Wall was part of the Old Dark or linked to it in some way. Yet it was that same pragmatism that had forced her hand and turned her into a traitor to the South, or so Nia reckoned. In Kelandra's mind, the approach of an even more terrible enemy necessitated the alliance that she had helped forge.

It makes sense to me also, she thought, *but who would have thought a Watcher- no, several Watchers- would go against everything that they...*

Nia stopped herself. She had almost forgotten the awful truth that she had learned. She wondered suddenly who Kelandra might have been, long ago, before...

"Are you going to get on that horse or do you expect me to help you up?" Teryn demanded. A thick-set man with short blonde hair and a scarred scalp, Teryn was the Warden's chief guardsman, and- rumour had it- a man who dabbled in sorcery. But despite his station Nia could not help but answer back as she leapt up. "In Luudhoq, it's considered gentlemanly to help a lady onto her horse."

"You're no lady," Teryn retorted. "Are you ready at last? Good. Let's ride."

Within a short while they had left Darkbrook behind and headed east across sweeping hills and past close-set woodlands of pine and fir.

Luncheon time had come and gone and Nia's stomach had already started to growl again when they spotted the remains of a camp fire near the bottom of a hilly slope where tall grass met thick scrubland. The ashes in the clearing lay cold and wet from partly-melted snow. The riders dismounted and took a cursory look around. Carcasses of deer, goats and sheep littered the area, all of them gutted and thoroughly ransacked. The faintly sharp smell of blood came across to them on the wintry breeze.

"Is it common practice among huntsmen to consume every digestible part of the animal?" she asked, peering at the carcass of a deer. The creature's skull had been cut at the top and the contents removed in their entirety. So cleanly had the cavity been scraped of its meat that Nia found herself imagining not an implement cutting it free but instead an extensible set of jaws and a long, thickly barbed tongue.

Teryn shook his head. "Even when times are dire, the hearts and brains are given to the dogs to fight over."

"Maybe they had dogs." Nia took a closer look at the camp fire remains and then frowned. "That's odd."

"What is?" Teryn demanded.

"There isn't a trace of cooked meat about the place." Nia glanced back at him. "What sort of people make a camp fire and then eat every conceivable scrap of meat on a carcass entirely raw in the depths of winter?"

The men looked grimly at one another. "Another sign of the Old Dark," Saryth, one of the older riders said eventually, scratching at his beard. "How many more do we need to witness before anything is done?"

"Would you spread chaos amongst our people so quickly?" Teryn rejoined. "We'll track them and see what more we can find out about their purpose here." He glanced at Nia, who walked carefully around the camp, studying the ground, until she faced south-west. "They went this way." She crouched down to look more closely at the grass and the damp earth beneath. "Well, that's interesting. It looks as if one of them was walking barefoot. A captive, perhaps?"

"Not all the *kin* have need of clothing," Saryth told her, drawing his cloak about him with a shiver. "Many are not even born of human mothers."

"Be that as it may," Nia persisted, "these are human footprints."

"Are they?"

Nia looked thoughtfully at him and then turned to Teryn. "Would it not be prudent to return with the knowledge that we have rather than pursue these... kin?"

Teryn looked uncomfortable. "All we have here is the remains of a fire and some idle conjecture." He glared at Saryth. "We follow them, unnoticed if at all possible, and we find out whatever else we can."

Nia led them along the trail through the afternoon, stopping occasionally when she felt unsure about the direction without studying the ground in more detail. Finally, with the sun low they drew near to an area of scrub and woodland. A path wound through the close undergrowth and between windswept bushes and trees towards a woodland of tall chestnut trees that sloped away into lower ground.

"I can hear voices on the wind," Nia said a moment after they had halted. She pointed towards the woodland. "And the trail leads down there. Perhaps it's time we..."

"...determined who and what they are. Agreed." Teryn motioned for her to dismount. "Follow the trail on foot for as long as you can, Nia. This scrub is too uneven for the horses, and besides you'll be quieter on foot and on your own. We will wait for you here until sunset. Make sure you're not seen, let alone caught. The Warden has said you're an expert in such matters."

Nia glanced at the other men and sighed in resignation. "I'm a little more used to cities," she muttered, swinging her leg over the saddle and jumping to the ground.

She headed through the scrub and on into the woodland, glancing back only once to see the Warden's men waiting, lit up in the bright afternoon sun. The path continued between the trees and Nia crept along it as quietly as she could, stopping once in a while to listen intently to the voices she had heard carried on the wind before. As she pressed on, eventually she could make out scraps of conversation. Finally she came to the western side of the woods and caught glimpses of half a dozen or so people sitting on the grass. Nia positioned herself behind a tree to listen, breathing as quietly as she could. Fragments of conversation came across the light breeze. "...blood rite in Woods Ford" she heard one man say. Then a woman: "...a miracle, Leon, and now a witness to other miracles!"

"Why must they die?" she heard another man speak up. He sounded younger, she thought.

"The greater good," the first man said. Nia finally dared to creep forward a little further, and between gently rustling leaves she caught sight of them. She almost gasped in shock.

Two of them looked normal enough, but three were anything but ordinary. A woman- perhaps the one who had spoken- looked a little like a prisoner Nia remembered being tortured by Watchers a few years ago. The prisoner had been repeatedly placed in a vat of boiling water and then burned in all manner of other ways. Somehow the Watchers had kept her from losing consciousness. But this creature actually had no skin that Nia could see. *How is she held together?* Nia wondered, fascinated as much as horrified. *Is she in pain? Is she the product of some kind of witchcraft?*

Her gaze turned to another of their number- a male, as far as she could tell, which had no mouth where a mouth would normally be, but *two* huge mouths instead, one on either side of its face, each equipped with lips and- she quickly noticed- an array of needle-shaped teeth.

A third one, muscular and more wolf-like than human, sat next to it. She could not tell whether this creature was snarling or grinning, or even both.

Despite these horrors, Nia found her gaze drawn to the man whose words she had heard first and who appeared to be their leader. At first she looked upon him and thought he appeared quite unusual- fairly young, of slim build and clean-shaven with short dark hair. But then she realised that he too was extraordinary, just in a more subtle way.

Something about his movements and gestures and the way he sat made her certain of the fact. He enjoyed an oddly languid, graceful poise, as if he had all the time in the world and would still possess that luxury even if they were suddenly attacked. When he spoke his words had a quiet certainty to them; he commanded as if it was second nature.

Although his face was not turned more than halfway in her direction, Nia still could see the intense look in his so-dark eyes. No, it wasn't a look, but more a presence, a force, pulling in those who looked upon him. *Sorcery,* Nia thought faintly. *There can be no doubt. These are the* kin *that Saryth spoke of.*

She listened to them for a while longer, long enough only to confirm what she already suspected- that they were planning some sort of attack on a place called Woods Ford. She had no idea where that was, but the Warden's men would.

Nia turned and began to creep back along the path. Once she judged herself to be far enough away from the *kin* she ran as quickly as she could through the woods and on to where the men and horses waited. There she breathlessly told them everything she had seen and heard.

"Woods Ford is two days' ride north from Darkbrook," Teryn said as soon as she had finished. "We'll head back."

Such was their near-panic that they almost left Nia behind while she was still struggling back into the saddle. She hastened after them, certain that her horse felt something of her unease. *Let's hope we make it back and I never have to set my eyes on any more of these* kin, she thought, her knuckles white and cold as she clutched the reins.

Full darkness had all but fallen by the time they arrived back in the town. Teryn dismounted swiftly, urged Nia to stay by his side, and gave instructions for the men to get the horses stabled and say nothing of what Nia had told them until told otherwise. Then he hastened through the gates of the Warden's fortress, throwing an impatient look back at Nia to ensure she kept pace.

Protocol and hierarchies were far simpler in Darkbrook than anywhere in the south, Nia had already observed. Teryn merely demanded audience with the Warden and the guardsman to whom he had spoken ran off and returned a short while later to confirm. Teryn strode on to the Ghoreth's chambers and knocked on the door, not waiting before opening the door and striding in. *His head would have leapt from his shoulders for such a transgression in Luudhoq,* Nia thought.

"You found something, then?" Ghoreth stood by a bookcase at the far end of his study. Placing the book he had been perusing back in its place, he walked back to his desk. "Go on."

Teryn turned to Nia. "Tell the Lord Warden everything you told us. All of it."

Nia gave her account of everything she had seen and heard while tracking and then spying upon the *kin*. Teryn paced fretfully back and forth, but Ghoreth's expression did not change. When finally she had finished, he sat back in his chair, steepled his fingers and said nothing. Nia and Teryn exchanged glances and waited as patiently as they were able. Finally Teryn could no longer bear the silence and asked: "What command should I give, my lord? We need to..."

"Do something? Agreed." Ghoreth stared back at him, forcing Teryn to drop his gaze. "Then do this. Send fifty men to Woods Ford at first light. Pick the best of those who can be spared from the town watch. Speak with Arkim and tell him that he is to accompany them. Go."

After Teryn had left, Ghoreth sighed and leaned forward. Nia read the look in his eyes, and before she could stop herself she had already blurted out, "It won't be enough, will it?"

"They have a chance. Much depends on how powerful these *kin* are."

Recalling what she had seen Nia added, "I hadn't seen anything like them before. Even those that looked human..."

"...were not human," the Warden murmured. "I mentioned Arkim just now. He has a certain talent with the Old Powers, but it's nothing compared with the *kin*. Besides which, if these half dozen you saw can call upon others..." He sat back in his chair. "We have no great armies here, Nia, no Watchers. Other than Darkbrook, no town has anything more than a small garrison to defend it. A village like Woods Ford would have less than that, no more than two or three militiamen who report once a tennight, even less frequently in the winter season."

Nia said nothing. She could not help the situation, and decided that no remark existed that could serve any meaningful purpose. *What if these* kin *then attack Darkbrook?* she wondered. *If there are more of them, they may feel that they can win such a battle. I certainly wouldn't bet against them.*

Uneasy and restless, she did not sleep until near dawn.

VII - The Slowing of the Clock

I

If it wasn't already an open secret then it will be soon, Phaedra thought as she stood on the parapet watching the group of Watchers striding through the square far below. *Yet even now, no official announcement has been made.*

Her restlessness had grown in recent days. The troubling suspicion she felt- a nagging feeling that matters had begun to spiral out of control- had grown into an insistent, shrill inner voice. The sight of Watchers marching east out of Luudhoq to bolster the defence of the Border Wall did nothing to allay those worries; in fact it worsened them. Phaedra recalled the recent news of strife in the untamed North and shuddered. She recalled her own vision of the vast rabble pouring forth from those territories to put out the light of civilisation- witches and monsters and madmen falling over one another in their eagerness to destroy everything in their path.

In an attempt to distract herself from these black ruminations on apocalypse, Phaedra had directed her energies towards trivial matters. Often she would seek out Daniel on a whim (or occasionally he would find her first) and they copulated wherever they chose, determined to find some kind of distraction in their loveless union. They talked about any pointless, irrelevant subject that came to mind. They even discussed the possibility of finding a way into Garret's inner chambers to locate and play his precious music, although Daniel's fear of retribution remained just a little stronger than his curiosity and Phaedra reminded him twice that she would provide an alibi but wouldn't accompany him. They argued about the end of the Existence- *we learned that word from the people of Harn,* Phaedra recalled, *and no longer do we call it the Universe-* the theory

139

of sudden contraction and rebirth as opposed to slow death by the leaking away of energy until all things became cold and still in their entirety.

By one means or another our end will come far sooner, Phaedra reminded herself morosely, *unless we spirit ourselves away to a place of safety. But no sanctuaries remain, or if they do then we have no way of finding them.*

She had wondered idly if the *marandaal* would rend them apart so completely that their constituent fragments had no chance whatsoever of rejoining their companions. *Dust and vapour,* she thought. *No cells, no molecules even. Immortality itself torn beyond repair.*

Phaedra heard the sound of someone approaching behind her. Issele stopped when she turned round, and Phaedra laughed at her apparent reticence. "You remind me of a time when you were far less timid, Issele. Do you remember?"

The older woman's lips curved briefly. *The cruellest smile in all of known history,* Phaedra thought generously. "I recall that day with perfect clarity. I pushed you from the balcony in your quarters, and down you tumbled to the courtyard below. I observed your unfortunate state in some detail. You must have been dead for a fair while."

"Not dead, but nearby as my body mended." Phaedra nodded. "I'll grant you, it made for an interesting experience. I hovered somewhere above the mess you'd made of me, ghost-like, invisible. At least, I assume I was invisible."

"Feel free in your assumption. I saw no wraith or ghost of you."

"Why would you? It was only my consciousness, I expect. In any case, I soon felt warm again, and looked out from behind living eyes. Every single path and junction of my brain swiftly wired again as it should be, more or less. *That* is the closest event to a true miracle that I can attest to. Although I guess it took longer for me to heal myself properly- I was dizzy and a little forgetful for a month afterwards, and kept walking into things. And getting up off the cobbles hurt *immensely*."

"Oh! Then my playful little push was not entirely in vain."

Phaedra shrugged, suddenly tired of their verbal jousting. "Enough of our joyful memories, Issele. Why are you here?"

"Anya and Omir requested that a meeting be held. The others have already agreed to it. As usual, you are the last to be located. You're like an errant child."

Phaedra smirked. "Well, they'd know about errant children. I recall that one in particular escaped their clutches. And what might the agenda be this time? More escaped prisoners? More Watchers that have misinterpreted their duties and fled for the North?"

"One of us should go the Border Wall to lead the first line of defence. The question is who."

This time Phaedra laughed with genuine amusement. "A pointless exercise! You will each vote for the one you hate the most. Let me think. Garret will receive the most votes. You yourself would vote for him twice if you could. But then he'll refuse to accept the result of the vote. So why go through with such a charade?"

"I didn't ask for your opinion on the outcome, Phaedra. I asked only for your presence at the meeting."

"Well, you shan't have it. I don't especially care who you send to the border. And if you happened to choose me in my absence- that would be an attractive option, would it not? Then, like Garret, I'd refuse to go. I don't intend to play at being a heroine to the people." Phaedra tilted her head thoughtfully. "Maybe you should volunteer yourself for the task, Issele?"

Issele had nothing to say in response, which Phaedra counted as a minor victory given the woman's reputation for a swift riposte. She watched as Issele turned and left, and then dismissed the news of the meeting from her mind, turning once again to survey the city and its human ants crawling about their tedious, irrelevant business far below.

But through the remainder of the day Phaedra's curiosity nagged continuously at her until she eventually gave in and told the first of the Seven she found- it happened to be Omir- that she would attend.

The Seven convened a day later in one of the great draughty halls on the south side of the fortress. Phaedra shivered in the chilly air and sat down to watch as the game played itself out. At first it proceeded more or less as she had expected. Votes were cast, Garret received more than anyone else, and he coldly rejected any notion of him leading the defence of the border. *Just as I thought,* Phaedra told herself. *How have we maintained our empire for so long when we remain so predictable?*

Then Stephan spoke up. "I will go to the Border Wall. If you all fear the *marandaal* so much, if you all fear your own demise at their hands, I will lead the first line of defence."

Silence enveloped everyone sitting at the table. Phaedra thought that she hid her shock at one of them volunteering for the task rather better than the others, but even she could not help but stare appraisingly at Stephan. *I suppose this way he gets to play the hero and gives himself an honourable suicide,* she thought sardonically. *Although since when have any of us ever cared about honour? Perhaps the joy of working with Omir in the Sanctum simply isn't enough for him. All those ruined bodies and half-made Watchers must be a frustration. Or it could simply be that he'd rather die separated from the rest of us. That much I can certainly understand.*

Phaedra recalled asking Stephan some years ago what he thought his work in the dungeons of the Sanctum amounted to. *Which is it, a failed technology or a dead art?*

she had inquired. She also recalled that his response had been less than pleasant.

"So be it," Garret said eventually. He made no attempt to hide his smile as he sat back in his chair. "May I be the first to wish you luck, Stephan."

Thus ended their meeting.

Two days later, Stephan headed through the main thoroughfares of Luudhoq, flanked by five High Watchers. Phaedra's first theory about his motivation appeared to be playing out true; a message had gone out beforehand to be spread around the city as far and wide and as quickly as possible. Even in the steady, cold rain that fell from leaden skies, throngs of people stood and watched, several rows thick in places, as they rode slowly past.

Stephan paused in the central square to make a brief speech. Phaedra could hear from up on her high balcony in the Fortress of the Seven as Stephan announced that he and some of the High Watchers would be joining the Watchers who had already gone to the eastern border to defend Harn. The crowd cheered on cue, although Phaedra detected an undercurrent of unease in the sound. Did they doubt his words? Or did she simply hear a reflection of their natural fear, as an audience to one of the Seven and an entire group of High Watchers? She had no doubt that the people nearest to them could glimpse the faces of the High Watchers under their hats and hoods, and that was generally enough to spread fear in itself. *Those unfortunate enough to look upon the face of a High Watcher see a visage utterly alien to their world,* Phaedra reminded herself.

They should be fearful. They have known nothing but peace for many centuries. When was the last time any of them had to worry about the imminence of war? The very fact that one of the Seven is heading out to defend the border of Harn is surely proof enough that times are changing, and swiftly.

Phaedra wondered if and when the anxiety nestling within the people of Luudhoq would find an uglier voice-looting and rioting, perhaps. All for one and every man for himself. *Those were popular pastimes in the old world, I seem to remember. In fact I recall the chaos of those final days at least as clearly as anything afterwards.*

She watched Stephan and his entourage make their way through the city streets until she lost sight of them in the distance.

Sometime after sunset, Phaedra wandered through the Hall of Measurement and observed an array of machinery that had either broken or ceased to work as it ought. Clocks that were entirely mechanical in nature and bore no obvious defect had stopped; Watchers assigned the task of mending them had been unable to identify the faults. As she stopped by one such device to regard its unmoving hands, the odd thought occurred to Phaedra that these breakages were a minor symptom of a wider catastrophe- the slow demise of the world itself, a winding down to nothing. *Perhaps light itself will fail soon,* she thought morbidly as her gaze drifted from one silent instrument to another. *Lanterns and torches will be impossible to light. Flames will die away.*

She knew that the idea was nonsense. She reminded herself that she had always been a woman of cold logic and reason, a product of the old world, a technologist. Aona could not change so quickly and so randomly. That would defy all universal laws.

But still the dark notions beset her. She had witnessed many things over the centuries for which she had no explanation. The people of this world called them sorcery. Certainly her miraculous, if slow and painful rise from the cobbles on that long-ago day would be considered *great* sorcery.

A Watcher sat at a workbench on the far side of the hall. Phaedra wandered casually over to her, and the

Watcher quickly stood and bowed. "How may I be of use, my lady?" she asked smoothly.

"What an excellent question." Phaedra stared at the multitude of pieces strewn across the workbench. "Have you gleaned anything today? Discovered anything?"

"I have not," the Watcher admitted.

I think I have though, Phaedra silently responded. *All that's logical and dependable in the world is slowly unravelling. The remnants of our recreated technology are fading away.*

"May I be of any further use?" the Watcher ventured when Phaedra failed to respond.

"I doubt it." Phaedra had already started to walk away.

II

She lay with Daniel later, and found her own disquieting thoughts mirrored in his eyes. "Do you remember what it was like to feel afraid?" she asked him.

"I feel it now," he said. "Aona is in danger of disintegrating under the yoke of the *marandaal.* I'm sure they've already consumed every world throughout the Existence."

"That could be millions, but I agree," Phaedra said. "I haven't been able to come up with an escape plan."

He laughed at that. "An *escape* plan? I doubt there would be anywhere to go- and if there was, how would we know about it? Even if we managed to create a Gate of our own?" His smile faded. "The technology has been rotting away for all these centuries. It's as good as crumbled to dust. And all our remarkable powers that were given to us- they're useless in the face of this."

"Perhaps we should see what we can resurrect," Phaedra mused, trying not to think about the unresponsive machinery littering the desks and tables throughout the Hall of Measurement.

That same evening they made their way down into the dust and the gloom of the Sanctum.

Phaedra tried to remember how long it had been since her last descent into the lower reaches of the Sanctum. She couldn't. All she knew was that over a hundred years had passed, and she could recall very little of that day. The long and winding passageways of cold stone, the empty and desolate rooms were all part of an underworld that had existed before the Seven built their great fortress. They had not even known of its existence at first, and yet by some odd twist of fate they had built the symbol of their rule directly above it. As they had tunnels and prisons dug beneath it by labourers, eventually the existing labyrinth was discovered, and old and new became joined.

Over time they would use small parts of the Sanctum as a workshop, where they would attempt to rebuild the shattered remains of technology that they had brought with them to Aona. They would labour here, in vain far more often than not. The Watchers represented the only fruit of that toil, and their creation had been a partial victory at best. Phaedra had pondered the matter of the rebel Watchers and had come to the chilling conclusion that however overwhelming their transformation, still there remained a small spark of humanity. *How?* she had asked herself. *How could that not be wiped away? How could it remain in the face of such physical and mental conditioning?*

All other efforts to restore the powers of the old world had failed, or they had offered up faint glimpses of success. Even now, in a few of the passageways the lighting that they had tried to set up would occasionally burst into life- but such flickering moments would swiftly pass. *We should probably have destroyed it completely,* Phaedra told herself as she walked with Daniel down one such corridor. *It* does no good. All it does is remind us of what we once took for granted. And yet here the two of us are, walking in hope amidst the ruins.

They walked through a doorway into a large square room where debris and junk littered parts of the floor. Larger items stood propped up against the walls. Phaedra was drawn to one in particular- it looked like a vast mirror of black glass edged with metal. As she walked over to it she could see her reflection shimmer and move as if she was staring down into water. Her image stared back at her like some dark-eyed wraith, and Phaedra took an involuntary step back. "I'd forgotten about this," she murmured.

"We could never get it to work properly." Daniel walked over and stood beside her. "But perhaps we gave up too soon. In any case, there are other powers down here- inexplicable things that we've never been able to understand." He paused, pondering the matter. "An interface of sorts, between what we know but cannot make work, and what we cannot know yet which works regardless."

Phaedra laughed. "And you hope to understand it now?"

"This is our hour of greatest need. What better time to try?"

"Since when has the insidious power that runs through this world cared about that?"

"Why can we not die?" he rejoined. "Don't you think there's a plan for us?"

Phaedra frowned. She could think of no worthy response.

"I understand your scepticism, Phaedra. Up to a point, I agree with you. But we must try. Perhaps see if we can coax it into working, even scanning the Existence for a world untouched by the marandaal."

You really are a dreamer, Phaedra thought scornfully. And yet she found his words persuasive. Supposing we could get it to work. Supposing it found a

147

world to which we could flee. And if it could open a Gate, just for a moment, long enough for us to step through- and leave the others to fight the marandaal...

She glanced across at Daniel. *I could spend the rest of my days with him if I had to,* she thought. *He amuses me a little more than he irritates me. I could die a natural death, perhaps, if we escape this world. And a natural death is by no means guaranteed if we stand against the* marandaal.

Again her eyes were drawn to the mirror. "We need to keep this to ourselves," she said. "Are we anywhere near the rooms that Omir and Stephan use for creating Watchers? If any of the others found out..."

Daniel shook his head. "We're about as far from their area as we can be." He looked appraisingly at her. "I suspect I picked the right ally," he said eventually. Phaedra thought he sounded a little grudging, but she hid her anger with a grateful smile. "You did?"

"If any one of us could be called an outcast, it would be you- and I would be second in line for the honour."

"You almost make it sound like a compliment, Daniel."

"It is. They bicker and fight and sneer and plot, and all the while oblivion draws nearer."

"Maybe it's what they want."

He shrugged, and turned his gaze back to the dark mirror. "It isn't what *I* want. What happens if somehow the *marandaal* are destroyed and our empire prevails? More of the same is what happens. I will not bear another thousand years of bitterness."

Phaedra fell silent, imagining. *It would be worse than bitterness,* she thought. *If no enemies remain to threaten our immortality, what then? We persist, we wear on until each day becomes an unbearable torture. But I don't think we'll ever taste that victory.*

She wondered suddenly how it was that the *marandaal,* all powerful as they were, could not move through the air or water. *That can only be an effect of this world,* Phaedra decided. *We were changed when we came here. The* marandaal *have perhaps been changed as well, except that a few of their powers must have been weakened. They can't fly, nor can they swim. They have to break through the Border Wall to begin the destruction of Harn, and that will delay them.*

"Aona made us what we are," Daniel said quietly, interrupting her thoughts. "This planet. Some force stilled the ticking clocks inside our bodies. Maybe it wasn't a gift at all, but a punishment."

She stared at him. "First you say there's a plan for us, and now a punishment? Which one is it, Daniel?"

"How do *you* see it?"

Phaedra smiled. "Just because something feels like a punishment doesn't make it intended as one. How can we even say if there *was* any intention? Anyway, we're hurtling towards the end of our thousand-year empire one way or another- so why does any of it matter?" She pointed to the mirror, but could not bring herself to look directly at it. "Making that work is all that matters."

They discovered enough that day to encourage them a little. Some dormant power still rested within the mirror-portal- enough perhaps to coax the device into at least sending out searching signals into the void. Phaedra eventually forced herself to stare into it for a while. Her indistinct reflection shimmered and stared coldly back at her. Daniel ceased his work with wires and coils and sat watching her. "What did you see when you stared into it?" he asked finally. "It plays tricks with the mind."

"Only myself," Phaedra told him. In fact she had caught glimpses of something behind her, but knowing that the mirror conjured optical illusions, she had not turned round to catch sight of the mysteries. *It happens a lot now,* she thought. *Objects or non-objects of which I see the merest glimpse. Maybe they exist and maybe they don't.*

Over the next three days they set up the components that had been used centuries ago to make the gateway and the signaller work. Inexplicably, power remained in the two generators that remained unbroken, although as she stared at the multitude of lights next to the display Phaedra thought of the strange events she had witnessed and wondered if the innate powers of this undercity had seeped into their ancient equipment and caused it to work.

I remember that we tried everything to make our technology work when we arrived, she thought. *But all our attempts failed. There's no reason why it would come to life now unless some other entity, some force, compromised it somehow.*

"It's helping us," she decided. Daniel turned to look at her. "What do you mean?"

"There's a presence- a force, an entity of some kind, I don't know what- here in the underbelly of Luudhoq," Phaedra reasoned. "The unexplained energy that you mentioned the other day. Maybe that's why Omir and Stephan managed to create any Watchers at all. If all our other technology died when we arrived in Aona, then it should always have been impossible. But we've never questioned the idiosyncrasies and puzzles of this world, have we? We were too busy congratulating ourselves at having found a little corner of the Existence untouched by the *marandaal,* too busy swiftly building an empire and crushing dissent, too busy killing off the savages and the hedge-witches."

"Aona was invaded by the *marandaal* once before, according to the legends in the north," Daniel pointed out, "but when they were defeated, the world was hidden from them for thousands of years."

"An entire planet subjected to some sort of cloaking?" Phaedra was unconvinced. "Well regardless, there is something insidious here that we can't explain. It has energy, it appears to have purpose- and it's helping to power the gateway, directing a part of itself towards our endeavours. Who knows, perhaps it's been seeping into our dead and abandoned devices over centuries, knowing that one day we would try to use them again."

"We were amongst the most learned people of the old world," Daniel observed, "and yet here we are working on instinct and hope, making use of power that has- you claim- been given to us for the purpose."

"In the absence of a rational explanation, an irrational one must do," Phaedra said with a shrug.

After they had left the Sanctum on the third day, sealing the door to their workplace behind them, Phaedra wandered for a while around parts of the fortress where she would not normally walk. She wandered past one of the Water Halls in which she hadn't set foot for decades, and after a moment her curiosity got the better of her and she stepped into the room.

Phaedra stared at the one of the stone bowls on the table and then the other. Both were filled with the water used for farseeing, one of their more potent powers that had developed over time. On a whim she placed her hand in the water and moved it quickly to splash it halfway across the hall. But the result of her petulant swipe was far more astonishing than she could have expected.

The water moved, and then remained fixed in the air only several paces away from where she stood. *It's as if time has stopped,* Phaedra thought in wonderment. *But it can't have done, no matter what the broken clocks and other devices in the Hall of Measurement tell me. So how can anyone explain this?*

It could not be explained any more than the telekinetic and regenerative powers of the Seven. Phaedra had once hated the word *miracle*- it was, after all, nothing more than a symptom of being unable to explain something- but she had thought the word and even used it with increasing frequency in recent decades.

Phaedra walked towards the water, then around it. She could not decide whether or not she ought to fear this phenomenon. *Some unseen force is keeping it in place,* she thought, almost daring to touch one of the sprays of water before pulling her finger back at the last moment. But whatever that force might be, it remained not only unseen but undetectable. Phaedra could not sense any change in temperature, any movement of air, any difference to gravity.

Then, without any warning, the water fell and splashed to the floor.

Phaedra thought for a moment that some presence within the hall waited for her to react- perhaps to try something else. Push the stone bowls over the edge of the table perhaps, or create some other minor mayhem. But instead she turned and left in a hurry.

She strode through a dozen passageways towards her quarters, unanswered questions clamouring for attention. Wherever they presented themselves she stopped by windows to look out and down at the city but also to try and compose herself. *There,* she thought. *The world is in place. Luudhoq is the same, at any rate. Calm yourself, you stupid woman.*

It was difficult, however, to see much of the city. Rain lashed against the glass, and the further she looked into the distance the dimmer and less distinct the outlines of architecture became, until they merged into a formless mass somewhere near the perimeter of her vision, almost like the work of a painter who had lost the will to fill in the background. *Which will come for us first?* she wondered suddenly. *The* marandaal *from the east, destroying all in their path, or the hordes from the north driven onwards by their mad witches and warlocks?*

She decided that it would be the *marandaal*. The people of the so-called Free Territories existed in factions; they were set against one another as much as the South. *My vision of them pouring forth towards Luudhoq was just that and nothing more,* Phaedra told herself as she walked on. *No matter how persuasive, how* real *it may have felt.*

But shadows danced in corners, odd sounds came and went in a moment and the hard rain hissed outside. The wind sighed like a restless soul weeping to be let in.

Phaedra thought of going to Daniel, but steeled herself against the act. She was not dependent on him. If anything *he* was dependent on *her*. She would go to him in her own good time, perhaps tomorrow.

A while later she stood in the corner of her opulent bedroom staring at her vast white bed, made immaculately as ever by her servant girl. *The perfect room,* Phaedra thought, taking in the familiar symmetrical design and ornamentation. *So quiet. So sterile.*

She longed to ruin it, but instead she lay down and listened to the rain. Thoughts of all their enemies assailed her.

If we can't escape, if the power of the Gate-mirror has truly leaked away forever, then may it end soon, she thought.

May all of this end soon.

VIII – Vultures

I

Phyqor glanced across at his daughter as they sat in the outhouse, watching and waiting for the wintry downpour to end. Over the last few days she had become sullen and withdrawn and uttered no more than a few words. Both he and Alexia had tried without success to find out what ailed her. She suffered nightmares less frequently now, but Phyqor felt certain that some other problem had replaced them. The most Yui would say on the matter was that she didn't want to talk about it.

"We'll be beyond the reach of the Seven soon, with any luck," he spoke up. He had said something very similar a short while ago, but could think of nothing else to utter. He wanted only to break the grim silence, and Alexia looked lost in her own thoughts, listening to the rain with a far-away look on her face. She also had seemed distracted since they had left the Green Road. Phyqor wondered if that had to do with what had happened to her in that place.

Yui had gathered strands of straw and bound them together in a shape that crudely resembled a human. As Phyqor watched, she tied more straw around it to tighten the figure further, her eyes full of cold hard anger as she stared at the strange effigy.

"What is that you're making?" Phyqor ventured after a while.

"What does it look like?" Yui retorted.

"A person?"

"I wish it was Nia," Yui said quietly. "I wish she was just a straw figure and then I could crush her and tear her to bits." After a moment she added, "I found her."

"You *found* her?"

154

"I attached myself to her for a while and I could frighten her through her dreams. But she got someone to break my link with her." Yui looked as if she might be about to say more, but instead she just gazed angrily down at the ground, tossing the straw figure to one side.

She's uttered more just now than in the last three days put together, Phyqor thought. *Is this what's been preying on her mind this whole time? Could she really have somehow linked her mind with Nia's? Or is she just making it up because that's what she wants?*

He moved over to where she was sitting and put his arm around her. Yui did not respond in any way; she simply stared ahead and through the doorway at the rain, a picture of icy resentment.

"You seem to be sleeping better," he said eventually.

"Well at least I won't interrupt *your* sleep so much," Yui muttered.

Phyqor sighed. He closed his eyes for a moment, recalling the troubled but loving girl she had been. The memories that came back to him were many, and they followed one another swiftly, each one bittersweet. *We can never go back to the days we knew,* he reminded himself sadly. *Everything that was, is no more.*

The rain ceased, and a short while later they headed north under a cloak of miserable silence.

Yui woke suddenly in the middle of the night, convinced that someone or something was tugging insistently at her arm. But when she sat up everything was still and silent. Her father and Alexia were both asleep, which struck her as a little odd; she recalled them mentioning that they would take turns to stay awake during the earlier and later parts of the night. Whoever's turn it was at the moment, they were clearly so tired that they simply couldn't stay awake.

And knowing our luck, the people hunting us would choose tonight to finally find us, she thought bitterly.

Yui glanced across at her father and felt a pang of guilt. She had been mean to him, and knew that he felt hurt by some of the things she said. But more and more often recently it seemed that only bad things would come out of her mouth. Usually they would spill out before she even thought about them properly. She felt tired and angry and fearful, and it was just easier to be miserable and hurtful than to be grateful that he was here with her- and that they were all still alive and still free, at least for now.

She even thought about waking him up to tell him that she was sorry. He would forgive her. He would give her a big hug and she would fall asleep again in his arms. It would make him happy if she just smiled and told him she loved him.

But she didn't wake him, because a shadow loomed in the doorway and in her fright she forgot all about apologies and forgiveness.

"It's all right," the owner of the shadow whispered. The voice was male, quiet and clear. He moved a little so that she could see the faint moonlight- Archaon had disappeared and Ildar was less than half-full tonight- upon his face. He looked fairly young, she thought. Perhaps younger than her father- about Alexia's age. His hair fell in waves as far as his shoulders. It looked dark, but it was difficult to tell *how* dark.

"I'm not one of those hunting you," he continued softly. "I'm from the Free Territories, which is the land you've just reached."

Yui threw a look towards Phyqor and Alexia, but they continued to sleep. "They'll not wake until the morning," the man said, watching her. "I made it so. I need to speak with you, Yui, and I have to do so without being interrupted."

Perhaps it was the fact that he somehow knew her name that spurred her into sudden, desperate action. She scrambled over to Phyqor and shook him, shouting at him to wake up.

But he would not, and neither would Alexia.

Yui turned fearfully to the man in the doorway. "They'll wake in the morning, quite refreshed," he said mildly. "Those who pursue you are still some distance away..."

"How far away?!" she blurted out. "Are the Seven coming for me? I can't let them..."

"The Seven?" He smiled at that. "No, but at least one High Watcher pursues you." He looked thoughtfully at her. "Did you know that you crossed the Never-Built Wall today?"

Yui stared at him and shook her head. She had heard the phrase a few times, and others a bit like it, but still wasn't sure exactly what they meant.

"That means you're in the Free Territories now. But your enemies have also crossed the Wall. They continue on into lands that are not theirs. Not quite an act of war, but certainly an act of insolence. They want you desperately, Yui. It seems that their masters are willing even to sacrifice the hard-won, fragile peace between North and South in order to capture you."

"Please." Yui heard her voice trembling uncontrollably. "Please don't let them..."

"Well, you're in luck. They won't have you. We'll make certain of that."

"Can you truly destroy them?" Yui's eyes widened in disbelief and sudden wild hope. "Even High Watchers?"

"Even High Watchers," he affirmed, "tough creatures though they are."

"How?"

"In truth, Yui, I'm a little like you. The Old Powers move through you- that's what drew me here- and they move through me also. Of course, I don't have *your* talents- I doubt that anyone else in all Aona does, which is what makes you so very precious- but we borrow from the same dark earth, the same whisper of the wind."

Yui shuddered at the sound of his words; for some reason she felt exhilarated and horrified at the same time, as if she had suddenly found herself at the top of a mountain or great spire in the dead of a starlit night, with a cold wind swirling around that might send her tumbling into the blackness below.

"You're too young to understand the true importance of your powers," he said, "but you knew one thing for certain, didn't you? You knew that you could not let the Seven know the things that you do. The places where the Gates are and where they will be."

Yui nodded and closed her eyes, trying to will away the memory of the countless days she had spent as their prisoner. But instead a memory of one of her visions swam into her mind, sharp and virulent.

Ashhar inhaled softly. "I see it," he whispered. "Make it stop, Yui, or there's nothing I can do to protect you."

With an effort she made the image in her head disappear.

"My own abilities are also a little different to yours," Ashhar said after a moment. "However, they can and shall be used to thwart the creatures of malign sorcery that have pursued you all the way from the Black Citadel."

"What's your name?" she asked him.

"Ashhar. It's a First Age name. Do you know about the First Age?"

"A little." Her father and Alexia had taught her a fair bit about the history of the world in between her writing and reading and her numbers. She remembered some of it, but would have remembered a lot more if she hadn't been daydreaming a lot of the time.

Ashhar crouched down so that he was at roughly the same height as herself. Yui didn't usually like it when adults did that- more often than not it meant they were about to speak as if she was too stupid to work something out, and that by lowering themselves down to her level they might get her to understand.

But he didn't speak to her in that sort of way. If anything, she felt grown-up and important as she listened to his quiet, clear and serious words.

"This is what will happen tonight, Yui. My friends and I will head south to meet the nearest of your enemies. We will destroy them. I want the three of you to keep heading north for the moment. Don't tell anyone about our meeting here tonight."

"Why not?"

"I am granting you the favour of your life, child, and you reward me with questions."

"What else do you want?" Yui frowned, not entirely understanding his words.

Ashhar smiled and shook his head. "Never mind. Only do as I say."

Yui looked beyond him, suddenly hearing what she thought might be a faint whisper out in the night, a word or two spoken from across the distance of the field.

"My friends," he told her, "are best kept away from you and your family. You may hear them, but you'll not see them. I am a man of courtesy, Yui- and there are things in this world that little ladies should not see."

"I've seen more than you think," Yui retorted, before biting her lip and looking down at the ground. "I didn't mean to be rude," she added hastily. "And thank you for your help."

Ashhar stood up, the movement lithe and smooth. "I will come to you again three days from now," he said. "Sleep."

He turned and ran swiftly across the moonlit field. Yui watched him sprint until she could barely see anything but vague movement. The shadows at the far end of the field, where a gate and hedge marked the perimeter, looked a little darker than they ought, she fancied. Perhaps those were the shapes of his friends.

She fell asleep without realising, and woke with low wintry sunlight pouring in through the doorway. For a moment Yui thought she could see Ashhar's silhouette framed there, but as she shaded her eyes from the sun she saw that it was her father. He was talking quietly with Alexia.

She got up and went over to the doorway, grimacing as the sun hurt her eyes. "What are you doing?" she asked as she saw them both peering at the ground.

"Nothing you need to worry about," her father said, but Yui glanced at the muddy grass and saw a faint symbol scratched into the soft ground. *Ashhar,* she thought as the memory of her encounter came back to her. *What does the symbol mean?* she wondered. *Is it something to help protect us?*

By the time they left, the sign in the grass had disappeared, as if it was no longer needed and the sunlight had burned it away.

II

Three days later, Ashhar found them in another abandoned outhouse further north. Phyqor was awake when he approached, but a word whispered in their direction was enough to send him to sleep in an instant. Ashhar watched the companions through the doorway of the building, content to sit and ponder the journey ahead for a while.

Ilumor found him thus, sitting cross-legged half a dozen paces from the sleeping companions. Ashhar jumped lithely to his feet at the *kin*-man's approach, then relaxed a little as Ilumor came into view.

"I know who you are," Ashhar said finally, and returned the knife to his belt. He inclined his head in a brief mark of respect.

Ilumor smiled inwardly at that. Even he no longer knew who he was. "Good. But tell me, who are *you*? Why are you with these people?"

Ashhar frowned in puzzlement. "You don't already know? I have been tasked by our Lords to seek out descendants of the First- or if I cannot, then anyone with strength in the Old Powers. They led me to these people. Against the starspawn, one descendant is worth a hundred men."

"A thousand," Ilumor said.

"Well, the child is much more than that. She..." His eyes gleamed in Archaon's light as he struggled for words. *Take your time,* Ilumor thought as he stared expressionlessly back. *I already have a good inkling of who and what she is. I have found my quarry just as you found yours.*

"She is of the First's line, there is no doubt about that. Yet she is something more besides. She sees Gates. She *knows* them, to a point. She knows where and when they will appear."

"And you know that how?"

"The knowledge requires no proof. When she speaks of them- well, when she imagines them or invokes a vision that she's had, you can see a measure of what she sees. You know the truth of it without understanding, and without the burden of proof. Do you recall the moment when you became *kin,* if I may ask?"

"Of course," Ilumor lied.

"The knowledge is something that comes into being as she imagines it, but for a little while it's not unlike that exquisite lifting of the veil. The sharpening of the mind and the realisation that we know and understand not yet one hundredth of the world's secrets. In truth I'm glad you arrived when you did. The Seven continue to hunt her. She escaped them once before. We killed one of their High Watchers, but it took no small effort. Half a dozen *kin* fell."

"She escaped from the Seven?" Ilumor was further taken aback. He cast a glance at the sleeping child, finding her entirely ordinary, if as dishevelled and dirty as a city street urchin. *Now I begin to understand,* he thought. *A Descendant, with visionary powers beyond those of other Descendants, who for good measure managed to foil the sorcerers of the Black Citadel. She's more remarkable than I suspected.*

"They realise her importance, of course." Ashhar looked quickly to the south as if he expected a legion of Watchers to bear down upon them. "There's a place to which I must take them within the forest of Mordenglen. There she will be given over to the direct care of our Lords. But in the meantime, enemies hunt us and will not rest." He looked weary, and Ilumor wondered how long it had been since the *kin*-man had slept. Many of their kind required very little sleep but even so, no mortal whether *kin* or common could deny themselves the sweetness of slumber indefinitely.

Of course they hunt you, Ilumor silently retorted. *This child is the key to the destruction of the* marandaal, *if all you say about her is true. Legends tells us that they are weaker in the moment that they step from the void into the physical world. If we could know where and when they will step forth...*

Ilumor looked again to the sleeping child, and suddenly saw not only two opposing choices but also a third one that was both insane and entirely rational.

He could do as the light commanded: kill this *kin*-man and shepherd his charges to wherever it wanted. Then perhaps it would finally release him. Or he could travel with Ashhar to Mordenglen to ensure that the child reached the *choragh,* and once there perhaps his Lords could cure him of this curse and break the invisible collar of the light. *If it even lets me reach Mordenglen,* he thought.

But there existed a third choice.

His gaze took in the girl's pale unprotected neck. *If I kill Ashhar,* he thought, *and then slit the child's throat, what then? Surely the light will destroy me in an instant for letting the hope of all Aona bleed to death in her sleep in a hay barn. And if it does not, my Lords will make an end of me. One way or another, what remains of my life will be crushed in an instant. The light has ruined my desire to live on, no matter who I serve. This path will lead to my swift ruin.*

"A remarkable child," he agreed, and walked next to Ashhar, ostensibly to gain a closer look at the sleeping girl. Then in one swift movement he stabbed at Ashhar's chest with his hand, using every ounce of force he could. For an instant he felt every facet of the attack in exquisite detail; the snapping of bone followed by the wet, pulsing heat of the *kin*-man's heart, still a very human organ, and pounding healthily until Ilumor's fingers tore through it and in moments stilled his blood.

He pulled his hand free, and Ashhar sagged to the ground, eyes wide in astonishment until the moment when life fled them. Ilumor peered at his crimson-bathed hand as he held it up in the night air.

The unexpected choice, he reminded himself as he breathed in the sour odour of Ashhar's drying blood. *The one that no master could have foretold.*

He turned to the child and unbuckled his knife. *One last deed and I'll rest forever.*

For a moment he caught a glimpse of his desperate face reflected on the blade.

When he looked at her again, Yui was staring directly at him.

III

For an instant, Ilumor felt as if his power to make an unforeseen decision formed the very core of the Existence itself, a situation upon which everything else depended. But the sensation was far from exhilarating. It terrified him. Instead of staring down at a plethora of possibilities, he plummeted towards an abyss that led only to another and then another. Aona herself would find a way to entrap him, wrap him up in an embrace whose reality was horror itself- a place where death did not exist but the sheer terror of dying was eternal.

And yet he still held the dagger. His hand clung tightly to the handle of the weapon as if by doing so it gave him free will. Ildar's reflection trembled on its blade as his hand shook.

Kill her, he urged himself, *and that will be the end of everything.*

But he couldn't.

Then Yui's lips moved, and Ilumor caught a faint whisper. A moment of silence passed, and then he started to burn from the inside out.

Phyqor and Alexia woke to the sounds of screaming. They saw the man writhing on the ground just outside the doorway of the outhouse, ragged shrieks of agony rising into the night. Yui stared at him, her eyes cold and vengeful. When Phyqor placed a protective arm around her, drawing his longknife, Yui jumped, startled. As if that had broken her concentration, the stranger's screams subsided to a pitiful weeping, and he rolled back and forth on the grass as if he was trying to put out invisible flames.

"He is *kin*," Yui said quietly. "The Old Dark. Just like the one he killed." She pointed to the body lying further out into the field. "The other one said he would protect us. But he wanted to take us to his masters instead."

"I'll slit his throat," Alexia muttered, but Yui spoke up again, more urgently. "No! There's something else about him." She frowned. "I don't understand."

The man stopped moving and lay staring up at the night sky. Steam drifted up from his mouth and an acrid stench filled the air. "What did you do to him?" Phyqor asked quietly.

"I taught him a lesson. He wanted to kill me, but he's being forced to do something else, *by* something else. Something far more powerful." She shrugged. "He'll live. His body is half made of sorcery. I'm not even sure I *could* kill him."

The burned man moved his head slowly to face them. A faint, alien light gleamed in his eyes for a moment as he addressed Yui. "You can try," he whispered. "I know you can. Destroy me. Give me peace everlasting."

"He's a lightdreamer," Alexia murmured. "Maybe it *would* be a kindness..."

"Lightdreamer?!" The stranger spat the word as if it was venomous. "I defended this world against the *marandaal-* and my reward? I was wrenched away from those I served, and forced to obey the will of the most feared mistress of all. Yes, it must be her. The light. The pain. It must be her. Aona will not let me rest."

"Why are you here?" Phyqor demanded.

"To do Aona's will, against my own. To lead you to those you seek." He fixed a baleful stare upon the three of them.

"I know who you mean," Alexia said suddenly. "I'd forgotten. I was given the names when we were in the Green Road. I remember them now." As Phyqor and Yui stared at her she continued, "Kian, Anlerran and Ileana. And there's one other- whose name I still can't recall. A man. One who can sense Gates as and when they form, just like Yui."

He smiled thinly. "I know those names. They are Inerdyr's enemies. I'm not entirely surprised to hear them mentioned." Slowly he sat up, grimacing in pain. "My name is Ilumor, in this life." He listened as they hesitantly introduced themselves, and then he told them, "The light of the world sees fit to punish me further. Your enemies have become mine."

"That doesn't make us allies," Phyqor said.

"I'm afraid it does, for now. I have been robbed of choice."

"Do you know where they can be found?" Alexia asked him.

"The witches?" Ilumor's lip curled contemptuously. "They're nothing but untamed *kin*. The same Powers pulse through us all." He looked at Yui. "Through her also, stronger than anyone I've known. She's like a dark river. Is she your child?"

"Mine. Not Alexia's," Phyqor said uncomfortably.

"Odd that you have no such powers yourself," Ilumor remarked. "Perhaps you're simply due a late awakening. The Powers never skipped a generation in the old days."

"Do you know where they can be found?" Alexia demanded. "You know their names now. Can you take us to them?"

"I don't know where they are as yet," he confessed, "but I suspect I will soon. In all likelihood they won't be together, you realise. But I can also keep us far from the *kin*."

"We have to try," Alexia said. Phyqor saw an urgent look in her eyes. "We have to bring them all together. Yui won't be safe until we reach them."

Ilumor laughed, but the sound cut off as pain seized him. "That would make sense," he agreed after he had recovered. "That would be what Aona wants."

Alexia turned to Phyqor. "When I became separated from the two of you in that place, I was shown things. I don't remember them all, and I don't think I understand the things I *do* remember- but the heart of the world is slowly dying. It's up to the few people who can locate the Gates to save it." She smiled wanly. "I make it sound so simple. But I know it's true."

"We can trust him," Yui said quietly.

"Yes, you can trust me." Ilumor moved a little nearer and stared intently at her. "Child, will you promise me something? When my work is done and the three of you have been delivered to these wildling sorceresses, will you promise to make an end of me?" His words suddenly sounded sharp and eager. "Will you, if you're able?"

"I would gladly end your life," Yui said quietly. "I know what you are. When I hurt you just now, I saw pictures in my head of some of the things you'd done."

"I'm sure you did." Ilumor bowed his head. "Thank you. You offer me an undeserved kindness, I know. I've lived too many lives. My will and my soul are long spent and yet my mind and body wear on, sharpened and honed through the passing days. I'm nothing but the blade of my mistress, just as before I was a conduit of the Earth Lords. I retain the Powers but not my link with the *choragh*. How can that be?" He shook his head. "I long to be returned to my former masters. They seldom hurt me. Certainly they never tortured me. But now..." His words drifted away into a faint, unintelligible whisper.

Ilumor said nothing more. He stared out across the field as Ildar sank below the horizon and eventually the sky began to lighten in the east. Birdsong began in earnest. A chilly breeze swept through the field, bending the grasses and sighing amongst the stones of the walls.

IV

A cold breeze angled across at the four travellers as they struggled on along the muddy track. Ilumor walked at the head, lithe and unyielding. Whatever Yui had subjected him to the previous night, he appeared to have recovered well enough. Phyqor stared at the *kin*-man's back and wondered just how resilient he was. *What sort of wound would it take to be rid of him?* he asked himself. *Yui said he's half-made of sorcery.*

Phyqor tried not to think about it. They needed him for the time being. *What about these witches that Alexia mentioned?* he asked himself. *They can teach her to control her powers, perhaps. But what if they're much as Ilumor described them- like the* kin *he mentioned but wild, untamed, dangerous? What if they were barely able to control themselves?*

He feared that despite everything, he hadn't done enough to help her and she would be consumed by her powers.

The weather improved during the afternoon. As the companions headed along a path that led through a large meadow and stopped for a brief rest, Alexia suddenly felt as if someone or something was whispering to her. The sigh of the wind in the tall grass, the rustling of the leaves in the larch trees that stood in the near corner of the field, somehow combined to sound like a voice.

She stopped, transfixed as she turned and a shaft of sunlight passed from between the gently moving leaves of the nearest tree. Where that beam hit the still-frosted ground, steam curled slowly up into the air. Alexia saw faces within it.

This was some kind of sorcery, she told herself, and wondered if it might have something to do with Yui or even Ilumor.

"Alexia?"

She jumped and turned to see Yui staring at her. "You brought part of it back with you," Yui murmured finally, and turned to walk on towards where Phyqor and Ilumor were discussing the way ahead.

"What do you mean? Part of what?" she called, but Yui did not even turn round. Alexia looked across the field again towards the trees but saw no sign of any apparitions. The sun had dipped behind a cloud, and the field appeared oddly dark. The breeze had lessened almost to a standstill.

Alexia shivered and hurried after her companions, drawing her cloak more tightly about herself.

That evening, Yui fell asleep soon after they stopped to rest but woke suddenly a little later. "I had a dream," she said quietly.

Phyqor glanced at his daughter. Her eyes looked distant, but at least she was not reliving the entire dream again as if it was happening in the waking world. "What did you dream about?" he asked finally, although he wasn't sure if he wanted to know.

"I was back in that place." She stopped and frowned. "The Green Road. That's its name. I was there, but this time it wasn't so bad because I knew deep down that it was just a dream. It was like one of those I had when I was younger, before all this happened. A normal dream."

A normal dream, he thought. *I would do anything for you to only ever have normal dreams, and be rid of the lure of Gates and monsters from the void.*

"I was in the middle of a city," Yui continued, "but it wasn't Luudhoq. It was some other place. I was staring out across a lake, and I saw an island in the middle of the lake. On the island I saw a tall building, a tower that went all the way up to the sky. It touched the clouds. And inside the tower, there was something... a Gate maybe. A place where the Green Road was weak and could be pulled apart. I remember thinking to myself that no one else knew about this. It was a secret way for the creatures to get in- the ones from my dreams. The light ones and the dark ones."

"The light ones and the dark ones?" Alexia repeated.

"She means the *marandaal* and the *choragh*," Ilumor spoke up without looking in their direction. "The eternal battle raging for Aona's heart."

"I can't help but think it might be true," Yui said, turning her troubled gaze to her father. "What if there *is* a

Gate somewhere inside the Green Road? What if the dream is trying to tell me about it?"

"It's possible," Ilumor said.

"How can it be possible?" Phyqor rejoined.

The *kin*-man laughed. "Open your eyes. You must have seen your share of miracles in recent times. Do you think shaping your daughter's dream to bear such a warning is beyond Aona's powers?" He looked thoughtfully at Yui. "Supposing the *marandaal* had a hand in its creation somehow and are working to open it, to force their way into Aona's heart."

None of them spoke for a while. Rain pattered lightly on the leaves of the trees and a damp breeze whispered through the trees. Yui shivered suddenly, and Phyqor put his cloak around her.

"What would happen if they did that?" Alexia asked.

"Something beyond our comprehension, I expect. I've seen many things over a long time, but I can't begin to imagine what would happen if Aona were destroyed from the inside out. One thing's for certain. The fight against the *marandaal* would be for nothing."

IX – Through the Valleys of Ill Will

I

During the first twelve days after they left the *illeagh* fortress, the companions made faster progress than they had expected, with the air cold and crisp and the skies thankfully clear of snow except for brief flurries.

Late in the afternoon of the twelfth day they made their way down a wide valley into the lower Rhunin, patches of which were even free from snow, towards the first human settlement they had seen for tennights. Torches flickered in the distance and tendrils of hearth-smoke rose lazily into the still air from some of the chimneys. The sun hovered close over the rugged horizon and already the village lay cast in deep shadow.

"Raven's Ford," Ruhal said.

Dusk had melted almost entirely into night when they reached the middle of the village and made their way to the unnamed guesthouse. Anlerran glanced around and saw suspicion and even hostility in the eyes of the fur-clad villagers who had stopped and gathered to watch their arrival. A dark thought occurred to her. *Could it be that Inerdyr's poisonous words concerning us have reached even this far-flung corner of the land?*

She sighed and pulled her cloak more tightly about herself, disliking the pensive mood of the settlement and the temptation to look left, right, forward and behind at the same time. *It's to be expected,* she reasoned. *After all, we travel with servants of the Black Citadel. What more is needed to arouse disquiet amongst these people?*

"We need rooms here for one night," Ruhal called out to a servant who was brushing the side yard. The man cast a nervous glance to the half dozen or so villagers who had gathered in the track, their forms half-lit by the lantern light

171

pouring from the bar room of the guest house. Now and again shouts and raucous laughter would rise above the general cacophony of the place. The villagers who had stepped out into the chilly evening air, however, had a forbidding look about them. They shared an expression that Anlerran had become familiar with in her recent life-loathing tempered by fear.

"You're not wanted here," one of the men gathered nearby spoke up. Relief lit up the face of the young servant. Temporarily freed of the need to answer, he quickly took the opportunity to sweep elsewhere.

"You must trade with travellers whose route takes them near to Raven's Ford," Ruhal pointed out as he dismounted. "Or are you so wealthy that you turn folk away?"

"Few travellers come this way. Fewer still in the winter." The man, a thin, mean-looking fellow with jet black hair took a step forward, a hard look upon his face. Anlerran suddenly thought he looked a little like a carrion bird. "And even fewer than that from the *north,* in the winter. Yes, some of us saw you approach."

"We have silver for when you trade in the summer months," Ruhal said as the companions led their horses to be tethered by the reluctant stable-hand. He pointed to a few of the saddles and bridles that were hung up in the rear of the stable nearby, their metal fittings gleaming faintly. "Those were made in Mornkastle, if I'm not mistaken."

At Ruhal's signal the companions made their way into the guest house. Thankfully crow-man and his friends made way, though if anything their mood had blackened further.

Enough empty rooms were available for everyone. Anlerran looked pensively around as Ruhal paid the innkeeper for the rooms and meals. Thankfully he appeared less reticent about accepting their money. She almost interrupted when it became obvious that Ruhal had only procured the one room for them both, then stopped when he looked at her. *I would embarrass myself by protesting,* she thought, *especially in front of all these strangers.*

When they went upstairs to inspect the room he closed the door quickly behind them and lunged for her almost desperately. With great effort she pushed him away, breathlessly explaining, "I need to bathe, Ruhal, and so do you. We both stink."

She thought for a moment that she might have angered him, but instead he laughed and nodded. "You're right. We'll order a bath. We have enough silver- and your father has gemstones if we need to use them."

"Does he?" Anlerran hadn't known about that.

After they had bathed it occurred to Anlerran that her clothes could do with a wash as well, but she needed to wear them. Nonetheless she felt a little more comfortable than earlier as she made her way downstairs with Ruhal. The tap room had become quieter. Many of the villagers, uneasy with the new arrivals, had returned to their homes.

No sooner had the companions sat together than they heard a low keening sound from somewhere outside, bestial and shrill. A moment later, the fire in the hearth at the back of the room leapt up taller, brighter and fiercer than before, as if in answer.

What happened next confounded them all. A sudden blast of air blew out one of the tavern windows, sending shards flying. Through the broken window a lump of damp, dark earth was flung, landing on the boards with an ominous thud. Anlerran thought for a moment that she could hear chanting, but another gust of wind drowned it out, shaking jagged pieces of glass from their foundations.

Culos stood, staring intently at the window. He snarled, teeth bared so that suddenly he became transformed into a terrifying creature.

Anlerran's gaze flickered again to the earthen clod as she became increasingly attuned to the strange powers that that swirled around her. Her eyes widened as they beheld a slow, menacing transformation. The earth began to stretch away in each direction, forming a shape of five sides. Smoke began to swirl from it.

The air crackled with energy. A strange humming filled the suddenly warm air, and the fire in the hearth roared as if with terrible rage. For a moment, Anlerran thought she could see a face in the flames; two dark slits of eyes, a row of glittering teeth.

The earth changed shape again, and to Anlerran's dismay it grew, becoming larger and taller. In a moment it had taken on a rough-hewn humanoid appearance, growing to six feet in height. Anlerran could see the fabric of sorcery that wove this being together; she could even hear and smell it, the vileness assailing all of her senses at once. She also knew that Kian stood next to her without needing to look, and could even sense the girl's own powers.

As the earth-creature turned and lumbered towards them, knocking over chairs and tables, Anlerran saw Jahar suddenly switch his attention to the fire. Something loomed in the flames; a dark shape with sharp, angular features like shards of black glass. It reached out a thin, impossibly long arm of smoking ruin to them, but Jahar struck palm-first at the entity suddenly. The action somehow withered it, and sent the apparition howling back into the flames with a blast of freezing air that all but extinguished the fire.

Anlerran's eyes stung. She closed them for a moment, and to her shock found she could see the earthen being just as well without her sight. The web of power that held it together hummed and glistened in her mind. With an effort she set about locating the weakest knots in the force that maintained its shape. She found herself able to visualise the way in which this abomination had formed, and when she caught sight of the corrupt heart of this evil framework she attacked that core with all her might.

As if it instantly knew her intention the creature responded with unbridled fury, hurling chairs and tables and glasses at her. But each object struck an unseen barrier, something fashioned either by her father or Jahar, and shattered, the fragments returning at speed. Seeing that she was shielded from its attack, Anlerran redoubled her efforts. Eventually she heard and felt something snap. The creature uttered a shriek of agony, and in an instant it had lost its shape entirely. Nothing stood before them but smoking ash that collapsed to the floor. Even then the sound of its demise lingered in the air.

Jahar slumped wearily forwards over the nearest table. Elluron exhaled and hung his head in relief. Anlerran almost swooned suddenly, but her father reached out to steady her. Anlerran glanced warily at the hearth as she sat, and saw that the fire and its dark inhabitant were no more.

"What were they?" Kian whispered. "What were those things?"

Anlerran shook her head. "I don't..."

"*Diafagh!*"

Ruhal's bellow from near the door shook them from their exhaustion. Iyoth strode towards him along with Kian, and the others followed. Outside, they found a shambling *diafagh*, and another came stumbling after it, from the dark field behind the village.

"There will be more," Elluron said quickly. "The ground must be fairly soft across the field. It may be as easy to turn the earth to mud before them. That will slow them down."

At that moment Ildar rolled out from behind a bank of cloud and by its light they saw the oncoming horde more clearly. For a moment the companions were rendered speechless by the awful sight of more than a hundred restless dead, stumbling and scrambling their way across the field, some lurching like foul puppets on two legs whilst others scuttled on all fours.

"No matter how many, they all walk the same ground," Elluron said, and turning to Anlerran and Kian. "The two of you already know what to do. Follow my lead. You will see when you close your eyes."

Anlerran took a deep breath, closed her eyes to the world around her, and for a moment she found herself enveloped by a curious light and shifting colour. She looked around, without opening her eyes. What her mind's eye beheld appeared as a strangely oblique version of their surroundings. Her father stood next to her, all light and movement, shimmering like a beacon of strange fire. Anlerran gazed in sightless wonder. *His* illeagh *form, or something akin to it,* she thought, but she had no time to ponder that further as her attention was forced through the air itself and away towards the oncoming *diafagh.* As her gaze wandered further, heading towards the oncoming foe as if she were an invisible bird, Anlerran marvelled: *I can see the living things of the earth, and the roots of trees gleaming with life. I hear the sounds of the world.*

But sudden fear gripped her when her far-sight reached the multitude of once-beings that stumbled relentlessly on in silence across the landscape. She heard her father whisper within her mind: *Now we send them back into the earth and crush their bones for all eternity.*

Anlerran felt the ground *change* suddenly. Clumps of earth became smooth mud, with water drawn from nearby sources, rivulets forcing their way through the dark earth to where the *diafagh* walked. Yet it was too slow to stop their advance.

Anlerran! Kian! I need your help. I cannot do this alone.

How? Anlerran thought desperately, but a moment later she knew. The process was nothing more than a knot and she had found the place to pull at it. A subterranean sound filled her ears; she almost cried out as the taste of earth filled her mouth. *Don't fear it,* Elluron whispered.

The ground beneath and before the Blood Lords' silent minions grew softer still and the progress of their enemies slowed. Within moments, those that had walked upright were on their knees, arms raised towards the sky as if beseeching some celestial power to free them from the mud. They sank, and the mud tightened and hardened around their flailing, putrid forms to crush them. Iyoth and Lura and the Watchers stepped forward to behead those few that had managed to reach them.

Back, she heard Elluron call faintly.

Only when she opened her eyes did Anlerran realise how exhausted she was. Elluron staggered to his knees next to her. Culos barked urgently and a little later, faces she knew appeared. Only then did she realise that she was already lying upon the ground.

"It's done," she whispered.

"They continue to gain in strength," Jahar said later as they gathered inside the guest house. An *erythragh* was raised. It would have taken one of the *choragh,* or a powerful member of the *kin*, to bring it into being and have it lie dormant, to be evoked upon our arrival."

"Erythragh?" said Kelandra doubtfully.

Jahar gave her a cool look. "You would not have heard of them in the Citadel, I expect. They have not been seen in more than a thousand years. The *erythragh* are elemental beings- created from elemental matter in the same way as *diafagh* are created from the abandoned flesh of creatures." He shook his head. "Another foe to fear. Let's hope we never have to face more than one at any time."

Elluron said quietly, "Every time we survive we invite them to come against us in greater numbers."

More sounds could be heard from outside. Some of the villagers had plucked up enough courage to make their way to the tavern. A few had also gathered in the nearby field where one or two remnants of the *diafagh* could be seen by their torchlight, still twitching on the ground. Anlerran could hear angry mutters of "Sorcery!" *True enough,* she thought tiredly, *but not of our making, no matter what you may believe.*

As her companions gathered near the doorway, eight men of Raven's Ford approached, their faces grim by the light of the torches they bore. One of them spoke up: "We want you to leave. You've brought evil to Raven's Ford." He took a deep breath and addressed Ruhal. "We know who *you* are. The Warden of Mordenglen, a traitor who abandoned his people, a felon who consorts with Watchers. Inerdyr of Mornkastle has vowed to cleave your head from your shoulders."

"That news has reached you then." Ruhal looked scornfully at the villager. "Inerdyr and his minions are corrupt liars and you people listen only to their poisoned hearsay. In their misguided foolishness they would condemn Harn to an enemy far worse than you could imagine."

"Inerdyr's men came here, yes," the man replied. "They said that servants of the Black Citadel travelled with you. You're all cursed and you've brought your ill luck here."

"So Inerdyr made a vow to behead the Warden of Mordenglen, then sent his thugs in his place?" Jahar asked with a thin smile.

Anlerran suddenly decided to speak up despite her exhaustion.

"You have the truth of it," she admitted to the villager, who frowned and looked her up and down doubtfully. "If we had not passed this way, then I expect your village would not have been troubled."

"Not so soon at any rate," Jahar added, giving her a sidelong glance.

A babble of angry argument ensued amongst the villagers. Anlerran fixed her gaze on the crow-like man who had accosted them earlier. Perhaps fittingly, he lurked behind the man who had spoken out.

She continued with emphasis, *"Not so soon,* as Jahar pointed out. The foes of Harn gather everywhere, and misinformed folk unwittingly do much of their work for them. Some of you have already seen the remains of *diafagh* in the field over there. We sent them back into the earth this time. Consider how you might have fared had they come against you a night earlier."

"They came against *you,"* the same man pointed out. "Not us. You brought mayhem to Raven's Ford. *You* brought your conflict here, whatever its nature."

"It would have come for you sooner or later regardless, fool," Kelandra said coldly.

"Ancient enemies thought long vanquished are rising to rend each other apart - and all Aona," Ruhal spoke up. "The *choragh* and the *marandaal* are your enemies- not us. We risk our lives in the hope that folk such as you will not have to do so. Help us and you help yourselves, no matter the lies spread by Inerdyr of Mornkastle. Or you can slink back to your houses and content yourselves with whichever beliefs comfort you instead."

The companions stood silently by as heated argument erupted. Finally the man who had made himself spokesperson spoke up again. "You may remain here tonight, but be gone in the morning having paid for the damage caused." He scowled. "Inerdyr is not our master, but he has defended the North for many years against the wiles of the Black Citadel and its overlords."

Anlerran looked back at the ashen-faced men and women, many of whom had been in the tap room when the *erythragh* attacked. They still looked numb with fear, staring around continually as if they expected more creatures from their worst nightmares to burst through the walls or the floor and reach out to tear them to pieces. *Certainly they will have interesting tales to tell their fellows in the days to come,* she thought. *This at least is one village that would in time to come need no convincing that the* choragh *have stirred from their long rest.*

Jahar pointed to the dark stain upon the floor of the guest house, not that many of the villagers could see inside the place. "A powerful servant of the Blood Lords came for us tonight. *Sorcery*, as one of you rightly said, but not our own." He continued, lifting his voice slightly over the dismayed mutterings around them, "Inerdyr wants the head of Ruhal, Warden of Mordenglen, who along with these Watchers of the *Black Citadel* has defended this place tonight, and perhaps saved many of your lives. But in the distant east, the starspawn have already started to lay waste to Aphenhast. They come to Aona to resume their old war with the Blood Lords. The Old Dark yearns to enslave us. The starspawn desire one thing only- to obliterate us."

Murmurs of confusion spread amongst the gathered villagers. "Have none of you heard the stories from Aphenhast?" Jahar snapped.

Silence fell for a moment, and then one of the other men spoke up. "What do you want us to do about it?"

"Only this," Jahar said. "When others come, or if any of you travel elsewhere, tell them the tale of this night and the truth we have told. Tell them about the *diafagh* that swarmed from out of the dark and that we saved Raven's Ford from those creatures."

The companions watched as the villagers gradually dispersed, and sat down to rest inside the bar room again. Later, when the time came to sleep, the Watchers elected to sit downstairs resting but not sleeping, in that eerie way that Anlerran could never get used to seeing. "Any hint of another disturbance, and we will know about it," Kelandra said by way of explanation. "Besides, bedchambers are for those who need sleep."

Anlerran wondered to herself if the Watchers would sense the proximity of creatures of the Old Dark before it was too late. She saw Ruhal and Jahar talking quietly together by the entrance to the guest house, but surely they would not remain awake for much longer.

Then she saw Culos facing the broken window and stared out into the night. Briefly the hound turned his head to look solemnly up at her. *He will know better than anyone if the Old Dark returns for us tonight,* she decided. She turned and began to make her way upstairs, glancing back only once to see the hound bathed in Ildarian moonlight, statuesque.

As she continued up the stairs, Anlerran lost her footing and stumbled and Lura, who walked a little way behind, placed an arm around her. "I'll help you," she murmured.

The two of them progressed slowly up the stairs, to a small low-ceilinged room of whitewash and black beams, where Lura helped her to her bed. "Thank you," Anlerran murmured through her exhaustion. "My friend."

Lura looked uncomfortable. "All I did was help you upstairs," she said finally. "That doesn't make us friends."

"Does it not?"

"Attachment is a doorway to pain. Furthermore, you're a witchling who's seen little of the world and I'm a common mercenary. A walking wound, more or less."

Anlerran felt her eyelids drooping. Something about the jealous, bitter sound to Lura's words disquieted her. "Would you... rather... be me?" she asked, her eyes closed. If Lura responded at all, Anlerran did not hear the answer. She barely heard the woman walking away and closing the door behind her before she swiftly drifted off into a deep and dreamless sleep.

II

The following morning Anlerran woke to find Ruhal already up and dressed and standing by the window. His attention was fixed on something outside but he turned as she stirred and sat up. "I was thinking about how you stopped the *diafagh*," he remarked. "The Old Powers are truly awakened in you now."

Anlerran blushed at the compliment, but thought it mistaken. "I could have done nothing without my father's guidance. Or without Kian, more than likely."

"In time, you may even surpass your father." Ruhal walked over to sit on the edge of the bed and continued, "I can't say if the people of Raven's Ford or anywhere else will listen to us, regardless of what they've seen. In the meantime, Inerdyr will raise his army, as we knew he would. But with more than one purpose. He has an eye to the east where the *marandaal* destroy all they encounter, but remember that we are supposed to be dead and rotting inside the prison of stones he had made. That in itself is an affront to his authority. He will use at least a part of the forces at his disposal to crush us, and all those who will not bend the knee. And when a madman plots, the results are almost always insane."

"We already know he'll come for us," Anlerran pointed out.

"But there are certainly *choragh* agents amongst Inerdyr's people, working some insidious weave, instilling fear and obedience," he continued. "I can't prove it of course, but that's what my instinct tells me. Inerdyr was always thirsty for power, but in happier times he used it to bring order and stability to the middle North. Perhaps over time he came to enjoy that influence too much, the obedience he had instilled in so many. But this is something I heard from my grandfather a long time ago. Inerdyr has lived for more than three centuries. He and I have been at cross purposes more or less since I became Warden of Mordenglen."

"Why?"

Ruhal shrugged. "I can't fathom it, but at times I have questioned the laws he saw fit to pass- and which a majority of the Council of Wardens agreed to. Then there was my association with the *orkar*. They have never had any liking for Inerdyr, nor he them." He looked away. "And *then* there remains the matter of Wistport, the conflicting accounts of the battle fought there."

Wistport, Anlerran thought. *I keep hearing about that place.*

They left Raven's Ford as soon as they could, after purchasing provisions and horses with some of the Elluron's gems. Anlerran had only a vague idea about the price of horses, but to her the agreed price seemed lower than it ought to have been, so desperate were the townsfolk to see them leave.

Four days passed during which they made good progress. Snowfall remained minimal, and each day dawned and remained clear, bright and cold. At the villages where they rested the welcome was never better than cool and suspicious, but luck favoured them otherwise. No creatures of the Old Dark appeared, although Anlerran and Kian both thought they could sense them at times, distant, faint and perhaps not even following or hunting them. Such sensations made their skin crawl but were fleeting.

"I thought it puzzling how our lives ran in similar ways for so long," the *du-luyan* girl remarked on the fourth evening as the two of them sat together. "Just think- we were both adopted, albeit in different ways. We are both descendants of the First, though for so long we had no inkling of the fact. Well... in truth a part of me always knew, but still it felt hidden."

"Like a memory from a dream," Anlerran said.

Kian nodded. "Yes. That's exactly what it was like. And one more thing- we both found our fathers after many years." She looked across at Anlerran. "Despite these things, a passing glance would convince the onlooker that we're two utterly different creatures."

"Different only to look upon," Anlerran pointed out.

"To most folk it's the only difference that matters." Kian stared moodily into the distance for a while before changing the subject. "One day, if peace ever comes I should like to reclaim Mirkwall. Shimlock would have passed it to me." She shrugged. "Who knows if I would have made a good custodian? But if I ever have the chance, perhaps it can be restored to a measure of its former self. Then again, it might already have been reduced to rubble. Or if it hasn't, perhaps the minions of the *choragh* have made it entirely their own and are too strong to be overcome. They had already threaded their way through much of the place before I fled."

"Even if it lies in disarray, you might rebuild it with enough help," Anlerran asserted. "I've heard a little of the story of that place. Did it not come into being after a great battle- one of the last against the *choragh* in the First Age?"

"From stone, blood and sweat. And a dream. A vision." Kian's eyes had a faraway look to them for a moment. Then she smiled suddenly. "You have a way of pointing out the light in the darkness, Anlerran, no matter the situation. Maybe that's why you were born into this desperate Age."

Anlerran shrugged uncertainly. She felt humbled but embarrassed by the *du-luyan* girl's words. "I try, Kian. I confess it's often a struggle, but it's in my nature. And my upbringing. My guardians taught me that people are often their own worst enemies and some of the greatest battles are fought within yourself- against the despair and darkness that floods in unless you're determined to see the light in things."

She looked across to the other side of the fire where Iyoth, and Lura were talking, and picked up enough fragments of their conversation to know that they were talking about swordsmanship and combat. *The art of killing,* she thought.

"I find it odd," Kian remarked in a low voice, "that creatures like these Watchers, fashioned by the sorcery of the Seven, should have been made to look like humans. They even possess gender. But can they reproduce?"

"I don't think so." *Not any more,* Anlerran thought with a shudder.

"So why then would they be made male and female?"

"The people of Luudhoq are human," Anlerran reasoned carefully. "The Seven perhaps feel that their subjects better identify with Watchers if they look a little like them." Then she continued in a softer voice, "They may be able to hear us."

Kian shrugged. "We're simply pondering their nature. I'm sure they've done the same regarding yours and your father's."

Observing her companions in silence, Kelandra felt the oddest sensation for a moment. She neither understood nor recognised it, yet it had the effect of inducing a decision that felt almost involuntary in its suddenness.

She stood up and began walking away from the campfire. "Do we have company?" she heard Ruhal ask.

"No," she responded without turning round.

Kelandra offered no explanation. She let them assume that she was simply going to pass water, and walked across to where the ground began to slope. Rocky scrubland fell sharply away into the depths of a valley where the moons cast pale light and thick shadows.

"Do we have company?" she murmured, echoing Ruhal's words.

She tried to rationalise her actions. *I suppose I reflected on the situation,* she thought. *I reflected on its unusual nature. Watchers, humans and* du-luyan *together, all of us with a price on our heads, all of us bonded to a common cause. If I stood outside of that circle as a passive observer looking down on that scene, would I not dismiss it as reckless, illogical and futile? Certainly I would. And yet I do not leave them, and neither do the other Watchers.*

Kelandra stared into the night sky as if an answer might be conjured from the heavenly patterns. She could not ascertain whether she and the other Watchers followed the correct path or not, and yet she *did* remain certain that Harn needed the help of these witches and renegades.

The feeling that she had something *wrong* with her would not leave her thoughts. *Might that be why I took this path?* she wondered suddenly. *Could it be that some power of which I'm unaware caused a kind of madness, which then obscured my ability to reason? Might it even have been the* marandaal *themselves? We already knew that many people in Aphenhast and some in Harn had become affected by their proximity. Lightdreamers, heralding the coming of some God of Light.*

But regardless of the truth or falsehood behind her theory, what was she to do now? There could be no going back. She and the other Watchers would be destroyed. In fact they stood a better chance of survival by remaining with their fellow-traitors.

Kelandra felt a peculiar, directionless hatred almost overcome her. *I'm mimicking human behaviour,* she thought. *Spending time in their company has led to my taking on some of their emotions without consciously deciding to.*

Again, that should not be so.

Eventually she made her way slowly back to the campfire. She returned the stares of her companions with her well-practiced, serene lack of expression. Anlerran smiled uncertainly as their eyes met and Kelandra immediately wondered at the reason behind that expression. The girl was possibly the most guileless of their number and yet Kelandra often found her behaviour incomprehensible.

That may well be because of what she is, Kelandra reminded herself. *She is not entirely human, and the part of her that isn't I cannot understand at all. We have no data at all on these* illeagh. *How could they exist, even as well-hidden as they are, without the Seven at least knowing about them?*

On the fifth day after leaving Raven's Ford they caught sight of Mordenglen's northern edge ahead in the far distance, and open land between them and the great forest. At noon, Ruhal called a halt, and they gathered together on the windswept plain. The breeze sighed through the long grass; here and there patches of snow lingered where the sun could not reach.

"The only luck we have is that our various enemies are also ranged against one another," he began. "Yet we cannot rely on such enmity, however strong it may be. If we watch and wait, or if we run and hide then Harn will be consumed. As you know, the time has come when we need to raise our army against Inerdyr. But we can't do that by recruiting in the villages. Even if some folk join with us, it will not be enough- and you saw everything that happened in Raven's Ford."

"And that after we saved their skins," Alturus added.

"True. So, we need to do more."

Anlerran looked across at Ruhal. *He knows we need a plan,* she realised. *But he no longer has one. What sketchy plan he had is in ruins, or as good as. We can never convince folk of the need to follow us by going from village to village. Our own strange unity is considered unspeakable amongst the people of these settlements. But we must remain together regardless. If we drift apart, with neither plan nor purpose, no others will take our places. All others seem caught up in factions, preparing to fight one another. How easily all Harn could fall to chaos- and then the* marandaal *will sweep across this land finding only feeble resistance if any.*

An idea came to her suddenly. "Your friend Garrok the *orkar* lord leads a force of some might. He spoke of seeking aid for his people against the return of the *choragh*.

Although I suppose he may already have gone to Inerdyr in desperation, and can anyone blame him?"

Ruhal shook his head. "I don't think so, Anlerran. Garrok would rather gouge out his own eyes and eat them than side with Inerdyr, or even beg for his help. But he *is* a possibility. We have no other allies. We should at least ask for his allegiance, if we discover where his force are to be found."

"Bringing creatures such as *orkar* to our cause will only harden opinion against us," Kelandra spoke up. "They are known throughout the south as savage beings, bent on mayhem and destruction. They cannot be trained and they cannot be relied upon."

"That is a myth," Lura said, glaring at the Watcher. "And we are in the Free Territories, lest you forget."

"...seeking to unite the two parts of Harn," Kelandra argued.

"It is a myth, and yet in some ways it isn't," Jahar spoke up. "As a race they are honourable, proud, but they *are* warlike. Southern tales of their kind are, however, nowhere near accurate. Caricatures are made of them by the people of the south, and then stories are told as befit the monsters they imagine. It suits the powers of the Black Citadel to fashion demons from hearsay and half-truths." He stared shrewdly at Kelandra.

"I could ask for no better allies," Ruhal reasoned. "Let's make an alliance with the *orkar* first, if we can. Then we can offer peace to Inerdyr, if he will accept it."

"He won't," Jahar stated. "We already know this."

Ruhal smiled at that. "No, he won't. But if we ever have the choice, let's show our intent by *offering* him peace."

"What about the device that the *illeagh* gave you?" Anlerran suggested, turning to her father. "If they answer its call then that might be enough to defeat either Inerdyr or the Seven."

"It may be used once only," Elluron pointed out. "Remember that, Anlerran."

"Why, if they chose to help us once, would they not do so a second time?" Iyoth frowned. "They came to our aid once, in the Rhunin."

"I can't be entirely certain that they will help us at all," Elluron told him. "But it may be that they *cannot* do so. They are no longer connected to the world as they once were. They have faded, lost something of their hold upon Aona. I share a part of their heritage, but precious few of their secrets."

"I am inclined to make use of the *illeagh* device against Inerdyr," Ruhal spoke up. "Powers know that he is under *choragh* influence, and I'm certain that creatures of the Old Dark will fight alongside him. If the *illeagh* come to us then, if we call them, surely they will see that for themselves."

"Ruhal, it is not that simple." Elluron's words sounded grim. "I wish only that it were. The *illeagh* would fight against the *marandaal* simply because to do so is a part of their nature. But I cannot say what will happen if they meet *choragh* on any battlefield to which they are called. I cannot say for certain that they will fight one another. The ancient First Race has been divided for eons, but that in itself does not mean they will seek to tear one another apart should they meet again. I can't even be sure that they are *able* to kill one another, or what happens if they try."

A long silence followed. Not one of them had considered that possibility.

"Then we use the device outside the gates to the Black Citadel," Ruhal said finally. "The prerequisite to a united land, a united people, must be the destruction of the Seven." He glanced at the Watchers in turn. "Is this not so?"

"We have made them our enemies, and that will not change," Ildoron reflected. "Be assured that they will fight until the very end."

"The device will be used when I determine that the time is right," Elluron said quietly. "That is why it was given to me. It was a rare demonstration of trust, and I will honour it."

Ruhal stared at him but said nothing.

We may never find ourselves outside the Black Citadel, Anlerran thought. *Should we not call the* illeagh *when first we need them, regardless of what my father says? But then, he knows their nature more than any of us can hope to.*

Ruhal remarked finally, "I say we go to Garrok, and then we speak plainly with him. We tell him that we seek to raise an army against the might of Inerdyr, and ask for his alliance with us, though it may mean the annihilation of his own people."

"Any means to the end, Ruhal," Jahar said. "Or else we may as well turn eastwards and prepare to be turned to ashes as we grovel."

"Whatever our alliances may be now, the Seven brought enlightenment to the South and sent the witches and warlocks scurrying," Kelandra spoke up, as if Ildoron's words had been the last she listened to.

"Odd that you should still speak well of the very same sorcerers against whom you committed treachery," Jahar observed.

"Is it?" The Watcher looked unimpressed. "The fact remains. They civilised the South. Some of the lore they brought with them is known to all Watchers. There's a gulf in knowledge between us and the people against whom some might say *you* have committed treachery. For instance, you people know so little of the ways in which worlds are arranged around the sun..."

"Other worlds?" Anlerran asked, startled.

Kelandra gave her a look of faint contempt. "Yes, Anlerran. Worlds other than Aona and its moons. They are distant, yet they circle the same sun. Their paths can be plotted and foretold with the art of numbers, as you might call it."

"What about the stars?"

"The stars? They are other suns. Some of them exist alone, hanging in the Void, but others are accompanied by worlds of their own."

"Are any of them..."

"Like Aona? Is that what you wish to know?"

"Yes," Anlerran said uncertainly.

"No longer," the Watcher told her, taking a bright silver coin and spinning it on the back of her hand. Both flesh and metal appeared white by Ildar's light.

"They are all dead, or they were never alive," Kelandra continued softly as the coin slowed and fell.

III

Six days later they arrived at a place called Heart's End on Ruhal's map. An abandoned settlement less than five leagues from the eastern edge of Uythar, it had lain forgotten for some considerable time. Lichens and mosses grew in a thick carpet over much of the rubble that remained of the huts and houses.

Tired and hungry, the companions drew to a halt with dusk hastening and the harsh calls of carrion birds above as they wheeled in the dim sky. The few villages they had passed through on the way had been low on provisions and lower still on welcoming faces. The sight of this desolation improved no one's mood.

The largest of the buildings still retained most of its roof and walls, and they built a fire in the old hearth and gathered around it after tethering the horses at the side of the building where some shelter could be found for them.

The companions warmed themselves by the flames and thoughts had started to turn towards the meagre provisions they had left, when Iyoth suddenly jumped up and placed a finger to his lips. The others sat pensively and listened, unbuckling blades as quietly as possible. Presently they heard the sounds of people approaching. Whoever these newcomers were, they approached from north and south. Jahar extended a hand towards the fire in the hearth and the flames dwindled swiftly to nothing.

From the windows of the ruin torches could be seen, appearing to float in the darkness as their bearers drew quietly nearer.

Kal-myrran, who was nearest to the south-facing window, whispered, "Humans and *luyan*. Dozens."

"Inerdyr's followers," Ruhal muttered.

"If so, then his hand has been forced by our progress," Jahar whispered. "We're almost into Uythar, and they have no mandate over those lands."

Kal-myrran spoke up once more, urgently. "I count more than fifty on this side alone."

The words resonated through Anlerran's mind. *Too many*, she thought, her hand shaking as she gripped the handle of her knife.

Suddenly the entire place became bathed in searing white light. The walls shook. A moment later Kal-myrran sank screaming to the floor, her body wrapped in shards of lightning that crackled and writhed around her shuddering form. Then Jahar fell to his knees. His head jerked backwards and his eyes inexplicably darkened to become utterly black. As his skin became paler, almost translucent, so his eyes became like holes in that haunting visage. Caught up in silent, terrible agony, he reached out an arm as if to implore some invisible force for mercy.

The first wave of their foes reached the settlement, charged down the earthy track and pressed on towards their shelter, abandoning stealth for speed. Anlerran felt a shimmering in the air in front of her, as if a small pocket of the Existence itself was about to explode or bend outwards. As their enemies rushed towards them the Watchers stood close together and raised their arms, and it was as if the oncoming rabble suddenly ran into an invisible wall. Many of them fell where they were, eyes bulging, hands scrabbling at their heads as if unable to bear a sudden increase in pressure.

Anlerran felt helpless, unable to summon anything of use herself. Their enemies were not creatures of the Old Dark even if they did its evil work. They were, she reminded herself, simply the hired swords of a mad sorcerer. Her hand gripped the handle of her knife even harder, for all the good that could do.

From the other end of the building, splintering and shouting arose, and more of the enemy poured forth. Elluron cried out a word that Anlerran had never heard before, and a dozen or more of the oncoming human and *luyan* fighters tumbled to the floor, crying out in agony. The few who somehow reached them were cut down by Ruhal and Lura, and others by Iyoth and Kian who stood back to back each with twin curved blades that shimmered in the gloom.

Blood and gore spattered the floor, the salt stench rising like madness amidst the carnage and mayhem. Anlerran glimpsed one *luyan* man as he staggered towards her screaming something in his own language. She slashed at his throat with her knife and he sank to the floor clutching helplessly at himself as his life leaked violently away.

But their enemies pressed forward relentlessly. For every foe the companions cut down, another or even two more appeared from out of the night. *We're finished,* Anlerran thought bleakly, watching as on one side the Watchers struggled to maintain their shield against wave after wave of the enemy, and on the other, Elluron called words of power but with diminishing strength.

She saw Elluron stagger and fall to one knee, but she could not get near him. Too many enemies stood between them. Meanwhile Ruhal roared in tired defiance, streaming with blood. Their foes pressed on with renewed eagerness, sensing an imminent end to the battle.

The world slowed to a single heartbeat. Anlerran turned to see the Watchers staggering and the barely-visible shield disappear and then flicker into being again. *Soon,* she thought. *Soon this will all be over.*

A hand gripped her arm and pulled her around gently. She beheld Lura's stricken features. Leaning forward the mercenary said quickly into her ear, "Make them pay dearly. Kill as many as we can."

Anlerran's eyes welled with tears of rage and despair. *Powers, I will send as many of these vermin to the underearth as I'm able to,* she swore.

The rabid wave came at them, and the world became a blur of metal and hot blood.

A sound of horns cut through the night air followed by a vast, low chanting. There came a lull amongst the enemy, followed by a growing murmur of confusion. Anlerran pulled her knife from the chest of a still-twitching *luyan* woman, the red mist clearing long enough for her to hear other, more distinct sounds- the drumming of hooves and a collective bloodthirsty roar.

Moments later, *orkar* riders thundered into the settlement. For a short while the enemy fought back, but they were hopelessly outnumbered and soon the survivors turned and fled into the night, scattering in all directions.

Ruhal sank to his knees, laughing almost hysterically. After a moment he raised his blood-smeared face to the heavens and exclaimed something that Anlerran thought must be in the *orkar* tongue.

Hardly daring to believe, Anlerran staggered slowly over to the broken doorway and watched the sight of *orkar* warriors hunting down the stragglers and the wounded amongst those who had fled, spearing them and lifting them up on those spears as if to show them off to the moons high above. Some remained on horseback to chase down the escapees, but others, though they looked like lumbering giants, ran at frightening speed out into the surrounding land to apprehend and slaughter. The companions watched the butchery, and then gathered in numb, exhausted silence around Kal-Myrran and Jahar who lay dead upon the ground.

Presently one of the *orkar* dismounted, tethered his horse nearby and walked over to them. "Garrok," Ruhal said, his voice dry and cracked. "Did you know we were here? We had hoped to find you."

"We knew." Garrok pushed a two-headed axe through his belt. Anlerran watched blood, dark in the moonlight, drip from its blades. The *orkar* man's eyes glittered like hard gems in the half-light. "We knew also that Inerdyr's men had been recruiting from amongst the villages. A man by the name of Hanric led them." Garrok spat upon the ground. "We know him well."

"I also know him," Ruhal said quietly. "A man with a fondness for atrocity."

"But our scouts also tell us that *kin* joined with them," Garrok continued, "and for one reason or another Hanric was slain."

"These people who attacked us were not *kin*," Kian spoke up. "I would have known if they were." She glanced at Anlerran, who nodded tiredly.

"They were not," Garrok agreed. "The *kin* are strengthened by those that die in their name- or the name of their masters. These people were simply convinced of your evil, and sent forth to destroy you at any and all costs. They were sent amongst the human and *luyan* villages to gather folk to their cause."

Anlerran found herself looking at Garrok in a new light. That he knew those who had attacked them were not *kin* was a surprise to her. *Are some of his people able to channel the Old Powers?* she wondered.

She gazed mutely at the bodies, feeling only a numb sense of detachment. Then, as she looked away and out into the moonlit night, her eyes took in the sight of the *orkar* casually butchering those of their enemies who had survived the battle but were too badly wounded to flee, or had been chased relentlessly across the dark fields until caught. She even saw some who were wandering aimlessly, even heading back towards the *orkar*, who had commenced a low singing as they cut through their enemies. A hot rage swept through her. *This is all they deserve,* she thought, fists clenched so tightly her nails dug into the palms of her hands. *May their heads fly from their shoulders. May they die pleading and in terror.*

But the red mist swiftly cleared. *These are people of the human and* luyan *settlements hereabouts,* she reminded herself. *They are the very same folk who we might have recruited ourselves had they listened to us. They simply fell in with the wrong side.*

"Some should be allowed to escape," she heard Kelandra reason. "If we cannot win their respect through reason, then fear will do instead."

"Agreed," Ruhal said. "Garrok, will you allow this?"

The *orkar* leader walked away towards where his men continued to hunt, to bark out an order. Anlerran glanced briefly at Ruhal, and saw a hard, cold look in his eyes.

I have seen a similar look before, she thought, *but only in the eyes of Watchers.*

The sky lightened slowly. The dense and salty odour of blood hung in the cold air. Those of their enemies who had been allowed their freedom had long fled.

Anlerran listened to Garrok and Ruhal talking. "Your reputation for speaking out has become a reputation as an outlaw, a traitor, one who makes oaths with the powers of the Black Citadel," Garrok observed, "although I'm sure you're already well aware of that. There is talk of the Council of Wardens convening in order to formally strip you of your title."

"A title is nothing," Ruhal said dismissively. "I'm surprised that they haven't done so already."

"Mornkastle is with Inerdyr, you realise."

"Perrian the Warden of Mornkastle?"

Garrok nodded soberly. "Yes, from what I've heard. Of course, that may change."

Anlerran saw Lura walk a little distance away, and decided to go after her. She stepped through the wreckage and then lingered nearby as Lura sat on the remains of a low stone wall.

"Are you badly hurt?" Anlerran asked.

"No worse than yourself," Lura said quietly, wiping blood and dirt from her cheek. "Is that why you followed me?"

Anlerran sat with her for a while, saying nothing. Lura, it seemed, was content to do the same, but eventually she spoke up. "Vengeance," she said hollowly. "The need for vengeance eats at me. Its hunger is never satisfied."

"At us all," Anlerran acknowledged. "But we must learn to keep it from consuming us."

For a long while after that, Lura said nothing. She appeared to be engaged in some inner struggle.

"I should consider myself lucky." Lura's voice became low, reflective. "I've led a violent life, Anlerran, and others who've done the same have paid a far greater price. Jahar, for example."

"Perhaps the sharing of your pain may help in time," Anlerran said quietly.

Lura laughed at that. "Pain cannot be *shared*, Anlerran. How old are you? Seventeen summers?"

"The next will be my eighteenth," Anlerran agreed, a little reluctantly.

"You have much to learn. Grief lies ahead." Lura frowned, picking dirt and caked blood from her nails. "I could easily have laid down to die during the night," she remarked eventually. "I am so tired sometimes, Anlerran- tired of this bitter journey."

Anlerran could only silently agree. *I am also tired,* she thought, *and sometimes the bitterness and hatred pours from me, as it did for a moment when I saw the* orkar *going about their bloody work in the night.*

I understand you, Lura. A little, at least. And you're right. I don't have any words to work as balm for your sorrows, and I can't show you a better path than the one we walk.

IV

Jahar was cremated, and Ruhal, Lura, Elluron and Anlerran each said a short farewell. "In another life, old friend," Ruhal murmured finally, and the pyre was lit, with the help of some firepowder that Jahar himself had carried.

Ruhal turned to Kelandra, Ildoron and Alturus. "What ritual marks the passing of a Watcher?"

They looked at one another. "Very few Watchers have ever died after being brought from the Void into Aona," Kelandra said at last. "Those few are always taken back into the care of the Seven for their own rituals."

"We cannot leave Kal-myrran where she lies," Alturus pointed out. "It's possible that our enemies may find the body and use it in some way- glean something of importance from it."

"Then it must be burned," Ildoron said.

The Watchers created a separate pyre, placed Kal-myrran's body upon the wood and set light to it, standing back as the flames swiftly caught. The fire burned more fiercely than had Jahar's, and an intense white glow formed within and around Kal-myrran. Everyone stepped back as

198

the heat grew unbearable. Finally the flames died away, leaving nothing but fine ash.

Do they even know any natural death? Anlerran wondered, *or do they die only through wounding, or some enemy sorcery?*

Watchers have metal inside them, she thought, recalling Kelandra's wounds as they recovered in Fhaarluy, *and some magic runs through them- magic such as I can't hope to comprehend. And yet everything that was Kal-myrran turned to ash.*

When the companions made ready to leave, the sun had begun its descent. Garrok, who waited nearby, spoke up. "The towns of Targmal and Darkbrook may join with you. Many fear that the Old Dark is stirring."

"That much is plain to see," Ruhal said.

"Some name you traitor, others remember the injustices that certain allies of the sorcerer have heaped upon them in the past, each time a hint of dissent is heard. You know these places well, Ruhal. Dark superstitions linger there like shadows. If you can show yourselves to be stronger than Inerdyr..." Garrok shrugged. "You will have the makings of an army, perhaps. And Ghoreth the Warden of Darkbrook has never been a friend to Inerdyr."

Dark superstitions, Anlerran thought with a shudder, as her memory of the crazed man who had mutilated himself in a tavern taproom came sharply back. That feverish violence still felt far too fresh in her mind.

Ruhal looked thoughtfully towards the west. "Ghoreth has a reputation as a fair man. He would at least hear us out."

"I expect that's more than you've become used to of late," Garrok remarked.

"I take it the *orkar* are still on good terms with the folk of Darkbrook?"

"As good as ever."

"Will you come with us and speak in support of our cause? I know we already owe you much."

"Your lives," Garrok pointed out. "But yes, we will. We can set up camp outside the town."

Anlerran watched as Garrok strode away to give orders to his troops. She wondered if he had any idea what grim misfortune he had wandered into.

They reached the town of Darkbrook shortly after nightfall two days later. Torches and lanterns lit the streets, and by their light folk poured from out of their shops and houses as the news spread of new arrivals riding down the main street. A few of them even called out greetings to Garrok, who along with a half dozen of his fighters had ridden with them into the town.

They accept us because we are with the orkar, Anlerran realised. *But they will know who Ruhal is, and they will know the nature of his companions. They will want answers soon enough.*

As they reached a stable next to the village's largest inn and the crowd gradually dissipated, Kelandra suddenly said, "*No.* It cannot be her."

The nearest of the companions stared at her. "Who cannot?" Iyoth demanded.

Kelandra pointed across the street to a human woman perhaps in her twenties, who was accompanied by two men of Darkbrook's militia. She stared back at Kelandra, equally transfixed. *Horrified,* Anlerran thought briefly. *They know each other. But how?*

"I arranged for her to be sent down into the Sanctum before we left Luudhoq," Kelandra said grimly. Her fingers beat a rhythm on the pommel of her sword. "The *Sanctum!* No one ever escapes that place. How can she be here?!"

Anlerran felt alarm and dismay surge through her. *For once we actually appear to be welcome somewhere,* she thought. *The last thing we need is this.*

"Kelandra," she murmured, "you are no longer a Watcher of Luudhoq. Whatever time you speak of, it's over." She wondered why the Watcher had incarcerated the girl in the grim depths of the Sanctum in the Black Citadel- a prison that Lura had told her more about than she wished to know over the last few tennights, although she suspected that Lura herself had never been imprisoned there. *Kelandra spoke of that place as if it were impossible to escape from,* Anlerran reminded herself. *Now she's found that it isn't.*

Kelandra blinked, and fixed Anlerran with a forbidding stare. "No one has ever escaped the Sanctum before," she said quietly. "It is the greatest prison ever built."

Anlerran opened her mouth to reply, but no words came out. All she could think was the fact that she had given a Watcher a direct order- though she had no authority to do so.

"Someone clearly *has* escaped the greatest prison ever built," Lura spoke up from behind them. "Tell me, do you count all the people you have sent down into that place?"

"Why would I do that?" Kelandra retorted, as if puzzled at the question. Her eyes remained fixed on her prey.

"Stay here, all of you," Anlerran said quietly and swung off her horse, relying on one of her companions to halter it before it strayed. Ruhal swiftly calmed the creature, though not without a curse. She made her way across the road to the other woman, who suddenly shook herself free of her helpless shock, and turned to flee- but the two militiamen grabbed her quickly.

"Make an end of her," Anlerran heard a woman call out as she ran over. Immediately the sentiment was echoed by several other folk.

"You're in no danger," Anlerran said, and the girl laughed at that, her sullen eyes full of fear. She had a defiant watchfulness about her. *A survivor,* Anlerran thought. *A survivor of the Sanctum.* "No danger?! You *do* know who your companions are? Ah, perhaps you've not heard of me. How strange- even here I've become well-known. *Especially* here, in fact."

"Known as a murderess who walked free," someone nearby muttered.

"Quiet," one of the men spoke up.

"Kelandra is no longer a servant of Luudhoq," Anlerran said.

"Please," the girl whispered. She turned to both of the men in turn. "Kelandra will slay me. Let's return to the Warden's fortress. Those people who've just ridden into town- some of them are Watchers."

"She would not dare," Anlerran said softly, hoping by all the Powers that that was true. "The folk of Darkbrook have welcomed us, or at least they've welcomed our allies the *orkar.* Is that not so?" She glanced at one of the men and then the other, who shrugged warily. Perhaps the mention of Watchers had unnerved them. "Best you keep the peace," one of them said, "or it won't matter who your friends are."

The girl's stare strayed to her companions, who still sat gathered on horseback across the road. None of them had moved. The girl smiled wanly as she looked at them all. "That man holding your horse for you- is that Ruhal?"

Anlerran's jaw dropped. "It is," she said finally. "How do you know him?"

"I don't. I only know *of* him."

Anlerran suddenly considered that somebody who had escaped from the Black Citadel might be of great use to their cause. Certainly she would at least have an interesting story to tell. *She fled all the way to Darkbrook, presumably. Many questions remain unanswered.*

"I'd like to talk with you," she said abruptly, and gestured to a small alehouse down the side-street, called the *Stick and Shovel*. She glanced back at her companions and saw Ruhal point to a large inn that had prime position in the market square up the hill. The companions headed on up the street, although Kelandra's stare lingered in their direction for longer than anyone else's.

Although there were only several drinkers in the *Stick and Shovel*, Anlerran chose a table near the back where no one was likely to pass by without being noticed first. The woman's guards waited between them and the door, close enough to intervene if need be but too far away to eavesdrop.

Having bought some wine for them both, she began: "My name is Anlerran."

"Mine is Nia."

"The Watchers we travel with are no longer servants of the Black Citadel, Nia. You have nothing to fear from them."

That statement elicited a mirthless laugh. "Do you expect me to believe that? I don't think even *you* believe it. They will find a way. Kelandra will find a way. I *know* they are no longer servants of the Black Citadel as you call it. I know they are traitors. They can never return to the southlands. I've known all this for longer than anyone- do you know why?"

Anlerran shook her head.

"Because I was once *Kelandra's spy*. I worked for her. I was a thief, an assassin, a fact-gatherer, a rumour-monger. Anything that could only be done by mingling with the populace, or through extortion or coercion, or the slitting of throats, I did for her."

Anlerran frowned in bewilderment. "Why would she have thrown you into the Sanctum?"

"Oh, she told you already? Well, it's obvious when you think about it. How do you think I knew of Ruhal?"

Anlerran thought for a moment. Finally she had her answer. "You sought him out, and set up their meeting. The band of companions... came together because of your work." She sat back and took a gulp of wine. This was a profound revelation.

"And of course, once I returned to Luudhoq for my payment, Kelandra realised that she could ill afford to have me continuing to live my life freely, knowing all that I knew. By the time I was able to speak of what I knew, there was no point as it had become common knowledge. She and her fellow conspirators had already fled Luudhoq, and I was left to rot in my cell. I should have left the city as soon as I'd delivered the message. Then again perhaps the gate guards had already been told to let me in but not out. And to think that not so long ago she allowed me a wide degree of freedom, in between my... assignments."

Anlerran pondered Nia's words. "Yet you escaped the Sanctum," she said finally. "Is it true that no one else has ever done that?"

"Oh yes. I am truly one of a kind." Nia's voice had an oddly sardonic edge to it, as if her words might have two meanings. Suddenly a kind of darkness fell upon her. She downed the rest of her wine in a few gulps and sat back. "You seem like an honest girl, Anlerran. Would you grant me one favour before Kelandra and her companions slay me?"

"I told you already, they'll not slay you."

"Let's agree to disagree on that little detail. *Especially* after they hear what I have to say." A vengeful look loomed in Nia's eyes. "I'll tell you the truth, for what it's worth. The last few months have not been kind to me. In fact, you could say life itself has not been kind to me. I have no interest in lingering on for much longer- although funnily enough this place provided a distraction from such thoughts for a while. I want to tell you- *all* of you, your friends and those Watchers- what I discovered when I escaped from the Sanctum. I want to see their faces. I want to see Kelandra's face as I tell my story."

Anlerran found herself both intrigued and alarmed. "Why? At least tell me why it's so important that she..."

"Kelandra used me for all I could give, and left me to be beaten and raped in a cell for the rest of my miserable days!" Nia shouted. The few locals in the tavern turned to look briefly. Nia paid them no heed. Her expression was etched with both misery and a kind of lurid triumph as she fixed her eyes on Anlerran's.

"Yes- I'll tell you what I found in their glorious Sanctum," she said quietly, "and when I do, it will make the Watchers' world fall apart."

Anlerran realised she had a decision to make. Beyond Inerdyr and his allies there loomed the Black Citadel. *It isn't so dark to its inhabitants perhaps,* she thought, *provided they keep their eyes down and obey. On the other hand, I heard tales of the malice and might of the Seven as I was growing up. I was taught that they were invincible and that their cruelty knew no limits.*

But now Nia's words appeared to promise some unsuspected weakness, a secret that the power of the South perhaps even feared.

She leaned forward. "Nia, do you know why Kelandra and her colleagues wished to meet with their sworn foes- Ruhal and his companions?" Kelandra would surely never divulge information that she had no need to, although at the same time she reckoned even the arrogant Watcher might have felt the need to explain to her agent why she plotted treachery against her kind.

"She sought to unite Harn, of course," Nia said. "At least, she may have believed she was doing it for Harn. I can assure you, that fact does not make me hate her less."

"Well, I understand her reasoning. It's perhaps the only thing that binds my companions together. The *choragh*, ancient foes of all the younger Races stir, rising again to resume their old war with the starspawn."

"Starspawn?" Nia stared at her.

"The *marandaal*. Did Kelandra neglect to mention them?"

"She spoke briefly of them. It meant nothing at the time, but I've heard much about them since."

"Kelandra and Ruhal made their pact so that Harn may be united and strong, to face the *marandaal* but never under the yoke of the *choragh*."

Nia shrugged. "They may as well chase rainbows."

Anlerran regarded her curiously. "I realise that life has not been good to you, Nia," she ventured at last. "But will you not aid us? Your skills and above all else your knowledge may be of great use."

"No." A hard little smile flickered upon Nia's lips. "I would rather continue the tedious life of servitude into which I've lately fallen. I'm already *useful* here. I ask only one thing of you, Anlerran- keep Kelandra away from me for as long as you and your band of mercenaries are here. I'm not afraid of death, but I would rather she was not the one to deal it."

"Will you at least share with me the story of your escape from the Sanctum?" Anlerran asked. "I would like to hear about whatever it is you discovered."

When Nia paused, she added, "I will go to Ruhal afterwards and ask him for whatever coin we can spare to give you, such that you may live in some comfort here."

"I live as a servant under the protection of Warden Ghoreth," Nia interrupted. "Those two men are my bodyguards today. I only came here to collect accounts from a number of shopkeepers. There's nothing you can give me that I want."

"All the same, I would like to hear your story."

"So be it. Buy me another cup of wine. A large one."

Anlerran sighed but did as Nia had asked, and the girl gulped down over half the cup before she sat back and took a deep breath. Presently she began her tale, and by its ending, Anlerran's world also had changed forever.

"I escaped from my cell," Nia began quietly. "I don't need to tell you how- that's not important. But I did, and I wandered the lower reaches of the Sanctum for a long while, perhaps a day or more. I found a place where the wall had come away, and it revealed a passageway of sorts- a cavity between two walls in truth. So I made my way through it, became lost all over again... and then I heard the worst noise I have ever heard.

"*A sound from another world,* I remember thinking. A scream that cut through me. Then I saw a small hole in the wall up ahead, and I looked through it into some sort of chamber beyond. I saw light everywhere. White, then a silvery-grey glow- then it dimmed... and it went on and on, round and around, over and over in the space of moments. I saw smoke, and cogs and wheels some distance away.

"When the smoke cleared, I saw a human man. He was naked, legs and arms stretched out to either side. His arms and legs were held in place by coils of metal, and these coils also went into his flesh in many places throughout his body, as if they'd become a part of him.

"At first I thought this was a place where the Watchers brought people to be tortured. But I then saw two other men in the room, observing, noting. I listened to what they were saying, and knew then that they were two of the Seven. The prisoner started sobbing and pleading. Then the two men talked about him, about *others* they had captured over decades, centuries even..."

She leaned forward intently, and whispered, "This much I learned, Anlerran. Watchers, all except the High

Watchers, *are made* in the Sanctum. They're *fashioned from human prisoners. They were all once human.*"

Nia sat back, lost for a moment in the enormity of her statement. "I guess they are captured by High Watchers or agents of the Seven, the pain of their torture makes them lose their minds. As for their bodies..." She shuddered. "Well, that was what the room was for. The man's body... I saw long, thin lines of metal, or perhaps something else, being drawn into him by the *things* in that room. I don't know whether they were creatures or just objects powered by sorcery... but I know that what I saw was a human man *becoming a Watcher.*"

Both women remained silent for a while after that. Anlerran struggled to comprehend the enormity of what she had heard.

"They heard me, or saw my movement eventually," Nia said sometime later. Her words slurred a little. The flames had died down in the hearth and the innkeeper had put another load of logs on. "But I escaped them. I found a way out of the Sanctum... into the hell of the Bonemord. But there's another story. Suffice to say that the Seven would have identified me as the eavesdropper, once they found that I was no longer in my cell. I know their terrible truth, and they'll not rest until I'm slain. Oh, they're not worried about me telling people in general- I would be laughed at for creating another rumour about Watchers. But if I happened to tell a Watcher, that would be a very different matter."

"How so?"

"Watchers can *always* determine whether or not someone is telling the truth, Anlerran. One of their many potent abilities."

"Why do they do it?" Anlerran murmured.

"The Seven, you mean? I suspect the magic that made the High Watchers is forgotten lore. From what little I heard, it was lost or somehow became diminished when the Seven and the High Watchers they had with them came to

Harn. So, as High Watchers eventually perish, maybe the Seven try to create replacements. Perhaps they study the corpses- I don't know. Sometimes they succeed but most times they fail, and the *results* are used for other experiments, or just slain."

Anlerran felt numb. She could find nothing to say. *The* choragh *make slaves of the dead,* she thought, *while the Seven are content to torment the living.*

"Will you leave me a few coins for more wine?" Nia asked her. "My wages are three days away."

Anlerran handed over four copper bits. Nia thanked her and pocketed all but one of them. Anlerran left her buying another cup of wine at the bar and leaning against a nearby wooden pillar for support. *Wherever she chooses to end up, she'll not be going far tonight,* Anlerran noted, glancing across at her guards who had long tired of loitering and were sitting at a game of fourdice whilst taking turns to watch Nia with no little degree of frustration. She wondered briefly why they put up with the girl's behaviour and didn't simply drag her unceremoniously back up the road to the Warden's fortress.

Anlerran made her way outside and took a long, deep breath of the frosty air, lost for a moment in the enormity of what she had heard. That Nia spoke the truth she had no doubt. *I must decide what to do,* she thought as she made her way up the road. *But what?*

Kelandra turned to her as soon as she had seated herself at the table in the *Western Star* inn where her companions waited. "Does Nia still think I intend to kill her?"

"Do you?" Anlerran rejoined. She forced herself to look the Watcher in the eyes.

Kelandra gave her a faintly contemptuous look. "Why would I? What can she do to harm our cause here of all places? If she wandered the streets shouting about us turning our backs on Luudhoq, it would do only good. No, she has nothing to fear from me, and I certainly have nothing to fear from her."

Anlerran's heart lurched at that statement. *Powers, how more wrong could you be?* she wondered, looking away lest the Watcher see the sudden alarm in her eyes.

But Kelandra was otherwise occupied. She sat back in her chair, arms folded, looking thoughtful. "Nia has a dark secret," she said finally, "but with some thought we could put it to use."

"What secret?" Iyoth frowned.

The Watcher leaned forward and lowered her voice. "She is one of a kind, as far as anyone knows. A *natural shapechanger*. She has the ability to turn from female to male and back again, at will. I can assure you that it's true. We need to think of a way in which she might be of use to us. In fact, if we ever do reach Luudhoq she would be of great use. Few know the streets of the city better than Nia. And she has that most... *unique* ability. I'm sure we can put that to use somehow."

Kelandra turned to Anlerran, who could scarcely believe what she had just heard. "Bring her here, Anlerran, if her guardsmen will permit it. If not, then we should approach Warden Ghoreth tomorrow and ask that she be allowed to at least discuss matters with us. I swear upon the Watchers' Oath that I will not harm her." She glanced at the other Watchers, who nodded and repeated the vow.

Anlerran turned helplessly to Ruhal. "What do you say?"

"We would do well to make every friend we can in Darkbrook," he said. "Even this Nia, who appears to be largely despised. The Warden has seen fit to place her under his protection. She will remain unharmed- so let's welcome her if we can."

VI

Anlerran felt nothing but dread in her stomach. *Bringing Nia into our group, even without the secret she bears, would be like having an unstable sorcerous device that might blow up at the slightest touch. I can't shoulder this burden alone, but neither can I tell anyone.*

"I will see if I can find her," she ventured finally.

Anlerran stepped out of the tavern and walked down the winding street towards the *Stick and Shovel*, but stopped after a short while, taking a deep breath of the icy air. No one was around except a couple of drunks much further down the street leaning on each other's shoulders. She watched them until they disappeared down a side street.

Powers, what do I do? she asked herself. *This is precious knowledge, but it may also be a catastrophe waiting to happen. Letting Nia journey with us may even hasten such a disaster, but I see no better option. I've been told to bring her to the others, and I can't give them any excuses.*

Am I certain that Nia told me the truth?

I am. I have no doubt.

She wondered if Nia was still there or if her guards had lost patience and dragged her back to the Warden's fortress. As she approached the tavern she found her answer. The door opened and Nia emerged, the Warden's men holding her by the arms. She looked up as Anlerran approached, and smiled. "So good of you to come... back for me," she muttered, slurring her words.

"May I talk with her?" Anlerran asked the guards. "In private?"

When the guards had stepped away sufficiently, Anlerran said quietly, "We want you to join us, Nia."

Nia laughed softly. "What does Kelandra think of that? Oh, and have you seen fit to tell my master?"

"Kelandra thinks you will be useful. She and the other Watchers have sworn an oath to not harm you."

Anlerran paused, then added in a whisper, "She also told us about your... *changing* ability."

Suddenly Nia was alert. "Well," she said finally, her voice trembling slightly. "I can do nothing about it now. Have you told anyone else what we talked about earlier?"

"No one, and it must stay that way until the time is right for it to be told."

"There is no right time." Nia shook her head. "I should never have told you, but my rage coaxed it from me. If it becomes known, chaos will consume the land. Is that what you want?" She laughed bitterly. "Even *I* don't want that!"

Nia's expression became solemn, almost apologetic. "You've spun yourselves a web that will only destroy you," she said quietly. "Believe me, I know about these things."

X - The Chasm Opens

I

Vornen sat bolt upright. Bed sheets clung to his sweating, shaking body and his blood pounded. He found his attention drawn immediately to the east-facing window, as if something waited for him beyond it. *Go to sleep,* he told himself, but instead he got up and walked slowly over, taking deep and measured breaths to try and calm himself. *Open the window,* he thought. *A little cool night air will help you sleep.* But by the time he had walked unsteadily across the floor his sweat had already cooled and he started to shiver.

I had a bad dream, Vornen told himself, although he couldn't explain why he had wandered all the way across the room.

He ached for *kyush.* It would calm him. It would blunt his dreams. It would, he also told himself, help with the sweating, which had grown steadily worse over the last tennight. He knew that that was nonsense- *kyush* made its users sweat more, not less, and some healers claimed that it made dreams more vivid and less easy to distinguish from reality. But he told himself the opposite in the faint hope that repeating it often enough might make it true.

He glanced back at Amethyst. She still slept soundly. His gaze took in her slender form as she lay partly bathed in Ildarian light. One arm stretched out to her side and over the edge of the bed. *If a year ago someone had told me that this would be my fate, I'd have laughed in their face,* he thought. *I may still dream of Gates, but I'm no longer pulled towards them. And I'm with a woman who I want to stay with for the rest of my days.*

But even as he looked longingly at his lover and prepared to return to her warmth, the dream refused to fade. If anything it became sharper.

He recalled a vast, grassy hill, shallow-sloped. He could not remember being there before dreaming about it, and yet he somehow knew the place intimately as if during his long-forgotten childhood he had laboured up that slope with the aim of running heedlessly down it, laughing and unafraid.

Oh to be unafraid, he thought, *and to meet each day with hope and a smile.*

In his mind's eye he walked up the hill now, but a strange energy took a tighter hold of him and his every step was both larger and quicker than its predecessor, until he bounded at terrifying speed towards the flat, featureless summit of the hill where the windswept grass met the sky. By now his heart pounded as if it had expanded to fill his entire chest. His legs felt as though they were on fire as he came to a halt at the top of the hill, struggling for breath, indeterminate shapes and colours looming at the edges of his vision.

Then the air shimmered before him. Something began to materialise, and as it did the ground itself gave out a vast groaning and cracking sound, a response to some mighty astronomical force that had been brought to bear on the landscape.

The sky grew darker, but the air directly in front of him grew darker still. It took on the form of a doorway. The doorway opened. From within...

Vornen jumped violently, startled out of the vision by a gentle touch on his shoulder. The scene melted away, replaced by the incomplete darkness of the bedchamber. He was kneeling on the floor, hands together and fingers entwined as if in supplication to some higher being. Amethyst sat in front of him, wide-eyed and concerned.

"You were shouting," she said softly. "Did you have another nightmare?"

"A dream about a Gate," he murmured, "and not for the first time." He shivered and wiped cooling sweat from his forehead.

"At least they're only dreams, and they no longer draw you towards them."

"What if that happens, in time?"

Amethyst gave him a sharp look. "I won't contemplate that, Vornen. Were the worst to happen, I'll... no, I won't even consider it." Suddenly she leaned forward and kissed him full on the lips. Her breasts pressed lightly against his chest, and Vornen felt the lingering images of his dream recede further and fall away. "It's cold," she murmured. "Come back to bed. I'll make you forget your dreams. I can't sleep now anyway."

For a short, blissful while he did forget. They made love in near-silence. Vornen stared mutely up at her as she sat astride him. Amethyst moved slowly as if she felt the need to not only savour but keep and treasure every moment of their union. *And every moment we have remaining to us,* he thought, crying out as finally she coaxed the seed from him. She smiled and bent forward to kiss him. A moment later she said quietly, "You're mine, Vornen, and I'm yours. No powers will take you from me."

Oh, if only I knew that could be so, he thought, even as he stared up at her and brushed back a strand of her hair. *I'll hold on to you with every ounce of strength I have, but there are powers far greater than you and I can hope to withstand.*

"If this war is ever done with and the *marandaal* defeated," Amethyst said a while later, "I should like to go back to Darkenhelm. I need to know if my family survived. If they did and I can find them, I'll introduce you."

"I will be on my best behaviour," he said lightly, but a cold weight formed in his stomach. *Don't think so far ahead,* he silently implored her. *Don't think ahead at all. Live the days you can, and watch over your shoulder for the coming darkness.*

The next morning Vornen stood and looked out over the cold, windswept courtyard, feeling oddly pensive. His thoughts turned to something Ileana had said as they dined together the previous evening. *Something is about to change. It has to do with Inerdyr.*

He had asked what she thought it might be. *Something bad,* was all Ileana said.

He didn't trust Inerdyr any more than Ileana did, but there was little they could do. Everyone who lived and worked within the castle was clearly fearful of the sorcerer. Vornen suspected they remained here for the pay and protection offered by castle life. "I won't be a part of his plan," Ileana had said several times over the last tennight. But none of them had a choice in the matter. They were refugees from a foreign land, guests of honour in name at least, and Inerdyr was possibly the single most powerful man in all the Free Territories. Certainly as far as Vornen could tell the Wardens of the nearby districts and their militias were in his thrall. He had needed only to eavesdrop on a few conversations to learn that.

Amethyst shared Ileana's suspicions, as did Jak to a lesser degree. "If I could take Ileana away from this place I would do so in an instant," Amethyst had said vehemently several times already. Vornen had smiled at that, recalling how their relationship had changed beyond recognition. At first Amethyst had sworn to give her over to the witch who had forced her on the journey to find the girl. Now, he couldn't imagine Amethyst giving Ileana over to anyone for any reason. To all intents and purposes Ileana had become her little sister, to be protected and looked after no matter what.

But there were things here that Amethyst couldn't possibly protect her against.

II

That evening, a winged messenger landed on the balcony of Inerdyr's bedchamber. Inerdyr took the rolled paper from around its leg and the bird perched on the wall, peering at the sorcerer as he stood and unfolded the message.

> *Your man has had to be put down. The killing of the mercenaries and Watchers will, I presume, be given to others. Our Lords have placed me on a different path.*
> *Ferrin, of the kin*

Almost blind with fury, Inerdyr grabbed at the crow. But he caught only cold air. Perhaps having sensed his intended action, the bird had taken flight into the dark before he could bring the Powers to send it crashing to the ground.

The insolence of the kin *astonishes me,* he raged silently. *With each passing day it seems that they consider themselves a rung higher in the order of things. What purpose did orchestrating Hanric's demise serve except to mock me? Surely they know I desired the heads of the traitors. Will they now keep them for themselves, or give them over to our Lords?*

He did not know what to do. Undoubtedly he stood above the *kin*, whatever they themselves might believe. His Lords had gifted him many things, and one of those gifts had been allowing him to retain his humanity and not give his body over to them utterly. *There are many ways to serve,* he reminded himself, *and mine shows how they value me as I am- a master of the Old Powers, a servant of them, yet still human. I am an example that the* kin *detest. Certainly Arrko and Ilumor are both mired in jealousy.*

I should make an example of the kin, he thought. *But I cannot do that.*

217

The urge to wound, maim and cause suffering would not ebb away. Instead it served as an appetiser.

Hanric won't be coming back, Inerdyr reminded himself. *So I must work for both of us.*

He made his way down to the dungeons, the urgency of his steps matched by a quickening of his heart. He waited as the jailer opened the cell in which Sarros languished, and then he sent the man away.

Inerdyr observed his prey in silence for a short while. Sarros had always been slightly-built, but little remained of him now to cover his bones. Naked and dark with dirt, he had been reduced to a creature of sharp, painful angles. His cheeks were sunken and one arm shook uncontrollably. His chains rustled faintly as he squatted by the back wall. Inerdyr breathed in the mingled stench of excrement and putrefaction, which he had enjoyed for as long as he could remember, and continued to stare at the fragile body cowering before him.

He recalled being fascinated by the extent to which Hanric would violate those he had marked out. He had been almost mesmerised by the sheer beauty of the man's brutality, and often wondered how someone who appeared to be of no more than average strength could deliver such damage, such agony. Hanric had possessed no talent in the Old Powers, so Inerdyr suspected that the answer to that puzzle lay somewhere else entirely.

Imagining what Hanric might have done had the *kin* not unnecessarily slain him, made the blood pound and sing through Inerdyr's body. Simultaneously he felt a familiar urge shiver its way through him, and knew he could not leave unsatisfied.

"You let a great prize slip from my grasp," Inerdyr said softly, "and you've yet to be suitably punished for it. Do you think a beating from a man as lacking in imagination as Ayvin is punishment enough for what you have done? I don't."

Sarros could do nothing except utter a faint croak and weakly spit blood onto the floor.

"Hanric would have loved this duty," Inerdyr continued. "But Hanric cannot be here." He peered at Sarros, certain for a moment that the man was grinning at him, even though his mouth was near closed.

Inerdyr crouched near his broken prisoner, where the odour of the man's beaten and diseased body was especially sharp. He moved Sarros so that he cowered on all fours even as his emaciated arms were still held up by iron rings in the wall. The prisoner could utter nothing more than a faint yelp of agony.

Then he sighed faintly and his head dropped forward.

Spitting his frustration, Inerdyr slapped him and kicked him in the groin, but he would not stir. He checked for a heartbeat and a pulse and found none. Sarros' tortured heart had given its last beat and his blood had stilled and started to cool.

"Could you not have held on to life for a little while longer?" he asked.

Then the rage that had seethed within him like a poison finally surged forth. He rained blow after blow upon the body. He kicked it so hard that the chains almost came free. Flesh ruptured and bones cracked and snapped under the weight and fervour of his onslaught.

Finally the red mist and mad heat faded. Inerdyr gathered his breath, spat slowly on the corpse for good measure and strode over to the door, turning the key in the lock.

"Done with me already, are you?"

He turned slowly. Sarros half-lay and half-sat suggestively, his entire torso opened up and rib cage snapped wide apart as if inviting Inerdyr to rummage around in its contents. His intestines gleamed, pink and pungent in the dim light.

The castle is doing this, Inerdyr decided. *This is just its latest trickery.*

"I made you, and I can unmake you," he said quietly, staring at each of the walls in turn.

"Who are you talking to?" Sarros' apparition asked. It picked up a portion of intestine and waved it accusingly at him. "No matter, old man- I'll be waiting for you under the earth. Who knows, maybe we shall be as one, my flesh and yours. You'd like that."

Inerdyr did not favour it with an answer. Vaguely aware that he needed to be somewhere else, he opened the door and stepped out into the passageway, shutting and locking the door behind him.

He made his way slowly up to his quarters lost in a chaos of thoughts that came and went, and when he opened the door to his study he could no longer remember what those thoughts might have been. His gaze turned slowly towards the wall as he slowly flexed and relaxed his blood-stained knuckles. For a moment images flooded his mind of all the castle folk he could observe and listen to. *Somewhere one of them will be plotting against me,* he decided, *or thinking ill thoughts at least. Plots can be punished. Ill thoughts should be punished too.*

But as he stepped towards the wall- *my blank canvas,* he often liked to call it- the lantern light in the room grew dim and the flames in the hearth leapt far higher, roaring as if in joy. Inerdyr felt a dread certainty stir within him, and when he turned towards the fire he saw a figure standing near the fireplace that itself looked like a vast flame, only entirely black.

Inerdyr went down on his knees and bowed his head. *Close your eyes,* the *choragh* commanded him, and when he did an icy finger traced a line down his weathered cheek. *Loyal servant,* a voice whispered in his mind. *Most loyal servant. The time has come for you to lead by example.*

He dared not speak.

It is time for you to become kin- *the highest of all the* kin, *Inerdyr.*

Despite his lord's command, his eyes flickered open. Panic flooded through him, and he felt the same touch as before, only this time inside him, wrapped around his heart like an icy coil. When the *choragh* spoke into him again, the words held a dangerous edge. *Many of the* kin *have dreamed of this honour. Some have killed others of their kind in an effort to prove themselves worthy. But we find it fitting that it should go to one who has not yet taken the ceremony.*

Somehow Inerdyr found his voice. "Lord, I have always believed that I can best serve Aona through maintaining my humanity, by remaining close to the peoples of the Free Territories." The words began to tumble freely and urgently from his mouth. "In so doing I have brought many to our cause, whether or not they realise it, and..."

Be silent. You have served us well. The time has now come to serve us better.

Inerdyr had no time to plead further. A sliver of darkness reached out from the greater mass and swirled before him, splitting into tiny fragments that sank like barbs into his taut, struggling flesh. His body jerked backwards, held in place only by thin black threads. He could not only feel but see each line, powered by irreversible sorcery as it burned through him, remaking each and every part of his physical form that it touched. Even through the intense agony of this internal havoc he could feel these changes happening. Staring wildly around his study chamber he could see each individual speck of dust on the shelves. He knew the precise amount of heat within every spark of the fire in the hearth. He could hear the sounds made by people in all the nearby parts of the castle, and could even concentrate on particular voices so that they became louder and clearer. Each of his senses became sharply magnified and enhanced, as if they had previously been muddled and improperly focussed.

Had any of his serfs been present to witness this transformation, they would have cowered in terror at the sight of the black, pulsing veins spreading like cracks across his rapidly shuddering face. They would have turned away from the look in his wide, astonished eyes, of terrible pain and equally terrible knowledge.

A babble of voices in his head sounded their varied reactions to the violation of the body they occupied. Some howled in sheer terror. Others screamed their unbridled rage at the remaking of Inerdyr's inner and outer form, while a few shrieked their joy as they discovered new powers, new talents. All these voices eventually burst from his mouth, and the sum total of their chaos reverberated around the castle. The walls could not hold them; they seeped through rock and wood as easily as air. Servants and guardsmen alike abandoned their duties and stared at one another in wordless horror as the ululating bellow echoed through every far-flung corner, leaving nothing untouched by its resonance.

III

Ileana sat up in her bed, overwhelmed by sheer terror. Her certain knowledge of what had happened made it far worse.

Now we have no choice, she thought numbly. *I'm not anywhere near ready to leave. I'm just as likely to kill my friends as save them. But if we stay, we'll all die. We have to flee now.*

"Jak," she muttered, and shook him when he failed to wake up. When he opened his eyes and stared at her, she said immediately, "Get dressed. We have to leave."

He sat up, suddenly alert. "What are you talking about? We can't leave!" He frowned. "Are you still dreaming?"

"I'm awake," she said grimly. "Did you not hear that sound? Get dressed!" She tried to be calm, but inside she wanted to scream at him.

She quickly dressed and waited impatiently as he got out of bed and struggled into his clothes. "We *can't* leave," he persisted. "There's nowhere to go, Ileana. Are you sure you're not still asleep?"

"Wait here," Ileana told him, and slipped quietly out of their room and across the landing. She knocked on the door of Amethyst's and Vornen's room and waited in frantic silence for them to respond.

"Come to our room," she whispered as soon as Amethyst opened the door a crack. "Both of you."

Amethyst stared at her for a moment, but thankfully instead of asking questions she just stared at her for a moment and then nodded.

Ileana waited, pacing a few steps back and forth, until Amethyst and Vornen emerged. She ushered them impatiently through to her room and closed the door behind them. "We have to leave now," she whispered.

Amethyst stared at her. "Leave? You know that we..."

"Yes, I know. There isn't time to explain any of this."

"Is this because of the noise that we heard?" Vornen asked quietly. "We heard it too."

"I expect the whole castle heard it." Amethyst shivered.

"I heard nothing," Jak told them. "I must have slept through it. What noise?"

"You could sleep through a war, Jak." Ileana turned to Vornen. "Yes, it's because of what we heard. It was something to do with Inerdyr. I'm certain of it."

Vornen and Amethyst exchanged glances. "Ileana, there's nothing we can do," Amethyst said eventually.

"There is." Ileana took a deep breath. "There's somewhere we can go, and I can take you there. I know I can. But we have to be linked together. Holding hands."

She could barely look at the confusion in their eyes. "Let me try," she said forcefully as soon as Amethyst opened her mouth to reply. "Don't say anything. Just *let me try*. If it doesn't work, so be it."

In the uncomfortable silence that followed, Ileana found a deep, hard rage growing inside her, and a desperate need to be gone from this place. *Inerdyr will come for me,* she thought. *Something's happened to him to make him even worse, and soon he will come for me, or send someone.*

And my friends won't believe any of this until it's too late.

She could feel the Powers seeping through her, a trickle at first and then a steadily growing stream. But within moments that stream had become a raging river that threatened to carry her away. *I knew it,* she thought. *I knew I could make them stir, even if there are no creatures of the Old Dark here. Or perhaps it's all because of Inerdyr. They rise inside me because of what's happened.*

The sheer magnitude of this unknowable force still frightened her, but no longer did it feel entirely alien. She would struggle to control it, but on some deep and distant level she *knew* it, and that faint knowledge lessened her fear a little.

Ileana grasped Jak's hand, and almost recoiled as she saw a look in his eyes just like when they first met at his father's cottage in Fhaarluy. *I love you,* she wanted to tell him, but she couldn't speak at all. *Does he fear me?* she wondered desperately. *Do the Powers change the way I look and turn me into some sort of monster?*

Trying to put those thoughts to one side, Ileana took Amethyst's hand. She watched as Vornen linked hands with Jak and Amethyst so that they formed a square.

As those forces soared through her Ileana felt everything around them somehow becoming more *distant,* as if the four of them stood at the centre of a world that had started to retreat in all directions. *Take the step,* a voice whispered in her mind, almost buried in the avalanche of growing chaos. *You have no choice. Take the step!*

Ileana closed her eyes, feeling an ebbing away of the noise and mayhem in her mind. It roared dimly as if suddenly far away, and then faded into silence. For a moment she felt as if she was standing still and the world spun around the four of them.

She opened her eyes a while later. They appeared to be in the same room. But she turned and looked across at the window, and out at the featureless sky, knowing in an instant that they were not. Her heart pounded in exhilaration and fear. *I did it!* she thought. *Somehow I did it!*

"What happened?" Amethyst whispered. "What did you do?"

"I brought us here." Ileana scarcely dared to believe it. "This is it. This is the place I told you about. It's..." Suddenly a name came to her from nowhere. *I knew it all along,* she realised. *It would have been passed down through generations of Descendants- and somehow I know it even though I never knew my birth parents.*

"The Green Road," she murmured.

Amethyst stared helplessly at her, but Ileana could tell immediately that Vornen and even Jak knew the name. "Gods, it can't be," Vornen said. He walked over to the window and stared out into the dark. "I've seen some strange things," he confessed. "But this...no, it can't be..." He laughed uncertainly.

Amethyst turned to Ileana. "Does this mean there's no one else here? No guards? Is Inerdyr able to reach this place? Where *are* we exactly?"

"I'm sure he isn't," Ileana said. "And there are no guardsmen or any other people that I've seen. But there are... other things here. That's why we need to go now."

"What things?" Jak demanded.

"It's best that we don't talk about them." She walked to the bedroom door and opened it. The others followed her out, along the landing and down the stairs, and then through corridor after empty corridor down to the great entrance hall and into the inner courtyard. "There's really no one here," she heard Amethyst mutter. "This isn't possible!"

As they approached the castle gates in the outer courtyard, a swift transformation occurred before them. In a heartbeat the gate bars rusted, snapped and fell apart, the brittle pieces clattering to the ground.

"Nothing here makes sense," Jak whispered as they stared at the fragments.

Ileana looked across at him. "It isn't the same place."

The companions stepped over the broken remnants of the castle gates and beyond the walls of the fortress and the broken gateway. Ileana looked down at the sweeping grassy slope and the silent city far below and recognised the scene immediately. As they stood at the crest of the vast slope she imagined herself running at full pelt down it, allowing herself to rush out of control, further into...

Into the heart of the world, she thought. *This place isn't about directions. It's about how far you allow yourself to become a part of it. If I lost control I could end up so far inside, so deep within the world that I might even cease to be.*

She closed her eyes for a moment in an attempt to force away the frightening, compelling scene that she had conjured up, even as part of her felt an urge to run and run, to lose herself and be free of cares and worries for all eternity.

"What is that place?" Vornen asked as they stared down at the city.

"I'm not sure," Ileana confessed, "but I *think* it's somewhere that used to exist but has long gone in the world we know. Like a memory or a ghost of a city."

"There were no cities there *ever*," Jak pointed out. "Mornkastle would be to the south, this city is to the west. But there were never..."

"The Green Road doesn't follow the rules of maps," Ileana said. "That might not be west. Directions don't really exist here as far as I can tell. Not exactly. There's just further in, and out. And I think we have to go further in."

"Into the city?"

"I think it's a path to where we need to be."

"And how do we leave this place?" Vornen asked quietly.

Ileana looked down the ground. She had been dreading the moment that that question would be asked. "I don't know," she said finally. "I know I can work out how to do it, but I... I just don't know how yet." She felt the heat of shame in her cheeks, and couldn't look at her friends. *Maybe I really have trapped us all here forever,* she thought. *I'm not even certain that people can die here. There are things worse than death, and perhaps they're waiting for us down in that city.*

Before she knew it Ileana had fallen to her knees and started to sob. *I've destroyed any hope we had,* she told herself over and over. *I've destroyed all hope and condemned my friends to an eternity in this place.*

She felt Amethyst's arm around her. "We'll find a way," Amethyst said, and such was the iron determination in her voice that Ileana almost believed her. She took a deep, shuddering breath, rubbed her eyes and before anyone could say anything else she set off down the hill, taking slow and careful steps. *I want to run and run until the world swallows me up and I no longer know who I am,* she thought. *But I can't.*

They drew near to the vast iron gate of the citadel. Ileana regarded the great rusted bars and tall spikes. The entrance looked almost as she remembered it from before, except that in one part of the gate the bars had fallen apart entirely. A space had been created, large enough for them to step through.

What kind of things will we find here? she wondered. *If this place is an echo of a city that once existed, will ghosts of people wander the streets? Will events from long ago be played out over and over?*

They stepped through the broken gateway and into the city.

They encountered no ghosts as they walked down the wide street that led towards the heart of the city, but as they walked Vornen became increasingly certain that something was following and watching them. Ileana looked across and grabbed his arm suddenly. "You can sense them," she said.

"Yes." He drew a deep breath. "What are they?"

"I don't know," she whispered. "But if you see one, look away immediately. If it makes a sound, don't listen to it."

"I didn't see or even hear anything," Vornen said. "I just... *felt* something. Some presence. Might there be other people here?"

Ileana stopped and considered. "If there are then I think we should avoid them. They will probably be stronger than me, and they'll know how this place works far better than I do. They might want to do us harm. I'm just learning as I go along. I only brought us here because we had no other choice."

"No other choice?" Jak frowned.

"Inerdyr would have come for me." Ileana gave him a meaningful look. "And *your* usefulness to him would then be at an end, Jak."

They walked on along the street as it sloped downwards and began to curve around. Buildings of many shapes and sizes stood on both sides. Some were vast monstrosities with row upon row of square glass windows, whereas others stood tall and perilously thin. Most were made of stone but some glittered in the faint light and looked as if they might be made entirely of glass or crystal.

Occasionally a sound like the sighing of wind around the stone would start up, but no actual wind accompanied it. The air remained still, the temperature constant.

As Ileana had warned, Vornen caught faint glimpses of things he could not hope to explain from time to time- ephemeral shadows and shapes that appeared for an instant and were then gone. *What are they?* he wondered, looking steadfastly away if he happened to glimpse such an apparition. *Manifestations of the Old Dark? Or just part of the very fabric of this place?*

He found his hand gripping the pommel of his longsword, and smiled grimly as he removed it. If there was any place where a physical weapon would be rendered entirely useless, surely this was it.

He looked at Ileana, marvelling at how composed she now appeared no matter how she might feel inside. He tried not to think about how little she knew of the Green Road, that she led and made decisions by intuition and hope as much as anything else. *Only recently she was little more than a captive of ours,* he thought. *And now we are helpless in this place and rely on her- a girl who's little more than a child.*

Why are the Old Powers awakened in those who struggle to deal with them? Vornen wondered a moment later. He recalled his journey out of Aphenhast with Jaana, during which he saw for himself the growing resentment and bitterness within her, a burden lightened only when she seized the Old Powers and destroyed the *kin.* The last of them had laughed even as she tortured him- amused because he knew in that moment that she may as well have been *kin* herself. *Might that have been their purpose?* he asked himself. *To serve as a sacrifice in the name of the* choragh, *simply to make the river of Jaana's powers run a little darker? How many others like her have they tainted in the same way?*

Vornen stopped suddenly, his gaze drawn to a tall, thin tower set on an island in the middle of a lake to their left. The island was perhaps a thousand paces away. Light glowed behind some of the windows in the curved walls of the tower, but it had a dim, sickly yellow colour. As he looked more closely Vornen saw faint movements behind some of those windows, nothing more than quick shadows flitting from place to place within the tower's interior. Staring at the light, he wondered what it would be like to step inside that place, to walk beyond the threshold and be bathed in that curious illumination. He felt certain that mysteries and miracles abounded within its walls, and the further he walked into the place the more astonishing they would show themselves to be.

Before he knew what he was doing Vornen had taken half a dozen steps forward and stood up to his ankles in the water. His skin crawled as invisible threads of force pulled at his body, as if to entice him further in, to wade or swim through the lake and reach that distant shore. The water appeared to be rippling gently *towards* the island.

He heard his name called, but couldn't be sure which of his companions had spoken or even if the voice was male or female. The sound was faint. It could have come from leagues away, carried through the air. *No*, he decided. *No one called me. They're just waiting. I'll just walk a few more steps and get a better view of the tower and the light. There's something in there that needs me to see it, just for a moment. Then I can go back and tell the others what I've seen. The island doesn't look that far away and the water isn't getting any deeper. I'll bet it's this shallow all the way to the island shore.*

Hands grabbed him and hauled him back out of the water. His thoughts came swiftly back into focus as he was forced to turn away from the lake and the tower. He heard what sounded like a collective sigh somewhere behind him, as if whatever entities populated the tower were regretful of his turning back. *We'll see you sooner or later,* he imagined them whispering.

"I warned you," Ileana said, turning his face so that he looked into her eyes. "There are things here that will try to pull you further in."

Vornen shuddered. Although fainter now, still he could feel the pull of *something* inside the tower, and the sensation was not entirely unlike...

Then he knew it for certain, and quiet horror filled his thoughts. "There's a Gate here," he murmured. "Maybe on the island, even inside that tower. It's faint, but it's there."

"No," Amethyst whispered. "That's impossible!"

I want it to be impossible as much as you do, he thought. Aloud he said, "I can feel the pull. It's different to anything else. It's a Gate."

"I won't lose you again," Amethyst said fiercely, grabbing his arm. "I will not."

"It isn't drawing me in," he said. "At least, no more than anything else here."

"And what if that changes?"

Vornen had no answer to that. He shivered. Had he said the same thing to her just recently? He could no longer remember.

They moved swiftly on, to an area where the buildings around them looked ancient. Many had crumbled away to little more than piles of rubble.

"Is it safe to eat or drink anything we find here?" Jak ventured.

Ileana smiled faintly. "Are you hungry, Jak?"

He frowned, considering, then shook his head. "No. Although I feel as if I ought to be by now."

"I don't think we need to eat while we're here," Ileana said.

"What about water? No one can live without water for several days," Amethyst pointed out.

Ileana frowned. "I don't think we should drink the water here."

"But we *are* here, aren't we? Surely we *will* need water soon even if we don't feel that we do."

They looked at one another. Finally Ileana took a deep breath and shrugged. "I don't know," she said quietly. "I hadn't thought about it. I didn't have time."

After walking on for a while they came to a wide, slow-moving river at the edge of the city. The land on the other side stretched away, flat and grassy, for as far as they could see. "We spoke of water, and here it is," Vornen noted.

Ileana approached the edge of the river and peered down. The water looked unusually clear, and she could see down as far as the river bed perhaps a dozen paces below the surface. *Is this a test?* she wondered. *Are we supposed to notice how clear and clean the water looks and then decide here and now if it's safe to drink?*

"It's flowing more slowly," Jak murmured. "Look! It's *stopping.*"

It's not just stopping, Ileana thought as she took a step back from the water's edge.

It's waiting.

IV

Jaana listened to the sounds of Inerdyr's voices as she lay on her bed- the pain and ecstasy that cut like a knife through the noise.

After the sound had ebbed away she got up, dressed and left her chamber. She headed in the direction of the sorcerer's quarters, padding barefoot in near-silence. Even though it was no longer audible she felt that howl continue to pulse and echo through her body. Her skin crawled as if invisible creatures slithered across it. The sensation was

232

familiar. The imminence of *kin* and *diafagh* produced such an effect. But somehow it no longer disgusted her. Her reaction to it had begun to slowly change.

No guardsmen stood outside Inerdyr's quarters. Jaana guessed that they had scurried away in fear of the unknown. She knocked on the entrance door, but heard nothing from within. After a moment's hesitation she made her way in unannounced and a short while later opened the door to the study chamber. At the exact same time, the scream of a dozen voices inside her head stopped abruptly.

Inerdyr knelt facing the fire, naked from the waist down. He didn't turn as she closed the door behind her, but he said quietly, "Good evening, Jaana."

She didn't reply. Inerdyr shrugged off his shirt, and as it fell to the floor behind him Jaana saw that his body appeared younger, more taut and muscular. His hair, although still silver, now looked lush and plentiful. "My veil has been lifted," Inerdyr murmured, and somehow Jaana thought he might be talking not only to her but to the fire as well. He spoke like a man caught up in the throes of a rapturous dream. "If you could see what I now see, you would beg me to make you *kin* here and now. There is true beauty in true power." Slowly he turned to face her. "The time has come for all those who wield the Old Powers to be made again as *kin*."

Jaana came to sit at his side and looked across at him. The dark fathomless pools of his eyes drew her in. "When your senses open to the inner secrets of the world," Inerdyr told her, "then you will wonder how you ever could have existed without that knowledge."

"I want to know those secrets," Jaana whispered. She could not pull her gaze away from the look in his eyes. "I want..." She swallowed, unable to speak as a powerful, raging *need* almost overwhelmed her.

"The power." He looked knowingly at her. "It sings to every part of you- a song you've known for as long as you can remember anything at all."

"I have spent my life as nothing, waiting for it to begin," Jaana murmured. "I want to lead a legion to destroy the starspawn. I want my name to be carved into legend. If you can do so, I beg you to make me *kin* before anyone else. Because *you* are *kin* now. I can tell."

He smiled, and when his lips parted briefly Jaana imagined an abyss lurking behind them. "You'll have your legion," he said softly. "You'll lead many of the *kin* into battle, Jaana. But I need you to do something first. Bring Ileana to me. Find some guardsmen to go with you, in case her friends decide to give you any trouble. That girl's rebellious streak will end here tonight."

"*I* should be first," Jaana whispered. She could not bear the thought of Ileana becoming *kin* ahead of her.

"Do as I command." One of the black veins in Inerdyr's cheek looked as if it might burst, but instead it rippled and split to form several smaller vessels as if it sought to burrow through a previously unexplored area of his flesh. "Bring me that insolent little bitch. As for her boy-friend, have him thrown into the cells. He'll live out the rest of his days there." The warlock's voice had become lower. Jaana felt her skin writhing even more, as if Inerdyr's proximity had somehow agitated it. "I will teach her what it means to invoke my fury. I will break her, and then I will remake her."

Jaana felt a ripple of excitement. "Can I watch?" she pleaded. Her voice sounded different to her own ears. "Isn't it important that I learn from your example?"

Inerdyr smiled. His hand reached out to caress her cheek, and the touch was like a raging fire. A tear rolled down from one of his eyes, bloody and dark like a deep crack breaking apart his cheek. "You're a true servant to the

Powers, Jaana. Yes, you may watch. You may do more than watch. Would you like to hurt the girl?"

"Yes," Jaana whispered. "Yes. I want to hurt her." She swallowed. Her throat felt dry and she could not stop trembling. A small inner voice still screamed at her from a distant corner of her mind. *This is wrong! Take this step now and you can never go back. You can never again be who you were!*

I have nothing to go back to, she told herself, *and I have no wish to be the woman I once was.*

"I'll let you," Inerdyr said as Jaana watched his swiftly growing state of arousal. "I demand only that you keep her alive with her wits intact. Otherwise, you may do whatever you wish to her."

Jaana received no answer when she knocked on Ileana's door. The fact did not surprise her in the least, nor was she at all shocked to find the girl gone from the room when she used the key Inerdyr had given her to open the door. She checked under the bed and inside the wardrobe but did not expect to find Ileana whimpering there in the dark, nor was she.

When she couldn't find Vornen, Amethyst or Jak, Jaana allowed herself a contemptuous smile. Clearly Ileana knew what had happened this evening, only her reaction to hearing Inerdyr's transformation had been one of ignorance and fear. She would have gathered her companions and fled; only there was no point in hiding anywhere in the castle. They would be found, and Ileana had only invited greater punishment upon herself by trying to hide.

Jaana returned to Inerdyr, growing fearful of his likely response as she drew near to his chamber. But instead of reacting in fury he laughed. Finally he said to her, "Did you know that all that's needed to summon the Powers, aside from the innate talent itself, is the brain and a torso with a heart?"

Jaana almost told him she didn't understand, but a moment later she understood perfectly. She smiled and nodded as he continued, "Nothing else, Jaana. No arms or legs. No reproductive parts. No tongue, or teeth, or even eyes."

He looked her up and down. "Ileana can wait. She'll be found. But in the meantime your loyalty will be rewarded, Jaana."

"You mean... now?" She could barely believe it. "You will make me..."

He said nothing more but merely beckoned to her, and she went mutely to him.

V

As Ileana gazed down into the motionless water, she glimpsed what she thought at first might be a reflection of the night sky, with stars shimmering- until she remembered that as far as she knew, no stars were ever seen in this inner world. Nevertheless she looked up quickly just to make certain.

"It looks about ten paces deep," Jak pointed out.

Ileana looked away from the water and its mysterious points of light, which she suspected that her companions couldn't even see. "I think it's far deeper than it looks."

Vornen looked both ways along the river. "I don't see a bridge."

Ileana nodded. "We need to find a way under it instead."

"Maybe we don't even need to cross the river," Amethyst suggested. "Do we?"

Ileana stared down into the water again, watching as several of the points of light moved together, merged and then slowly drifted apart again. *What are they?* she wondered. *I don't expect I'll ever know.* "We will need to do

236

something," she said, oddly certain. "It marks a boundary between one part of this place and another. It's a way through."

She glanced quickly behind them, suddenly fearful. Drawn to the shapes of the nearby buildings, she thought for an instant that some of them had begun to change. One looked as if it had more windows than it had only moments ago. Another seemed wider and shorter than before, its contours rounded, as if it had begun to slowly melt and spread outwards across the landscape. *Eventually this place will become something entirely different,* Ileana realised. *Something even more terrible. The world is slowly dying, and that's what I'm seeing.*

Ileana had not stopped thinking about how they could find their way out of the Green Road. She had managed to escape last time by thinking about Jak, and somehow that had given her the strength to force her way back. But Jak was with her this time, and so were Amethyst and Vornen. The only three people she loved in the world were all with her.

She reminded herself that this city through which they walked might well be Aona's memory of a place that had once existed in the outer world. And because Aona was beginning to die, so too was the memory. The Green Road was a reflection of what had once been, half secret inner world and half ghostly nightmare, and it slowly disintegrated just as Aona's life force did.

Ileana looked across the river into the indeterminate distance and marvelled at how she could be so certain of such things, even as that cold certainty filled her with horror.

The marandaal, she thought. *And perhaps the* choragh *also. The conflict wears away at the world itself. And the Gates- holes in the world that lead only to the void...*

She turned to Vornen. "Are you certain that it was a Gate you sensed earlier?"

He nodded, grimacing. "Without any doubt."

And you should know, Ileana silently replied, recalling when she met Vornen for the first time. He had been tied to the Gates then, pulled towards those that eventually opened far to the south. Somehow their influence upon him had extended all the way to Ethanalin Tur-morn from where they had started to form in Nisstar.

"Further in to be further out," she murmured, staring at the points of light as they shimmered in the water. *They are not stars,* she reminded herself again. But she could not help but think of them as stars, the waypoints of the external heavens.

This is a test, she thought. *Aona tests my belief and my courage. Maybe, even though they're not stars they're part of a map of the Green Road. But a map of a place where directions mean nothing sounds impossible.*

She turned to her companions. "Can you all swim?"

As they gaped at her she added, "Follow me, whatever you do. Stay here and you'll be lost forever. Promise me?"

Ileana waited only for them to nod in agreement. She didn't give herself a moment longer to be too frightened to take the plunge. She jumped.

The water pulled at her, rose like a maelstrom around and then over her body in an instant. As it pulled her down, Ileana could sense her companions nearby. *They came with me!* she thought, her relief immeasurable.

Her surroundings were a little like she imagined the inside of a waterfall being. She had stood on a ledge under a powerful waterfall once while walking in the Tur-morn Hills. The power and the roar of the water then had been a deafening crescendo, yet it held almost no comparison to this overpowering vertical river that had seized them as they touched it, and sent them hurtling into a watery abyss.

Ileana felt a deep sense of wonder rise through her fear. As she fell, she caught glimpses of miraculous things beyond the liquid veil- places from long-forgotten ages, perhaps many thousands of years before the *choragh* rose. Lights, sounds and shapes from this unknown time filled her senses, fragmented yet sharp and detailed. She even thought she could hear snatches of conversation, spoken in languages that no one would have remembered even a thousand years ago.

Above and beyond everything else, Ileana saw her own self and her friends, pouring along with the vast stream of water from one vast platform to another far below. *Deeper,* she thought, falling and watching herself fall at the same time.

They slowed and came to rest in a shallow pool in a wide valley. Silhouettes of great mountains rose up wherever they looked. No evidence remained of the deluge that had borne them to this place.

Ileana sat up in the pool, and as she did the water evaporated swiftly from her clothes, leaving them entirely dry. The pool itself began to dry up, until nothing remained of it. She turned to see her companions staring down at themselves in stupefaction.

The greenish tinge remained in the sky, but Ileana could also see stars. She looked more closely at the patterns formed by those distant points, and could not recognise the constellations. Either the stars were in the wrong places or they were not the right stars at all.

Ileana looked across at her companions. "Vornen," she said suddenly, "can you still sense the Gate? Do you know where it is?"

"It's faint," he said after considering for a moment. "It moves through this place. Sometimes I feel as if I know which direction it lies in- left or right, up or down- but then it's gone."

"It has to be destroyed," Ileana said grimly.

Vornen just laughed quietly to himself.

They headed along the valley floor. The ground here was entirely flat and made of packed earth through which thin cracks occasionally ran. The companions' footsteps made almost no sound. Near the edges of the valley they could see what looked like streams and pools that glistened and slowly changed shape, as if they filled with water or some other substance which then receded.

They walked on for a long while. Days might have passed, but the heavens remained unchanging. They uttered no more than a few words each; the sense of wonder and disbelief they had initially felt now began to ebb away, replaced by the ever-present fear that they might not find a way out of this place.

They rested sometime later. Ileana shivered suddenly, wondering why the air suddenly felt much colder. Nothing around them had changed. Slowly she struggled to her feet, certain that she would sway and fall down as soon as she stood.

Then something else caught her eye. It glistened on the ground and melted away in a moment.

That was a snowflake, she thought, dumbfounded.

Looking up she saw more of them spiralling silently down. Ileana felt sure that it never snowed anywhere in the Green Road. No natural weather of any sort existed in the Green Road as far as she had seen.

Somewhere out in the gloom she could see the faint outlines of low, rolling hills. They were no longer in the valley through which they had been walking. The distant silhouettes of the surrounding landscape had changed slowly, to form something entirely different.

Slowly she turned to the others. "We're back," she tried to say, but the words came out as a tired whisper and were snatched away by the breeze that had begun to blow across them.

Ileana's legs gave way and she collapsed to the cold ground. *No,* she thought weakly. *It can't end like this. Not after everything that's happened. There has to be a reason. There has to...*

She became dimly aware of four or five figures materialising from out of the shadows. They spoke a language she couldn't understand a word of. Confused, Ileana tried to raise her head but couldn't. She tried to speak but was unable to manage that either. She heard her companions speaking, but failed to make out what they said before someone or something lifted her up and everything around her faded away to nothing.

V

Three days passed before Ayvin was asked by Serith, the commander-at-arms, to walk down to the cells with him. Serith opened one of the doors, and the two men surveyed the scene within the gloomy confines of the cell.

"He was left here to rot," Serith said quietly as Ayvin took in the sight of the mutilated remains in the far corner. "Even a traitor deserves better than this."

Ayvin looked slightly away from the broken, ruined mass of flesh, trying not to let his nausea show. He had known of Inerdyr's persuasions for years, but like any sensible man who valued his life he had pretended to know nothing. Talking about it could do no good for anyone- least of all himself.

"You have a family, don't you?" he asked. *Powers,* he thought, *the air stinks of gore.*

"I do," Serith said guardedly.

"Then you should choose your words more carefully," Ayvin told him. "Listening to you just now, some people might think you spoke critically of Lord Inerdyr."

Serith paled and looked around the room as if expecting the sorcerer to appear from out of one of the walls. "I meant only to... I mean..."

"A word of advice," Ayvin cut across. "Before you next think to speak loosely, consider what might happen to your family if such a transgression was to be found out. You have a wife and two young children, I believe."

Serith took a step back. "Why would he harm them?"

Ayvin shook his head and gestured to the mercenary's barely recognisable body. Could the man not see the truth for himself? No one, no *creature* even, existed outside Inerdyr's limits. Men, women, children and infants, animals, the living and the dead- he would torture and despoil any and all of them.

Serith nodded, finally understanding. Powers, the man was slow sometimes. How had he retained his job for so long? "You won't speak of this?"

"I won't," Ayvin said, "but for their sakes, learn to rein in your emotions."

He cared nothing for Sarros. He had barely known the man, and only as one of Ruhal Dalmorn's mercenaries. Sarros had been the weakest of them and the most easily persuaded, which was why he had initially been of use- but then he had neglected to mention the descendant of the First who had been travelling with their group. That alone warranted the man's execution. A traitor deserved to die. A traitor who turned not only against the Free Territories but then against his own fellow traitors- truly a rat amongst rats.

But the sheer glee and obvious pleasure with which the man had been torn apart disturbed him. He saw that Inerdyr, often in favour of putting out the eyes of those who crossed him, had left Sarros with his intact. Ayvin suspected that that look of frozen terror and agony would remain fixed until the man's eyes rotted away.

He wondered why Inerdyr had left his handiwork here rather than have it cleared away or burned to fine ash. Had he thought to strike fear into those who encountered it later? Or had he intended to return to play with the man's body as it slowly putrefied?

Ayvin felt faint. "Have the body burned," he said suddenly.

"A funeral pyre?" Serith looked doubtful.

"No. Of course not. Take it out into the yard, douse it in alcohol and set it alight. Let the wind scatter the ashes, and if any bones remain intact then let the dogs amuse themselves with them. And Serith- speak of this to no one. If you must have the help of one of your men, demand the same of them. Then, have a servant clean this place."

He left swiftly, eager for the fresh and bitter air outside.

XI - Revelations

I

Nia arrived at the inn with the hour still early. Anlerran looked up from her breakfast of bread, cheese and saltmeat and saw that the woman was accompanied by two different guards. *Those two from yesterday evening certainly deserved their sleep*, she silently remarked. "Have you thought further about our offer?" she inquired.

"Offer? It sounded more like a demand to me," Nia said, seating herself at the table. "I have no life to lead except the one given to me by Ghoreth, Warden of Darkbrook. It will be up to him whether I aid you or remain in quiet servitude. I should prefer the latter. Quiet servitude suits me well. I expect he will wish to keep me."

"You may not have a choice," Anlerran warned her.

"That would certainly be in keeping with my life to date," Nia agreed with a smirk. Anlerran frowned. *I don't like her desperate unhappiness*, she thought. *I'll wager she's always been alone, apart, something of the shadows even before she worked for Kelandra.*

"I haven't yet told you about the Bonemord," Nia added, and disquiet stirred in Anlerran's heart. "The Bonemord? What could that place have to do with any of this?"

"If I may, I'll explain when you're all together. The Watchers will be interested in this," Nia said politely, and she sauntered away, followed closely by her guards.

"I don't like that girl," Lura said quietly from her table across the room.

"No one likes her," Anlerran answered, with a twinge of sadness.

244

"Nia seems to think that the Warden of Darkbrook may deny her leave to travel with us," Anlerran told Ruhal when he arrived in the breakfast room. At least, that's her hope."

Ruhal shook his head. "We'll pay him whatever we must. Wardens are raised to their responsibilities partly because of their having a practical nature. She may possess a certain value to him, but his first responsibility is to his people. We have to keep her with us, Anlerran. Kelandra knows her well, it seems, so if she believes the girl might be useful, we'll hold on to her."

The Watchers arrived a little later, and a short while after that Nia returned. Kelandra turned to stare at her, and Nia glared back at her as boldly as she could. "You are quite remarkable," Kelandra said finally.

"Am I?" A flicker of amusement crossed Nia's lips for a moment. "I suppose I am, Kelandra. Thank you for telling your companions about my... ability."

"You should be thankful for it," Kelandra said dismissively. "It makes you useful. If you were not useful, you'd be dead at my hand. You can be assured of that."

The companions gathered in one of the rear rooms of the inn to hear Nia's tale, and Ruhal convinced the guards to wait outside the room. Nia waited until everyone sat around the table in the dimly-lit chamber, and then she began her story.

"When I escaped from the Sanctum," she said, "I found myself in the Bonemord, another place from which supposedly no one had ever escaped."

"And yet somehow you managed," Kelandra pointed out.

"Yes." Nia met her gaze unblinkingly and continued, "Even as I emerged from the tunnel, I knew I was being hunted by the Seven's men and a tracking beast. I heard the creature. I looked across the waters and decided to choose the fate of being ripped apart and eaten alive, rather than allow myself to be taken back to the Sanctum. So, expecting to die quickly, I dived into the swamp and began swimming. Of course, they didn't follow. I disappeared into the mist and I suppose they arrived a little later, looked around and turned back. But nothing pulled me under the waters." She shrugged. "Sometimes I was awake and aware, sometimes the whole world became like a dream. I drifted. I ended up lying on the bank of a muddy island. I was captured, taken..."

"Wait." Ildoron leaned forward. "Captured by whom? Are you telling us that there are people, *alive,* within the Bonemord?"

"Well, my lord Watcher, that's the purpose of my story. There might well be thousands of them. Most are deformed in some way... I suppose you might call them monsters. I was taken to a man who lived on one of the hills. He told me that they are people from *Luudhoq,* taken first by the Seven to be the subjects of experiments in their Sanctum, and then out of the city and into the Bonemord. They have no hope of escape. Some have apparently tried, but even if they reach the edge of the swamplands..." Nia pointed a finger between her breasts. "Their captors place something in their chest, something that kills them if they try to leave the Bonemord. I suppose even those who are born there have that same affliction. Like... an extra part of their bodies that's somehow passed on through some sorcery, from the parents to the child. Not that I expect many infants survive for long."

"What is done may be undone if the weave is known," Elluron said eventually. "But therein lies the problem. The powers of the Seven are alien to us."

"I cannot think of anything the Seven have done that may be reversed by anyone else," Kelandra pointed out. "Still- an interesting tale, Nia."

"Thank you, Kelandra," Nia said icily. "I'm so glad you enjoyed it."

"How did you escape from the Bonemord?" Kian asked. "You wouldn't have had the curse that these people have- but how did you even reach the edge of the place? How did you escape your captors?"

Nia smiled ruefully. "The man to whom I was taken decided to let me go."

"Decided to let you go," Ildoron frowned.

"I told him my life story- well, a shortened version of it- and I suppose he took pity upon me," Nia said. "His name was Barrik. He led me to a place where he kept a rowing boat, and told me to keep rowing north from there. I'm no boatswoman, but I managed to reach the northern edge of the Bonemord eventually. I owe him my life. Without his help I would never have escaped, and soon enough my *difference* would have been noted even by the Bonemord people. In fact, they were coming for him even as I left. If they'd caught me a second time, I would more than likely have ended up as serpent-food. I suppose folk of faith might call the entire episode a miracle. Perhaps a song will be written about me, to be passed down to the children of those who witnessed my passing through their lives." Her expression soured. "Perhaps not."

Iyoth finally broke the silence that followed. "Surely for these people to have remained unknown for all this time, something must happen to those fools who decide to explore the Bonemord from the lands outside it. Yes?"

The Watchers glanced at one another. "That would make sense," Kelandra agreed finally. "I know nothing of the sorcery they used to build this barrier," Iyoth continued, "but we know this much, if Nia's story is true. She only escaped because she did not have the taint, the weave of power that the denizens of that place have. And perhaps the opposite also holds true- only those who *have* that sorcerous weave already can enter the Bonemord."

"No bodies have been found near the place, as far as I know," Alturus said, "but there are recorded instances of folk wandering into the mists, never to return."

Later that morning the Warden of Darkbrook and the senior men of his militia met with Ruhal and Garrok, and Ghoreth told them about his fears for Woods Ford. "You're here to recruit," he said bluntly, "and if you can go to their aid, then I will give you a half of Darkbrook's remaining force."

"Are your men willing to take up arms against Inerdyr?" Ruhal frowned. "Many will die in so doing."

"They will die anyway if war comes," Ghoreth pointed out, "and one way or another, it will. The mad sorcerer's people will think of this region as treacherous anyway. They will see traitors wherever they look. It suits their plan. Besides, my men would rather fight alongside *orkar*. They have done so before."

"They have never fought alongside Watchers," Garrok pointed out.

"And until now, neither have you." Ghoreth turned to Ruhal. "I understand from one of my servants that you wish to add her to your ranks."

"The Watcher Kelandra informs me that Nia may be of great use to us." Ruhal shrugged. "How much do you want for her, Ghoreth? She may well be good at her job, but she's just a southern footpad when all's said and done."

"And yet your Watcher reckons she'll be of great use to you. Which one is it, Ruhal?" Ghoreth looked thoughtfully at him. "One hundred silver, or whatever equivalent you have. But she's to be returned here when this is all done."

"If she survives."

"If any of us survive," Garrok echoed, and grinned when they looked to him, almost as if he relished the imminence of war.

After the Warden had left, Ruhal and Garrok returned to the *Western Star.* "There is something we need to decide," Ruhal said as the companions gathered in the yard and prepared to leave. "The device that Elluron carries is a thing of great power, but may be used once only. So we have a stark choice to make: do we use it *if* and when we ever come within sight of the Black Citadel, or against Inerdyr's hordes? I am for the latter."

"You presume two things," Elluron said finally. "That the *illeagh* will come, and that they will fight and destroy their own kin. But whatever assumptions we make, remember that long ago the *illeagh* and the *choragh* were one. Also, did I not say that the decision is mine to make?"

"Then what would you have me do, Elluron?" Anger flashed in Ruhal's eyes. "If we do not deal with Inerdyr then we never take the South. We never unite the land. We never bring together the people of Harn to face the greatest enemy of all."

"If we cannot think of a third way," Kelandra said, "then perhaps the matter should be put to a vote."

"There will be no vote," Elluron said, "because none of you can even begin to comprehend the nature of the *illeagh.* You cannot make an informed choice on a matter beyond your understanding. I am partly of their race and yet even I can never hope to understand them more than a little. I don't believe they would heed a call to destroy their dark cousins, no matter what you think is possible."

Anlerran sat uncomfortably as Ruhal and Elluron stared at each other. She felt certain that what Ruhal proposed was wrong, not only in seeking to use the device of the *illeagh* against Inerdyr but in his desire to move so quickly against the sorcerer. *There are others who will support us if approached,* she thought. *There have to be. We must stay our hand. We are surely nowhere near strong enough even with the* orkar *and the people of Darkbrook. I know nothing of warfare but I know odds well enough.*

Kelandra said quietly, "Ruhal, you struggle to rein in your emotions. Can you not accept that Elluron knows more about these *illeagh* than you do?"

"You know nothing of emotion, Kelandra- of what it is to be human," Lura spoke up before Ruhal could respond.

The Watchers regarded her dispassionately. None of them uttered a word, but Kelandra's lips curled slightly as if in casual contempt. *One day your world also will be torn apart,* Anlerran thought.

Briefly she recalled something that Jahar had once said during her training. *In some of the* diafagh, *it's as if a dim spark remains, a few scraps of memory perhaps- nothing that might even make a conscious thought, just a collection of fleeting images without meaning- the ghost of a memory, perhaps, disconnected from its owner but still lingering within its remains.*

The Watchers appear not to have even that, Anlerran thought, looking at Kelandra once the Watcher's attention had shifted elsewhere. *All that was can never be found again. The Seven burned away everything that made them human.*

To everyone's surprise Kian spoke up. "I don't think we should employ the device against Inerdyr and his forces."

"Do you not?" Ruhal glanced coolly at the *du-luyan* girl. "Do you have a particular reason?"

"As Elluron said, the *illeagh* may refuse to fight their own cousins in a war they may not see as their own," Kian continued. "But in any case, if we somehow win then what hope have we against the might of the Seven or the *marandaal*, if we cannot call on the *illeagh* again?"

"Unless we have no choice, I do not think we should use the device even against the Seven," Elluron added. "It must be saved for the *marandaal*. The starspawn are the enemies of the Elder Races since the dawn of Aona herself, or as good as. I would say a call to fight against the *marandaal* is the call most likely to be heeded."

"How do we even know that this *device* does anything at all?" Alturus asked.

"We don't," Elluron admitted. "We can only hope. That is the simple truth."

Kelandra pointed out, "The Seven will not surrender. The High Watchers in turn are utterly dedicated to the Seven. There is only one way to take Luudhoq and the south—by total, unquestionable force. I say again for all those who may think otherwise: be in no doubt that we will have to grind their bodies to dust beneath our feet. I am in agreement with Elluron. For now at least, we must not use this device."

"In the south we know much about Inerdyr," Alturus added. "He will execute his doubters, and perhaps their families. The more he fears desertion amongst his ranks, the more he will use fear as a means by which to maintain control of his people, whatever the cost. He is not used to any kind of uprising, and he will have only one answer to it."

"Much like the Seven," Lura observed.

"Well, you've made your decision," Ruhal said, staring at Elluron. "We'll head out to Woods Ford as soon as possible. Be prepared." He walked outside to the stables, and after a short moment Anlerran decided to go after him.

The Warden of Mordenglen stood staring angrily at nothing as he saddled his horse. Anlerran wandered cautiously over to him. *I'm not sure I can think of anything wise to say,* she thought, *and so I'd best say nothing at all. Maybe I should just leave him alone.* But just as she was about to turn and leave, he spoke. "I wonder so often how things came to be this way. Are there not other places dotted about the Existence? Kelandra said that some worlds share the same sun as Aona. And she spoke of other, distant worlds."

"All of them dead," Anlerran reminded him, wondering why he had suddenly thought to talk about this instead of the *illeagh* device.

"But *this* place, *our* world, has been chosen as the battlefield between two great evils."

"Perhaps the same war is waged elsewhere or has been in the distant past," Anlerran murmured.

"I don't doubt that. Many stories tell of the *marandaal* claiming place after place, to destroy all life." Ruhal turned to face her. "But I think there's a great secret to this world, Anlerran. A terrible truth that dwarfs such revelations as the discovery of a true shapechanger, or the forgotten people imprisoned within the vastness of the Bonemord. No, there is something far greater at work."

Anlerran said nothing. She had no idea what he was talking about, and yet on some deeper level she did. "It's like something in the corner of our eyes, that we may never see properly," he said softly. "Some innate knowledge that our waking selves simply cannot grasp. I have known many witches and warlocks, Anlerran- my mother was such, no matter what she might call herself. You must have known that from the fateful evening when you met her. So I know the stories of such places as the Silver Road, and even the Green Road. There is one tale, seldom told..." He paused, exhaled deeply, and then said, "A tale that shows how all these roads lead eventually to the same place, if followed for long enough."

"What place?" Anlerran asked quietly. "Somewhere far beyond this world?"

"No." Ruhal shuddered, drawing his cloak about him as a gust of icy wind swept down the street. "Somewhere *far within*. The very heart of it all. My mother once said that when she was a little girl, she heard her grandfather talking with a guest of honour, a warlock from the abandoned desert realm of Alhar. His theory was that it is all the same. That the entire Existence is Aona, in its heart. The outside is only a reflection of the inside, and yet the inside is the outside." He shook his head. "I cannot understand it. I never could- it's always sounded like a meaningless riddle to me. But then again, she taught me that you don't need to understand something to believe in it."

Anlerran had no idea what to say to that. Ruhal glanced across at her and abruptly changed the subject. "Tell me, Anlerran- do you think those who would gather under our banner need *me*? Is that the truth as you see it? Or do you think it's the *cause* that they need? The hope of a united land that can stand against the starspawn? Do you think they have even given consideration to such things? People here live day to day, hand to mouth. Few of them have held a weapon in battle. Many still think of the *marandaal* as a fearful rumour and nothing more."

"Undoubtedly they need you." Anlerran's head was still spinning from his previous ramblings, but she gathered her wits sufficiently to give some force to her words. Nevertheless she looked away as she spoke, fearing that he might see her heart's doubt reflected in her eyes.

"Your father thinks not."

She stared at him. "Why do you say that?"

Ruhal gave her an exasperated look. "He would prefer to control events himself. See how he already protects his precious *device*? It gives him a measure of power over us."

"I have something else to tell you," he said abruptly as soon as she opened her mouth. "I will not do this without you, Anlerran. I haven't the strength without you at my side. You're my hope, my light." He laughed suddenly. "You're my voice of reason. Sometimes I feel a great darkness around me, and it has nothing to do with the *choragh* or Inerdyr's minions or the still-distant *marandaal*. No, it's a darkness of my own making. It wells up inside me, and sometimes..." His eyes held a haunted look. "Sometimes it comes to me like a madness, Anlerran. It possesses me. The more I lose, the less

I see reason to hope, the more this bitter violence surges. But with you at my side, and allies who I can trust...”

Say nothing, Anlerran thought as she smiled at him, hoping that he read no treachery in her eyes.

“Perhaps we *can* stay our hand and keep Elluron’s device unused,” he added suddenly. “If we have the *orkar* and perhaps some of Darkbrook’s militia- assuming Ghoreth is true to his word- we may have an army after all. Our force will grow. That’s my hope.”

“I think we all hope for that. I’m certain it can be done.” *As if you know!* a voice in her head silently scoffed.

Ruhal walked over and slipped his arms around her, pulling her against him in a strong embrace. *“My voice of reason,”* he whispered in her ear, and Anlerran could not help but shudder, as if Ruhal’s unseen shadow in his mind had now become hers also.

II

Ruhal’s words would not leave her mind, and as they prepared to ride out once again with the *orkar,* Anlerran was reminded of the mystical places her father had told her about during their discussions and her training. *The Silver Road and the Green Road are the inner places of the world,* he had said. *They are outside of the world we know, but they are also inside. They exist not in the world we can touch and see and hear, and so they cannot be mapped, yet they are nevertheless a part of Aona. They have no beginning and no end. Those of sufficient strength in the Old Powers may reach the Silver Road, but to do so is fraught with danger and often difficult. It’s like a night where an especially bright, full Ildar has risen- as if the light of the small moon shines down, yet the moon itself is nowhere to be seen. The Silver Road is somehow brighter than such a night, almost as bright as day.*

What about the Green Road? Anlerran had asked him.

254

Her father had smiled at that. *I have certainly never walked the Green Road, and I know of no one who has. Legend has it that the Green Road is a spiral down into the very centre of the world, and to walk it for long enough is to learn the secrets of the entire Existence.*

Anlerran started suddenly as she walked out of the stable, slowly leading her horse into the daylight. Elluron had been waiting at the entrance and she hadn't noticed.

"Be cautious around Ruhal," he said quietly without preamble.

Anlerran stared at him. Without warning, he traced his hand slowly down her cheek, then brushed back a strand of errant hair. "The Warden of Mordenglen does not deserve you," he said softly.

Anlerran swallowed. "Be that as it may..."

"Yes. You love him, or at least you *think* that you love him, perhaps because he saved you or because he awakened your nature. And he would no doubt point out that he made a woman of you."

She took a step back, slapping his hand away. "That's no business of yours!" Realising that she had spoken up, she looked quickly around but no one appeared to be within earshot. Ruhal had already gone somewhere to talk with Garrok about the best route to Woods Ford.

Elluron's violet eyes fixed intently on hers. "If you let him, that man will ruin you whether he means to or not. Keep him at arm's length, I beg you."

"It's too late for that," Anlerran said. She turned and walked swiftly away into the paddock.

As noon approached, Ruhal returned from a meeting that he, Kelandra and Garrok had attended with the Warden of Darkbrook. "Ghoreth has agreed to give us two hundred of his militia in return for securing Woods Ford. He has also agreed to give us Nia, and she will ride with us to Woods Ford. She may as well become used to our company."

A short while later they left Darkbrook, the thunder of hooves fading into the sigh of the morning breeze.

They stopped before nightfall at the edge of a thick woodland of pine and larch. To Anlerran's surprise Nia sat nearby when she was talking with Elluron by their fire, and asked to speak. "Of course," Anlerran said guardedly, wondering what new shock might be revealed this time.

"I'm surprised that Kelandra has not mentioned this already," Nia began. "When I returned to Luudhoq from Aphenhast, I brought with me three people from that land. I enticed them to Luudhoq with the promise of a better life, more or less. A child called Yui, her father and a woman who was a friend of theirs. The child... had visions of Gates. Powerful visions. I'm certain that she was seeing places where Gates would appear."

They stared speechlessly at her.

"I told Kelandra about them, and of course she had them taken into the Sanctum. I knew full well that the Seven would torture them. I knew that they would be incarcerated in the Sanctum for the rest of their miserable days. And..." She stopped, glancing fearfully at Anlerran, who frowned. *Something else,* she thought. *Nia fears something else that she's not spoken of yet.*

"The child's powers have grown," Nia said brokenly. "They've grown far beyond the ability to see the places where Gates may appear. When I was fleeing north after I escaped the Bonemord, she entered my dreams each and every night. She taunted me. She swore vengeance upon me. I only escaped her by..." Nia shook her head. "That doesn't matter. Maybe Warden Ghoreth will tell you all about that if you ask him. But she'll reappear when we head south again. I'm sure of it. The dreams she caused..." Nia shuddered. "I thought I might go mad. I feared that I might lose myself in my own nightmares and never wake up."

She sighed wearily. Anlerran could think of nothing to say, and neither could her father.

"It's all I deserve," Nia murmured after a while. "If I was her I'd have more than likely done the same. Wouldn't you? Perhaps not. I find you difficult to read sometimes, Anlerran."

And I you, but twenty times so, Anlerran thought to herself.

She was not entirely surprised when Kelandra spoke up. The Watcher had been listening intently to Nia's story from the other side of the fire. "It is true," she said, "or at the very least the child is real. She was lured by Nia's promise of being healed of the visions and nightmares that plagued her. Yui was handed over to the High Watchers and the Seven for examination and research. I believe the Seven hold her in a special prison and look after her personally."

"By examination and research you mean torture," Lura stated.

"Discovery of the truth by any means necessary." Kelandra fixed her cold gaze on the mercenary. "And I'm certain it will not endear you to me any further, Lura, to have discovered that *I* was responsible for handing her- and her father- over, once Nia had informed me about her... special guests. That was my duty."

Lura spat into the fire and looked away in disgust.

"Oh, but Nia should take some of the credit for this," Kelandra remarked, glancing at her former spy. "As she herself has pointed out, were it not for her all three of them might well still be free."

Nia gave Kelandra a furious, hateful look and said nothing.

Ruhal spoke up. "Kelandra, you said that the Seven hold her captive *personally*? Is she truly that powerful?"

"Apparently, yes. She is a dreamreader, quite clearly. Yet her most useful talent is something completely different. As we know, the eastern lands have fallen to the *marandaal,* and surely more of the creatures will soon arrive and press on towards Harn. The *marandaal* can use and manipulate

Gates. As Nia said, this child somehow senses when and where new Gates are about to appear. In other words, she can foretell the coming into existence of Gates, and therefore the movements of the *marandaal*."

As everyone gathered nearby tried to comprehend those words, Kelandra said to Nia, "Did she really find you in your dreams, Nia?"

"Yes," Nia spat. "And may she find *you* in yours."

"That would be impossible." Kelandra shook her head. "Watchers do not dream."

Nia spoke up again, softly so that only Anlerran could hear her properly. "Will someone watch over me? When Yui finds her way back into my head?" She laughed bitterly. "Listen to me, Anlerran. I already sound like a madwoman. Well, that's nothing to how I'll be when she breaks into my dreams again, more vengeful than ever."

"We will look after you," Anlerran assured her. She almost put an arm around the girl but hesitated at the last moment, thinking that Nia would react badly to such familiarity. "Surely powers exist that can protect against even such sorcery as hers. We may even be able to communicate with the child."

"I think that would be a bad idea," Nia said faintly.

III

The following afternoon, as they drew near to Woods Ford a stiff breeze blew from out of the west and carried with it the sour, acrid stench of burning. A little later, as they neared a line of trees that stood no more than a stone's throw before them, great plumes of smoke rose into the air from beyond.

Anlerran regarded the billowing smoke with dismay as mutters of consternation rose all around. *Might the whole of Woods Ford be on fire?* she asked herself, wondering who or what could have been behind such evil.

Or it might be the result of an accident, she tried to tell herself. *Someone knocked over a lantern, or a hay barn has burned down. Still, it doesn't necessarily take even a small army to burn a town if those involved know what they are doing and place small fires here and there, intending for them to grow quickly out of control.*

Ruhal looked across at her. "Do you sense anything of the Old Dark?"

Anlerran shrugged wearily. She felt uncomfortable and saddle-sore, and she wasn't at all certain she could concentrate enough to detect malign Powers even from a closer distance.

"If you do sense them..."

She nodded. "I know."

They made their way slowly between the trees and into the open land beyond. Woods Ford was a close-built settlement of ramshackle cottages and huts in the lower area, and stone buildings built upon the slightly higher ground to the north-west. A river ran through the place, but the companions could see no one fetching water from it to put out the dozen or so fires that had all but destroyed the town.

"If there were any survivors, they have fled," Elluron spoke up suddenly, "and the only creatures left here are lower *kin,* who have started these fires." He pointed to a large central pyre. Through the flames, piles of white bone and scorched flesh could be seen. "The unlucky ones already burn."

Along with the acrid odour of the smoke Anlerran suddenly detected something else that assailed all her senses at once. On an impulse she looked across at Kian, and knew from the look in the *du-luyan* girl's eyes that she felt that same sensation.

She knew instinctively the nature of the lower *kin*—lesser minions of the Old Dark, heterogeneous creatures that adopted various horrific forms. She hated them more than she feared them, but to ordinary folk they must be nightmares that had forced their way into the living world. She closed her eyes for a moment, wondering what it must have been like for the men, women and children of Woods Ford to have witnessed this onslaught of terror on their homes.

Elluron urged his horse onwards a little way along a track that led towards a wooden bridge arcing over the river. Anlerran followed him, and after a moment Kian did the same, followed in turn by Iyoth. Anlerran vaguely heard Ruhal calling out to her but he sounded faint and distant, and soon all the sounds of her companions faded behind her, replaced by the noise of the *kin-* scuttling, clicking, slithering and thumping, and occasionally words, none of which she could understand. But still she could not see them amidst the chaos they had created.

As they drew nearer still to the burning village, Anlerran's sense of the *kin* became stronger still, and for a moment her confidence faltered. Could they destroy so many? There might be hundreds here, thousands even.

Then she caught sight of at least a dozen, inching their way out of dwellings, taverns, grain houses and shops. Not one of them looked the same as any other. Some had body parts of various well-known creatures, but others were dreadful amalgamations comprised of a dozen or more disparate fragments, and a few defied any description.

"Over the bridge," Elluron said. Turning round, he saw Iyoth for the first time. "Your weapons can do little good here."

"My place is with Kian," Iyoth retorted, "just as yours is with Anlerran."

Kian looked dismayed, but rather than argue she simply said nothing as Elluron dismounted and tethered his horse to one of the trees at the edge of the woodland. "Riding against them will be impossible," he said by way of explanation, and after the others had left their horses behind they set off towards the bridge.

By the time they were halfway across the bridge many more of the *kin* could be seen. They emerged from the buildings they had ransacked, some of them glistening with the blood of those they had killed. Some of them appeared to be swaying amongst the flames as if compelled by a higher power, or performing some obscene rite. *Powers, there are hundreds,* Anlerran thought. Aloud she said, "We can't destroy them all."

"We've no choice," Kian pointed out. "They've seen us."

As if Kian's words had goaded them, the *kin* rushed eagerly forwards in a wave of indescribable, seething chaos.

Time slowed and became a blur of sound and fury. Anlerran lashed out with an almost overwhelming rage. The closest of the creatures rushed at her, clicking and scrabbling, a multitude of needle teeth snapping in the cold air. They died, crushed from the inside out. *I know you,* she thought madly. *I know you all, no matter what shape you take. I can reach within and crush the life from you.*

Some burst into flames; others simply fell and died despite bearing no obvious wounds. Some tried to flee back across the bridge, or through the river. But Anlerran saw from the corner of her eye that those *kin* who fled ran into three *orkar* wielding huge iron weapons, and many met their demise at their hands. Anlerran was dimly aware that some form of sorcery entwined itself about the *orkar* weaponry. Despite the great weight of their weapons the *orkar* moved swiftly. Often they appeared to be little more than a blur as they left devastation in their wake, sending pieces of the desperate *kin* flying into the river or through the air, so that everywhere about them the gore of their enemies rained down.

Despite this, the four of them found themselves pushed back towards and then onto the bridge. "We can't win this!" Anlerran heard Kian shriek, even as she crushed the skull of a many-clawed creature that came snapping at her.

Before long they had been pushed back over the bridge. Elluron shouted something that almost sent Anlerran and the others reeling back onto the ground, and he stretched out a shaking arm towards the bridge. A moment later the spans and legs of the structure split apart and sent a great mass of the *kin* tumbling down fifty hands into the river.

Elluron gasped suddenly and staggered to the ground, and Anlerran almost did the same, feeling a measure of his weakness. *What now?* she thought as her sense of the *kin* suddenly snapped. *Is the river strong enough to drown them or carry them away?*

It was not. Most of the *kin* could swim, and they made their way towards the river bank in their dozens.

She then watched open-mouthed as one of the *orkar* warriors, badly wounded but able to walk, staggered to the water's edge and threw a vast two-handed sword into the river. *Has he lost his mind?* Anlerran wondered, and then her eyes widened in astonishment as steam began to rise from the waters.

A great keening sound came from the river and rose in pitch as the water began to seethe. The *kin* were being boiled alive. The few that managed to struggle to the shore were dispatched with ease, most of them by the *orkar*.

"It's done, Kian," she said, barely able to speak. "It's done."

She turned to look at her companion when she didn't reply. Kian knelt with head bowed forward, sobbing by Iyoth's still body.

From their vantage point on the terrace of an abandoned storehouse at the distant end of the smouldering village,

Ferrin and Ithia had watched the battle, the bloodshed and the eventual demise of the lower *kin* that had been sent to raze Woods Ford.

"Interesting," Ferrin said eventually. "Who would have thought that *orkar* beasts would not only have the ability to steal a measure of the Old Powers for themselves, but keep it hidden until now?"

"A large measure at that," Ithia commented, and Ferrin silently agreed, recalling the transformation of the river from languid flow to boiling mass. *We need to capture and study them given a chance,* he mused. *I haven't seen the Powers used quite like that before.*

"What do you think they'll do now?" Ithia asked.

"Who knows? Their little army contains such opposing elements. It's a mystery to me how they've remained as one for so long. I suspect they'll rest and head back to Darkbrook." Ferrin observed the smoking ruin of Woods Ford with satisfaction. "This place has been given utterly to our lords as commanded. There is nothing they can save. The bodies have been burned, the rites performed."

"They may try anyway. Folk like that always do," Ithia sighed. "What should we do about them? They use the Powers wildly. How much longer can they be allowed this rebellion?"

"That, my crimson beauty, is for our Lords to determine." Ferrin yawned and stretched. "We'll head back to the camp for now, and then south. Perhaps to join with Inerdyr's force. That would be interesting."

They headed back up through the scrubland towards their camp, treading through freshly-fallen snow. Ferrin still found himself amused at how Ithia's steps melted the snow all around wherever she walked. "I would rather we forged our own path, if our Lords permit it," Ithia ventured after a while, as they pushed through bracken and bramble.

"There is only one true cause- why not one true army?" Ferrin countered.

"Inerdyr is not *kin*."

"The crows tell me otherwise," Ferrin said. Ithia was so shocked that she almost stumbled. When she had righted herself she stared at him in astonishment. "Are you certain?"

"I am. The mad wizard of Mornkastle has bowed his head and taken the ceremony, forsaking his misjudged pride. Either that or it has been forced upon him. Now he sees as we see, Ithia. Now the detail and the wonder open up before him. How much use that is to a madman, I don't know. But that's not our judgement to make."

As they pressed on towards their camp, Ithia wondered if it might have been better to simply have Inerdyr slain and a leader chosen from amongst the higher *kin* to take his place. True, Inerdyr held influence with the folk of the middle north- they either respected or feared him, but...

She almost felt cold, as they walked on under the grey sky.

XII - Bones for the Battlefield

I

Do you remember the Stillwater?

That faint whisper and the caress of his master turned Inerdyr's blood to a seething chaos. He sat up in the stink and gloom of his bedchamber, head uplifted so his eyes stared directly at the ceiling where a faint shimmering betrayed the presence of the *choragh*.

You were young then, newly given to us. Even so, you knew of your own sterility.

Cold hatred cut through him as he recalled. "They had to die!" he whispered savagely. "I was the only one born strong in the Powers in that entire century! That other men should father children but I- *I,* who could turn them to smoking ruins, even if they had no talent themselves- could not!"

You will return to the Stillwater.

When he failed to respond a finger of darkness cut into his side and Inerdyr felt a multitude of scrabbling digits spawned from their single parent, sliding over and through his innards. Yet not a single drop of his dark *kin* blood was spilled. The touch of the *choragh* reached his heart in a moment, and tendrils of primordial force cupped that pulsing organ in the darkness of its cavity.

Even now you retain some of your weak, human emotions and urges. That displeases us.

Inerdyr shuddered as the grip around his heart tightened ever so slightly. "I exist only to serve you," he managed to say eventually. To his ears, the words sounded thin and pitiful.

Summon as many people of these villages as possible. Anyone who can walk. Take an army to engage the wildlings. Ensure that those strongest in the Powers are with you. When you prepare to do battle, call to us and we shall appear. Through us, the Powers that pass through you shall be multiplied many times. Stand at the summit of the highest hill and send the masses into battle.

Inerdyr did not remember closing his eyes, but when he opened them his lord had gone. He shook and his lips moved wordlessly. But his eyes held something terrible; a recollection of the great revenge he had wrought long ago in Stillwater. Centuries had passed and yet a whisper from the *choragh* had brought back that memory in potent detail. He could even hear the anguished weeping of mothers whose babes had died in the seclusion of their wombs.

Inerdyr smiled. Stillwater. It made sense, not only because of the history of the place but because of the sacrifices to his lords that would be made there when battle was joined. In fact, the peasants were not even foot soldiers; they were there to die- either during the march or during the battle, and for their blood to leak into the cold earth, strengthening the power of the *choragh*.

He had Ayvin and his officers bring anyone who could fight from the outlying villages, while Serith marshalled the people of the castle. Within three days the camp that his men had set up next to the castle numbered five thousand, and Inerdyr judged that they could recruit others from the settlements they passed as they headed north.

"The aim is to crush them quickly and absolutely," he told Ayvin as they watched the marching preparations from one of the west-facing towers. "Did Jaana discover anyone else strong in the Powers, in the villages?"

"Two more," Ayvin said, "but neither as strong as Parril, she says."

"No matter." A smile played on Inerdyr's lips. "Soon we'll have everything we need."

Ayvin hurried away from his meeting with the sorcerer, glad to immerse himself in overseeing the preparations being made for the march north. He had never enjoyed Inerdyr's company but over the last few days he had found an irrational fear rising within him whenever he had to endure a meeting or briefing with the master of the castle. To a lesser extent he felt a similar feeling, when he rode out with Jaana. That frustrated him immensely; Jaana might be strong in the Powers but surely she was no threat to him. She was just a woman, a Hastian refugee, cold and withdrawn. But in recent days she had developed a quiet arrogance that made him oddly uneasy. Ayvin felt sure that she somehow mocked him when she spoke, although he could not say why. She brought her *luyan* girl-friend whenever they went from settlement to settlement, although Lyya looked perpetually downcast as if she accompanied Jaana only because she felt the alternative would be worse. *If I was Lyya I'd return to my own people,* Ayvin had thought more than once. *There's nothing for her here.*

As he listened to his officers report on the levels of food, clothing and weaponry around the camp, Ayvin found himself pondering the matter of Ileana's disappearance. Once it became obvious that neither the girl nor her friends were anywhere in the castle, Inerdyr had summoned three of the servants charged with tending their rooms, and had them beaten so badly that even their own families would no longer recognise them. Two would never walk again, and the third would never again be able to speak or even feed herself. Ayvin had seen no reason for the punishments, nor could he understand the reasoning behind allowing the servants to live after such severe beatings- after all, they were useless now. But he had always known better than to question Inerdyr on matters of punishment or indeed anything else.

"We don't need these peasants. What use will they be?"

Startled, he cursed and looked round to see Jaana scowling as she observed the comings and goings of the camp. *How did she creep up on me?* he wondered. Aloud he said, "That isn't my decision to make, Jaana, nor is it yours. Did you want something? I'm busy. We march at first light tomorrow."

The witch either ignored him or perhaps didn't even hear what he said. "Look at them," she continued. "They mingle idly because they have no idea what to do. They squat and defecate wherever they find a patch of grass. Many of them don't have the clothing for a winter march. Most have poor weapons if they have any at all. Half of these people will be dead by the time we reach Stillwater, from diseases and frostbite."

Ayvin silently agreed with her, but instead he found himself replying, "Thank you for your expertise, Jaana. Perhaps Inerdyr will make you commander in chief."

She gave him a contemptuous look and wandered away. *I should have held my tongue,* Ayvin thought angrily. *She's unpredictable. Who's to say she won't think on that idea and even approach Inerdyr, asking for that position? And who's to say that he in his madness won't give her that responsibility?*

He listened distractedly to the reports of his men, all the while wishing that he had had his way and Inerdyr had given him permission to raise a smaller army, made only from the castle and district militias. *A smaller army, of trained and motivated men,* he reminded himself. *Not a vast rabble of peasant folk with their women and children in tow. From everything we've heard, Ruhal Dalmorn's army is nothing more than a few mercenaries, renegade Watchers and maybe a few hundred orkar. We don't need a huge, unwieldy hammer to smash a small nut.*

Day wore on into night, and the following morning the rabble headed north, flanked by the better-armed militia. Ayvin rode in silence, trying to ignore the occasional mad, dangerous thoughts he had of turning and riding headlong the other way for as far as his horse would carry him.

II

Lyya would have understood some of Ayvin's thoughts. Her instincts continually implored her to flee if ever the chance presented itself, but she'd sworn not to abandon Jaana. Jaana had no other friends. She was surrounded by enemies, even in this army of which she had become such an important part.

I can't leave her. I won't leave her.

As befitted her station, Jaana had a well-made canvas tent to keep out the chill at night. At Inerdyr's command, several of the castle men helped set it up each evening. Lyya was glad enough of the warmth, but found herself thinking of those people who had only fires and blankets to keep the cold at bay. When she hesitantly mentioned this, Jaana pointed out, "Would you have us shivering through the night? Even if you did, still there would be thousands suffering." In a lower voice she added, "Between the two of us, I don't agree with these folk from the settlements being a part of this. But focus on the task at hand. We'll quell the rebellion in the north and we'll have the heads of the traitors. Any means to the end."

Lyya had neither the inclination nor the energy to argue with her. Each night she lay down with the single wish that sleep would come quickly. But when eventually it did her slumber was restless and often interrupted by one commotion or another somewhere out in the camp. On the second night it was especially bad. Lyya listened to the sounds of screaming and weeping, and at one point peered outside. Somewhere out in the dark she saw several people being pinned down by others, struggling and shouting what sounded like nonsense.

269

"Lightdreamers," Jaana murmured behind her. "Inerdyr wanted every able-bodied man, woman and child for the march. Lightdreamers often remain able-bodied even as their minds fall apart." With that she turned over, pulled her blankets closer and went back to sleep.

Lyya watched as two of the people were led away. Two others remained where they were. She saw someone raise a large stone to bring it down on one of their heads, and quickly looked away and retreated to her blankets. She shuddered and closed her eyes as she heard the sound of a skull being crushed.

Before the march began for the day the following morning, Jaana went to meet with Inerdyr, Ayvin and Serith. Lyya sat on a boulder watching the bustle and activity, and looked up as Fauli approached. She was a little surprised; the *du-luyan* woman had barely been seen at all since they left Inerdyr's castle. It occurred to Lyya that she had perhaps waited until Jaana had gone elsewhere before approaching.

Fauli sat next to her and remarked, "Where do you think they went?"

Lyya didn't know what she meant at first. "Oh, Ileana and her friends? Who knows? But good luck to them. Wherever they escaped to, surely it's better than this. For Ileana, certainly."

"Even if they had somehow escaped the castle by getting through the gates or over the walls, they would have been quickly found," Fauli reasoned. "Hunting dogs would have been sent after them. You must have heard the dogs at the castle."

"I heard them most nights. Now my sleep is interrupted by other things."

"So they must be still hiding somewhere deep within the castle. That's my guess." Fauli sighed. "Anyway, I thought it would be polite to bid farewell. We have, after all, been companions for what seems an age."

Lyya had the good sense to look around before speaking, and to be just as quiet when she answered. "You're leaving?"

"There's nothing here for me," Fauli said with a shrug. "And there's something evil working its way through this ragtag army. Don't tell me that you can't sense it yourself. The Old Dark, or the madness of these lightdreamers, or both... I don't know what it is, but I want to be away from here. I'd suggest that you come with me, but you've made up your mind to stay with Jaana, haven't you?"

When Lyya nodded reluctantly, Fauli extended her hand in farewell. "I'll wish you the best of luck then, although I fear your compassion will be your undoing."

Lyya shook hands with her and even smiled for a moment. "I will at least miss your blunt honesty, Fauli. Take care of yourself."

She watched as Fauli made her way through the encampment until she was out of sight. Long after that, however, her companion's words remained lodged in her thoughts. *I fear your compassion will be your undoing.*

Lyya found herself praying to all the old *luyan* gods that Fauli was wrong.

Fauli found it easy enough to leave the sprawling encampment. It was large and not especially well organised, and parts of it were poorly guarded. She walked away to the west, and quickened her pace further once she was out of sight.

She headed down a hill of scrub and bracken that led into a wooded valley. As she hastened along she wondered what Lyya's eventual fate might be. Fauli had grown to tolerate her over the time they had spent together. She even grudgingly admitted to herself that she didn't *entirely* dislike her. But she certainly couldn't respect her. Lyya was a poor judge of character and even now, after Jaana had become Inerdyr's most favoured and more than likely one of the *kin,* still she clung to the vain hope that she might somehow make Jaana see what she had done to herself. Fauli had realised days ago that the woman was beyond such redemption.

Leaving them had nevertheless been less easy than she expected. Lyya- and Jaana, for that matter- had been the only companions she had left. Now she was all alone in the world. She had no family, and all her friends and comrades were either dead, or vanished without trace, or had chosen a path that could lead only to their destruction.

"So be it," Fauli said to herself, speaking in the language of her own people. The words sounded strange to her, almost unfamiliar. A long time had passed since she had spoken with any other *du-luyan*. She had seen a small number of them in Inerdyr's army but noticed that they carried the banner of Wistledge. They would have given her a cold shoulder at best, so she had stayed out of their way.

Shivering in the chilly breeze, Fauli drew her cloak more tightly about herself and hurried towards the shadows of the woods. Dry scrub and dead bracken crunched under her boots. Milky sunlight seeped through the cover of grey cloud just as she reached the cover of the trees.

A sudden, dismal thought made her stop briefly. She was on her own, as the world slowly but surely descended into chaos. What, then, was the point in persisting?

After a while she trudged on, but the grim question would not leave her be. She was done with travel and adventure. She had nothing and no one. Where would she go, and what would she do to survive?

Fauli felt tears prickling her eyes. Angrily she swiped at them.

A figure loomed out of the undergrowth up ahead. Instinctively Fauli drew her longknife, but when she saw the creature that approached she almost dropped the weapon.

The *diafagh*'s head turned crookedly so that it faced her. Its mouth opened and closed and something black and viscous escaped from the creature's bloated, rotting lips. One side of its head had been struck a powerful blow so that the skull had fallen partly away; the soft and putrid contents swarmed with a sea of maggots. The stench was overpowering even from a distance.

It got through the Border Wall, Fauli thought in despair. *The one that was meant for me.*

She had no further time to think. The *diafagh* came rushing at her.

Fauli side-stepped the creature's charge and sliced at its outstretched arm with her longknife. The weapon should have cut through bone and severed the limb with ease, but instead it cut less than halfway through the dead flesh. The *diafagh* gave no indication that the wound had hampered it at all. It turned and came for her again. Fauli swiftly moved to the other side and struck at the exposed remnants of the beast's brain, driving the blade deep into that writhing filth. It staggered, then turned and reached for her far more quickly than she thought possible. Moving back and then forward, Fauli attacked desperately, hacking at the *diafagh* and dancing swiftly away. But the creature's corrupted flesh was tough as leather wherever she struck it, and its endurance appeared boundless. Fauli grew increasingly tired, and the *diafagh* managed to cut her with its claws, drawing blood in several places.

Finally as it lunged at her, fetid jaws snapping less than a hand away, Fauli stumbled backwards over a fallen branch. She fell to the ground and the *diafagh* uttered a faint rasping and rustling noise as it leapt on her.

By now Fauli was too exhausted to even raise her longknife to try and summon a last defence. She closed her eyes, preferring to die in darkness rather than see the *diafagh* kill her. *What a stupid, pointless life,* she thought.

Just for an instant the air became much warmer, prickling her skin. Then a sound like a dull, wet explosion filled her ears, and a rain of rotten flesh and maggots fell upon her. Fauli screamed and opened her eyes, her arms flailing as she frantically wiped the foul gore from herself.

Someone came into view and stood over her. Fauli reached for her weapon, but froze, confused. She recognised him.

It was Parril, the boy who Jaana and Ayvin had taken from the village of North Vale.

III

"Don't send me back!" Parril warily stepped away from her. "Please!"

Fauli stared incredulously up at him. "Did you... did you just..."

"I killed it." Parril stared numbly at the ruins of the *diafagh*. "I didn't even know what I was doing. I just felt... I don't know, *angry*. Full of power. As if I somehow knew how it was made and how it could be unmade."

Fauli got shakily to her feet, trying to collect her thoughts. "You saved my life," she said finally. "I wouldn't send you back even if I could. Did you ever want to be part of all this madness?"

He shook his head solemnly.

"I thought not." Fauli threw a glance back in the direction they had walked. "How by all the Powers did you escape? Mostly they're a shambles, but surely they had you guarded the whole while?"

"I..." He paused and then continued reluctantly, "I confused them. I told them that I didn't need guarding because I was already so securely tied, and that they should join the drinking and carousing going on elsewhere."

"And were you securely tied?"

"No. But I gave them the suggestion that I was, and that was enough. It's something I've been able to do sometimes when I've needed to. I put on this spare cloak and drew the hood forward to cover my face. I suppose the rest

274

was just luck. They weren't guarding the edges of the camp very well. I suppose they felt they had nothing to fear."

With the Old Dark already running through that army there's plenty to fear, Fauli thought. She wiped her longknife in the long grass and flicked an errant maggot from her thigh. "They'll realise soon enough that you've gone. We need to be away from here and swiftly."

"If they find me with you, they'll kill you too," Parril warned. "Maybe I'd better go a different way."

Maybe you'd better, Fauli silently agreed, and she was about to suggest just that and wish him the best of luck in evading capture when she made the mistake of looking directly into his eyes where she saw such fear and misery that she could think of nothing at all to say for a moment.

He saved my life, she reminded herself. *He may well have destroyed the* diafagh *anyway if they crossed paths, but the fact remains. I can't abandon him. Perhaps helping the boy will bring about my demise in any case, but wasn't that something I expected and almost welcomed only a short while ago?*

She tried not to think about that. Amongst her people, to even contemplate self-murder was despicable.

"How old are you?" she asked abruptly.

"Thirteen next summer."

"So you're twelve? You'll stand no chance on your own. You'd better stay with me. My name is Fauli, by the way."

"If they find me..."

"We just have to make sure they don't," Fauli interrupted him.

The two of them hurried along, eventually finding a broader path that continued west through the woods. The day grew dim as they reached the edge of the trees and low, rolling hills rose in the distance. "We'll need shelter," Parril pointed out.

"*You* certainly will. Humans are not the hardiest of creatures." When he stared at her she added, "But they have their uses." She caught the odour of the *diafagh* again in the breeze and looked down at herself. "I doubt any farmer or smallholder would care to give us shelter. A *du-luyan* woman still dripping with gore, and a boy sorcerer on the run. How would you rate our chances, Parril?"

"I'm not a sorcerer," he said quietly. "It's just... when I saw that..." He shuddered at the memory.

"You are what you are, like it or not." Fauli looked into the gathering dusk and sighed. "We'll press on through the night if you're able." When Parril gave a weary moan she looked sharply at him. "Your enemies won't wait for the dawn."

"It'll be too dark with the cloudy sky," he persisted. "We won't have the moons to see by."

"When it becomes too dark for you to see further, hold my hand," Fauli told him. "On the darkest of nights I can see as clearly as if Ildar's full face shone down from a clear sky."

He looked doubtfully at her. "Most of my people have the same ability," she added. "Don't you know any stories about the *du-luyan*? Did you know, for example, that we kill and eat every second child we give birth to?" When his look turned to horror, Fauli sighed. "I was jesting, Parril," she said sadly as they set off again.

Wherever possible, Fauli led them along routes that would have been difficult for Inerdyr's men to follow on horseback- although she had no doubt that the sorcerer would send out runners as well. They crossed three wide but shallow and slow-moving rivers, moving downstream to a different extent each time while they crossed, and Fauli took the opportunity at the first river to stop so she could wash her clothes and body free of the *diafagh*'s stench. As she cleansed herself, naked in the icy water, she threw a glance back at Parril and smiled to herself. He was peering in her general direction but his gaze shifted continuously as he tried without success to make her out properly in the near pitch darkness. *Young boys are the same no matter their race,* Fauli reminded herself with a smile.

They rested infrequently and only for a short while each time. Occasionally, if the ground lay flat and featureless up ahead they would jog, at least until Parril begged to stop. Despite his protests, he proved himself to be fit and strong for a human, and blessed with endurance. "Every onward step lessens our chance of capture," she encouraged him, which was of course nonsense. Common sense, hiding their trail and pure luck were all that stood between them and Inerdyr's soldiers.

As dawn broke and Fauli allowed Parril to sleep for a short while, she reflected on the oddness of fate. She had been about to perhaps give up on everything, despite the instincts with which she had grown up. Then the *diafagh* had appeared as if to hurry her destiny along with a cruel, ironic twist. And then...

Fauli looked at the sleeping boy as he lay curled up on the ground in his stolen cloak. *I'll do what I can,* she thought. *I have to.*

But as if to make a mockery of such determination, the drumming of hooves sounded from the east.

Fauli reached over and shook Parril awake, pressing her finger to his lips when his eyes flickered open. She had no idea what to do, but as she stood up and looked around, she saw a lake several hundred paces away. An idea came to her. *Nowhere to hide but underwater. But with my help we can do just that.*

She led him swiftly to the lake shore. "Either you trust me or they capture you," she said when he hesitated, and that was enough for him to make his mind up. They waded into the icy water until it came chest-high to them.

Fauli grabbed Parril by the shoulders as he shivered violently. "Whatever you do," she said quickly, *"don't panic."*

She kissed him full on the lips, opening his mouth with her hand. Then she pulled him under the water with her.

Fauli breathed into him, waiting for him to breathe back. After panicking for a short while he relaxed.

She reckoned that the horsemen had been perhaps a thousand paces away when she first heard them. She had no idea if they would pause at the lake or not, but factored in that possibility as she counted steadily.

Then she almost lost count completely.

Somewhere in the icy murk behind Parril she caught sight of a faint, pulsing glow, like the sun through thick mist. It floated somewhere in the distance but she couldn't tell how far away it was. It intensified and then faded slowly until it could no longer be seen at all. *A trick of the eye,* Fauli tried to tell herself as she continued breathing and counting.

Finally, she guessed that the horsemen had more than likely passed by. In any case she could not hold her breath for much longer- certainly not for both of them.

When she hauled Parril to the surface, she could still hear the thundering of hooves, but the sound faded swiftly. Fauli helped Parril wade out of the lake and then went over to inspect the hoof prints. The riders hadn't stopped at the lake. They had headed roughly north-west across the flatter grassland between the hills.

Parril could barely speak for shivering but still managed, "H... how... how did..."

"Another *du-luyan* talent," she told him. "And now we really do need to find a welcoming homestead and a fire."

They found no welcoming homestead, nor did Fauli expect them to. Despite the risks of the smoke alerting their enemies to where they were, after a short while she took the sealed tin of firepowder from her still-soaking pack and eventually managed to start a small fire. They huddled nearby to dry off, and eventually Parril stopped shivering. Once her cloak had dried she draped it over him.

"Yours is an interesting name," she commented a little later. "There was a famous man by the name of Parril in the First Age. One of the heroes of that time, you might say. He played a part in vanquishing the *choragh* and helped build the ancient fortress of Mirkwall in Aphenhast."

"I've never heard of Mirkwall," Parril said with a tired shrug.

"I'd be surprised if you'd heard of Mornkastle," Fauli retorted. She fell silent for a moment, recalling the legend. "One of the great leaders amongst the Younger Races, a *du-luyan* woman Eluren took him as her husband. Even then, it was considered a little unusual. Now it's almost unheard of."

"Did they have any children?" Parril asked.

"I believe they did, but the bloodline didn't continue after that. The offspring of humans and *du-luyan-* or humans and *luyan* for that matter- are always infertile. The seed of the men is dead and useless and in any case no infants can form in the wombs of the women."

"That's sad."

"It's the way things are, neither more nor less."

IV

They set off later that morning, continuing west through low wooded land, skirting around marshes and hills. Fauli noticed that many of the farm tracks and paths were well-worn and muddy and covered in dozens of boot prints, so judged that their own would soon become lost amongst them. *But if we see any folk before they see us we'll avoid them,* she reminded herself.

One such path led them towards a sprawling village of huts and a few surrounding farms and mills. Fauli suggested they head a little north through a thick woodland instead.

After a while spent walking along a narrow, partly overgrown path they saw that the trees cleared up ahead, revealing the edge of a marsh. "We need to head north for a little while," Fauli said. "We'll have to ascend. Stop complaining," she added sharply when Parril sighed and muttered something under his breath.

A moment later however, he pointed across to the edge of the woods where the treeline met the water's edge and murmured, "Look."

Fauli peered through the foliage and saw perhaps a dozen ragged-looking figures gathered near the shallows. Something about their spasmodic movements struck her as horribly familiar, and when she heard their babbling voices raised suddenly she knew what they were. "Lightdreamers," she said flatly. "You must have seen others like them before. Probably harmless enough to us, but best avoided. No sense in making ourselves known if we don't have to."

She walked on a few steps, then turned and frowned when she saw Parril still transfixed by the sight. "Come on!" she hissed.

"They're about to do something." Parril's voice shook a little. "Something terrible."

She walked back to him and grabbed his arm. "Listen to me. They are the mad folk who dream of the *marandaal,* who are possibly even affected by them, possessed by them. Do you not know that? They are to be avoided. They are sick, and nothing can be done for them. Do you understand?"

Parril wrenched his arm free and glared at her. "I know about lightdreamers, Fauli. But we need to see what they're doing."

He set off slowly towards the woodland's edge. Fauli ground her teeth in frustration and considered quickly knocking him unconscious. *They're all trouble,* she fumed, not sure whether she meant humans or boys. After a moment she walked after him as quietly as possible.

As they hid behind a thick oak tree and looked more closely at the lightdreamers, Fauli noticed that the air here was much warmer. It felt more like late summer than winter, and the breeze had died down completely. All they could hear now were the faint babblings of the lightdreamers as they clasped hands to form a circle. One of them, a boy not much older than Parril bobbed his head backwards and forwards continuously. A thin trickle of blood dripped from his ear. Next to him, an old woman dressed only in a thin damp robe growled softly to herself.

"Parril," Fauli whispered in her companion's ear. "Let's be gone from here." The oddly warm air was making her itch and sweat, and she had to fight the urge to run away as fast as she could. She recalled how the air had also felt warm and somehow *thicker* when Parril had rescued her, but felt certain that this had nothing to do with him.

An odd humming started up. Fauli couldn't be certain where it came from- the circle of lightdreamers, somewhere in the middle of them or somewhere out in the drifting mists of the marshland. Then she felt a rippling sensation over her skin. Parril gasped and shivered. "They're trying to evoke something," he whispered. "All these people must have had some ability in the Powers, but..."

They're lightdreamers, so perhaps their innate powers were buried or couldn't be detected, Fauli thought. Her mind raced. *What are they doing?*

Something she remembered Vornen saying one time came back to her. His description of the mayhem at Ethanalin Tur-morn, the air, the invisible currents of force pulling at the body...

"No," she breathed. "That can't be possible..."

These people were just mad fools. Had their innate powers suddenly been awakened? Were they truly powerful enough to create a Gate between them? Or was some hidden power doing it through them somehow?

Parril turned to her. "We have to stop them," he murmured. Fauli nodded but found herself looking at them all. She noticed that a few were even younger than Parril. *What if I'm wrong?* she thought desperately.

The humming grew louder. Fauli wiped sweat from her brow and scratched at herself. She glanced at Parril and saw that his eyes appeared darker than before. Tiny dark fragments moved around his pupils. For a moment she thought she could see a faint shimmering around his hands.

Without another word the two of them stepped from behind the tree and walked towards the lightdreamers.

XIII - Severed

I

Caul sat and listened to the rhythm of the rain as it pattered incessantly on the leaves. He had drawn his cloak tightly about himself but nothing could stop the chill from sinking in.

Arian sat just as quietly nearby, but even through his despair Caul knew that hers was a different silence. Whereas he could find no reason to hope, she would be planning how the two of them could fight back against the destruction of all Cai's people. He could have told Arian that it was a futile cause, but that would have infuriated her. They had known each other since they were both young children, and he knew that she would fight until her final breath. *The woman's insane,* he told himself, but he nevertheless admired her for that iron determination, no matter how misguided it might be.

Her deep orange eyes stared straight ahead, probably visualising some improbable victory. Her long hair hung partly over her face, divided into a multitude of intricate braids. Her jet black skin gleamed in the faint light. The situation could hardly have been more desperate and yet she stonily refused to be anything other than a warrior-sorcerer in the making- Merithen's prodigy but in truth more powerful than Merithen had ever been.

No, he thought, feeling a twinge of sadness. *As I've long known, it's something far more than admiration, not that she...*

"Why are you staring at me, Caul?"

He almost jumped. "I just wondered what you were thinking, that's all."

283

"I was considering our options," she said, confirming his suspicions. Then she added, "But the truth is I have no idea what to do. Have you?"

He shook his head in frustration. "No. I think all we can do for the moment is try to survive, and band together with others from Cai if we can find them..."

"No," Arian said quietly.

"Why not?" he demanded, perplexed.

"Because the *kin* mean to hunt us down to extinction, or subvert those who they can," she reasoned. "Those who surrender will become like them. The more of us who exist in one place, the easier it will be for them to annihilate us. There aren't enough of us to make a force to be reckoned with."

Caul sighed. "Then what? We all live as refugees wandering the land, scavengers until the end of our days? What kind of existence is that?"

"We'll find a way," she said stubbornly.

But Caul could not shake off his own fears. "What if the two of us are the only ones left?"

"I would think that quite unlikely, Caul."

"But supposing that we are?"

"Then we find the safest place we can, wherever that may be," she said, and turned to look at him. "And in time, we raise a family."

He swallowed, dumbfounded. "You and I?"

Arian frowned. "Who else, if we were the only two *du-luyan* who remained in all Aona other than those who became *kin*?"

He nodded, feeling a heavy weight inside him. *I should have understood,* he told himself. *Arian has always been relentlessly practical.* "Of course. It makes sense."

"But I hardly think it will come to that," Arian continued. "We are a resourceful people. Others will have survived and they will be thinking along the same lines. A way must exist to defeat the *kin*, and we'll find it."

Caul wanted to believe her, but couldn't.

"We should sleep," Arian said abruptly. "Will you take first watch?"

She sat back and bowed her head without waiting for a reply. Caul shivered and listened to the rain fall. He found his thoughts drifting and imagined what it might be like if he and Arian really were the last two of their kind left in all Aona. He could not help but picture it vividly in his mind.

So lost in thought did he become that Caul only heard the *luyan* bowmen when they stepped as one from their hiding places, arrows levelled at himself and Arian. Almost without thinking he shook her awake. He could not look at her as a moment later she cursed and said bitterly to him, "Well done, Caul. I asked one thing only of you."

One of the *luyan* stepped closer. A well-built man with deep violet eyes, he stared from Caul to Arian and back again. Long strands of transparent hair reached down as far as his waist where a belt of hunting knives, each one a slightly different shape to its companions had been fastened. Caul reached instinctively for the Powers, but they would not stir. *These people are not* kin, he reasoned. *But they may yet be agents of the Old Dark, and even if they're not they may decide to kill us anyway. There's no love lost between our peoples.*

The *luyan* man addressed him, speaking the trading language. "With whom does your allegiance lie? Speak truthfully."

Caul blinked. "Allegiance? I'm not sure what you mean. I have... we have no allegiance except to our people."

The bowman scowled. His sharp nails tapped against the metal studs of his belt, mirroring his evident irritation. "Where are you from? Your accent is strange."

"Cai, in Aphenhast," Caul said. The man who had spoken regarded him coolly, and a woman nearby muttered something under her breath. Finally the man addressed two of his nearest comrades. "Tie their hands and feet securely. We will place them in one of the wagons."

Caul sensed Arian readying herself to fight. He turned swiftly to her as the two *luyan* men approached. *"Don't,"* he hissed, fearing that she would ignore him. But she relaxed with an effort, her expression one of cold and stony anger as she reluctantly allowed herself to be tied with rope.

They were dragged to the edge of the woods where a train of wagons and horses waited along with another two dozen *luyan*. Caul and Arian listened to the discussion that commenced, but their captors now spoke in their own language so neither of them could make out more than a few words here and there. They were hauled into one the few wagons with enough space for two captives, and a short while later the small *luyan* army set off.

For much of the day the wagon rolled along a muddy track as they headed east, often shaking and rolling from side to side. On one occasion it very nearly tipped over on its side. Arian and Caul did their best to sit upright, which was far from easy with their arms and legs tied together.

"What do you think they'll do with us?" Caul ventured finally, having judged that Arian's fury had subsided enough for them to at least converse.

She shrugged. "Enslave us, perhaps."

He shook his head. "The *luyan* don't take slaves, Arian. They never have."

"No, and *du-luyan* have never been *kin,* have they?"

They fell silent for a while and listened despondently to the thump and groan of the wheels and the steady drumming of fat raindrops on the wagon roof. Caul stared out of the little window at the passing countryside. From time to time he caught sight of travellers in the distance, many of them in long, strung-out lines as the less able amongst them fell behind. Some groups headed east, others west. Caul's sharp sight identified most of them as humans. As the day wore on he observed that somewhat fewer folk were headed east, but of those that did at least half had something strange about the way they walked, the way their heads moved- their entire manner. He couldn't figure out why but the sight of those folk made him uneasy.

The wagon stopped briefly late in the afternoon and the *luyan* huntsman who had spoken to them earlier got in. "Greetings, dark cousins," he said. His smile did not waver even when Arian spat at him. "My name is Torral." He looked Arian up and down. To Caul it looked as if he was undressing her in his mind, and he quickly spoke up to distract the man. "What do you want with us?"

Torral sat on one of the boxes and unfurled a detailed map that he had brought out from the inside pocket of his cloak. "You say you came from Cai, in Aphenhast. That would be a long way." He traced a slender finger all the way from the far eastern edge of the map, to its western edge where the Wistledge had been drawn. "A *very* long way."

"We fled the *kin* and waited in the Silver Road," Caul found himself saying. "From there, eventually we reached the Wistledge. But the *du-luyan* of the Wistledge, at least those we encountered, had been..." He stopped, aware that he had in all likelihood said far too much already. Arian cursed under her breath and threw him a furious look.

Torral peered thoughtfully at him, then smiled. "Sorcery of some considerable power must have been brought to bear. And the look in your eyes betrays you, I'm afraid. Two *du-luyan* sorcerers have found their way into my grasp."

"We are only two," Arian spoke up. "There are others, and if they find you..."

"If *we* find more of your people skilled in the Powers, then we will count ourselves fortunate indeed. There are no *kin* here. None of us were fashioned by the *choragh* or have the Old Dark hissing in our veins. And if either of you were strong enough to use the Powers against ordinary folk, you'd have done so already. Nonetheless, the two of you may be most useful in the war to come, against the starspawn. The *marandaal*."

"Where are you taking us?" Caul asked.

"A castle just to the north of the city of Mornkastle. Others like yourselves have already been taken there. As luck had it, we were headed there regardless, but now we have two more good reasons for hastening."

"So we remain your captives?"

"No." Torral folded the map abruptly. His smile had vanished. "Not mine."

II

So many days passed that they became almost routine. The only event of note occurred when a small group of humans approached and begged to be taken east under their protection. They were a desperate-looking lot and in poor health. Two of them didn't even sound and look like sane people at all. Torral's men sent them all away.

Caul and Arian were given adequate food and water once a day, and twice a day, whenever the wagon train stopped they were allowed outside to pass water or defecate if they needed to. Their *luyan* captors remained cautious; Caul reckoned that they appeared more nervous than before. Perhaps Torral had spread word of their talents around the camp.

But as he said himself they're of little use against these people, Caul reasoned. *Oh, I might be able to cause some sort of disturbance, but as soon as I did I'd be full of arrows.*

He wondered which lord of these lands they were to be handed over to. Both he and Arian had demanded that Torral tell them, but he wouldn't and neither would any of his followers. *And then what? Are we to be forced to turn our powers towards the starspawn? From the little I remember hearing of them, it would take far greater powers than we can bring to bear.*

The nights were uncomfortable and restless, not only for himself and Arian but apparently for the *luyan* as well. Camping under the stars was second nature to their kind, but from what he could tell by peering through the window of the wagon and the odd visit outside to relieve himself, the onset of dusk made them uneasy. *Perhaps they too have encountered the* kin *during their recent travels,* Caul mused. Every time a creature out in the wilderness made a sound loud enough to reach them, many of the *luyan* would flinch and a few would even draw their weapons. *Brave warriors all,* he silently scoffed, but their reactions made him almost as ill at ease.

Perhaps eight or nine days after their capture, the wagon train drew to a halt and a short while later Torral opened their door to proclaim that their journey was at an end. "Yours, at least," he added for good measure as two of his men hauled Arian and Caul out.

A great castle stood before them, surrounded by high, grey stone walls and an ornate gateway at which the first of the wagons and horses waited. But from the muttering of voices amongst the *luyan* men and women, it appeared that all was not well. Many of them were talking in groups, some of them animatedly. Caul tried to listen to what they were saying, but he could only understand a few of the words. Arian murmured in their own language, "Wouldn't you expect a place like this to have guards at the gates? But there are none that I can see. In fact the gates lie open, yet we're waiting outside them."

"It feels too quiet," Caul said uneasily, wondering if the entire castle had been abandoned. Squinting in the bright, low winter sun he stared at the vast structure. As he found his gaze drawn to the high towers he listened intently.

Meanwhile Torral also listened and watched, taking time to look in each direction. Caul suspected that those eyes missed very little. Finally the *luyan* leader nodded. "You may be right. In fact, I suspect your talents may be of use here. I will send a half-dozen of my people with the two of you into the castle to determine the nature of this... silence."

"At least cut us free," Arian said, holding out her arms. "We'll be of no use bound." That statement was not true of course, but Torral appeared to have forgotten the fact.

He sliced their bonds with one of his shorter knives while a dozen or more *luyan* watched cautiously nearby. "A word of warning," Torral spoke up, looking meaningfully at Arian. "Please don't decide that two against six makes for good odds. Against *luyan* fighters it does not."

Arian merely stared back as if she might go for him there and then, and to all seven hells with the odds.

Accompanied by six *luyan,* Caul and Arian made their way through the gateway and into the empty courtyard beyond. Arian stopped and looked at the great stone ramparts of the vast structure. Caul watched her breath dissipate in the cold morning air. Finally she turned and looked at them all in turn. "There are *kin* here."

Caul followed her gaze. "Are you certain? Why can't I..." But then he suddenly felt a faint presence, perhaps from deep within the castle. As he concentrated, hoping to determine its nature, it shifted abruptly and vanished from his senses entirely.

"There is something, but I can't say if..."

Caul couldn't finish the sentence. His mind became flooded with a multitude of sounds and sights, as if the *kin* were swiftly emerging from wherever they had hidden themselves. He recognised the awful likenesses that crawled or scuttled or staggered from the nooks and crannies of the castle. Beneath the fear and revulsion he felt hatred burn brightly- for these were of the same ilk as the creatures that had attacked Cai and forced them to eventually flee. *The lower* kin, he thought. *The bestial army of the* choragh, *every one of them a living, breathing nightmare.*

He could sense one of them lumbering towards a tower window. Larger and more powerful than the others, it flung them out of its way, seizing slow or ill-witted *kin* and snapping their bones. Even before this beast appeared Caul saw it in sharp and terrible detail- a creature that might once have lived either as a human or a dog but which now bore features of both, twisted into a lurching obscenity. As if to emphasise its ambiguous nature it alternated between using four legs and two to cover the ground, and all four limbs could have been either arms or legs. Short-haired and with patchy, diseased skin all over, an expression of directionless rage on its face, the creature snapped at the air as if dispelling invisible flying tormentors from its vicinity. Its huge yellow teeth were permanently bared, swollen gums drawn back. Its bloated stomach hinted at the late stages of some unspeakable pregnancy.

Caul sensed all of this in a moment, and then the *kin*-beast appeared at one of the high windows. It turned its head to them immediately, perhaps sensing him and Arian in much the same way as they had sensed the lurking multitudes. But by the time he had the presence of mind to point to it, the creature had disappeared from the window.

The revulsion in his veins quieted enough for him to gather his thoughts and turn to speak with the *luyan.* "Arian is right," he told them. "There are *kin* within the castle. Many dozens. Perhaps hundreds. We can't fight that many."

One of the *luyan,* a female, shook her head. "It can't be so. This is the castle of Lord Inerdyr, the single most powerful man in all the middle lands, perhaps all the Free Territories."

Caul shrugged. "Perhaps he and everyone else fled before the onslaught of the *kin.*" He almost added, *My own people had to flee them eventually, and they have ten times the resolve and courage of soft human folk, many of whom would not even have been trained in the use of weapons, let alone the Powers.*

But whatever disbelief the *luyan* held, it was gone a moment later. From the great entrance doors and the lower windows of the great castle the *kin* swarmed, many of them scrambling over one another in their haste. Their cacophony filled the wintry air. They were of every conceivable shape. The huge dog-like creature appeared last, padding along unhurriedly in the wake of its shrill and snapping brethren.

As the *kin* rushed headlong at them, Caul and Arian directed their powers towards the enemy, turning many to smoking, molten shells. At Cai they had been at the vanguard of the desperate effort to beat back the rampage, but had nevertheless struggled to control their own fear. Then, they had never seen such monstrosities before and had heard of them only through myths and scare-tales. Now the fear was tempered with rage.

The *luyan* stood their ground and attacked those who made it past the defensive wave of the Old Powers, but the *kin* healed quickly and no sooner were they beaten back than they surged forward again. Weapons could only delay them unless they somehow cleaved the head from the body, and even then some of the *kin* would continue forward, headless but still somehow knowing where their enemies stood. One many-legged beast leapt at the face of a *luyan* fighter and tore flesh from bone in an instant. The man died screaming under a mass of scuttling chaos.

Caul felt the forces within him raging almost out of control. The world became bright, the battle an extended moment in which he stood against the *kin* as a conduit. He remained dimly aware of *luyan* men and women perishing around them, but it was the death of each *kin* creature that he felt most acutely.

Yet there were too many of them. He and Arian were forced back beyond the castle wall, and the *kin* poured on through the gates.

Eventually the remaining *luyan* turned and fled. The wagon horses had already done so, taking the vehicles with them. Those horses which had been tethered pulled and stamped, frightened and desperate, rolling their eyes in terror.

Caul sensed Arian stepping slowly back, and he did the same alongside her. Abruptly she turned to calm one and then another of the horses. The *kin* surged forward and Caul redoubled his efforts to destroy them.

"Ride!" he heard Arian scream then, and he turned to see her already astride one of the horses and holding the reins of the other.

Caul needed no further encouragement. Swiftly he leapt up into the saddle, and he followed Arian as she turned her steed and rode from the chaos at a fierce pace.

XIV - Scarlet Over Snow

I

Kian sat sharpening her knives, placing each one back on the large scrap of leather once she judged it to be keen enough. Her mind strayed continually from the task. Every once in a while she would put the chore to one side, restless and unable to look at her father's still form upon the makeshift bed any longer. She would get up and walk to stand outside the tent where he had been placed, listening to it flapping in the stiff breeze as she looked across the river at the devastated town of Woods Ford.

No buildings still stand, she observed. *Even those few that were made from stone have somehow melted. This is simply a place where a town once stood. The pyre of bodies we found burned so fiercely that the bones turned to fine ash, and soon the ashes will have all blown away. A year from now there'll be nothing left except fragments of char hidden in undergrowth.*

Kian's sharp eyes picked out a figure wandering by itself on the outskirts of the town's charred remains. *Nia,* she realised. Occasionally the woman would stop and stoop as if to look at something, before moving on. *Is she scavenging?* Kian wondered, and frowned, not certain how she felt about the act. *You were nothing but a thief yourself not so long ago,* she reminded herself.

Kian's gaze fell nearer then, to the river where devastating sorcery had been unleashed by the *orkar* to boil the *kin* alive. The water had stopped its seething and boiling that same afternoon. Kian guessed that the water temperature was now more or less normal and that the shallows might even freeze tonight. *That was some considerable power the* orkar *brought to bear,* she thought. *I*

294

suspect we'll see it again, if they can call upon it so soon. That's twice they've saved us now.

All she wanted to do was find a bed and collapse on it, sleep for at least a week and wake up to find her father healed and up and about. Even after two days her head felt thick and turgid from the effects of using the Powers. Her body ached as if she had been wrestling with *orkar* warriors. Anlerran's exhaustion was even greater, which had led to their return to Darkbrook being delayed.

But beyond her physical wretchedness Kian felt worse than ever before- lost and cold, and alone. The only time that even began to compare was that night after Iyoth had left her, and then it had been entirely different, her grief and confusion cut through with a dark fury.

Please, she thought, looking back into the tent for a moment. *Please let him live.*

She knew that to plead with some imagined higher power for good fortune was pointless, and yet desperation had driven her to the act twice already. *He'll live or he'll die,* she told herself now, watching the faint movement of his chest as his body laboured to pull the breath of life into itself.

Kian could not look at him without tears welling up. Instead she forced herself to watch an ongoing discussion between Ruhal, Anlerran, Elluron and the Watchers. They were too distant for her to hear the conversation, but she used her sharp vision to lip-read at least half of what they said and then piece together the rest. They were talking about the arrival of more *orkar* from Uythar forest in the north, and also about those few people who had fled Woods Ford and been found since. Most of those wretched survivors had been moved together in an area protected by *orkar* warlocks. They had, after all, nowhere else to go unless Darkbrook welcomed them, and the possibility of protection and food, however meagre, was more than enough to entice them. Kian had heard some of their stories; they were horrific but no more or less than to be expected. *I know the* kin *better than any of you can,* she found herself thinking, then immediately felt ashamed of thinking such a thing. These people had lost everything.

She heard someone approaching behind her and turned to see Lura. The woman nodded in greeting and looked into the tent. "He's the same," Kian said quietly.

"No worse then." Lura came to stand by her side. "He's fighting the wounds as fiercely as your people are renowned for."

Kian smiled thinly. "I don't think my father ever stepped back from a fight, whereas I'm standing here as good as useless. I want to be able to heal whatever poison or sorcery the *kin* have caused to flow within him. But I've never had much talent for healing."

Lura nodded sympathetically and turned to go. As she did, Kian heard her gasp and swiftly turned. "Is he..."

But as she looked inside the tent she saw for herself. Iyoth was sitting up, gaunt and swaying. His eyes, lurid with fever, stared wildly at nothing as he clutched at the thin blanket that had covered him.

"I'll fetch a healer," Lura said, and ran towards the centre of the encampment.

Her father could barely speak, so Kian urged him not to even try as she waited impatiently for a healer to arrive. When the stout *orkar* woman entered the tent, she waved Kian to one side and began her ministrations as the *du-luyan* girl looked fretfully on. Iyoth lay back and his eyes closed.

Time passed. Kian almost wore the ground to a trough of mud as she paced restlessly back and forth. Lura waited outside, silent and watchful. Kian wondered how it could be that Lura had nothing better to do than to watch the healer attempting to save her father. For a moment she even considered that the human woman felt attached to him somehow. They had become friends, she knew that much. Lura saw her looking and smiled hopefully; Kian did the same and then looked away. What business was it of hers? She ought to feel grateful that Lura had brought the healer so quickly and cared enough to wait.

"He will live," the healer said eventually, without turning round. "He'll be weak for a few days, but that's only to be expected. I expect anyone other than a *du-luyan* man would have succumbed to so many wounds. Particularly unnatural injuries such as these."

"He followed me," Kian told her as the healer gathered up her potions in a cloth bag. Iyoth was asleep once again, and appeared to be breathing more easily. "He refused to turn back. He said his place was with me."

"When I first saw him I thought to myself, even for a *du-luyan* he has some arrogance," the healer said. Before Kian could respond to that comment she continued, "A proud man, and a father. What else would you expect him to have done?"

"I should have said something," Kian said quietly, "but I didn't."

The healer bellowed a throaty laugh at that. "Oh, and would he have listened? I very much doubt it. I wager he'd do the same again in an instant given the chance."

"I won't let him," Kian said fiercely, but the healer laughed even harder as she trudged out of the tent. Kian heard her still chuckling to herself as she headed back to the *orkar* encampment.

"I'll leave the two of you in peace awhile," Lura said. Kian turned and saw Iyoth stirring, and quickly went to kneel at his bedside. *Don't you ever follow me into battle against the* kin *again,* she wanted to say, but she couldn't. She found herself unable to say anything at all, and when his hand reached out to stroke her cheek all she could do was look down at the muddy grass and weep silent tears of relief.

As Kian rightly suspected, Lura had grown fond of Iyoth. Yet she held in her heart a love that she had kept buried and tried to forget for years, but which had slowly found its way back into her waking thoughts. Now that Iyoth was more than likely going to be well, or as well as could be expected, his fate no longer distracted her and those feelings rose to the surface again.

I should never have agreed to this madness that Ruhal proposed, she thought as she made her way through the muddy camp. *I should have told him that we had both already lived a lifetime's worth of pain and weariness and killing. I should have said to him, "Was Wistport not enough for you?"*

But she had gone against her better judgement, enticed by his grand words, his vision and his crazed optimism. She had believed in him, and despite the horror of everything that had happened since, she still believed in him. *And perhaps I would have accompanied him on this mad venture regardless,* she told herself. *I'd rather be with him than without him, even if it meant the end of us both, which it surely will.*

She knew that this was not a good love. Driven mainly by lust and need, it had always had about it a certain savagery and desperation fuelled by her desire to escape her innate unhappiness.

It would be so much easier if I hated Anlerran, she considered as she strode along between the tents. *But I can't. I pity her, for her wide-eyed innocence, her gentle heart and generous nature.*

Then again I envy her, for her firm and doubtless fertile body.

Lura stopped to take a few more sips of sourgrass from her flask. She had bought it in Darkbrook after begging some coins from Ruhal. It should have been enough to last her a tennight or more but half of it had already gone. *I'll beg some more from the* orkar *when I run out,* she thought absently. *They have more than enough to go round.*

The welcome fire spread through her insides and she walked on, buoyed by the temporary courage it afforded and the smile it put on her lips.

Presently she caught sight of the tent where Ruhal and Anlerran slept. Anlerran was somewhere on the other side of the encampment with her father at the moment, being trained. "Being taught how to control herself," Lura murmured, wondering if she ought to be taught the same thing.

She took another sip of sourgrass and made her way over to the tent, ducked inside and smiled as Ruhal turned round. "I just wanted to discuss a few matters with you," she murmured.

He frowned. "With me alone? Should we not wait until the others can be present?"

"I really don't think they'd have any interest in this," Lura said lightly. She swaggered over to him and put her arms around his waist, pulling him against her. "It's been a long while, Ruhal, but I still..."

"Lura, stop." He took a couple of steps back.

"Why?" she said dangerously, following him.

"You know why. I'm with Anlerran now."

"I don't see that little chit of yours anywhere. In fact I made sure she was training with her father before I came to you. She'll not be back for a while."

"That was not my meaning." He rubbed a hand through his hair, confused. "Why now? Why after all this time?"

"I think you've forgotten how good I was, Ruhal." She looked searchingly into his eyes for a moment. "Ha! No- I was wrong. You hadn't forgotten." She knelt down before him. "Your young charge can't possibly know the things I know. I'll wager her lovemaking is clumsy and ill-directed, or passive. What does she do? Open her legs and lie there for you to do all the work?"

"Don't talk about her," Ruhal growled.

"Let's talk about us then. Do you remember our last time, my Warden?" Lura's smile broadened as she allowed her gaze to drop. "Ah. *Part* of you remembers, that's for certain."

She began to unbutton his trousers. He made as if to resist her for a moment, then sighed. Lura glanced up and saw him staring straight ahead as if in stubborn denial that any of this was happening. *He already looks guilty,* she thought. *How will he look afterwards?*

Nia watched from a distance as Lura emerged from Ruhal's tent a little later. *I don't need to have heard anything to know what happened there,* she observed as Lura wandered away, looking a little unsteady on her legs. *Someone who wished to make trouble amongst these people would tell Anlerran.*

Nia sighed and looked into the wintry distance, and decided it would be better if she kept her mouth shut. The personal relations of her companions were no business of hers, and setting the fox amongst the chickens would not serve her well.

Besides, she reasoned, *what's one more little secret added to those I already keep?*

II

Snow drifted down again later, to cover the ash and further cool the dying embers of the fires. Ruhal walked with Anlerran along what had been the main street of the village. Mud and ash squelched under their boots and an icy wind cut across their path, but Anlerran welcomed the chance to stretch her legs after being virtually bedridden for the last few days.

"No bodies remain to be given burials," Ruhal remarked, looking left and right in turn. "The people of Woods Ford have been given utterly to the *choragh.*"

"Except those few who escaped and have since joined us," Anlerran reminded him.

As if on a sudden impulse, Ruhal seized her arm and drew her up against him. Even through his thick cloak she could feel his heat, and she wondered if he had a fever. "Are you well?" she asked earnestly, but either he didn't hear her or he chose not to listen.

"Gone without a trace," he said quietly. "As if they never existed." His hand traced a course down her cheek, hot and tremulous. "Life is fragile, Anlerran. We must live each moment and not let it pass by."

Anlerran agreed with him, but she could not find words to say. Something about the grief and anger in his eyes made her feel as if nothing she said would be enough, and so she could only bring herself to nod solemnly.

They walked back over the bridge to the camp. Anlerran felt relieved that they had spent only a short while in the place where Woods Ford had once stood. She could not understand why Ruhal had wanted to walk there again today; she could think of no purpose to the act. Had he not pointed out that no bodies remained to be properly buried? *Let them be dust on the wind,* she thought. *We can do nothing for the dead, so let's not walk where they once walked, lamenting our failures.*

Before sundown the companions met in one of the larger tents set up by the *orkar*. The purpose of their gathering was to agree a way south-east passing through a number of settlements on the way, after their return to Darkbrook. Two separate maps were shown, but they disagreed with each other in several places. Anlerran watched quietly from the rear of the tent, her heart sinking a little further every time voices were raised in argument. *How have we even remained together for this long?* she wondered at one point, observing the bristling animosity between *orkar* and Watchers.

"I do not think the time will come soon for us to move against Inerdyr," Elluron spoke up. "Even if we are strengthened by reinforcements from Uythar and Darkbrook."

"The time has come for us to move against him," Garrok grunted. "I grow weary of waiting."

"We will not be party to a decision based around your impatience," Kelandra told the *orkar* leader.

"I agree with Garrok," Ruhal said, looking up from one of the maps which had been rolled out on the ground with daggers to hold each corner. "We begin the march south from Darkbrook as soon as we can."

"The survivors of Woods Ford will be taken to Darkbrook where they can be looked after," Elluron spoke up. "Responsibility for those people lies with the Warden of this territory. We cannot have them travel south with us, nor would many of them wish to once they know where we're headed."

"I did not suggest that we arm and enlist them," Ruhal said quietly.

"Regardless, we have other problems," Elluron continued. "Woods Ford has not been saved. Will the Warden of Darkbrook honour his promise? What do you have for him, Ruhal? A village destroyed, and a plea for more fighters? How do you think he will react?"

Ruhal stared stonily back at him and said nothing. Finally he continued with poorly-concealed anger, "We will recruit along the way after we head south-east from Darkbrook. Regardless of which map we refer to, at least five settlements stand on or near our path, if we head towards Stillwater."

Elluron was not yet done. "Can we feed all the people you intend to gather? They would need to bring their own provisions, pack animals, weaponry..."

But Ruhal had already dismissed him from his thoughts. He turned back to the *orkar* leader. "Garrok, how long do you think it will take Korrinn to arrive with more of your people?"

"A day, perhaps. There are more ironmasters amongst them. Inerdyr's army will not have seen such sorcery before- of that much I'm certain. It was a closely guarded secret until we used it at the river yesterday."

So that's what they call the orkar *sorcerers who destroyed the* kin, Anlerran thought. *Ironmasters. Wielding and shaping the Old Powers through weaponry.*

"It suited us that so many even in the free North thought of *orkar* as nothing more than blundering beasts, thoughtless and good for nothing but bashing heads together," Garrok added. "But it will not be the same now."

"We cannot lose sight of the greater battles to come," Elluron said. "The less blood of Inerdyr's people spilled, the better. We're in danger of taking the wrong path."

"Be cautious with your words," Ruhal said quietly, and a murmur of disquiet rippled amongst those gathered.

"Allow me to finish, Ruhal, if you have the patience. I was about to say that the less blood of *our* people spilled, the better also. The less the *choragh* will be strengthened. They are not called the Blood Lords for nothing, as you well know. We may even find that Inerdyr's forces fall apart."

"Are you saying that we should offer him peace?" Ruhal shook his head in disgust.

"No. Only that we should not be seen to make the first move."

Ruhal said nothing at all in response. Perhaps he could think of nothing to say. He perused the map once again, tracing his finger along its surface. Finally he looked up at Garrok. "We'll head back to Darkbrook at first light tomorrow," he said.

Even as Garrok nodded, satisfied, Anlerran saw from the corner of her eye her father turning and leaving without a further word.

She made her way through the encampment to find him, but when she did, he would not speak of Ruhal. Instead he turned and looked searchingly into her eyes. "Is there anything else you wish to speak of? You've seemed preoccupied lately."

"I'm still tired, that's all," she said, looking away.

Finally, she returned to be with Ruhal under the cover of darkness. She found him in their tent sitting cross-legged with a couple of lanterns to view his maps by, an intense look of concentration on his face. "I am reacquainting myself with the lie of the land directly between us and Inerdyr's army," he said unnecessarily. "A league of open land first, then some low marshy woods we need to skirt around, and beyond that, farmland and five main settlements... then we head towards the Stillwater Hills."

He rolled up the maps carefully and tied them with string, then smiled. "Morale is high, generally," he remarked. "Garrok and I took time to walk amongst the people after the meeting was done."

High amongst which people? Anlerran silently rejoined. *The* orkar *who follow Garrok are hardened warriors. The survivors from Woods Ford are ordinary people- frightened, weak and hungry. How can he possibly see high morale as he walks about the camp?*

Not noticing her lack of comment, Ruhal pressed on, "Once Korrinn and the other *orkar* arrive the day after tomorrow, matters should improve further." He shook his head and laughed suddenly. "Ironmasters! Garrok hid that one from us all."

Anlerran wondered if she ought to talk with him about the march south. She shared many of her father's misgivings about it. But as she opened her mouth and prepared to speak, he gave her a different look suddenly- a look that Anlerran knew well by now. Her heart began to race as he turned and snuffed out the lamp. A moment later, a strong arm reached out of the gloom and wrapped around her waist to draw her towards him. She could feel a strange sense of urgency about him, made obvious by his quick breaths and shaking hands. *What's the matter with him?* she wondered for a moment, as he almost hauled her to the ground, pulling clumsily at her shirt.

But when she removed her trousers and smallclothes and opened her legs for him, he thrust himself into her twice and then withdrew, cursing. He knelt between her legs and said nothing. Anlerran could just about see him looking at her, but couldn't quite determine the expression on his face. "What's the matter?" she whispered eventually.

"You just lie there," Ruhal said. His voice sounded dull.

"I'm not sure..." Anlerran felt bemused. "What would you have me do?"

He didn't reply. After a moment he lay down on the blankets, perhaps a little further away than she had become used to. "We have a long ride tomorrow," he said eventually. "You should sleep."

The following morning they headed back to Darkbrook. Those people from Woods Ford who were unable to journey on foot travelled either with *orkar* on horseback, or in the few wagons that the *orkar* had. They huddled together where they could; men, women and children who may as well have been mute. They shivered and occasionally they wept. One frail old man died before they set off and the body was hastily cremated. Watching the flames, it occurred to Anlerran that the *kin* had done something similar only days ago. Perhaps the friends and neighbours of the dead man thought the same as they watched the smoke of his destruction rise into the low and leaden sky.

Anlerran rode alongside Ruhal, but wondered if she perhaps ought to allow him a little more space. He looked preoccupied, coldly angry and- Anlerran thought- ashamed.

He would not look at her, and eventually she decided to spend the rest of the day in the company of Kian and Iyoth, whose recovery had been speedy once he regained consciousness.

When they arrived back in Darkbrook the day after, Ghoreth rode out to meet them flanked by four of his guardsmen. He took a cursory look at the survivors from Woods Ford. "The *kin*?" he asked eventually.

Ruhal nodded. "The burning had already started. There was nothing we could save."

The Warden of Darkbrook said nothing for a while. "Then I'll give you half the men we discussed. I'll need the other half." As soon as Ruhal opened his mouth to argue, Ghoreth raised his hand. "Half or none at all, Ruhal. I will not have Darkbrook undefended. Furthermore, these refugees will need to be accommodated within the town somehow. And this entire matter should have gone before the Council of Wardens."

"We had no time for meetings," Ruhal pointed out.

"Your militia will be as good as useless against the *kin*," Garrok spoke up. "Better that they fight against Inerdyr's foot soldiers."

"Darkbrook will not be left undefended," Ghoreth repeated.

"My lord Warden," Elluron spoke up. "Half of your previous offer is generous given our failure to protect Woods Ford, and we gratefully accept it."

Ruhal gave Elluron a long, cold stare but said nothing. Ghoreth simply nodded. "They'll be ready to ride tomorrow morning."

Late in the afternoon, Garrok's lieutenant Korrinn arrived back in the encampment with close on five hundred *orkar* warriors. Anlerran wondered how many of the five hundred might be ironmasters, but even with her ability to sense others who were strong in the Old Powers she found it impossible to tell. Perhaps they were able to cloak their talents somehow. All the *orkar* wore piecemeal leather armour with nothing more elaborate than fur cloaks over it. She could certainly not differentiate between them by looking for markings or signs on the clothes they wore. It was difficult enough trying to tell males and females apart.

Once the Darkbrook militia had also joined them the following morning, they headed slowly south. The day remained clear and sunny, the good visibility allowing them to see in detail the low grassy hills that lay further south. The *orkar* bristled with spears and axes, and the more lightly-armed men of Darkbrook might have looked fearsome themselves had the *orkar* not been present.

Anlerran wondered for a moment what it would be like to be a lone rider who happened to notice them from a distance. *I would turn the other way at first sight,* she thought, *and I'd keep going for as long as I could.*

While they rested for luncheon, one of the *orkar*, a muscular female with braided hair, approached Garrok as he sat and discussed the route ahead with Ruhal. Anlerran was near enough to hear her say, "We felt some great power being used to the south. Four of us sensed it at the same time."

"Inerdyr perhaps? Or the *choragh?*" Garrok suggested.

The woman shook her head. "No. That much we'd have known. It was something else. Impossible to say what, but it needs to be investigated."

Garrok frowned. "Take a half dozen ironmasters and the same number of axemen. Locate the disturbance and determine its nature if you can. If need be, retreat so you can return and report. Whatever happens, we must know if it poses a threat."

"As you say." She gave a little bow and strode away. A short while later a dozen *orkar* rode quickly south.

The army had already begun moving slowly on when Kelandra, who had been using her spyglass, pointed ahead of them and called across to the others, "They return. But they bring others with them."

A short while later the *orkar* riders arrived with the newcomers, but Anlerran barely heard the commotion that rose up all around. Her attention was drawn inexorably to one of the captives, a girl several years younger than herself. On a sudden impulse she closed her eyes, and when she did it was as if she could still see the girl. Amongst the sounds and shadows of everyone else, she appeared as a beacon of brilliant, searing light.

Anlerran took a deep, tremulous breath, awed and troubled at the same time, for she knew without doubt that this girl was strong in the Old Powers; far more powerful, in fact than anyone she had ever encountered.

III

Amethyst, Vornen, Ileana and Jak were made to kneel, and a group of people, presumably the leader and his inner circle, stood before them in a half-circle along with at least half a dozen heavily armed *orkar*. Amethyst looked slowly up and glanced around, making sure that her gaze did not linger long enough on anyone for it to be interpreted as a challenge. They were, she had to admit to herself, a fearsome, strange group- humans, *orkar* and others who she felt certain must be Watchers although she had never seen any before.

"Who are you?" one of the Watchers- a dark-haired female- demanded.

Amethyst knew that she would have to speak on behalf of the four of them. Vornen remained exhausted, and Ileana and Jak lacked the guile and wisdom to tread the narrow path between saying too little and too much.

She looked across at Vornen, and for a moment an image of him standing almost knee-deep in the lake in the

308

Green Road came to her. *He would have waded to his destruction,* she thought. *I knew that as soon as we pulled him out of the water and I saw that far-away look of desperation. But now he has that same look in his eyes.*

"I will answer for us all," she said quietly, maintaining her level gaze in their direction even as she heard Vornen sigh and saw from the corner of her eye his head slump forward. His mind would be elsewhere now, and there could be no knowing when it might return.

"Why you?" one of the male Watchers responded, a cold look in his hard grey eyes. "Can they not speak?"

"The man beside me is exhausted. Question him after he's rested, if you'll permit that," Amethyst replied. "The other two are youths. I will do the speaking."

"As you wish." The man they called Ruhal, who she already knew to be their leader looked her up and down. Amethyst did not know what to make of him. *He looks like a common mercenary, if a tough one,* she thought. *I wouldn't have thought him a leader of people if I hadn't seen it for myself.*

"This girl"- he pointed to Ileana- "is strong in the Old Powers. Did you know?"

Amethyst did not say anything, but Ileana spoke up suddenly. "Inerdyr is a servant of the *choragh.* You're his enemies, aren't you?" She turned to Amethyst with a tired smile. "We found them."

Ruhal turned to her. "Inerdyr's allegiance surprises no one here."

"But now he is higher *kin* as well. Perhaps the highest of all the *kin,*" Ileana added, staring back at him. "More powerful and more insane than ever. Something happened to him. Perhaps one of the *choragh* themselves raised him to be *kin.* Did you know that?"

Ruhal said nothing, but a flash of anger in his eyes told Amethyst that here stood a man who detested being shown to be a fool or ignorant on a matter. *Yes, there's a man who thinks mostly with his heart or his fists,* she thought, looking away when he returned his gaze to her.

"Inerdyr certainly knew of *your* powers, and will do anything to recapture you," an older man next to Ruhal said softly. Amethyst thought he might be human or *luyan* at first, but when she looked more attentively at him she realised that she had no idea what he might be. "You said some interesting things to the *orkar* outriders who found you. Do you remember much of what you told them?"

"We must all protect her from the Old Dark, no matter the cost," he told his nearest companions when Ileana shook her head tiredly. *Gods, at least one of you talks sense,* Amethyst thought.

Then as he moved she caught a better glimpse of his face in the light, and she could not help but stare for longer. *Elluron,* she thought, astonished. *How could I not recognise you? And what were the chances of finding you here?*

Amethyst almost spoke to him unbidden then, to remind him of who she was- not that she was anyone of importance. But he looked at her and she saw a faint smile and the slightest of nods. *He recognises me. I wondered from time to time where he might be headed. He saved me from the servants of the Old Dark and cold and hunger alike. How did he end up here with these people?*

"Does Inerdyr hold others like Ileana?" Ruhal asked. "Even descendants of the First?"

Amethyst blinked and returned her attention to him. "He had sent his people out to look for them," she said uneasily. "But one we already knew of- Jaana. She's especially strong in the Old Powers, you would say. But she became an ally of Inerdyr, perhaps consumed by the same madness. I've met a number of mad folk during my travels, and I couldn't say I worked out what motivated any of them."

At the same time she thought, *Maybe it wasn't madness but despair that persuaded her that Inerdyr's cause represented the only chance of Aona's survival. Or perhaps*

Inerdyr simply twisted her unhappiness into hatred. It wouldn't have been that difficult.

It might be the truth, it might not, but either way Jaana had made her choice and would live or die by its consequences.

"There must be many who are convinced that Inerdyr is their saviour," Ileana spoke up quietly. She glanced at the boy kneeling next to her. "Jak's father Harqan is Inerdyr's man through and through." As he scowled at her, she added, "I'm sorry, Jak- but you know it's true."

"Harqan. I know that name. A ranger and protector of eastern Fhaarluy, if he's the same man," Ruhal commented.

"That's him," Jak said reluctantly, glowering at Ileana.

Alturus' cold voice betrayed a hint of impatience. "We need to know who amongst Inerdyr's followers pose the greatest threat."

"Jaana," Ileana said immediately.

"Another important question remains unanswered," the female Watcher spoke up quietly. "How did the four of you escape Inerdyr's stronghold?"

As all eyes turned to the girl, Amethyst smiled encouragingly. "You can tell them," she said, as the girl glanced doubtfully around at everyone. "We have no choice in the matter," she pointed out.

Ileana faltered slightly. "I'm not sure how I can even explain this," she mumbled, and looked down at the ground. "I don't think anyone will believe me."

"Tell them anyway," Amethyst prompted her.

"There's a place- a place which is a little like the world we all know, but it's... different," Ileana began hesitantly. "It's closer to the true heart of Aona. It's the inner world. It looks like the world we all know, but it's different, and things happen there that shouldn't be possible. I know its name. It's called the Green Road."

The effect of the girl's words on those who had gathered was twofold. Most responded with blank stares and shrugs, as the words meant nothing to them. Amethyst stopped the grim smile that almost came to her lips as she saw looks of utter shock upon the faces of Ruhal and Elluron, the girl standing between them and another of their companions, a *du-luyan* girl who stood nearby.

"You have been there?" Ruhal said finally.

"That's how we escaped. There was no other way. I had to..." She sighed, struggling for the right words. "I had to find a way for us to step somewhere else entirely. I think I only found a way through because I *had* to."

Elluron gave her a thoughtful look. "Tell me, Ileana," he murmured, "do you know if the *choragh* also know how to find it?"

She shrugged, and Amethyst spoke up again. "Inerdyr sought to unlock Ileana's knowledge of such things. He would often send Jaana to try to befriend her. By now, the two of them would have broken down her defences."

Elluron turned to Ruhal. "They will come for us," he said simply. "The *choragh* will demand nothing less, if they know about Ileana. It looks as if you will have your confrontation soon."

Events moved swiftly. Many of those who had listened to what Amethyst and Ileana had said now left, although the four of them were still guarded. Amethyst listened to the arguments that persisted outside the tent, until the protagonists left to conduct their quarrel elsewhere.

"What will they do with us?" Ileana whispered.

"I honestly can't say," Amethyst said, trying to offer a brave smile. "But we got this far. *You* got us this far."

"That's a good answer," Ileana declared, and she managed the faintest of smiles.

IV

Anlerran listened to the heated discussion with growing alarm and a sinking heart as it grew more animated and bitter. She chanced a look towards Ruhal, who was arguing the case for moving on Inerdyr's army with haste. *My voice of reason, he called me. Maybe I'm more to him than a girl half his age who satisfies his lust. He lays bare his troubles before me and questions himself. And with each day it seems that he becomes more desperate. Desperate enough to confront Inerdyr sooner rather than later. Even worse, he handles dissent poorly.*

What if I reasoned with him? Would he listen to me, if I chose my words carefully, if I uttered them at the right time and in the right place, perhaps late at night when he's sated and content? Then again, he's seemed far from content with me recently. I've no idea what I've done wrong.

Anlerran thought that he might already see treachery in every word of dissent. She saw the frustration on the face of her father and the cold contempt in Kelandra's eyes as Ruhal's arguments became shorter and louder and made less and less sense with each passing moment.

Elluron said forcefully, "There are other Descendants, Ruhal. There must be. In time, we will find them. To send those three into battle against the warlock is sheer folly. Would you have them killed on the battlefield, for you to claim your victory against Inerdyr?"

"I would never let Anlerran step foot on such ground," Ruhal shouted.

"I would never let you," her father said calmly. "Bring harm to my daughter- mercenary, ranger, or whatever you claim to be- and you will wake up under the earth. That is a promise."

Everything then happened in little more than a moment. Anlerran realised much later that had she not been so shocked, she would have plainly seen a degree of planning, a setting up of the event.

Ruhal drew his sword and made for Elluron. In the next instant, Kelandra had grasped Ruhal's shoulder. Anlerran heard her whisper something, and Ruhal stopped in mid-strike, seemingly unable to move. The sword fell to the ground with a thud.

Lura rushed at Kelandra, a longknife in her hand. A blur of swift movement, Elluron disarmed her, wrestling the weapon from her grasp and pinning her to the ground.

Garrok loomed in the background, his greatsword held in two huge hands. The blade shimmered oddly in the gloom. He neither moved nor spoke.

Ruhal's legs gave way and he sagged to the ground. "Tie him," Elluron said, and watched calmly as Kelandra did as bidden.

Anlerran tried to speak but couldn't utter a word. Her mouth had gone completely dry. Lura, however, found her voice and screamed obscenities at everyone around her as Ruhal, hands tied behind his back, was led away by Alturus and Ildoron.

"Given the chance, Ruhal may well have taken the device of the *illeagh,* used it and condemned us all," Elluron spoke up. "He is not fit to lead. He has shown himself to be irrational and dangerous and will therefore remain under close guard until we decide otherwise."

"Who do you mean by *we?*" Garrok asked quietly.

Elluron turned to him, but didn't answer the question. "Regardless of what happens now, we need your people to remain with us. Inerdyr's army will come for us all. That's a battle that cannot be avoided. And they will hunt you, whether or not we have your allegiance."

Still Garrok said nothing, but slowly he sheathed his sword. Elluron turned his attention to Lura and let her go. The mercenary stood up, still shaking with rage. "Peace, Lura," Garrok said quietly. "In all likelihood they'll kill you if you move against them. If Ruhal meant so little to them, imagine what they think of you. Don't give them the chance."

Lura favoured Elluron and Kelandra with a malevolent look, then turned and strode out. No one moved to stop her.

Garrok folded his arms and looked at Elluron and then Kelandra. "It's clear that you engineered this."

"Ruhal may have tried to kill Elluron in his rage," Kelandra pointed out. "Do you honestly believe him to be the right leader given what you've just witnessed?"

Kelandra's words echoed through Anlerran's mind. *Would he?* she wondered. She felt as if the reality of the situation had only just dawned on her. *And what then? Could I ever again be anywhere near a man who had tried to kill my father?*

"No," Garrok said finally. "But I trust neither of you. Assume control and you will lose it swiftly. The matter of leadership must be put to a discussion."

The *orkar* man turned and left without a further word.

Elluron finally turned to his daughter. "You have been closer to Ruhal than most. Are you so surprised at what you saw?"

"No," she said reluctantly. *I should have known a day like this might come,* she mentally added, and her shoulders slumped as she continued, "Ruhal told me once that darkness dwelt within him and that only I kept it at bay. I'm not surprised by his action. I'm only surprised that you had to goad him into it for your own purposes. A shameful act, father." She looked down, feeling a flush of embarrassment and anger in her cheeks.

"You will have to do as Garrok says," Iyoth spoke up. "You cannot depose your leader and leave all your people guessing as to what now happens. No one likes uncertainty. The *orkar* and the men of Darkbrook will follow a different path if it continues."

He left, and after a moment Kian went with him.

Anlerran found Lura sitting on a boulder near to a stream, a contemplative look on her face as she honed her sword with a small whetstone.

"May I join you?" she asked, a little more bluntly than she intended.

"Did your father send you?" Lura rejoined without looking up.

"No. In truth, I told him that his was a shameful act. But then, perhaps Ruhal would have killed him or tried." Anlerran regarded the swordswoman carefully, and suddenly an altogether different thought occurred to her. "How many people have you killed, Lura?"

Lura frowned, taken aback. "Why would you want to know such a thing?"

"Were you at Wistport with Ruhal and Garrok?"

The swordswoman gave her a half-amused look. "Which question should I reply to first, Anlerran? No, I'll not give you an answer to the first. Wistport? Yes, I was there. It was a bloody day. It was also a day when truth and falsehood could not be disentangled. There are some places in the Free Territories where they condemn Ruhal as a murderer for what happened in Wistport that day. They also believe that some of Ruhal's recruits and also the *orkar* ran wild, killing in cold blood, raping women and children- Powers, men as well. But to other people they were heroes, restoring the word of common law in a place that had been brought close to ruin by pirates from the Bay of Anvar. The Warden of Wistport and his enforcers were weak and the situation had been allowed to fester. Something had to be done."

"And where does the truth lie?"

Lura did not speak for a while. She placed her sword across her legs and stared into the nearby water as if lost in the past. "It lies somewhere in between," she said finally. "By and large the *orkar* left the citizens of Wistport unmolested.

Likewise, the majority of Ruhal's men. Wistport was a success by most measures, but by no means a *complete* success. Such forays rarely are. There are always bad apples, Anlerran. Some walk amongst us. The *orkar* are mostly noble warriors, but believe me when I say that some of those not far from us would ruin your insides in their lust given the chance, and slit your throat afterwards. Or at least cut out your tongue, so you may remember the violation but never speak of it."

Anlerran shuddered.

"It's started to unravel. Recall the folk of Woods Ford who we chaperoned as far as Darkbrook- they were fearful, angry, resentful. After all, we arrived too late to save most of them. The survivors remained with us as far as Darkbrook because they had no homes and they knew that any fate would be better than wandering the land aimlessly. Now we head south as little more than a rabble. The *orkar* and the Darkbrook militia are on good enough terms, but they will never trust the likes of Watchers- or your father."

"I think perhaps you could have said this when Ruhal and my father were arguing," Anlerran said ruefully.

"Could I? Perhaps. Well, it's done with now." Lura carefully ran a finger down the blade of her sword. "I've known Ruhal a long time, Anlerran. He's made mistakes in the past; he's misjudged things. Of course, anyone might have done the same- but Ruhal wears guilt almost like other people wear clothes."

"What should I do?" Anlerran sighed. "I've not yet seen eighteen summers. I know nothing of the world."

"Never mind the world," Lura told her. "There's nothing you can do. Your father and the Watchers and perhaps Garrok, and Teryn of Darkbrook, will preside over this sorry excuse of an army until it drifts apart."

"What are you going to do?" Anlerran asked.

"Do? I don't know. The fellowship I had is gone. Sarros proved himself a traitor, Jahar is dead and Ruhal held prisoner by the Watchers." She paused and looked across at Anlerran, then sighed deeply. "Powers, I may as well tell you now..."

"Tell me what?"

"A few days back, while you were training with your father I went to Ruhal. I laid with him."

Anlerran stared mutely at her.

"Men are weak when it comes to such things," Lura continued, "and if you didn't know that before, well you do now."

Anlerran felt tears pricking her eyes. "Why?" she said finally. "Why would you do that?"

"Because I wanted him to want me. Because I was drunk." Lura shrugged. "I don't know. For what it's worth, I'm sorry."

"It's worth nothing," Anlerran said bleakly. Unable to spend a moment longer in her company, she left the mercenary sharpening her blade again and staring at nothing as the snow began to drift down.

VI

Unable to rest until she confronted Ruhal, Anlerran pleaded with her father that she be allowed to see him. *I must know what he has to say for himself,* she reasoned. *I need to know why he betrayed me with Lura.*

Elluron took her to a large tent which to her surprise was guarded by two *orkar* men. "Have they turned against Ruhal so quickly?" she asked.

"The *orkar* are a pragmatic race," her father reminded her, "and their leader has given his thoughts on the matter, which changed after his initial disquiet. Their loyalty is to the cause, not to the man who once led it."

The guardsmen stood aside to allow her through, and Elluron waited outside, walking a short distance away.

Ruhal sat with his head bowed and turned slightly away from the light and attention; Anlerran could not tell if the position was one of exhaustion or shame, or both. He looked up at the sound of her approach and Anlerran tentatively stepped a little closer. The Warden of Mordenglen looked desperate, humiliated, a man who had been stripped of everything but the clothes on his back. "My father allowed me to see you," she ventured finally.

"Your *father*." Ruhal spat the word. "I've done much for him. I brought him his daughter, whom he had abandoned. I looked after you. I protected you. Your guardians did the same for far longer. Where was *he* all this time?"

Anlerran said nothing, thinking it wiser to let Ruhal spill forth his bile without comment. But instead he smiled suddenly. "They will decide shortly who is to be leader, now that they've usurped me. It should be *you,* my love."

Anlerran shook her head, aghast that he would think she could lead an army. "I have neither knowledge nor experience of such things."

"Age has no bearing," he said angrily. "They will follow you if you show courage. Will they follow your father? Of course not, though he himself may find the notion attractive. He is half-*illeagh*. To them he may as well be some being brought down from another world, from the stars."

"And he made me- a quarter-*illeagh*," Anlerran reminded him.

Ignoring the poor logic of his argument, Ruhal pressed on heedlessly: "Garrok is *orkar,* and in the middle lands they still fear and loathe his kind. Likewise, it cannot be one of the Watchers..."

Anlerran waited for him to continue, but he appeared to have lost his train of thought entirely. "Lura," he said eventually, a crooked smile upon his face.

"What about Lura?" Anlerran asked guardedly. She could not help but curl her hands into fists at the sight of him smiling and mentioning her name at the same time.

Ruhal leaned forward, his face half cast in shadow. "*She* could lead. And she will lead for us. We can advise her, we can... yes... perhaps Lura, if you'll not take what's yours for yourself."

Anlerran felt as if she was heading into the heart of some dark storm as she stared back at the strangely muddied look in Ruhal's eyes. He looked like a man trapped in a place where desperation and euphoria might even be the same thing. Anlerran struggled to conceal her dismay. *It's a wonder not that he succumbed to his internal darkness, but that he resisted it for so long.*

"You can see that what I say makes sense," he whispered. Listening to him, Anlerran realised that in his own mind it did. He had been deposed, but already he imagined a way of influencing affairs, perhaps through Lura- a figurehead to lead until such a time as he himself would be deemed fit once again. How could he possibly think that a self-hating drunkard would be fit for any sort of leadership?

Anlerran had no idea who might be best equipped to lead their ragtag rebellion, but she feared what might happen if Lura became leader. The woman was violently impulsive, damaged and rancorous, and aside from that her virulent hatred of the Watchers had shown no signs of abating in the time they had spent together.

She could not lead, and in all likelihood no one would follow her. In any case, she would laugh at the very idea.

"No. Not Lura," she said flatly.

"Why not?" Ruhal looked as if he had been presented with an unsolvable puzzle.

"Lura is not lacking in courage," Anlerran admitted. "But the leader who is chosen will be the man or woman who will lead all Harn to war against the *marandaal.* Can you truly see her leading Watchers, such is the hatred that runs through her veins? And would they follow her? I think not."

Ruhal scowled and shook his head, as if the problem was not insurmountable despite anything Anlerran said. "Lura *must* lead in my place. Who else can I trust?"

Trust? Anlerran silently echoed.

A sudden red haze came over her, and she struck him so hard across the jaw with her fist that she knocked a tooth out and drew blood. Ruhal's widened in astonishment as he gasped in pain and spat blood onto the ground. "What... why..."

Then she saw the sudden realisation in his eyes. "Yes," she said quietly. "You can't even trust Lura. She told me that the two of you..." Anlerran's still-clenched fist shook with anger. "She told me all I needed to know."

Ruhal's head dropped. *Can you not even look at me?* Anlerran silently raged. Finally he said quietly, "She came to me. The two of us were lovers once. I shouldn't have allowed it."

"But you did. Is she better than me?"

His silence devastated her.

She rose to take her leave of him, unable to spend another moment in his company. Ruhal spoke up suddenly. "These bonds shame me, Anlerran, and they shame those who put me in them."

No, she thought. *They don't shame you. They protect you from a far worse fate, which you would have otherwise surely brought down upon yourself by now.*

She left before he could see and worse still interpret the maelstrom of emotion that threatened to engulf her.

VI

Amethyst looked up as Elluron walked into the tent. He nodded and smiled faintly. "Amethyst," he murmured.

"You remember me." Amethyst almost laughed out loud.

"Of course. It's good to see you again. I often thought about your journey. Did you find what you were looking for?"

Amethyst glanced at Ileana, who smiled back. "I did," she said. "But matters took an unexpected turn."

"Ah." He looked briefly at Ileana. "Maybe there'll be time to tell your story. I should like to listen to it."

"What will happen to us?" Ileana asked. "Has it been decided?"

"We'll do our best to keep you safe. Inerdyr will determine your whereabouts sooner or later. That will give him reason to come to us with even greater haste."

"But we wouldn't have left any trace! We just vanished from inside his castle."

"From what little I know of the man, he would have known that some powerful sorcery had spirited you away once it became clear that no trail could be found." Elluron's gaze fell on Vornen. He walked over and lifted his chin gently. When he looked into his eyes, Amethyst saw sudden shock. *How much do you see?* she silently asked him. *Can you see everything that afflicts him, the torment he's in? Can you help him?*

"What is the nature of his affliction?" Elluron asked suddenly. Vornen half-smiled and murmured something incomprehensible. "Tell me everything you know as swiftly as you can, Amethyst, if you wish to save him."

I have no choice, Amethyst reminded herself, and she said, "He has dreams and visions of Gates sometimes. I've even shaken him awake as he sits screaming, clawing at the air. To Vornen, the dreams have become real. Can you help him?"

"Truthfully, I don't know. One of the *orkar* healers may have some talent in this area." Elluron sniffed the air near Vornen's mouth. "Do you give him the *kyush* or does he procure it elsewhere?"

"I would never give him the vile weed," Amethyst said. "I expect he bought it from someone at Inerdyr's castle when I wasn't looking. Has it made him worse?"

"It won't have helped, certainly. *Kyush* can have unpredictable effects. Those who use it over a long period of time sometimes fail to recognise the boundary between the real and imaginary. I will have this man taken to the *orkar* healers."

"Do you think they can heal him?" Jak asked after Elluron had left. "I didn't even know *orkar* had healers amongst their people."

"Of course they do!" Ileana exclaimed. "All races do. You don't seem to know much about *orkar*..."

"They don't live in Fhaarluy. Are there any in Aphenhast?"

"Not that I know of. I'd heard a little about them, but I didn't know what they looked like until I saw a picture of one in a book I read at the castle."

Their conversation drifted on, but Amethyst paid little attention to it. Her thoughts drifted back and forth between her fears for Vornen, and her wider concern for all four of them. *Even if we're safe for the moment,* she reminded herself, *these people are Inerdyr's sworn enemies.*

Food and water was brought to them a little later, and three *orkar* healers came to inspect Vornen and take him to a field hospital tent. The healers gave him a potion to make him fall into a deeper sleep. One of them explained that he was as safe and as comfortable as could be expected and the potion would have rid him of the dreams for the time being.

Amethyst, Ileana and Jak were shown to a small tent that had been made up for sleeping in, and two *orkar* remained outside, either to guard them or to stop them from escaping. *They don't know what to do with us,* Amethyst reminded herself before she sank down onto a blanket and was overcome by tiredness. *I don't think these people even know what to do with themselves.*

VII

Before darkness had fallen, Elluron gathered the companions together. Even Lura attended the meeting, although she stood furthest away as if she had already prepared to leave and remained only out of idle curiosity as to who would be chosen to lead.

"All of you gathered here know why Ruhal is no longer our leader," Elluron told them. "But who *is* fit to lead? We were brought together by one thing only- recognition of the need for unity. But unity is even more difficult to keep than to attain. Who can bind us all together? In truth,"- he paused and looked around at everyone- "in truth, I fear that *no one* is. I would propose, therefore, that our Council gathered here lead together. We make decisions by listening to opposing arguments, where any exist, and we then put the matter to a vote."

Alturus shook his head. "Were the situation different, I might agree. But do we have the time to argue and contemplate and pore over each decision?"

"Our choice should not bear a heritage of distrust from the past," Elluron continued. "We must present a united stance that all of Harn can put aside all grievances for, and believe in."

"But if anyone here nominates that we should have a single leader," Kelandra said, "then they must also nominate the person they think fittest for that task. Myself, I say there is no one figure amongst us who can unify us all, but by consensus we can be seen as factions that came together and stayed together."

Elluron nodded slowly. "Does anyone here, considering Kelandra's words, believe that a single leader of unity can be found from amongst us?"

324

Quiet murmurs and the shaking of heads ensued. *So much for Ruhal's plan,* Anlerran thought, and wondered how he might react if he found out.

None of them had any idea what would now happen. They formed a patchwork army of elements that coexisted uneasily, and a following of tired, hungry refugees. Winter's grip upon the land tightened by the day.

"Lura, you began this venture with Ruhal," Elluron said, turning to the mercenary. "I should like you to remain, but are you about to give up and go your own way?"

Lura stared back at him. "Nothing would give me greater satisfaction than to see the Sanctum razed to the ground, and the empire of the Seven adrift in ash. *Nothing.* So yes, I should prefer to remain. You know so little about me, half-man."

Elluron smiled. "You are much easier to read than you think, Lura. Tread carefully, and you will remain welcome amongst us. An unwise move would quite possibly be your last."

"Now that may well be the politest threat I've ever received." Lura's sardonic reply elicited a deep chuckle from Garrok.

"The furthest outriders returned from the south a short while ago," Korrinn spoke up. "A great army is on the move from the middle lands, and has been for some days. There's no doubt that this is Inerdyr's. There are many thousands, but most of them appear to be ordinary folk gathered from his territories, or those of Wardens who are in thrall to Inerdyr. They are not warriors. They are, for the most part, families who have been forced to march to war."

"He will send them first," Garrok said as everyone pondered the news. "His commanders will drive those folk to their deaths."

"Not if we don't kill them," Elluron said. "Other means exist to prevent them from even coming near." Without elaborating he continued, "I propose that three of us take the burden of leadership- myself, Kelandra and Garrok."

Anlerran glanced across at Teryn of Darkbrook, who stood at the back of the tent, arms folded. The militia leader said nothing, nor did his expression change, but she wondered what he thought of being excluded from overall leadership given the number of fighters he had under him.

No one spoke against Elluron's proposal. *Now do you have everything you want, Father?* Anlerran thought as she watched him talking with Kelandra and Garrok as the meeting dispersed.

They made their weary way south-east for the next tennight and camped near to settlements with the aim of recruiting from amongst the people there. Anlerran watched with a heavy heart each time Kelandra, Elluron and Garrok rode into one of these villages and more often than not returned under a cloud with no new followers. *The season is bitter and folk have no appetite for war,* she felt like saying when her father described them turning their backs or professing their inability to fight or perform any useful work.

With no more than a hundred additional recruits from the area, the camp eventually reached the vicinity of the Stillwater Hills in a black and fractious mood. The weather had become much worse of late with bone-chilling winds lashing from the north-east and wet snow swirling through it, partly melting on the muddy grass. More than a dozen of their number had died in the last few nights, most of them from frostbite.

Through the late afternoon's wintry haze they could make out the Stillwater Hills rising out of the flatter lands in the distance. The clouds there looked almost as dark as night, and forks of lightning occasionally stabbed down, a moment's lurid brilliance cutting through the suffusing grey.

As she shielded her eyes against the downfall, Anlerran fancied for a moment that something else loomed at the southern edge of those hills- a vast shadow that moved across the landscape as if made by the mass of clouds, although it appeared even darker than the storm. An army, Anlerran thought, though not as large as she had imagined Inerdyr's host to be. Where were the thousands of folk that Korrinn had mentioned? Certainly many of them would have died during their march, but surely some would have survived the journey.

Elluron rode nearer to her and pointed towards the distant hills. "What do you think of that storm?"

Anlerran frowned and studied it a while longer. "The lightning," she realised finally. She shook her head in bewilderment. "Once, then again, then a third time- and it repeats."

Her father nodded grimly. "Have you ever before known lightning that can be predicted?"

Anlerran looked again to the storm and fancied that she saw small black figures creeping across the landscape as another fork of lightning stabbed down to illuminate the hills. But a moment later, when another bright flash lit up the distance she saw only the grassy slopes, empty but for a faint covering of snow. *I imagined an army of our enemies nearing us,* she told herself, but feared that it was not her imagination and that they had been somehow hidden by sorcery.

Even directly above, the clouds began to swirl in one direction and then another, borne by currents that had nothing to do with natural weather. When Anlerran closed her eyes, she could feel a groaning and snapping as if from under the earth, and the strangest of visions came to her- a clear picture of ancient remains shifting, as if the proximity of the approaching forces agitated them in some unknowable way.

Might another battle have been fought here, long ago? Or some great magic evoked?

"Something will come for us from that blackness," Elluron said. "The *choragh* mean to make an end of us, and swiftly."

Anlerran felt her own mortality stirring to greet her. "We're no match for whatever they send."

"I would guess that they have sent themselves," her father said. "There's a faint legend that tells of life originally forming in the mud of some distant, forgotten world. Life so often seems to end in mud, also."

"What was it all for?" Anlerran murmured tiredly. "Why did you want to lead us to this?"

He kissed her on the forehead, the warmth of the touch gone in an instant as the wind whipped at her face. "We would have had to face them eventually," he said. "Better to go with courage."

Before she could reply he rode swiftly away to discuss with Garrok and the Watchers, and Anlerran remained to view the approaching mayhem. She heard someone drawing their horse near to hers, and glanced across to see Kian, taut-faced and silent as she surveyed the still-distant storm. Anlerran could tell from her single look that the *du-luyan* girl had seen something similar.

"There are too few of us," Kian said, "even with the *orkar* ironmasters. But we can't run. They would slaughter us as we fled."

"Yes. This is it." Anlerran reached across and squeezed her hand. "Kian, it's been an honour to know you."

"An honour shared." Kian smiled tiredly, wiping snow from her hair.

Ileana watched as thunder rolled and flashes of light cut through the air. Her skin crawled as she glimpsed ephemeral shadows and figures, some tiny and some vast, flitting shapes that would head across the open land and overcome whatever resistance their army might summon. Somewhere in the Stillwater Hills the *choragh* lurked, and a potent army of *kin*.

She looked at Anlerran and Kian. When she closed her eyes she could see them still, quietly glowing figures on horseback. *They're like me,* she reminded herself. *The Old Powers run through them. The three of us are the same in many ways.*

Ileana knew that even those strengths would mean little in the face of the evil manifesting itself before them in the distance. Inerdyr was now perhaps the most powerful of all the higher *kin*, and somewhere, somehow, he helped control this conjuration.

If I don't do something now, we will all die here for nothing, she thought. *Maybe most of us will die anyway. But if...*

Lost in her own thoughts and terrified by the enormity of what she was about to do, Ileana walked between Anlerran and Kian. "Dismount, quickly," she said. "I need to tell you something."

She could barely hide her relief when they looked at each other and did so without question. *It must be now,* she thought, *before they suspect me.*

Ileana grasped their arms, and raised her head to the sky.

A piercing shriek cut through the air, drawing the attention of all who heard it.

But when heads turned in the direction of the sound and eyes peered through the hastening blizzard, the owner of that cry and those she was with had vanished from the world.

XV - Paths to Oblivion

I

Anlerran found herself crouching on her hands and knees and staring down at the mud and grass. Everything around her had fallen silent. No snow lay upon the ground.

She raised her head, and exhaled softly, astonished and terrified in equal measure. What kind of sorcery was this?

For a moment she saw indistinct shadows dancing at the edge of her vision. But these were not the *choragh* nor their *kin,* nor anything to do with them. Nor were they her comrades, or the ranks of the enemy she had momentarily seen. She could see no one around her.

The ephemeral, dancing darkness faded. The air felt oddly flat and still. A lurid tinge marked everything around her. *I can see less every moment,* she thought, panicking. Instinctively she seized at the powers within herself, feeling the crackle of her inner energies as if they battled against some intangible blanket of foulness.

Someone or something grabbed her arm, and she screamed and whirled round, striking out blindly to no avail. The strength had suddenly left her, but in any case she saw Ileana kneeling at her side, a calm, bright presence and perhaps the only companion of hers remaining in the world.

"Come with us," Ileana said quietly.

"What's happening?" she whispered as Ileana helped her to her feet. When she stared around her in each direction once again she thought she could see the movements of people, and even faint sounds that they made, but these swiftly disappeared.

Then she saw Kian standing nearby. At the same time she imagined that she heard a voice from the bottom of an ocean, or deep within the earth, or lost in the heavens. It

330

came to her as if from all sides and all places but sounded desperately distant, and she had no way of telling who or what uttered the word. *Anlerran!* it shrieked, over and over and in anguish.

"This is the Green Road, or a small part of it," Ileana said softly, clasping her hand and motioning for Kian to join them too. "I'm sorry, both of you, but I had no choice to bring you here. I can't do this on my own."

"Do what on your own?" Kian asked. Even as she spoke, she looked sharply around as if she could see the same phantom images and hear the same whispered sounds as Anlerran.

"Destroy Inerdyr," Ileana said simply.

Anlerran stared at her. "Ileana, this is madness. How by all the world's secrets can we put an end to him? Please, you need to take us back."

Ileana looked around them and pointed in a direction. Anlerran realised suddenly that she no longer had any idea which way was north or south, or east or west. "Do you see a storm? Do you see any evidence of the *choragh* or the *kin*?" Ileana asked both of them, and Anlerran shook her head. But Kian asked, "How can we strike against Inerdyr and the *kin*, if they're not even here?"

"Send us back," Anlerran said softly. "We can do nothing here."

"We return when the task is done," Ileana replied stubbornly. "Have either of you seen the state of your army? Until Inerdyr is dealt with, people will be afraid to support you even if they want to. We all watched as Elluron and Kelandra and Garrok tried to gather recruits from the villages we passed through. In every settlement the folk saw a rabble. *Orkar* and mercenaries and Watchers. It looks more like a badly-conceived rebellion than an army."

And such it is, Anlerran admitted to herself. "It's all we have," she said disconsolately.

"No," Ileana argued. "It's not. The three of us together have the power to kill Inerdyr if we get close enough to him."

Anlerran stared at the young girl, wondering if she was deluded or simply insane. Ileana looked stubbornly back at her, her pale blue eyes wide and serious.

"I've never been able to use my powers against anything but the *kin* and others made from *choragh* sorcery," Kian pointed out.

"Neither have I," Anlerran echoed. "We cannot stand against the warlock. He's still human, no matter how long he may have lived."

Ileana smiled thinly. "But remember what I told you. Inerdyr has been made *kin*. Why do you think I gathered my friends and escaped when I did? I had no choice. I knew what had happened."

Anlerran and Kian glanced at each other. "Are you certain of this?" Kian asked finally.

"I'm as certain as I can be," Ileana said. "The storm we all witnessed has been created by the *choragh*. Such is the power being wielded that even here I can feel its effect." She pointed, and the others looked, taking in their shadowy surroundings, the faint greenish glow that dimly lit the landscape, and finally the outlines of what appeared to be the Stillwater Hills in the distance. *How near are they really?* Anlerran found herself wondering. She suspected that distance and direction were not necessarily all they appeared to be in this place.

"Are we truly here?" she murmured.

"We are," Ileana affirmed. "And if we go to the summit of the hill we will know where Inerdyr is standing. The storm has made the way between the worlds... *thinner* there. He won't expect an attack from out of nowhere."

If we can lessen the shedding of blood through Inerdyr's destruction, can we even weaken the lords of the Old Dark? Anlerran wondered. *After all, they're not called the*

Blood Lords without reason. I don't have a better plan. And if battle is joined, the blood of our companions and followers- and the foot soldiers of Inerdyr's army- soaks the earth and strengthens the choragh.

Impossibilities abounded as the three women headed over the soft ground. As they looked into the distance away from the hills Anlerran caught sight of places that made her jaw drop in shock. To their right, a version of a city that she somehow knew to be Mornkastle lay glittering with the light of ten thousand bright torches in the murky dusk. In the opposite direction and further away she saw an altogether different city, dark and silent like a shadow fashioned from stone. *I know that place also, although I've never been there,* she thought suddenly.

"This can't be possible," she breathed. Somehow, almost within reach stood Luudhoq, the dark citadel of their enemies.

Ileana stopped and stood in front of her errant gaze, so that Anlerran was forced to look upon her instead. "Everything is different here," she said quietly. "Distance and direction are not what they would be in the truly physical world. Sometimes they barely exist at all. I also thought it impossible when I first came here. Often the land is like... like a crumpled map."

Anlerran's mind raced suddenly with possibilities. *If Luudhoq is not necessarily as far from us as it might be, then could we reach it that much sooner? Could some of us- the three of us here, perhaps- somehow enter it unseen?*

"No," Ileana said, and Anlerran jumped, suddenly aware that she had spoken those words out loud. "There are great dangers there," Ileana continued, "far greater than you or I could fight against. The Road has become... *poisoned*. It's not so much a road as a cliff. Parts of it are crumbling away and dying. I saw it when my friends and I were there before. We had to go through it to get to you."

Anlerran wondered where such a precipice might lead down into, and swiftly banished the thought. When she glanced back towards it she imagined that the Black Citadel had grown a little larger and loomed a little nearer, simply by her thinking such a thing.

As they continued on towards the Stillwater Hills, Anlerran felt her fear growing. When she looked at her companions she saw the same terror in their eyes. "We could die," she murmured.

"If Inerdyr isn't destroyed, everyone dies," Ileana said, but her voice shook.

A while later they reached the foot of the nearest hill and began their ascent. Anlerran thought she saw long and black shadows somewhere up ahead on the slope, yet the three of them made no shadows themselves. The air, oddly warm during their walk across the lower land, now became bitterly cold, and grew icier still the higher they climbed, until soon it became almost painful to breathe. Anlerran's hands became numb and she tried to tell herself that this was an illusion of some sort, some powerful dream in which she had become ensnared. But it felt real.

As they stopped briefly to catch their breath, Anlerran became sure that she could hear faint whispers- mournful, despairing. Ileana had heard them too and warned her, "Don't listen to them. If you start to hear words you understand, speak over them or at least concentrate on other thoughts."

"What are they?" Anlerran whispered.

Ileana said something that chilled Anlerran to her core. "I don't know what they are, truthfully. Dark things from the heart of the world."

As they recommenced their ascent, the sounds gradually faded away into the backcloth of silence, but they returned a short while later, quieter, more distant and yet more mournful than ever, as if they pleaded with the three women to stop and listen to their lament.

They reached the summit of the hill. *This is where the storm was centred,* Anlerran reminded herself. *But Inerdyr is not here. The* choragh *are not here. This place is empty.*

Shivering in the icy air, she turned to Ileana. "What now?"

Ileana led them towards the centre of the summit. She looked in each direction and then nodded to herself, motioning for them to stand next to her.

"As soon as you see him," she said quietly, "strike with every bit of strength you have. Do so immediately. If we pause for an instant, we are done for. The *choragh* will be nearby. We strike at Inerdyr and then we flee back here. Whatever you do, *keep holding hands* with me."

"What if we can do nothing against him..." Kian began, but Ileana cut her off abruptly. "I told you. He is *kin*. We have the power within us to destroy him." She squeezed Kian's hand and looked intently at her. "You have to believe in yourself. All three of us do."

Ileana gave them no further warning. She seized their hands, and in an instant, the gloom of their surroundings brightened into the harsh violence of a winter storm. Shadows and shapes flitted and shimmered all around the slope of the hill. Before them the figure of a man stood facing away, naked and taut, arms outstretched to the roiling clouds, his body lit harshly by flashes of lightning. Fragments of light and darkness leapt from his hands into the storm. The ground shook as if it might split apart at any moment.

Kill him. Anlerran heard the command whispered in her mind, not knowing whether it came from herself or Ileana.

Inerdyr turned, perhaps sensing their presence. Anlerran felt a surge of the Powers rush through her, so strong that it almost knocked her off her feet.

Inerdyr cried out and reached his hand to his head, an expression of agony on his face. To her side, Anlerran sensed raw, intense power pouring from where Kian and Ileana stood. She screamed, her rage at Inerdyr drawing her own powers out of her body. Blood began to spill from the warlock's eyes and bone started to jut out from his skin. He sagged to the ground, his knees making a sickening sound as they snapped. Bloodied and enraged, he looked at them and his mouth opened; words she could not hear issued forth. Anlerran felt a wetness trickle down either side of her head, and her vision became dark and distorted.

At her side, Kian swayed, and Anlerran thought she heard a whisper from her. *I can't do this any longer.*

Fire, Anlerran thought as Inerdyr opened his mouth. *Consume this man before he can let loose more of his spellcraft.*

The flames leapt from beneath and around Inerdyr and licked eagerly at his flesh; even the fierce blizzard could not stop them. He bowed his head and tumbled to the ground, an invisible heaviness slowly crushing his body. *Ileana and Kian are doing this,* Anlerran thought as the fire burned his flesh and the unseen weight bore down upon him.

Great slivers of blackness rushed towards them from every direction. She knew what they were. She could feel their cold fury, their desire for vengeance. Pain flared in her head, more terrible than any she could have imagined. *We can't fight them,* she thought numbly. *We're no match for the* choragh. *May this end quickly!*

Abruptly the storm, Inerdyr and the ephemeral shadows in the distance- the *choragh*- vanished.

Anlerran looked around, wracked in pain as she staggered to her knees. *The Green Road,* she thought as she saw Kian kneeling next to Ileana, holding the girl's hand. *Ileana brought us back.*

"We have to leave," Ileana murmured, but she didn't have the strength to get to her feet. Anlerran and Kian helped her, and the three of them headed slowly down the slope.

The journey back down the hill and across the dark open land beyond took a long time. Perhaps more than a day passed; none of them could tell. They stopped often, hardly daring to believe that they had brought about Inerdyr's downfall, and fearful of what might happen to their companions if the *choragh* now unleashed the full extent of their fury upon them.

Ileana barely had the strength to return them to the world they knew. When she did, the three of them were found lying upon the muddy grass, unconscious but with their hands still clasped tightly together, as if an unbreakable bond had been formed.

II

A final boom of thunder rolled across the hills, followed by an ominous, terrible silence. Snow came down more thickly than ever to blanket the land.

Ferrin stopped in his tracks. A prickle of unease stirred within him. He looked to his right and saw Ithia on her knees. She looked this way and that as if she no longer knew the direction in which their enemy lay. To his left, another of the higher *kin* stood, a creature of raw sinew and vast jaws. It swayed on its feet as if the snow had already grown too thick to walk through, although the fall could be no more than a hand in depth.

On an impulse he turned and retraced his steps towards the summit of the hill from which Inerdyr had stirred up the storm and sent the elements into chaos to disguise their path towards the enemy. Looking up he no longer saw the quick-moving shapes of his lords, nor could he see Inerdyr.

His primal instinct urged him to turn and run. With an effort he ignored it, dismissing the sensation as the product of irrational fear. But when he reached the crest of the hill Ferrin was reminded of something else he had known, long before he had been elevated to *kin. Fear is not irrational. Fear has a reason. Fear exists for your survival.*

A charred ruin lay upon the ground, still moving spasmodically. The snow had melted away around it, and the nearest grass stood singed and blackened. Acrid smoke rose into the air.

Ferrin stepped nearer and squatted down to survey the body in detail. Every snowflake that fell upon the remains of its face hissed and became a momentary tear tracing a line down the burned skin before evaporating.

Burned terribly though the body was, Ferrin still recognised Inerdyr.

"And you were raised to be the highest of us all," he heard himself murmur as Inerdyr stared wildly up at him, or perhaps through him and into the descending snow. The cavernous remains of the warlock's mouth open and closed as if in astonishment at his condition. A spasm wracked the charred body and Inerdyr spat flecks of blood and small pieces of his insides.

Whatever powers he had possessed, he now owned none. Ferrin could sense that much. They had leaked away to some unknown place, or perhaps all that had been given to the warlock by their Lords had been taken back. Ferrin watched dispassionately as Inerdyr's movements slowed and became less frequent, until they stopped altogether. His eyes- *curious that they remained untouched,* Ferrin thought- remained staring up at the sky, sightless marbles desperately asking how he had earned this fate.

I have seen other kin *who were unable to control the powers flowing through them,* he recalled. *But Inerdyr should have been in control, and our Lords would have stopped him from channelling too much too quickly. No, something else happened here. An enemy force reached him, although that should have been impossible.*

Ferrin got to his feet and stood in each direction in turn, silently imploring the *choragh* to provide him with a sign. None came, but as he stood there the blizzard ceased and the snow clouds gradually disappeared. Ferrin watched the lifting of the veil as Ithia, Leon and then the others of his company joined him at the summit.

"What happened to him?" Ithia asked, staring at Inerdyr's still-smouldering corpse.

"Someone of great strength in the Old Powers, at a guess," Ferrin said. *We should be away from here,* he thought, but years of practice kept the fear he felt from showing on his face.

"But who could have got close enough? Our Lords were *here*, Ferrin. Even if all those witchlings had attacked at the same time, they would have been crushed. They couldn't have got close enough to him."

"There's a question I can't answer," he admitted, although he did in fact have a theory. It troubled him, and it was not one that he cared to share with the rest of the *kin*. Even to his own vivid imagination it sounded as mad as Inerdyr himself. *As Ithia said, no one could have got close enough. Inerdyr stood surrounded by our Lords. I myself saw them. I turned and saw them just before the storm was stopped. Surely only a Descendant of the First- or more likely a group of them- could possibly have done this, and they could not have reached Inerdyr with our Lords nearby.*

"We'll head back to our camp and await orders," he said, trying to shake his mind free of that troubling thought.

"What about the enemy?" Leon asked.

Ferrin pointed towards the lower land. "They now see us as clearly as we see them. Most of the lower *kin* that gathered for battle have been slaughtered. The anointed highest of the higher *kin* is no more, seared inside and out by some distant touch. Our Lords have gone from here. Do you see them?"

Leon shook his head, shivering as he pulled his fur robe more tightly about himself. "What do we do with Inerdyr's body?"

"Nothing. Let him lie here and the crows take him, if they can find a peck of unburned flesh in his body."

"Still some juice for them in his eyes," Ithia observed with a faint smile.

Ferrin looked around and swiftly counted his followers. Not one of their number was missing.

They headed eastwards down the hill. The Stillwater shimmered before them, pale in the afternoon light, its edges frozen. Behind them the sun hurried to burn through the western clouds before the horizon swallowed it.

I for one would sooner face the starspawn than Inerdyr's killers, Ferrin mused, not sure whether or not he would, or indeed if it mattered.

III

The stench of blood and death filled the harsh air. The lower *kin* had been routed, and several of the higher *kin* captured. The peasant army that Korrinn had reported had not appeared. Most of the higher *kin* had retreated as the storm lifted.

"What are we to do with those *kin* that were captured alive?" Elluron spoke up. "The ironmasters cannot hold them indefinitely."

"Put them under the earth or burn them," Kelandra said immediately. "Why are we keeping them at all? So far they've been impervious to questioning, no matter how much pain they're made to suffer."

I imagine you're well qualified to make that statement, Amethyst thought with a sideways glance at the Watcher.

A group of four ironmasters entered the tent, bearing with them a dark-haired Hastian woman. Elluron looked towards Amethyst. "Is this Jaana?"

Amethyst nodded, forcing herself to look unblinkingly back as Jaana fixed her malevolent stare upon her.

"Inerdyr's loyal lieutenant," Garrok said. "We should hear what she has to say." He motioned to the ironmasters and Jaana was thrown to the muddy grass. Her hands had been tied behind her back. Amethyst could also see a faint shimmering around the rope and wondered if it might be the effect of a binding by the *orkar* ironmasters.

"Help her stand," Elluron said to the two nearest *orkar* guards. "Let's speak with her properly."

They hauled her to a standing position and Jaana stared sullenly at Elluron and the others. "Your rebellion will fail."

"How so?" Kelandra demanded.

"Soon the Council of Mornkastle will know what has happened here. They will prepare for your eventual coming. Survivors will have sent messenger birds. Most of the higher *kin* will also come for you again. We will keep coming for you until you are all destroyed."

Jaana continued, "The news of Inerdyr's demise will travel fast. The man who kept the peace in the middle lands has been murdered by traitors, and you have declared open war. Defeating Inerdyr does not mean you defeat the true guardians of Aona. If you weaken them, you weaken Aona herself. You lessen our chances of victory against the starspawn. What do you think to gain by struggling against us?"

Jaana stared around, nodding as she saw that she had everyone's undivided attention. "Listen to me," she said. "Surely you are not *all* fools. Make peace with the Earth Lords and let us stand as one against the *marandaal*. A truce can be brokered with the South, even now. You do not need to take Mornkastle and needlessly waste lives there. You need not march several hundred leagues or more and sacrifice yourselves attempting to take the Black Citadel. We can stand as one, and our Lords can make peace with the South. Let no blood be shed until the time comes to destroy the starspawn."

"I have a question for you," Kelandra spoke up. "What became of the thousands of ordinary people enlisted in Inerdyr's army? We saw none of them in battle."

A look of unease flickered in Jaana's eyes. "Disease. Frostbite. Hunger. I myself would have spoken against bringing them, but it was not my place."

"All of them?" Kelandra stared at her. "They all died before you reached the Stillwater?"

"About half." Jaana looked down at the ground. "The others were buried alive in a mass grave near the eastern shore of the lake. A necessary sacrifice to magnify the powers of our Lords in the battle to come."

"Slit her throat," Garrok commanded as a murmur of disgust rose up, but when one of the *orkar* guards drew a knife, Elluron raised a hand and said, "No. Put your weapon away." The guard looked doubtfully at Garrok, who finally nodded, though he looked displeased.

"The *kin* are different to your witchlings only in their acceptance of universal truths," Jaana continued. "We work the same forces. We might have different ideals, but we're the same. Why don't we call a truce? Why not stop this fighting?"

She's a sly one, Amethyst thought as her gaze took in the oddly dark veins that criss-crossed Jaana's neck and cheeks in places. *Surely everyone here will recognise her words for what they are- an attempt to sow seeds of discontent amongst those who have only just fought a wearying battle.*

"Together, we can all send the *marandaal* out of Aona for all time," Jaana continued. "But divided, we cannot withstand them. Do you want to be the ones who helped usher in an age of darkness? I may be a descendant of the First, but I know that the powers were stolen from the rightful guardians of Aona. Our lords may in time have gifted them, but instead my ancestors took that which was not theirs to take."

Jaana shrugged at the collective silence and bowed her head tiredly. "Kill me and be quick about it," she said eventually. "At least then we'll all be done with this charade."

"It might prove useful if we tortured her," Alturus spoke up. "She must know secrets concerning the *kin* or even her masters. Such information could be important. We are experts at delving into the murk of the mind."

"I don't doubt it," Elluron said quietly, "but we will not torture her."

When Amethyst turned her head to look at Jaana again, the woman wore an indolent smirk on her face.

"The *choragh* wish to enslave the Younger Races again," Elluron told her. "Your own words make that plain. We do not need the help of your masters. *They*, however, need an army of slaves to empower them by blood sacrifice. Harn will not give that to them."

"I don't speak for my Lords," Jaana said sullenly.

"No?" His expression was thoughtful. "But you'll have a chance to speak *with* them soon enough. I will send you back to them. Doubtless your masters will be well pleased with you, captured and humiliated. Tell them we have no wish to wage war on them until the *marandaal* are banished from our world- and then only if they still claim dominion over the Younger Races."

Jaana blinked and swallowed, as all around her the gathering descended into uproar. Garrok strode up to Elluron. "You *cannot* allow her to go free," he hissed. "She is *kin*. She must die."

Kelandra stepped quickly forward until she was almost between them. "We could not hope to make her suffer as her masters will at their hands. And what better sight to give our soldiers than that of a broken and defeated *kin-woman* being sent back to her lords?"

Garrok uttered a harsh curse in his own language, spat on the ground and stepped back, angrily motioning for the two *orkar* on either side of Jaana to release her. They hauled the prisoner to her feet and cut the ropes that bound her wrists. Looking at her, Amethyst could not tell whether Jaana was relieved at being miraculously released, or fearful of her possible fate when she inevitably returned to the clutches of her masters.

"If we see you again," Elluron warned, "then you will be slain. If any of the *kin* attack us then the cold earth awaits them. Guards, take this wretched woman to the eastern edge of the camp and let her go free."

At first Jaana appeared to be rooted to the spot, perhaps still astonished at her reprieve. "Your mercy will come back to haunt us," Lura said abruptly as Jaana was led from the tent.

"I would prefer not to have to hear your opinion," Elluron said in a hard voice. "You are one step from being named a traitor."

"By defending the man who created this army you now lord over?" Lura looked him up and down. "You are no better than the *choragh* yourself."

Now there goes a woman with fury in her heart, Amethyst noted as she watched Lura turn and stride away, her face like thunder.

She made her way back to the tent where Vornen rested and told him what she had seen. He had gained some strength and was sitting up and drinking some foul-smelling herbal concoction that one of the *orkar* healers had made for him. "How is Ileana?" he asked quietly.

"Well enough, though she's said little and she looks as pale as a *luyan*, poor girl," Amethyst sighed.

Vornen put the cup to one side. "Not so long ago, I silently wished that you wouldn't look into the future at all," he said. "I saw no point in having plans or hopes. But after we came back from the Green Road, I think perhaps that's *all* that we have. Life is nothing without those little hopes, Amethyst."

"That's very philosophical," Amethyst commented. "Are you sure you haven't found some more *kyush* from somewhere?" But she found tears pricking the corners of her eyes, and silently fumed: *Why do his words always affect me so? Can I not love him without setting free all my emotions, like some giddy young girl?*

"I would be honoured to meet your family, if we can find them," he said. "I'm afraid I can't reciprocate. I've no idea if I have any family left alive or where they might be in the world. But I've contemplated many idle plans. I would like to have children with you one day."

"Gods, Vornen. You pick some strange moments." Amethyst tried to steady her voice.

"If we make it through all of this," he added as if he hadn't heard her. "Well?"

"If we make it through all this," she repeated. "It goes against all sense to bring a child into this world, but maybe my instinct has beaten my sense into submission. That often seems to be the case where you're concerned."

She squeezed his hand and then kissed him on the lips. Their eyes met and Amethyst forgot everything around her for a moment. *Your eyes reveal you*, she thought. *And I'll hope for whatever you want, for as long as I see your inner beauty burning brightly through the mud of your mind.*

IV

As she came within sight of Mordenglen's western border, Jaana's rage that had seethed for the last three days finally subsided, replaced by contempt and cool hatred.

Much of the animosity she felt was levelled at the witches who had apparently killed Inerdyr- descendants of the First like Jaana herself, but they claimed rights to the powers they held. They sought to use them for their own ends, even to help cobble together an army of the ignorant lorded over by *orkar* beasts and hired swords.

They're not your powers, witchlings, Jaana seethed as the snowfall paused and in the west a few shards of sunlight broke through the cloud cover. *The* choragh *are your masters and soon enough they will bring you to heel. Do as you will and wage war against the South; at least such sacrifices will strengthen our lords against the starspawn. One way or another your rebellion is done for, your murder of Inerdyr a hollow victory.*

Jaana pressed on into the dark interior of the forest. Soon she realised that this place truly belonged to the *choragh* now; their essence coursed through every fibre of the ancient woodland. It might have been the First Age again, when the world was young, Aona still unfound by the *marandaal.* Jaana almost smiled, and drew a deep breath of the cool, pine-tinged air.

Head a little to the north-east, a voice whispered. She had no idea if the notion originated within her own head or not, but it felt persuasive, and after a moment she led her horse along a path that led in that direction. But after only a short while the mount became restive and ill-tempered and even turned to bare its teeth at her. Jaana had neither love nor patience for horses, and decided that she would rather keep walking her chosen path than continue trying to cajole the fractious beast.

She gladly dismounted, and watched in silence as the horse turned and cantered away back along the path they had already trodden.

As Jaana soon discovered, the way ahead would have been unsuitable for such a creature anyway. The path became narrow and branches hung low overhead, besides which she soon found herself side-stepping great tendrils of bramble and patches of deep-looking mud, wondering why she felt so intent on heading along this overgrown route.

After a long while she arrived at a semi-derelict cottage whose front door stood wide open. Jaana walked slowly around to the back and discovered a hole dug in the ground- a grave, she decided immediately- and some tangled vegetation nearby. Jaana knelt down to cautiously touch it, and allowed herself a contemptuous smile. This was indeed a grave, and someone weak in the Powers had tried to ward it. In the face of her lords' growing power within Mordenglen, that warding had been rendered utterly ineffectual.

And what now of the bodies? she wondered, but as she walked round to the front of the house again and peered into the cottage she found her answer.

One of the *diafagh* sat at the kitchen table, slack-jawed and head leaning forwards. A great slash across its throat, bloodless now yet still gaping, pointed to a likely original cause of death. The other *diafagh* stood over a stove whose abandoned pots and pans still held the mouldering remains of a dinner never eaten.

They turned and looked at her, but did nothing more. Jaana would not have expected them to; she was *kin* now, and they would not attack her. They would do nothing at all unless she or another of the *kin* commanded.

She could destroy them if she wished, but she felt no compulsion to. Instead she observed them for a short while. It occurred to her that these two, perhaps awakened as the shadow of the Earth Lords swept across the forest, had adopted the positions they had occupied just before they had been killed.

Both of them now flowing with the old Powers, awaiting commands. But I have no commands to give them.

Eventually, as the light faded Jaana turned away from the scene and headed off east, deeper still into Mordenglen.

Jaana came across a disused stone hut sometime later. Full darkness had fallen, but her dark-sight was better now than ever before- another gift from the Earth Lords. She forced open the door and walked inside. An old straw-stuffed mattress lay in one corner. Aside from that the place was empty.

Frost already formed upon the ground outside, but Jaana felt a racing heat through her body, a strange force that energised and enervated simultaneously. Certainly the bitter chill with which the ordinary creatures of Mordenglen had to cope meant nothing to her. She felt the sharpness of the air but not its effect.

Jaana sat on the mattress for a long while, breathing steadily, inhaling the dampness of this place. She allowed her thoughts to wander in whichever direction they wished to take, and imagined herself standing before the army of traitors once again, only on this occasion her Lords had lent her superior speed with which to destroy the witchlings- for Jaana had decided they were beyond turning. She imagined slashing at their necks before any one of their allies had a chance to defend them. She pictured herself plunging her knife through the softness of their eyes, driving the blade deep into their delusional brains. She imagined inflicting a dozen unspeakable acts upon their still-twitching bodies as their companions looked on, rendered motionless with horror.

A faint presence pulled Jaana from the idle pleasure of her thoughts.

Someone is approaching, she realised, and she walked to the window. She could see no one through the glass, but nevertheless felt certain that soon she would.

I know who it is, she thought a moment later, dumbfounded by that realisation.

Lyya came into view, cast partly in Ildar's white light as she walked slowly along one of the paths that led up to the hut. She looked up, and perhaps recognised the face behind the glass, for she quickened her pace. Jaana went to the door and opened it, and the two women stared wordlessly at each other. *She looks lost in her own mind,* Jaana thought as she looked into the *luyan*'s green eyes. *Lost, but now she's found me. How did she manage that?*

She ushered her inside, and watched as Lyya took off her backpack, set it on the floor and sat on the mattress with a sigh.

"What are you doing here, Lyya?" she asked after a while.

"I came here to find you," Lyya said. "Your trail was easy enough to follow. I'm here for you. I left what was left of the army days ago, meaning to try and find you when the battle was done, if I could. Did you not notice?" Lyya paused, and looked meaningfully at her. "You gave yourself over to the *choragh* before we even began the march. Why would you do such a thing, Jaana?"

"Why would you come after me if I serve the Earth Lords?" Jaana rejoined. "Surely it would have been *safer* for you to fall in with those misguided fools who think they can fight against the true guardians of the world *and* withstand the *marandaal*. That, at least, is what they would have you believe."

"I came after you because I love you," Lyya said quietly.

Jaana stared at her. She had no idea what to say. She had never expected to even see Lyya again.

"And I know that you love me," Lyya continued. She got up and walked a little closer. "Powers, I wish I had done more to help you long ago. Perhaps then you wouldn't have been manipulated by Inerdyr. You could have been like the other Descendants- no, you still can."

"Why would I wish to be like them? They will die for their ignorance."

"Come back with me and we'll join them," Lyya pleaded. "They'll forgive you, if you only renounce the *choragh*..."

Jaana took two quick steps back, shaking her head. "Are you an utter fool, Lyya? The Earth Lords are the only true force standing between us and annihilation from the void. You cannot see that because you serve those who serve themselves- those Descendants who insist that the powers they hold *belong* to them. But they are only a part of the great scheme, Lyya. As are we all."

"I beg you, Jaana- please come back with me."

"No. I couldn't even if I wanted to. They captured and then released me. I can't fathom why, but they swore to kill me if they saw me again." Jaana stared thoughtfully at her. "Do you truly love me?"

"Upon my word. I wouldn't have said so otherwise. You know it to be true."

"Then stay with me. Give yourself to my Lords as I have done. I ask nothing more."

"I can't do that!" Lyya cried. "Why would you ask such a thing of me?!"

"If you love me, then do it. If you don't, then turn and join those fools." Jaana glanced out of the window at the thickening frost and listened to the deep silence of the woodland. "The *choragh* gave you safe passage to this place," she said quietly. "They understand your importance to me, perhaps." She smiled. "One more gift for my loyalty. Had you been of no importance, you would never have survived your journey here. A patch of mud might have suddenly turned out to be a hundred hands deep; a tree might have somehow entwined you and crushed your bones. No, you are here only because you're *meant* to be here, Lyya- for me and for our Lords."

Lyya stared helplessly at her. Jaana came closer until they stood so close together that they could have kissed. She reached out to stroke the *luyan* woman's translucent hair as it shimmered in the faint light. "I remember when I first saw you," she whispered. "I decided that you were the most beautiful creature I had ever seen. Do you truly fear that our Lords will harm you, when you mean so much to me? Give yourself to them- words are all they ask of you- and serve as I serve. Fight alongside me against the *marandaal*. You may not be a descendant of the First, Lyya, but the Earth Lords will gift you great powers as *kin*. Your eyes will be opened to the inner workings of the world. You will wonder why you could not see the truth of things before."

"No," Lyya whispered, but Jaana kissed her upon the lips, then again more urgently. "Stay with me," she murmured. "What else is there for you? I love you, Lyya. Those others do not. You are nothing to them but a *luyan* foot-soldier like so many others. Will they mourn you if you fall in battle as they attack Mornkastle or even Luudhoq? No, they will not. Stay with me and utter the words."

Jaana knew then that she had broken Lyya's resolve. Perhaps she had seen her possible future as one more faceless pawn in the traitors' all-encompassing madness. Perhaps she had simply decided that it would be a better life, shorter or otherwise, to remain with one whom she loved and take up arms for the sake of Aona herself, rather than march alone in a vast army to her eventual fate as a body face down in the mud of the battlefield.

"What would you have me say?" Lyya asked shakily.

Jaana felt heat burn through her hands and down to the tips of her fingers. "Kneel before me," she said, "and repeat these words."

Lyya sagged to her knees, although her will had not yet broken entirely. "Jaana, I beg you..."

"Enough begging. Repeat this after me. *I give myself to the Earth Lords, body and spirit. The* choragh, *the Earth Lords, are my true lords. I have no others, nor shall I ever.*" The words came automatically to Jaana. It didn't matter that she had never uttered them before. She had given herself without speaking a single word of obedience, made *kin* by Inerdyr. But that would not do for Lyya.

"I give myself to the Earth Lords, body and spirit," Lyya said quietly, half-sobbing. "The *choragh*, the Earth Lords, are my true masters. I have no others, nor shall I ever."

Jaana could feel a writhing sensation throughout her hands, concentrated at her fingertips, as if thousands of tiny entities had suddenly been awakened, agitated and excited by the promise of a new servant to the true powers of Aona. At the same time, Lyya looked up suddenly and Jaana could tell in that instant that now she indeed changed. Blackness ran through her eyes, the irises of which were now a much darker green.

"It's done," she murmured. "Rise."

Lyya blinked in confusion as if she had only now woken up. "Jaana, what have you done to me?!" One shaking hand reached for her longknife, and although Jaana did not reckon for a moment that Lyya would use it, still she grasped that hand until the *luyan* woman's panic had subsided a little.

"What becomes of us now?" Lyya moved to the side wall of the hut and stared agitatedly out through the window.

"We head towards the Border Wall and await the *marandaal*. What else?"

Lyya looked bemused as she turned around. "How can the two of us..."

"It won't be just the two of us, Lyya. Far from it. Others of the *kin* will join us at the Wall. That's where we're all headed eventually, no matter the movements and plots of the fools who slew Inerdyr and many of the *kin*."

"We'll die," Lyya said automatically.

"All things die, yet nothing truly dies." Jaana smiled at her own insight as she lay down on the mattress. "Are you warmer now, Lyya?"

"I feel a strange heat inside me," Lyya said quietly, turning to face her. "I've destroyed myself for you, Jaana."

"You've destroyed nothing of yourself," Jaana retorted. "You are simply reborn, and now you and I are the same."

XVI - The Box

I

As the army progressed south over the next tennight, some of those folk who had been part of Inerdyr's army joined them. Many of those later left, citing whatever reasons they could find such as ill health, or family to protect.

Over those same days, as they passed near small villages and hamlets during the journey south, around the same number joined their force, some of them entire extended families or even in one case an entire village of people. The council of leaders listened to reports of the reasons they gave for joining and found, unsurprisingly, that chief amongst them was the relative safety they hoped being part of the gathering would offer. The news of Inerdyr's death had also spread far and wide, and perhaps some of these people had decided to make use of their new-found freedom.

The weather remained bright and cold. The nightly frost grew savage, and around eighty of their people succumbed to frostbite, while a similar number died of one disease or another. Funeral pyres were lit nightly. Restlessness abounded and fights became common, and yet overall an uneasy peace remained in place.

Garrok did not hide his displeasure at the lack of discipline that blighted parts of the camp. "Amongst my people, to desert an army is to forfeit one's life," he said one evening as he sat with Korrinn, Iyoth and Kian, cooking a side of calf over a large fire. The *orkar* had taken it upon themselves to agree a price with the better-off farmers and landowners who joined their army, which as far as Kian could see amounted to payment in meat for protection provided.

"Killing people for trying to survive won't help our cause," Iyoth commented.

354

"So says the assassin," Garrok grunted as he tore off a part of the carcass with his claws and stuffed almost all of it into his mouth. The *orkar* man looked appraisingly at Iyoth. "Still, there's an old saying that a son or a daughter changes a man like nothing else can."

"Do you have any family?" Kian asked him before Iyoth could utter anything in return.

"No." Garrok chewed methodically, swallowed and then cleared his throat before adding in a quieter, more reflective voice, "Too busy fighting those who would do my people harm, and travelling. Maybe, if we survive all this and if I still have my strength and wits, I'll raise a family. Depends what kind of world is left for them to grow up in." He smiled, although the expression still looked predatory to Kian. "We're all dreamers," he said, "with one eye on a distant hope that never bears fruit."

Some distance away, Elluron looked up as Anlerran approached. "I have something I must tell you," she murmured, "and I fear you won't like it."

"You don't need to fear my reaction," he told her. "You may, however, have need to fear your own inaction, depending on what this is."

"Can you make absolutely certain that we cannot be heard?"

"I can," he said, frowning. Anlerran watched as he whispered something under his breath and closed his eyes. For a moment the air felt somehow thicker, almost as if she was underwater. Her father opened his eyes and motioned for her to sit next to him. "Tell me everything you need to," he said. "I'll say nothing until you've finished."

Anlerran dropped her voice further. "I have something terrible to tell you. I should have told you before now. Nia bears another secret- one which may bring about the downfall of the Seven. But it might also be the end of... well, everything."

"What do you mean?"

"Have you ever wondered where Watchers come from? I know this now."

Elluron stared wordlessly at her.

"Nia saw two of the Seven *creating* one, or attempting to. Making him from the tortured flesh of a screaming man. A human man. *That* is where they come from- they are human men and women, or at least they begin as such."

Anlerran took a deep breath and quietly related to him everything that Nia had told her about the origins of the Watchers. His expression barely changed.

"Are you certain that Nia spoke the truth?" he said when she had finished.

Anlerran blinked, taken aback. She had always felt absolutely certain of the story's truth. She thought for a moment, recalling how she had felt and how Nia had appeared that evening in the tavern in Darkbrook. "Yes," she said. "I am absolutely certain."

"And have you told anyone else?"

"No. I couldn't. It took me this long just to tell you."

"I should have learned of this earlier, Anlerran." Elluron appeared to relent a little. "But what's said is said, now. I think we have to play this card, and sooner rather than later."

"What do you mean?" Anlerran asked guardedly.

"Soon enough we'll be within striking distance of Mornkastle, and one thing is for certain- the powers that rule the city will send emissaries out to tell us their position. With any luck, there will be some sort of negotiation. That may be the time to reveal the truth about the Watchers- truth that they can ascertain for themselves."

"What if our revealing this awful truth creates a wave of bloodshed that can't be controlled? Don't you fear the same thing?"

Elluron fell silent for so long that Anlerran was on the verge of asking him again when he said, "We have no idea what will happen if Nia's story can be verified as truth by any of the Watchers present. Nevertheless we must make it happen. The South may well fall into chaos, but therein lies our best hope. Others may tell you differently, but we have little hope of taking Mornkastle or any other city by force. They all have a vast number of defenders and all the southern cities will be protected by Watchers as well."

"What do we do now?" Anlerran asked.

"We'll decide when we come near to Mornkastle. But the powers within that city must hear of this."

With the afternoon growing late on the tenth day since their departure from Stillwater, a small group of riders were spotted heading out of the grasslands in the south. The foremost among them bore a white flag that he held high as he slowed his horse to a halt still fifty paces or more away from the army's front line. Still holding the banner of peace aloft, he slowly dismounted. Two others held flags bearing a green background adorned with the moons above a wall. Anlerran knew that this was the coat of arms of Mornkastle.

Fighters had drawn their swords and longknives at the behest of their commanders, but the man who had dismounted paid them scant attention. Scarred and creased, he looked like a seasoned veteran of battles. "My name is Yan Hennicson," he spoke up. "Who among you speaks for this army?"

Elluron, Garrok and Kelandra exchanged glances, and finally, as if by some silent and mutual consent Kelandra spoke up. "The three of us, and then a wider council," she said, gesturing to Garrok and Elluron in turn.

"Interesting," Yan commented dryly. "May I meet with this... *council* of yours to discuss matters?"

The camp was set up and a short while later Yan sat before Elluron, Kelandra, Garrok, Anlerran, Kian and Iyoth in the meeting tent. Elluron had asked that Anlerran and Kian attend, and Iyoth had accompanied Kian without asking. Elluron had chosen to ignore the intrusion.

"Six of Mornkastle's ruling council offer to meet six of you, a league from here, directly south," he began without preamble. "The open area near the bottom of that hill." He pointed back into the southern distance although of course it could not be seen from inside. "At noon, tomorrow. In return for this audience your army will not move another pace towards Mornkastle in the meantime. Those are their terms."

"And how many of these six would be Watchers themselves?" Kelandra asked.

Yan shrugged. "I wouldn't know. That isn't for me to say."

"We have no way of determining if this is trickery or not," Kian pointed out.

"But we cannot progress on that assumption," Kelandra told her, and turned again to Yan. "Those terms are acceptable, but on these conditions. Our host will camp here, but by the same token no armed forces will move north from Mornkastle. No one at all should come near except for these six members of the Council."

"You would be wise to respect our terms," Elluron added. His voice was mild but carried an icy tone. "The mighty sorcerer Inerdyr now lies dead in the Stillwater Hills, little more than a scar on the landscape. Be aware, Yan, that transparency is in the interests of Mornkastle. Return to your masters and tell them that six of us will meet with them as requested."

"Of course." Yan looked carefully at each of them in turn. His gaze lingered a little on Anlerran and Kian, as if he could not quite believe that they too were members of this council. "It may however be better if you refrained from mentioning Inerdyr's unfortunate demise. The news of his death spread quickly along with some colourful rumours, and strong opinions of you have resulted. Inerdyr was not well loved, but he helped keep in place the uneasy truce that has lasted between north and south for so long. You could say that a powerful figure north of the Unbuilt Wall was essential to keep the balance and prevent the Watchers and their masters from a coup of Mornkastle and incursions into the Free Territories. Now, as far as the people of Mornkastle can tell, he has been replaced by a force of *orkar*, mercenaries, renegade Watchers and thugs from outlying settlements who have a bone to pick with the folk of the city. That is not my opinion, but it *is* the opinion of many."

So saying, he rose, turned and left.

Finally Anlerran broke the silence. "Who will the six be?"

Her father glanced across at her. "Nia must be one," he said quietly.

"Why?" Kelandra asked immediately. "What possible value could *Nia* bring to such negotiation?"

"Will you allow it?" Elluron responded mildly. "I think she will be of considerable use. After all, did she not help to bring us all together? I suggest you and I, Kelandra, along with Nia, Anlerran, Kian and Iyoth."

Kelandra stared at him but chose not to pursue the matter. Anlerran gave a quiet sigh of relief. "You may as well find Nia and inform her," her father said.

Anlerran was glad to leave their meeting, but felt Kelandra's coldly inquisitive gaze upon her as she hurried from the tent.

She headed across the encampment and spotted Nia sitting with her back against the roundstone wall separating the encampment from a bordering meadow. She was busy splitting grasses with one of her knives. Not for the first time, Anlerran wondered how she could spend so much time engaged in pointless activities. "How are your dreams?" she asked as Nia looked up, recalling that she had not asked her in a while.

Nia shrugged. "Yui still hasn't made an appearance yet, if that's what you meant. If she does I imagine you'll find me cold and stiff by dawn's light. But since you ask, my dreams have been entirely normal. You would probably call them nightmares."

Anlerran saw the haunted look in Nia's eyes. *Perhaps now may not be the best time to talk with her,* she thought. *But with Nia there's rarely a good time.*

"I have to speak to you about something," she said quietly, having made sure that no one was near enough to them to eavesdrop.

"What is it?"

"The time for your story of the Watchers' origins draws near." Anlerran raised a hand to placate her as she saw the sudden look of alarm in Nia's eyes. "You will be one of the six who attend the meeting with the representatives of Mornkastle. When that time comes, tell it as fact. Do not gloat, I beg you. Do not embellish. Recall and describe, nothing more."

Nia swallowed nervously. "I'll be too fearful to gloat, Anlerran. I should never have told you, and I wish by all the powers that I hadn't. Do you truly know what will happen when the truth is told- and Kelandra or one of the others determines the truth of what I say? Do you? Because *I* have no idea."

"Neither do I." Anlerran got to her feet. "But for better or worse I told my father, and he has determined that now is the time. Think of it as one less burden to be carried."

"Oh, there are many more," Nia muttered, but Anlerran had already hurried away through the gloom, a chill in her heart as she contemplated the day ahead and the dreadful secrets that would finally spill forth.

The following day, the six riders headed to the designated meeting place with the sun rising quickly towards its zenith. After only a short while they drew near to a large flag that bore Mornkastle's coat of arms, fluttering in the icy breeze. Six figures could be seen waiting near it. Anlerran felt her insides tighten with worry, and she took deep breaths, hoping that she could at least retain her outer calm.

As the companions drew to a halt a dozen or so paces away and dismounted, the figures approached. First came a tall, imposing man with shoulder-length silver hair, flanked by a younger man in soldier's attire. Behind them walked a stern-looking middle-aged woman, and finally three Watchers. That they were such, Anlerran could tell in an instant. *I still find it odd how I'm so quick to see the difference between them and those who are still human,* she thought, *even now that I know their origins.*

"I am Perrian, Lord Warden of Mornkastle," the man said as he surveyed each of them. "This is Elarin, also of the Council." He gestured to the two younger men. "Allin, a lieutenant in the city's defensive force." Then he turned to the Watchers. "Merran, Lerak and Ishar."

Allin was more than a soldier, Anlerran decided, looking at him as Elluron introduced each of his companions. She could sense that the young man had some strength in the Powers- not as much as herself or Kian, but still considerable.

Then her attention was caught by the looks that Elarin and Nia exchanged. *They know each other,* she thought. The fact was as plain as day even before Elarin remarked, "Nia! I must admit I never thought I would see you again."

"Nor I you," Nia guardedly replied.

"Without this girl," Elarin said to Perrian, "the army waiting to the north would likely not exist. She brought together Ruhal Dalmorn and this Watcher, Kelandra."

"Remarkable." Perrian fixed a cold stare upon Nia. "Although I can't say whether we should congratulate or condemn her actions." He frowned. "I am surprised that the Warden of Mordenglen isn't here in person. Ruhal was always one for imposing himself on any occasion he stumbled into."

"Ruhal is more a leader of men in battle than a negotiator of treaties, as I'm sure you already know," Elluron replied.

"I was simply Kelandra's messenger," Nia spoke up uncomfortably. "Nevertheless, I was locked up in the Sanctum for my troubles."

"You escaped the Sanctum?" Merran stared at Nia. "That is not possible."

"Sometimes, even now, I wish it wasn't," Nia replied. "A slow death in the darkness would have been a far less complicated fate."

Anlerran glanced at her father, who gave a barely perceptible nod. *It's time,* she thought, and felt her stomach churn with worry. She turned to Kelandra. "Do you remember speaking to me one time of how the Seven saved you from the Void and the *marandaal?*"

"I recall mentioning it in passing. And?"

"You told me that none of your kind have ever recalled any details of this event. So terrible was your time in the Void that your minds closed themselves to the memory. Or words to that effect."

"Is there a point to this, or are you seeking only to waste time?"

"Something did indeed happen for you to become what you are- but not in the way that you've been told. Nia can tell you the truth. She has witnessed the attempted making of a Watcher."

"Wait." Kelandra stared intently at Nia. "Do you believe anything this woman says? Nia is not a star-traveller. She has not survived the Void. She knows nothing of our origins. She was born into this world by parents who were eager only to discard her. She is a crawling nest of lies, bitterness and self-recrimination, perhaps only one misfortune away from succumbing to the skittering darkness inside her own head."

"Enough," Elluron said abruptly. "Your opinion of your loyal servant is well-known. Let her speak, Watcher, and then- as I believe you have the capability of doing- you may divine the truth or otherwise of what she says. Regardless, you must swear not to harm her."

"I have already sworn not to harm her, half-man," Kelandra retorted quietly, looking for all Aona as if she had sworn to do the opposite at her earliest convenience.

Elluron turned back to the representatives of Mornkastle. "Together we must ensure the peace of the city and the continued rule of law, for Mornkastle but also all of Harn. As you may know, the *choragh* desire to defeat the starspawn. But they also seek to impose their old dominion over the Younger Races and bring back the days of blood, the time of sacrifice. In short, they would turn Harn back to the grim First Age. All that has been built since that time- all civilisation and enlightenment- that would be swept aside."

"In *your* territories perhaps. The Seven would not allow that to happen in the South," Merran pointed out. "We are also aware that although you speak of civilisation and enlightenment, you yourselves killed one of the few figures in the north who sought to keep some kind of order."

None of the companions chose to answer that.

"Have any of your kind ever remembered anything of this emergence from the void?" Kian asked Merran.

A strange look entered Merran's eyes. "Not to my recollection, but the question is irrelevant. Our previous lives are of no consequence. We were brought to Harn for a reason- to serve the Seven and preserve the age of enlightenment in which the people of the South now live. Even you primitive folk in your so-called *free territories* have obliquely benefitted from the civilisation you choose to remain apart from."

Nia still looked petrified. She bore the look of a woman who had finally awakened into her day of reckoning. "Tell your story," Anlerran said quietly. "Remember what I said to you yesterday."

She would recall much later that the day that set so much in motion was itself drab, unremarkable.

The details came brightly and vividly to Anlerran as the girl spoke, faltering and even repeating herself on occasion. She described everything from her escape to her witnessing of the man in the chamber being tortured by two of the Seven, the conversation she had heard between them, and her flight from the Sanctum, pursued as far as the great swampland of the Bonemord.

Nia somehow managed to look Kelandra in the eyes when she had finished. "I don't think you or your kind came from any void. The Seven only brought the High Watchers with them from whichever world they fled from. I heard them talking about it. Since then, they have tried to make Watchers with whatever strange magic they have down in the Sanctum. Mostly they fail. But you and all the other Watchers... you're *human*. At least, you were. I expect you no longer look anything like you would have done as a human woman- they couldn't take the risk of you being recognised out in the city. The sorcery of the Seven must have changed you utterly, inside and out." Suddenly Nia seemed to realise the enormity of what she had revealed, although she must have dwelt on it for an age. "Changed all of you," she said faintly.

"You are lying," Kelandra said flatly. "It's an interesting tale, Nia, even for you- but a lie nonetheless."

"I suggest you determine that for yourself," Elluron said. "You can do that, I believe."

"There is no need." Kelandra's words were coldly dismissive.

"There is no reason not to," he rejoined.

"Put an end to this, Kelandra," Nia begged. "I've carried this knowledge with me for so long. Discover the truth for yourself."

"Very well." The Watcher approached Nia until she was standing next to her. Anlerran glanced across at her father, who stared intently at Kelandra. She had no doubt that he would defend Nia if needed, but couldn't say whether or not he would be swift enough

Nia bowed her head, and Kelandra's hand touched it. The Watcher also inclined her head forward slightly.

After only a short while Kelandra staggered suddenly backwards, her face ashen. She stared around, looking confused. Nia cringed as if she expected to be hacked to pieces at any moment.

Kelandra took a deep breath, closed her eyes for a moment, and then returned to where she had been standing. "It is true," she said quietly. Her voice shook, although outwardly she remained as serenely cold as ever. "I swear it."

I have never heard her voice so much as falter before, Anlerran thought.

She wondered what thoughts surged through Kelandra's head. A terrible thing had been done, but no other option remained open to them. Even the whole North aided by the *illeagh* would surely struggle to defeat the Seven and all their Watchers. And of those, how many might at the least be persuaded to abandon the Seven? How many might join their cause, Watchers and more common folk, to bring down the Seven?

Perrian spoke up suddenly. "We expected to be engaged in negotiation, not this nonsense. Kelandra is known as a traitor who abandoned her Watchers' oaths to help raise this patchwork army camped to the north." he motioned to Merran. "Divine the truth for yourself. I'd like to hear it from one who can be trusted."

Merran carried out the same act as Kelandra had, before removing her hand taking a sudden step back.

"Well?" Perrian demanded. Anlerran thought that his voice shook a little.

Merran nodded. "It is as Kelandra says. I also swear it."

Nia stood in disconsolate silence, not daring to look at anything but the ground. Anlerran felt troubled and exhausted, but after a moment a strange sensation of relief began to stir within her. *Come what may now,* she thought, *the deed is done, or at least the seed is sown.*

An eternity could have passed. No one spoke. Kelandra and the Watchers of Mornkastle stood like statues. Perrian and Elarin looked to each other in stunned silence.

Anlerran's father turned to the Watchers of Mornkastle. "The Seven cannot create and manipulate Gates- at least, they can no longer. I suspect the last time they did so was when they came to Harn with their High Watchers, fleeing the *marandaal.* But you and all other Watchers- you were once people of Luudhoq."

Still the Watchers said nothing. But then Lerak abruptly walked away to where their horses had been tethered. "Stop," Perrian called out. When the Watcher ignored him, he shouted, "As Lord Warden of Mornkastle I command you to stop!"

Lerak neither replied nor even turned to look. Within moments he had saddled up and ridden away back in the direction of the city. Anlerran wondered darkly what he might do on his return.

"The Seven brought many tales from their world," Merran said quietly after a moment. "One of them was the story of a magical box that many sought to open. When finally a key to it was found, and the box opened, none could control the events that occurred when its contents spilled forth into the world."

She continued, "We had a code. But now that code is meaningless."

"Surely we all create our own value," Anlerran ventured. "The code may have been built on a lie- but you can fashion your own code, founded on truth."

"What do you know of such things? You're a wildling, a creature of the darkness that the South has held at bay for centuries."

"I will attempt to destroy the Seven, or die in the attempt," Kelandra said suddenly. "There's my code."

"Then you will die," Merran told her, "because the Seven are immortal, and all-powerful."

Perrian looked at Nia and shook his head grimly. "You have no idea what you have unleashed, what may now happen to the world. It has always been up to us in Mornkastle to preserve the balance of power- for if we don't, then the land will fall to chaos far more easily than you might suspect. Your revelation has made that far more likely." He smiled and nodded to himself. "Of course. That was your intention."

"Not mine," Nia murmured. "I intended none of this."

"We sought to unite the people of Harn..." Anlerran began, but Perrian cut across her. "Unity through chaos? I warn all of you now- attack Mornkastle and we will destroy you all even if the city's streets run with rivers of blood. You have my word on that."

"By the way," Perrian added, as he leapt back on his horse and his companions hastened to do the same. "Yan was most surprised to find that Ruhal Dalmorn was nowhere to be seen when he was sent to talk with you. I would have thought he of all people would have been present. Perhaps you've murdered him as well?"

The Warden of Mornkastle turned his horse and rode away, his four remaining companions hastening after him.

III

Ruhal's thoughts festered as he lay in his tent, still securely tied hand and foot. He not only contemplated his displacement by Elluron and the Watchers but also still harboured simmering notions of unlikely revenge. He had reserved a special place in his heart for Elluron, who had repaid Ruhal's devotion to and protection of his daughter with poorly-concealed treachery.

I helped take his infant daughter to a place of safety, he reminded himself for perhaps the hundredth time. *I helped place her with trusted guardians, and watched her from afar, ready to protect her if and when needed. I led her from Mordenglen when the time came. Without my help she would never have made it out of the forest, let alone all the way to the Rhunin to be reunited with him. And how does he treat the man who gave him back the daughter who he willingly abandoned all those years ago? He sets me up to look like a would-be murderer and makes me a prisoner, then assumes control of the cause that I created.*

Ruhal's fists shook as he raged silently. Abruptly his thoughts, which flitted so quickly now between themes, turned to Anlerran. *I'll take her away from him,* he told himself. *That would be fitting. He doesn't deserve her. I'll take her away and we'll go somewhere, anywhere. The distant west, where there are few settlements. The* marandaal *may never reach that part of the world. I'm done with this rebellion. Aona and her people can die in the dirt and rot as the sky turns dark.*

Anlerran...

He ached for her. Powers, how he wanted her. *I'll beg her forgiveness for as long as it takes,* he swore. *I know she loves me. I saw it in her eyes when we were together in the* illeagh *stronghold. I still saw it even amidst the hurt, when she told me what Lura had told her.*

The rage came swiftly back. *Lura! She may as well have been a whore as a sellsword. She ruined everything. She caught me when I was weak. I should have pushed her away but I didn't. Yet that doesn't excuse her. She has even less shame than I thought. And to think she then told Anlerran about what we did. Why? Why does she hate me so much as to do that? I've been a friend to her for countless years, and she repays me with a calculated plan to destroy everything I hold dear!*

A picture of Anlerran sent the fury into the background of his mind. He imagined her coming to his tent unbidden and unknown to her father, quietly untying his bonds and tugging his clothes off before sitting astride him, sopping wet with lust. Ruhal groaned to himself in frustration, tugging his hands pointlessly against the rope that bound him. One of Garrok's ironmasters had weaved a spell into the knots, making them impossible to undo or even slacken.

Ruhal heard a brief discussion outside, and then a figure ducked into the tent. He turned his head to see the form of an *orkar* man approach. A moment later he realised that it was Garrok. When he opened his mouth to speak, the *orkar* leader pressed a finger to his lips. "Don't speak. Listen," Garrok said. "The guards have been told to allow you through the camp perimeter, should they happen to see you."

Ruhal stared incredulously at him as Garrok's knife cut through his bonds. "There is a condition." Garrok helped him sit up. "You must never again set foot within a league of this army. Go find yourself somewhere to hide."

"Hide? What sort of man do you think I am?" Ruhal whispered, rubbing his wrists. For a moment his dream of escaping to the distant west with Anlerran came back to him. *That's the sort of man I am.*

"I'm offering you a way out," Garrok said quietly. "You were a man of honour and a friend. But if they find you, and certainly if you come back, I will not be able to help you. I will stand back and let them deal with you as they will. My advice is to never be seen by anyone here ever again."

He tossed a hooded robe to the ground nearby, and turned to leave. Ruhal followed him. The guards who had been posted outside had gone, but a horse had been tethered nearby. "May luck go with you," Garrok said quietly, handing him the reins. "That way," he added, pointing west as Ruhal donned the robe and pulled the hood down low over his head.

The *orkar* leader strode away without a further word.

In a stupor, Ruhal got onto the horse and began riding slowly to the western edge of the encampment, following the exact direction to which Garrok had pointed. The guards had been posted far apart from one another in this area. If either of them caught sight of him they gave no indication of having done so.

He rode a little further and only goaded his mount into a gallop when he was some distance away, rushing through the late afternoon to put as much distance as he could between himself and what had once been his army.

He fled, but in his heart the desire for revenge burned more strongly than ever.

IV

Kelandra sat on a fallen tree trunk and watched the argument between Garrok and Elluron unfold. Her outward calm came naturally to her. It had been instilled into her, made a part of who she was.

Inside, she screamed continuously.

A ridiculous lie had been shown to be fact. Everything- her vows, her code of behaviour, her very nature, was a lie instead.

Once the initial shock had begun to ebb away, she had felt an urge to kill. She could have reached Nia and slit her throat before anyone could do anything about it. Elluron had been prepared to defend the self-satisfied little bitch, but she reckoned she would have been too fast for him.

Who else? Perhaps Anlerran- sanctimonious and self-righteous Anlerran.

Perhaps all of them.

But Lerak's departure from their gathering had stirred within her shattered mind the realisation that the truth was not hers alone to endure, and she knew then that the reactions of each Watcher to that truth would be as different as the code and oaths of the Watchers had been consistent. From total order would come total chaos. Some would rampage; others might even end their own lives if they could. A few would simply disappear somewhere.

She imagined one settlement after another ransacked, pillaged. *And the people of the South see us as a valid militia, as enforcers with whom they are acquainted,* she thought. *They would suspect nothing, perhaps, until sudden slaughter commences. Of course, tales of their deeds would spread, but that would itself foster rumours about all Watchers, not simply renegades.*

Soon we will all be renegades, and feared for the mayhem we cause instead of the laws we once upheld.

As they had ridden back in silence, Kelandra had felt the stares of her companions upon her. She could have blinded them- with a sudden movement she could have directed sharp, tiny gusts of air at their faces and sent them tumbling off their horses with their eyes leaking blood.

In her mind she had already murdered them all at least twice. But through the turmoil of that journey back to

the encampment she had somehow retained her outward
composure.

That had been two days ago. Since then word had spread
throughout the various commanders of the army and then to
the foot soldiers and refugees. Kelandra doubted that anyone
remained who had not yet heard. Ildoron and Alturus had
reacted quietly- so quietly in fact that Kelandra had almost
seen her own initial reaction mirrored. A day later, Ildoron
had come to her with the beginnings of what he had called a
plan. To Kelandra it sounded meticulous in one way only- in
its exact detail concerning the torture of the Seven, should
they be overcome. *Emotion over logic,* she thought. *We're like
a garment whose threads are swiftly falling away. Soon we'll
have neither purpose nor shape, and Watchers will be
remembered only as people who were taken apart, body and
mind, and built again. And then slaughtered the people of
Harn.*

Alturus, meanwhile, had not spoken a word.

With an effort, Kelandra concentrated on the
continuing argument.

"You allowed a madman his freedom." Elluron did
not raise his voice, but his anger was obvious. Kelandra idly
wondered what powers might be unleashed if he finally lost
his temper. The *illeagh* were utterly alien to her.

"You've set loose a far greater madness," Garrok
retorted, glancing at Anlerran who stood near her father.
Kelandra could not tell what the girl was thinking, but she
appeared distraught. "You call me reckless, half-breed, but
you have allowed the south to fall into chaos. You have
allowed hundreds of powerful lunatics their freedom."

He has a point, Kelandra thought with a grim smile,
even as Garrok, realising what he had said, swiftly looked in
her direction.

Kelandra found herself watching a man of the
Darkbrook militia as he wandered from one evening tinder

pile to another, lighting each with the fire from a stick around which an alcohol-doused cloth had been tied. As she watched fire after fire come slowly into life, the strident words of the belligerent *orkar* warlord- still warning that they had wilfully destroyed all their remaining hopes- faded into the background of general camp noise, and Kelandra suddenly recalled her own habit of lighting lanterns and torches around the rooms of her residence in the Fortress grounds of Luudhoq. *I lit them in a particular order,* she thought. *It had to be that specific order.*

A sudden, violently bright image rushed through her mind, so powerful that Kelandra uttered a gasp of pain and fear and leaned forward, clutching at her head. It poured through her, and for a moment it became her entire world.

"Can we light this one first?"

The child's voice was pleading, insistent. Celanne looked down at the picture of wide-eyed desperation and smiled.

"Please?"

"Very well. And you can light it yourself, but you must be careful. Remember, they can burn you."

Together, mother and son made their way around the room to light all three lanterns. With each one lit the gloom receded a little further. Celanne watched as her son stared transfixed at the flickering light, his serious countenance one of silent contemplation. Who knew what he was thinking, what he imagined in that instant?

On an impulse Celanne bent down and held him close. "I love you so much," she whispered. "More than you will ever know..."

Abruptly the vision dissolved into white light and searing pain, sending Kelandra back into the cold mud and stink of the camp and the continuing argument between her companions.

She could hardly bear to contemplate the scene she had just witnessed- a fragment of a memory that came from an unknown time.

"I had..." She swallowed, trying to stop her entire body from trembling with shock.

"I had a..."

But she could not bear to say the word.

It took half a day, but finally Elluron and Garrok appeared to put their differences aside sufficiently to agree to a discussion with the Watchers.

"Word will eventually spread to Luudhoq," Elluron said. "I'm sure the Seven will have a way of ensuring that their own story remains the official truth, but nonetheless disquiet will be rife throughout the city."

He paused and then added, "The scouts we sent to monitor Mornkastle returned a short while ago. As we feared, it seems that the smaller settlements in the area have fallen into mayhem. Refugees stream into the city through all gates bar the north. Mornkastle itself remains mainly peaceful, aside from isolated unrest. But once word of our revelation spread, most Watchers left the city. As far as we can tell, there were two main groups. One headed directly towards Luudhoq. The other began as one, and there are stories that it became three, or even four. There may well be a dozen or more by now. In any case, we know this much- that groups of Watchers rampage through the south, destroying whatever they can find."

"Presumably those who head to Luudhoq intend to attack the Seven," Garrok spoke up.

Elluron nodded. "Quite possibly. In which case, that will be to our advantage even though they will surely fail. A group of Watchers seeking to attack Luudhoq will raise all manner of questions within that city, no matter how many times the Seven remind everyone of their place. But one thing is for certain- we need to move swiftly on the Seven while the south remains in disarray. Mornkastle's leaders will be dealing with refugees and internal turmoil for some time to come. The same may soon be true of Waylorn. I believe we'll face no more than token resistance as we push south towards Luudhoq. The only serious threats will, I would say, come from groups of renegade Watchers."

Elluron looked meaningfully at Kelandra, Ildoron and Alturus. "But some may even be inclined to join us if they see that we have with us three of our own, dedicated to the destruction of the Seven. Whatever madness has afflicted them, and whatever atrocities they may have committed as they roam, a hatred of those who destroyed and remade them must burn brightly in their minds. We must do our best to convince them to join us."

"The people of Luudhoq have lived under the regime of the Seven for many centuries," Alturus said. As the others turned to him, perhaps surprised that he had finally spoken, he added, "They have never known the reality of war. The Watchers themselves have not known it. No one imagined it would ever happen. You are right to say there will be unease within the city- I would say violence may flare at some point. Already Luudhoq will be rife with rumours of the *marandaal* but also of rebellions and conflicts in the North. They fear that even if the *marandaal* are repelled, a vast barbarian army of witches, mercenaries and vile, savage creatures from out of legend will descend upon them. And in that, they are at least partly right."

"I can attest to that," Garrok said, staring meaningfully at him, "being a vile, savage creature from out of legend."

"The Seven will urge every man, woman and child to slaughter themselves defending the city," Alturus continued. His measured tone sounded detached from the terrible words he uttered. "The High Watchers will do their bidding with utter loyalty, ensuring that the human people of Luudhoq form the front line. Any dissent will be crushed with absolute force."

"What of the Watchers sworn to defend Luudhoq?" Garrok demanded. "What part will they play? Whose words will they believe? And what will happen when they face us? Will enough doubt have been created for them to question the facts they have always known- or will they help drive the people of Luudhoq to extinction?"

"No one can say," Kelandra pointed out when Alturus could find no response. Suddenly the vision of a past she could not properly remember flared in her mind again, and the hatred burned so brightly that she added without thinking, "But we will fight our way past whoever and whatever we need to, and we will find a way to destroy the Seven. What can we do if they place the citizens of Luudhoq in our way?

"I remember fragments of a life before opening my eyes in the depths of the Sanctum. Memories lurk in my head like shards of glass. I will make my so-called saviours pay the ultimate price for this, as will others- whether they flock to our cause or bring the city to its knees independently."

"And what about the people of Luudhoq?" Garrok asked.

"War is bloody, no matter how it's conducted." Kelandra smiled, quite unaware that her lips were trembling and a tear had escaped one of her eyes. "But the Watchers *will have their vengeance.*"

XVII - Mortality

I

During his tedious journey east, Stephan occasionally smiled to himself, recalling the looks on the faces of his comrades when he volunteered to lead the resistance to the *marandaal* at the Border Wall. Oh, some had looked more shocked than others, but he had grown to know their natures intimately over the centuries. Not one of them had expected that move. They had more than likely assumed that he had opted for a glorious suicide mission in order to hasten his own demise.

And for a brief while I did contemplate that, he recalled. *The idea of waiting in Luudhoq for the end to come was unbearable. I would rather have faced obliteration at the hands of our ancient enemies.*

His only companions on the journey to the Border Wall were the High Watchers, who remained silent until or unless given a question or an order. To Stephan that silence was as fresh as the continuous breeze that swept across the grassland from the distant southern coast, and it gave him the opportunity to work his way through a plan so simple that it was barely a plan at all, more a straightforward and logical course of action and one that he still found hard to believe the others had not thought of themselves.

They hold out hope of defending their little empire, he thought. *Even now.*

Stephan couldn't say for sure that they were wrong, but he no longer cared. He had grown tired of their company, their bickering and directionless hatred. He detested the continuous and pointless work of attempting to make new Watchers. His antipathy towards Omir, with whom he had spent so much time on that fruitless effort, was even greater.

One in fifty, he reminded himself. *I believe that was the ratio of success, more or less. And even on the rare occasions that we succeeded, how can we be sure that we succeeded completely? Why would the four renegades have acted as they did, against their vows, against the nature that we determined for them? Clearly there's a spark held somewhere deep that cannot be reliably destroyed.*

He glanced across at the High Watchers that ran alongside as he rode east, reflecting that these cold and mechanical creatures were altogether more trustworthy than both the Seven and the Watchers that they had tried to recreate. Somehow the powers that made the High Watchers- or *originals* as Stephan preferred to call them- what they were had persisted after their entry into Aona, even as the other technology swiftly withered away. They could not be replicated, and yet they had remained ever-reliable over the long centuries.

The Border Wall appeared in the distance. Stephan felt a chill as he observed the vast structure. Somewhere beyond that barrier the *marandaal* approached. How quickly would they fight their way through it?

But, he reminded himself, that would not be his problem to bear, nor with any luck would it be his fate to ever find out.

He slowed at the final approach, glancing up at the ramparts of the wall where men looked down. *I'll allow a little time to discuss the plan of defence with the commander at arms, give my orders to the originals, and then I'll head south under the pretence of gathering more people to the cause from the coastal villages.*

And I'll be on the first seaworthy ship to the South Ocean Islands.

He looked through the vast portcullis where he could see a mass of Hastian refugees on the other side of the wall. They had walked or ridden as far as the Border Wall to plead for entrance into Harn, but of course the authorities had denied them. That was their duty.

A short while later Stephan sat with Ilyan, the commander-at-arms of the Border Wall, listening to the man's report on what had happened thus far in the region. They had seen nothing of the *marandaal* as yet, but some of the people gathered at the foot of the wall on the Hastian side had spoken of seeing them approach and enter Darkenhelm as they fled. Darkenhelm had, Ilyan asserted, become a bloodbath and was now surely a smoking ruin.

Stephan listened impatiently to the man's rambling account of affairs and then accompanied him up onto the top of the wall to look down over the Hastian side as the High Watchers took positions along the wall, spaced a hundred paces distant from one another. Hundreds, perhaps thousands of people stared up at him. Some pleaded, others shouted angrily. Some sat and wept.

"We have warned them to leave and head north," Ilyan told him. "When the *marandaal* come they will be crushed underfoot in moments." He glanced at the nearest of the High Watchers. "I thank you for bringing the High Watchers, my Lord. I fear their powers will be required."

"Of course they will." Stephan almost told him that he might as well take all his men and flee, and leave the defence of the Border Wall to the High Watchers alone, but decided against it. It would be in his best interests to leave the Border Wall without complicating matters.

"If I may ask, my Lord," Ilyan continued nervously, "might we allow some of these people to pass through?"

He paled when Stephan looked sharply at him. "Forgive me..." he began, but Stephan cut him short. "What happens if we allow *some* of these people in? Everyone will fight to get through. It would be neither logical nor just to allow a fraction of these people into Harn. Furthermore, we certainly cannot allow all of them in. That would only cause friction and conflict between them and our own people. Do you understand how quickly matters might unravel?"

Ilyan nodded quickly. "I beg your pardon, my Lord."

Stephan looked north along the wall for as far as he could see, then beckoned to the nearest of the High Watchers. When it reached the two of them, he said, "Ilyan is now your commander. You and every other High Watcher is to obey his instructions as if they were my own. Confirm your understanding of this instruction."

"I understand." The High Watcher inclined its head slightly. The smooth material from which its face had been created so long ago almost glowed in the sunlight.

"Relay the instruction all your comrades and return to your position." As the High Watcher turned and left them, Stephan turned to the speechless Ilyan. "I have followed your career closely," he remarked. "You have always struck me as a most capable man. The task of defending Harn and commanding the forces gathered here at the Border Wall seems to me to be tailor-made for you."

"Tha... thank you, my Lord." Even in his confusion Ilyan drew himself up a little taller and puffed out his chest. *Idiot,* Stephan thought, *and soon to be a dead idiot.*

"I will head south to Ranith Tyr," Stephan continued, "in order to bring more recruits to the defence of the border. I will leave you in charge of matters."

Ilyan struggled to speak. Stephan waited as patiently as he could for the man to frame some kind of response. Finally the Border Wall's commander murmured, "No one except my lords and ladies the Seven have *ever* commanded the High Watchers before. I fear I won't know how... I mean to say... no mortal human can hope to understand them..."

"I have ordered them to follow your orders as if they came from me," Stephan said. "You have no need to understand them- and how could you anyway? They are machines, or at least it would be better for you to think of them as such. They exist to obey. That is their function. There is absolutely no question of them failing to obey. Is that clear enough for you?"

"Perfectly clear, my Lord."

"One more thing," Stephan added when Ilyan had finished bowing. "If a message arrives for me requesting information, you are to send a reply as if from me. Be sure to say that the preparations are underway and the *marandaal* have not yet been sighted. It's important that morale in Luudhoq is kept high. There is no need to say anything else."

Stephan had of course contemplated the likeliest possible futures and concluded that his best opportunity for survival would be to move himself as far as possible from the impending chaos. After dismissing Ilyan he left the defence station, and rode south along the wide trail that led towards Ranith Tyr and the coast. After a couple of leagues he turned south-west and took a less well-travelled track which led towards the outskirts of Aramor Forest and then on to the small port of Aramor itself. While resting during the afternoon he tied a handkerchief around the lower half of his face and pulled the brim of his hat down a little further to hide his short-cropped blond hair. It was unlikely that anyone would recognise him in a sleepy backwater like Aramor but it paid to be cautious.

Sometimes it's the more obvious details that pass by the most intelligent people, he mused as he sat leaning against a tree, enjoying the sunlight and cool breeze blowing from the coast. *If the* marandaal *could cross over water, or fly, Harn would have fallen already. Eventually they will force their way through the Border Wall, because they have no other way to reach Harn. But for whatever reason, they can't cross through oceans, nor over the land.*

Stephan took the gold coins from his pocket and passed them from one hand to the other and back again. He had more than enough to pay for passage to the South Ocean Islands. In fact he had enough to buy a ship of his own if he wanted to.

I could take it by force and leave a massacre in my wake, he thought.

The idea was persuasive, but it made no sense. He was not like Garret, a man who couldn't control his murderous urges. Instead he would approach the captain of an Islander ship and pay for passage south. He would leave no trace, and within a tennight he would be in the South Ocean Islands, where- according to the information he had gathered- no Gates had formed and no lightdreamers roamed. That might happen in time, but Stephan decided he would worry about that if or when it happened.

Laughing to himself, he pocketed his gold. A short while later he was riding south-west once again, imagining the distance between himself and Harn increasing to a yawning gulf as he looked back at the doomed empire of the Seven.

II

"Where have you been for the past few days?" Anya demanded sharply. "I have been trying to find you and Daniel."

"Oh, we've just been busy copulating, and keeping our distance from the rest of you." Phaedra shrugged. "Why?"

"You won't have heard the news then. It would appear that some of the Watchers in Mornkastle and nearby regions have been told, and have subsequently verified the truth of their origins."

"Oh." Phaedra felt her heart flutter for a moment. She tried to collect her thoughts, silently contemplating each dire event that might spring from this revelation. *Now Daniel and I really have to get that portal working,* she mused. *Chaos is coming a little earlier than expected.*

She sighed. "Kelandra's lackey ought to have been simply executed, don't you think? Why leave her to languish in the cells when slicing her head off would have meant this problem never happened?"

"Yes. I expect everything would have run so much more smoothly if you held single and absolute control over decisions," Anya observed.

"Oh, I don't doubt that," Phaedra said offhandedly, pointedly ignoring the woman's barbed tone. "Anyway, what would you have me to do? Then I can at least tell you if I'm going to do it."

"Nothing now. The four of us met in your absence."

Phaedra despised meetings, but she nonetheless felt a momentary stirring of anger. "Did you manage to agree on anything? Or did Garret and Omir maul each other again?"

"All the Watchers in Luudhoq have been summoned to the Hall of the Sunset Ceremony tomorrow at noon. Those High Watchers that were kept in the city will also be present, as will all of us."

Phaedra raised an eyebrow at that. "I see. Such a gathering hasn't happened for..." She frowned, tried to remember and gave up.

"One hundred and twenty-two years." Anya turned to leave. "We ask for your presence, and Daniel's. A united front is essential."

Phaedra had been about to declare her non-interest in the gathering on the basis that neither she nor Daniel had voted for it, but she found the notion of attending strangely interesting, even as a passive observer. "As you wish," she said with a shrug. "But if you'll excuse me for now- delightful though these rare conversations with you are, I am a little tired this evening."

"Yes. I expect you are." Anya gave her a look of distaste and walked away. Phaedra watched her for a moment, idly wondering which of the six she hated the most. Anya's cool, unflappable demeanour was entirely at odds with Issele's simmering rage. Garret and Omir were of a kind: monsters even to the monsters with whom they shared power. Stephan was the devious snake amongst them, which made his decision to defend the Border Wall even more interesting. And Daniel...

"Him, I can put up with," she murmured as Anya disappeared round the distant corner of the corridor.

That night she dreamed of a vast palace in which she ruled over a population of fawning subjects. She sat on a glittering throne of gold and jewels, surrounded by her most favoured. Frequently servants would appear with offerings of delicious food and drink fit for the goddess that she was. When she permitted one of her subjects to look her in the eyes she would see only pure, absolute adoration. Any one of them would give up their life for her.

When she woke up in the middle of the night, Phaedra realised that this dream was almost identical to another she had had as an eight-year old, in a distant age and a world now long gone. For just a moment she felt an overwhelming, desperate desire to return to her childhood. *Might everything have turned out differently if I'd chosen a different path?* she wondered.

Finally she drifted back to sleep, still contemplating the concept of her decisions affecting the fate of the universe.

Phaedra found Daniel the following morning as she made her usual roundabout way towards the Sanctum. Even before she had the chance to tell him the news about the Watchers, he quietly said to her as they walked down a flight of stairs, "It's *started scanning.*"

Phaedra almost tripped. "You mean it's actually *working*?!" She could scarcely believe it. "How did you manage that?"

He looked all around before continuing, although they were alone. "I don't know." He looked troubled. "In fact I'm not sure I did anything. It lit up and started going through the routine and I can't work out how. But it *is* scanning properly. I don't remember much of the time just before we arrived, but I do remember the exact procedure. It's as if the machine somehow remembered what to do after all these centuries. But the power boxes are all empty. They drained away long ago. The energy for all this is coming from somewhere else."

Phaedra found herself thinking of the water hanging suspended in the air. "The Sanctum has its own energy," she said. "This entire fortress shares it." She took a deep breath, put her arms around her co-conspirator and kissed him on the lips. "Well done, Daniel. *Very* well done."

"As I said..."

"It doesn't matter how it happened. All we can do now is wait. We may yet have a chance to escape."

He almost smiled at that. "You sound as if you've discovered hope again, Phaedra."

"I have," she said simply.

The sight that greeted them in their chamber deep within the Sanctum was exhilarating and frightening. The black mirror no longer reflected. Instead its interior was composed of nothing but utter darkness. Her gaze followed the mass of wires to the boxes and panels set to one side, where a bewildering array of lights flashed.

"We should check continuously," she said. "In fact we should sleep at different times, and wake the other if one of us finds anything."

Phaedra finally remembered to tell Daniel about the Watchers. "If Aona truly wishes to help us," he said a little later as they made their way into the great hall where Watchers were already gathering, "then now would be the perfect time for a gift from the heavens."

III

"Some of you will have heard rumours concerning the origins of Watchers," Omir began. "These are being spread by the wild and lawless savages from the lands north of Mornkastle. I tell you now that this is a lie concocted by their army of witches, mercenaries and wild beasts. It has one purpose- to sow seeds of suspicion, to allow chaos to thrive in our civilised territories. We face two threats- our ancient enemies the *marandaal* in the east, and this rabble in the north who know that they cannot overcome us by sheer weight of force. Instead they seek to divide us. That *must not happen*. It is your sworn duty as Watchers of Harn to defend the realm at all costs. We will crush them when they dare to approach Luudhoq."

Then we've already given up on the rest of the south, Phaedra thought. *It's been abandoned to the savages.*

She could not stop fidgeting in her chair. She had better things to be doing- poring over whatever data or findings the portal found not least amongst them- and she found the steady, unflinching the gaze of so many Watchers in one place unsettling, even if those stares were not directed at her.

Not a single one of the Watchers betrayed a hint of emotion in the wake of Omir's words, nor would she have expected them to. But she wondered how many of them might believe the rumours. *After all,* she thought wildly, *they're the truth!* She barely resisted the urge to laugh suddenly.

Luudhoq and the rest of our little empire can fall and burn for all I care, she thought, *as long as I find a path to another place. Provided I have air to breathe, water to drink and a supply of food, and I'm one of the higher predators of that world.*

"Each High Watcher will command a battalion of you," Omir continued. "Be under no illusions regarding the battle to come. We are threatened by a great evil, and it has one aim- the annihilation of this city and our people. They must be destroyed. There will also be some Watchers, many of them originally stationed in Mornkastle, who have been turned by sorcery, turned so that they no longer know the truth- that we the Seven, the High Watchers and all of you, journeyed through the Void to this place. Even now Watchers remain somewhere out there in the Existence, lost."

So much passion and urgency did Phaedra detect in Omir's voice that she reckoned he was only one small step away from believing his own words. As for the Watchers, their collective silence was almost suffocating.

"Together we will crush them and send their remnants scurrying back to the shadows from which they came!" Omir's voice grew terrible to hear. He had the ability to amplify it and radically alter the pitch and delivery at the same time, all in the space of a heartbeat. Although she had expected him to do this at some stage, still she almost flinched.

Directed at a human audience, his words would have brought about obligatory cheers, amongst those who had not been frightened out of their wits. But the Watchers, long washed free of such emotions, merely gazed back at their lord. Phaedra observed one, then another and another, unable to detect even a hint of whatever cogitation worked beneath the surface. Sudden late afternoon light poured through the window arches as the sun fleetingly rolled from under a bank of cloud. It illuminated some of the Watchers brightly and appeared to shroud others almost entirely so that they looked like silhouettes, or empty shapes.

Trickery of the light, Phaedra told herself.

She took a long, deep breath to calm herself. *They cannot turn against their masters,* a voice whispered in her mind. To Phaedra it sounded eerily like Issele's. *They are sworn to protect Luudhoq.*

Those who've turned against us or gone mad also had supposedly unbreakable vows, she mentally replied. *What about them?*

Then something once thought unthinkable happened.

One of the Watchers turned and began to walk out of the hall, followed by a second. "I command you to stop!" Omir bellowed. *They won't,* Phaedra thought, and Omir raised both his hands and clenched them into fists as his instruction was ignored. The Watchers' exit was halted. The further of the two staggered to the marble tiled floor, an invisible weight crushing his body. The second bowed his head and fell forwards suddenly. His body caught fire and burned fiercely, as the other Watcher struggled to rise from the floor. A great snapping, grinding sound rose, and he too fell forward, shaking uncontrollably until he lay still.

"Dissent will not be tolerated from any quarter," Omir said, returning his arms to his sides. "Turn your backs on Luudhoq, and you will be destroyed. Remain loyal to your oaths and your calling, and you will be rewarded handsomely. That is the choice everyone must make- not just the Watchers but the human people of Luudhoq."

Two days later Issele made a speech in the city's central square, to those citizens of Luudhoq who had gathered. The square teemed with people of all ages, social castes and professions. All those who could find a vantage point in the area had done so. Others lingered as near as they could, some of them standing on boxes or carts or even clustered on rooftops, to watch and hear her words. Soft rain fell and glistened on the cobbles and roofs.

"Over a thousand years ago," she began, "you the people of Old Luudhoq that was, joined us in our fight against the forces of chaos. We pushed them back into the distant north where until recently they have remained, enmeshed in witchcraft and sacrifice to their blood-deities, feasting on one another and committing all manner of depraved acts. Even now they are known to murder their own infants in the names of their dark Gods."

Issele waited for the inevitable murmur of disgust to ripple through the crowd before she continued, "With the coming of the *marandaal* in the distant east, they have seized the opportunity to press south from the Unbuilt Wall, ignoring the honourable truce that we created so long ago. They have slain their lord Inerdyr, who strove to control them and keep the hard-earned peace we enjoyed for centuries. As they press on through our lands they burn homesteads, they butcher and mutilate. Imagine the fate of your families if these creatures, seeping with evil, forced their way into Luudhoq.

"But that will not happen. They will not take this city. Together we will take up arms to defend our homes, our families, our loved ones. We all fight the same battle- the Seven, the Watchers and *you*, the good people of Luudhoq. Every man, woman and child who can wield a weapon of any sort must do so when the time comes. We all have our part to play. The savages *will not* breach the walls of Luudhoq."

Chaos knows no boundaries, Phaedra wanted to say. She imagined Watcher after Watcher questioning their origins, renouncing their vows, taking an unpredictable and violent path. She pictured blood seeping out through the cracks in the city walls in a peculiar inverse of her previous terrifying vision where the bloodshed had been wreaked by their ancient enemies.

And all the while the *marandaal* drew closer, perhaps already breaking down the Border Wall and its defenders.

On an impulse Phaedra turned and left her quarters as another dreadful vision threatened to overcome her. She walked swiftly in the direction of the Sanctum. Finally she sat breathless and crouching by the lights and faint sounds of her ancient equipment as it scanned the skies, somehow reaching through the reactivated portal. Energy that she could not comprehend powered her only hope in the world.

Occasionally Phaedra would stare into the inky blackness of the gateway, imagining that the beautiful orb of

an unknown planet might appear, hanging in the cosmos
and awaiting her arrival.

XVIII - As You Reap

I

Kian's eyes flickered open as a piercing shriek cut through the night. Immediately she sat up, listening to the pitiful sound of the quieter cries and sobs that followed.

On the other side of the tent, Iyoth stirred and pushed himself up on his elbows as Kian moved her blanket aside and grabbed her longknife. "That's just Nia," he pointed out. "Lest you forget, she suffers nightmares most nights."

"It's her, but she sounds different," Kian said quietly. She pulled on her boots and cloak quickly, glancing across at her father as he frowned and added, "Anlerran will tend to her if needed."

"Nia is one of us, for better or worse," Kian told him, "and it may be that my help is needed as well. She sounds worse than usual."

Iyoth muttered something to himself and lay down again, rolling over onto his side. Kian drew her cloak more closely about herself and stepped out into the frosty night air. It occurred to her that it was almost unnaturally bright tonight, with both moons near-full and arcing through a cloudless and starlit sky. For a moment her senses prickled as if the Powers were being used nearby, or someone strong in them was a short distance away. *Anlerran or Ileana, or even both of them,* she decided. *I've had that feeling before, just by being near to them. Although not at night when they're asleep.*

Maybe they can't sleep and that's why I can feel it, she considered. *But that didn't feel like them. Who else would it have been?*

Putting the matter to one side, she looked around and saw Nia a short distance away, kneeling on the ground with her head tilted backwards and arms flailing as if to ward away some invisible oppressor. Her eyes bulged in terror. Immediately Kian went to her and knelt nearby. *She's not wounded,* the *du-luyan* girl surmised. *It's just one of her nightmares, as my father said. But it sounded different to me. I don't know why.*

Nia's gaze suddenly fixed on her and she grabbed desperately at Kian's arm. "I knew it would happen," Nia whispered. Kian was vaguely aware of a few other people who had been sleeping nearby, coming over to see what was happening. "Give her a flask of sourgrass," she heard an *orkar* man mutter. "That'll put an end to this nonsense."

"What is it, Nia? Are you even awake? Can you hear me?" Kian wondered suddenly why Anlerran hadn't yet been roused by the commotion and come to help. She usually slept fairly near to the rest of them and as Iyoth had already pointed out, more often than not she got up and tried to soothe Nia whenever her dreams had been this bad. Her help provided no lasting solace as far as Kian could tell, but Anlerran would continue anyway.

"It's over." Kian had to bend nearer to hear Nia's faint whisper. "It's all over."

Then, hugging herself and laughing as if with mad relief she added: "It's Yui. *She's here.*"

II

Hulf walked slowly and methodically along the muddy grassland. He had left his rowing boat a while back. Sooner or later someone would discover it, and with any luck it would be a member of his miserable, hateful family. He fervently hoped that it would be one of them, and that the sight of the boat and his muddy footsteps leading away from the shore might even evoke the faintest stirring of guilt within them.

But deep within himself he knew that it wouldn't. They would shrug and see it as a good riddance.

Hulf's muscles knotted in his arms as he clenched his fists, still furious at years of ill treatment that had finally overcome even his considerable patience. He strode onwards, knowing that his torment would soon be at an end.

He stopped a while later, shivering. The air was colder here than he had expected. *I should have thrown myself to the water serpents,* he told himself as he began walking again. *But those who've seen the death by sorcery all say that it happens quickly and is over quickly. A small mercy.*

So wrapped up did he remain in his hateful misery that Hulf took a while to notice that the ground had become drier underfoot. *Soon,* he thought. *Just a few steps further.*

He walked on, and his thoughts drifted with the mist.

Sometime later, he looked up, aware that the air had changed somehow. The breeze felt colder than it ought. He could see far further than he could have imagined, and into a landscape that he had only ever heard stories about. No one from the Mists had ever been to this place. They could not. Only the young woman who everyone had said was a spy for the Gods of this wide-open world had ever escaped the Mists.

And now he had done it.

Hulf looked in each direction, including back at the drifting fog from which he had emerged. He waited for his heart to stop, for his body to burst into flames, for any number of other probable fates that awaited anyone desperate enough to end their lives at the perimeter of the Bonemord.

But he remained standing and breathing, and the blood raced through his body as if in excitement. Hulf walked forward another several hundred paces, then east. The murk of the only world he had ever known receded in the distance, and still his heart continued to beat.

Not only will I never need to go back and speak with them ever again, he thought, *but I'm still alive. I'm still alive!*

He began walking again, but then stopped suddenly.

What about everyone else? he asked himself. *They're not all like my family. If I can walk out of the Mists, then maybe they can too. I should tell them. But are there other people here? What will happen if they see us?*

Hulf's damaged brain could not process the implications and considerations of ten thousand people appearing from out of the Bonemord. But he decided that telling as many of his people as he could would be the best decision he could make.

Nodding to himself, he retraced his steps towards the starless world from which he had walked.

III

Phaedra was making her way down one of the many flights of stairs towards the Sanctum when she encountered Daniel on his way up and in a great hurry. When he saw her, he said nothing. He turned, impatiently beckoning for her to follow. Phaedra trotted down the steps after him, resisting the temptation to ask anything. All the while, her mind and heart raced as if in an attempt to outdo each other.

Daniel remained silent throughout their journey to the chamber where their enlivened equipment pulsed and searched. He only spoke when they had made their way through the archway and sealed it behind them.

"We're not going back," he whispered when she glanced questioningly at him.

Phaedra's voice caught in her throat. "We..." She felt faint. "You mean... it..."

Daniel walked over to the panel and turned one of the dials. An alien vista swam into view in the portal for a moment, showing lush vegetation, tall mountains and a lake in which stone structures rose like stalagmites into a sky of blue haze.

Phaedra stared enraptured at the scene until Daniel moved the dial again.

"Are you... certain?" she whispered as Daniel turned to look back at her.

He nodded. "I checked a dozen times. It's very similar to Aona. Less ocean, higher mountains, a little warmer, but otherwise..." He laughed suddenly. "It was meant to be. As you said, Aona had a plan. We've been offered this escape. It's up to us to step through."

Phaedra stared at the rippling darkness of the mirror. For a moment a sudden fear gripped her. Perhaps sensing it, Daniel walked over and took her hand. "We'll go together," he said. "Hand in hand, in the same instant. Agreed?"

"Agreed." Phaedra could not stop her voice from shaking.

Behind them, a muffled thump sounded against the wall. As they whirled round a great crack appeared, then another. Finally the area where the archway had been sealed broke apart into fragments.

Through the dusty gap, Garret appeared.

No, Phaedra thought desperately. *We can't let him take this from us. No!*

She hurled herself at him, slamming into his body with every ounce of force she could bring to bear. She tore at his throat and dug into his flesh, screaming. Bloodied and snarling, Garret drew back and then aimed a punch at the side of her head. So powerful was the force of the blow that it not only lifted her off her feet but sent her ten paces or more through the air and into the side wall of the room. Phaedra heard two distinct, sickly noises- the sound of her skull breaking when his fist connected with it, and then a second, louder sound on her other side as she struck the wall, cracking her skull open a second time and shattering her shoulder. Her vision became red and distorted. Blood filled her mouth. She could feel something dripping slowly out of her head on one side and past her ear.

But even through the agony Phaedra would not give up.

She staggered to her feet, and as Garret struggled with Daniel and finally aimed a kick that sent him across the room in the other direction, she went for him again, intending to send her fingers through his eyes and as deep as possible into his brain.

Garret was too quick for her. Almost without looking he snatched her outstretched hand from just in front of his eyes and bent her fingers backwards, then crushed every bone in her hand until the flesh oozed from between his own fingers. At the same time he rained blow after blow upon her head until the blood ran in stark rivulets from Phaedra's sightless eyes.

Garret threw Phaedra's broken form to one side and walked over to Daniel, who crawled slowly towards him. The kick he aimed at his head almost severed it from the spinal column. Gore painted the wall in lurid splashes as Garret repeated the move again and again, then- with the head almost separated from the neck- he stamped on Daniel's face with all the weight he could bring to bear, which was far more than his own. Bone and flesh disintegrated into a smear beneath his boot.

Garret walked over to the sensor and moved the dial again to ensure that the coordinates were still in place and locked.

He smiled to himself, and turned another dial. The impenetrable blackness of the gateway rippled violently and he felt its pull entice him.

He stepped forwards and through.

An immeasurable period of time passed. Garret became aware that the deep blackness of the void had been replaced by a murky, solid gloom which slowly solidified around him.

Low clouds roiled overhead, through which the reddish light of a vast sun weakly diffused. He choked as the warm and sulphurous air attacked his lungs. Suddenly he retched and coughed up a stream of bloody bile.

In the distance he saw vast mountains and weeping rivers of lava. The ground upon which he squatted was itself a hot plateau of stone and sand.

It did not take Garret long to realise that nothing could possibly live here. Nothing, apparently except himself. The air held no moisture. Baked dry and poisonous, it already attacked his innards. He convulsed and spat another stream of vomit and gore onto the rocks. It hissed and steamed and in a moment became little more than a stain upon the hellish landscape.

His skin began to blister and peel. At first he refused to even acknowledge the agony, just as a part of him refused to believe that this world was a vision of eternal damnation. But as that reality dawned on him he opened his mouth and screamed aloud. The sound became ragged and feeble as the tissues of his body continued to disintegrate.

Then he began to heal.

Through the agony of being slowly destroyed and remade at the same time, Garret finally discovered the answer to a question that all of the Seven had idly asked themselves and even discussed over the centuries. His greatest power of all- miraculously swift and near-perfect regeneration- had not been taken back when he fled Aona. That gift was still his.

In a world of the living, I would have been a God, he thought. *Again.*

Garret staggered to his feet, the impossibility of the situation defeating him. This air could not be breathed, and yet his lungs sucked it in. The gravity of this place bore down on his limbs and yet he somehow moved. The heat baked all liquid dry. He could not survive in this place where oxygen and water were surely non-existent. Survival was impossible. And yet his body implacably regenerated.

Even as time passed his mind retained the memory of what he had been- master scientist, fugitive, and then an immortal in Aona. Between the waves of agony that tore his consciousness apart, Garret considered that whatever entity powered the universe- he now suspected it was Aona itself- had created hell around all the Seven. And hell had followed him here.

The world rotated laboriously on its ancient axis. Many Aonan days had passed by the time the bloated red sun fell below the eastern horizon. Garret's body survived long into the lava-lit night, twitching and jerking as the great power that had made him a God fought against the inevitable shutting down of every cell, every spark of life.

Yet finally this lord of nothing lay still, burning inside and out as he kissed the poisoned ground of his new home.

9 781849 146753